RED-FIRE RAGING

"Belfas, no!"

But Belfas didn't appear to hear. He was running to where the Lady twisted in pain, his arms outstretched to pull her from the Dark Heart's fire.

He never made it. The red-fire turned suddenly toward him and flared. He screamed as the flames caught him.

"Ward!" Erin shouted. "Ward, damn you!" She sprinted forward. *No! You've taken everything else— you won't have him!*

And even as she ran, Erin saw the flame coil like a serpent and spring up to meet her . . .

INTO THE DARK LANDS

Michelle M. Sagara

A Del Rey Book

BALLANTINE BOOKS • NEW YORK

For Thomas, who must know, better than anyone, that a few pages a day is a poor return for all that you give me. I couldn't have written this, or anything that might follow it, without you. Proof? Read it; try to tell me where, in these words, you can't be found.

ACKNOWLEDGMENTS

I think that more work is done, by more people, on a first novel than on any that follow, and I'd like to thank the people who know best the truth of this: editor, Veronica Chapman, who saw something in the book that I first sent and was kind enough to put up with all of my ignorance about publishing; her associate Deborah, who *didn't* laugh when I asked about type-faces, among other things; and Gord Davis, who could probably, with humor and ease, sell a wolf to a shepherd—but wouldn't, on principle.

A Del Rey Book
Published by Ballantine Books

Copyright © 1991 by Michelle M. Sagara

Library of Congress Catalog Card Number: 91-92194

ISBN 0-345-37232-8

Manufactured in the United States of America

First Edition: December 1991

Cover Art by Tom Stimson

prologue

From the teachings of the Lady of Elliath, First
Servant of Lernan, God,
to the Lines of the Sundered.

All life has a beginning, and in that sense even the mountains
and the earth we dwell upon are alive. But imagine, if you can,
a thing which has no such life, and no unfolding: It is, it has
been, it will be. This is a hard task, but I ask it only for a
moment, for I will tell you of our beginnings, and I, too, must
start somewhere.

There was the Light, and there was the Dark. The Light was
glorious, ordered, strong; the Dark, ugly and twisted. Each slept
in perfection; each spread cold dreams in a wide net, reaching
ever outward. Thus did They find each other.

The Light touched the Dark; the Dark the Light—and both
were awakened. And where They touched, They frayed into
small, moving strands of Light and Darkness. Thus were the
Sundered born, the Servants of the two, like their parents to
your eyes, but lesser and diminished by the method of their
creation. Still, the Sundered of the Light cleaved to Light; the
Sundered of the Dark, to Darkness.

I was the first Sundered of the Light; I beheld the first Sundered of the Darkness and I knew him for my enemy. It was my
first thought, my only thought. With my brethren of the Sundered, I prepared for battle.

Battle we did, for the Dark would consume all without our
resistance. The voice of the Light was strong and sure. Stars
grew, stars died, and in the cadence of His words, we found
strength and glory; battle all but consumed us.

Yet neither Dark nor Light was victorious. The Sundered fell

1

around me until my Lord could bear their loss no longer. I
remember it well, for Light cut the void as He moved in a dwin-
dling spiral toward the Enemy. I knew there was danger, but I
did not know its nature and I could not follow the path that my
Lord made; it was too bright, too fast. Yet the Dark must have
felt His purpose and His boundless anger, for Darkness began
to trace His own path, His own menace, across the vastness. He
made no retreat, but instead moved to meet my Lord. The First
Sundered of the Enemy made haste to follow, even as I—but
who among the Servants, whether of Light or Dark, could hope
to match the swiftness of their masters? Although we traveled
with all haste, nothing was left for us in the end but to watch.

They joined, locking Their essences around each other. Neither gave ground, and neither retreated from the tight embrace
of Their struggle. We of the Sundered heard the voices of our
Lords grow weaker and fainter until they did not reach our ears
at all. Worse, we saw the Light dim and the Darkness brighten;
you who have always known dusk and twilight will never comprehend our terror. No more Light or Darkness was sundered;
They were too closely knit for that.

Thus was the Earth born, and gray humanity which holds in
equal portion a measure of Light and Dark and knows both life
and death, love and hate, pain and pleasure. And the Light and
the Dark slept again, Twin Hearts in the body of the world; the
Bright Heart and the Dark Heart as they are known now. We
cried out into the void all our ancient evocations—to no avail.
What slept we were powerless to awaken.

Thus the Servants were alone among humanity, each carrying
the heritage of his parents. All that we saw as we first wandered
the body of the world was ugly to our eyes, stained and impure.
We saw the mortals rise from folly to folly; saw them born and
saw them die. In time, we grew to hope that out of the gray we
might pull Light—or Darkness. The Sundered chose to mingle
with the mortals that had so displeased them at first, and from
these unions, you were born.

Thus began the battle we now fight. The Servants of the Darkness and their offspring furthered the ends of the Dark, as those
of the Light furthered the ends of the Light. Humanity proved
amenable to all of the influences of both: fear, love, hate, pain,
and hope.

And the Light and the Dark continued to sleep, untouched by
the conflict, until the battle of Pellen Fields and the fall of Gallin

of Meron, who was our foremost warrior, the champion of my choice.

The Bright Heart is not human or mortal; He knows no life as we know it. But the strength of Gallin's dying touched Him, where a living creature could not. And as Gallin died, the power of the Light—of God—flowed to him. And the Servants of the Darkness fled or perished as the power of their Enemy reawakened. And we who had served the Light since the beginning heard again the whisper of His voice and His purpose.

Thus did Lernan, God, return in power to us, His followers, lending us the strength of His purpose. Love, He gives us, and light, and hope. Yet even awakened, He was still lessened; the world that He had formed could not release Him to us. The void was no longer His home; nor would He wander it again in all His brilliant glory. He was interred. The Light of the Bright Heart would know no release from His body. Still, with His aid and strength, our victory was assured.

Or so we hoped.

But such was the nature of the Darkness that He could not sleep while His one Enemy awakened—and so did the power of the Dark Heart also enter the world, to speak once again to His ancient Servants, and the half-breed Malanthi that they had engendered. And to them returned the power of Darkness, the power of the blood ceremonies.

You, who are Lernari, bear some of the blood of the Light. You are the children of the Sundered and the mortals; you are our hope and our connection to the gray humanity. You will know death; we cannot prevent it. You will know time and feel its passing. More than this, you will know war.

And as the Sundered of the Light to the Sundered of the Dark, you will be enemy to the Malanthi, those borne of the non-blooded and the Darkness.

I ask you only to remember that you are kin to the nonblooded humans; you will live as they do and die as they do. Protect them and teach them.

chapter
one

The Lady of Elliath waited in shadowed silence. All around her, trees and flowers flourished under the light of no natural sun. This was her hall, and even the vagaries of the weather were trapped without. Still she knew, without seeing it, that lightning branched and forked its way through the gray and murky sky. The distant low rumble that followed would make itself known throughout all of her lands save these.

But war was never as distant as thunder. And from some tidings there was no escape, no matter where she chose to bide her time.

A sound, like a gentle chime, wafted across the breeze, and she rose, stately and elegant, to examine the details of a fresco that had been painted by one of her descendants. A whisper of foot brushing undergrowth grew louder as someone approached. She drew her light around her tall, slim form and let it trail like a cloak behind her.

A man stopped, ten feet from the sight of this glowing shroud, and bowed low. Without looking, she knew him for Latham, master scholar of Elliath.

She knew the hour, then, and the day; knew all that he would tell her in the sudden chill of the garden. A Servant's memory was perfect and endless.

Twenty mortal years ago, he had stood so before her, straight and tall, with a hint of gray pain about compressed lips and nearly closed eyes. Twenty years and more, she had chosen, for the sake of her line, to chance the veil of the future at the behest of the Bright God. She had not taken the trance lightly, and Latham had been among those to argue against it. But the war they fought had been dire, and the undoubtable outcome bitter.

She had retreated to her hall and begun the spells and openings of the ways. Here, she had taken her first step.

The paths of the possible were not easy to wander, and for the first year of her trance she had moved with care. Other minds and lesser Servants had been lost to the veils. Still, she was the First of Lernan, and as she had gained an understanding of those paths she had walked them more quickly and more confidently, changing what she chose to do, and how, to see what might come of it. Three more years had passed in her search for an end to the war, but she had found it.

One isolated path, one frail possibility, offered hope. She had walked that road, over and over, looking for any other answer. The fifth year had passed, and another three months, before she finally returned to the waking world with one secret hope for the lines—and bereft of any for herself.

It chilled her, even now, for Latham's presence here was a herald, the beginning of an end that was too clear.

She acknowledged him with a nod, but kept her back to him so he would not see her face.

He grimaced. Of the privy council, he could now boast to being the longest lived. His dark hair had paled to gray over the intervening years; a sign of wisdom. What wisdom now? Of all tasks assigned to him, this was always the worst, this bearing of ill news. But better to have it out.

"Lady, Cordan and his command were attacked twenty miles from our border. We arrived late."

She turned slowly, her face almost expressionless.

Did you see this, Lady? Could you have prevented it? He never asked aloud the questions that burned at his scholar's mind. She had spent five years, lost to them . . .

"They grow bold," the Lady murmured. "Twenty miles?"

"Inside our territory."

"Did any survive?"

He looked away and therefore missed the subtle change of her expression. "No. But five at least called their own deaths. None were taken by the enemy."

"Cordan?"

"One of the five, Lady. I'm sorry."

She turned away, her movements still regal and controlled. "Has anyone informed Kerlinda?"

"Kandor has gone to speak with her."

"I see." She said no more, but turned again, knowing that even she could not hide the look that transformed her face. If she had the courage, she would inform her daughter of the death herself; but this she could not face. It had started, yes, but the beginning had been the easiest.

It was dark, but the storms of the day had finally passed. Stars glimmered through the open windows, their blinking light no longer obscured by dense clouds.

Erin crept out of her bed. She glanced quickly at the crack of muted light beneath the door to her square, plain room.

Mother's still awake.

Taking a deep breath, she forced herself to move silently. Crady had been teaching her that; she still felt warm when she thought of how loudly—and long—he'd approved her progress.

But it wasn't for silence that she practiced now.

She crossed her legs beneath her and raised her small arms. In the dark, she began to draw a large half circle in the air.

The creak of a door interrupted her concentration, and she dove for the bed, heart pounding audibly. She waited a moment, then relaxed. Her mother wasn't coming; not yet anyway.

In a few minutes she found her way back to the floor and began to concentrate in earnest.

I almost did it yesterday.

Minutes passed while she tried to focus. It wasn't easy; fear that her mother would find her awake kept drawing her mind to the sound of steps on the floor below. But her father was coming back soon, and she desperately wanted to have something *real* to show him.

Come on. Light.

Her hands traced their silent pattern across the air, and she found the courage to utter an audible syllable.

Nothing happened.

I know I almost had it yesterday.

She tried again, with no results. Frustration warred with determination, and determination won—but only barely. For all her seriousness, she was still a child.

Arms passed in front of her again, but this time she forced herself to relax. She could feel the shape of the night surrounding her, feel the tingling at the base of her spine. She just wasn't sure how to use it.

Light. Light to cure darkness.

The words were comfortable because she'd heard them so often. She relaxed, starting yet again.

The room was lit by a gentle green glow that touched the

outline of bed, chair, and windowsill. In confusion she looked outside and saw that night still claimed the land.

I did it!

She laughed—she couldn't help it—but very quietly. Her mother was going to be pleased; her father proud. No one else her age had yet managed to bring the light up at command. Dannen was close, but it didn't matter anymore—she'd done it first.

Remembering her mother's stern admonition to sleep, she crawled back into bed, letting her feet dangle over the edge. She tried to lie down, but excitement made her bolt upward again. If she could show her mother what she could do, maybe she wouldn't be angry.

I could wait till morning.

She pulled the covers up under her chin.

But I want to tell her now.

The covers fell away. Maybe her mother wouldn't be happy at first—but surely once she saw the light, she'd forgive Erin.

That decided, she walked slowly to the door. Her hand trembled on the knob, but she opened it, allowing the firelight from the floor below to wash the room.

She headed down the familiar hallway to the stairs and, clinging to the banister—which was just above her shoulder—she made her way down, bare feet padding against worn wood.

She peered around the corner very carefully, then stopped, all caution forgotten.

Her mother's back was toward the staircase. But beyond her mother stood the most gloriously beautiful man that Erin had ever seen. She knew him at once for the Lady's kin—Servant to Lernan. He cast a light, obvious to her eyes, that put her achievement to shame, for it was white and pure, whereas hers was mere green. He was white as well, or as close to white as made no difference. Only his eyes, the deepest and clearest of green, had any strong color. These eyes looked beyond her mother to meet hers.

He looks like the Lady.

It was the first time that she had ever seen Kandor, Third Servant of Lernan, but it would not be the last.

Her mother turned.

Her mother's face was white, as white as Kandor's, but without Kandor's immortal beauty behind it. Erin took a step back.

"Erin," her mother said softly. "Did we wake you?"

Something was wrong. Erin shook her head mutely, and moved down the stairs.

"So this is your daughter, Kerlinda."

Her mother nodded quietly. "Come, Erin. Have you met Kandor before?"

"No, we have not met." Kandor looked at her then, his unblinking eyes taking in every detail of her strained silent face.

"What's wrong, Mommy?"

Her mother smiled and gathered Erin into her arms. Erin had never seen a smile like the one her mother gave her. It was too tight, as if it didn't fit her face anymore.

"I—"

"Kerlinda. Kera, let me."

Wordless, her mother nodded into Erin's hair.

"Erin, do you understand what the Line Elliath—and all the rest of the blooded lines—must fight for?"

"Yes." Why was her mother trembling?

"Do you understand how we must fight, and why we must train so long and so hard?"

"Yes." Why was he asking her these questions? Why was her mother shaking?

"Erin, your father, Cordan of Elliath, has been gone for two months, fighting the Enemy and those who serve Him."

Erin nodded, frowning. She knew this. Why was he telling her this?

"He was adult, as you are not. He fought well for our cause and aided it to the best of his ability."

"Mommy?" Her mother hugged her so tightly she could hardly breathe.

"Cordan of Elliath has finished his fight with honor."

The words were formal; Erin had heard them before many times. Without thinking, she said, "He rests in the peace beyond." It was what she had been taught.

"Yes, child. He rests now. We Servants of Lernan believe that in the beyond there is no war, no pain, no fighting."

Why was he saying this? "Mommy?"

Her mother pulled away, her face still wearing that awful smile. Erin was suddenly afraid to ask her mother any questions; something lay beyond that smile that she didn't want to know.

With a child's directness, she looked up at Kandor again. The Servant had not moved.

"Is my daddy dead?"

He closed his eyes, shutting off for the moment the glow of emeralds. "Yes, Erin."

"Oh."

She was silent as her mother watched her closely.

"Does that mean he won't be coming home?"

They wouldn't let her see her father. Her mother was called by the Lady, as were most of the adult members of the line, but Erin was left behind; the ceremonies of departure were, in this case, not meant for children.

Everyone had always said that Erin was not an ordinary child. She was cunning, in the naïve way that children are, and direct as well.

"Please wait here for me, Erin. I'll return as soon as I can."

And she had nodded without speaking, to make sure that she didn't give her word. But if her father was leaving, she wanted to give him one last thing: the gift of her newly discovered light.

Maybe, she thought, as she watched her mother disappear down the winding path, *maybe if he's happy, maybe if he's proud, he won't go away. He'll come home with Mommy and me.*

She remembered clearly the look on his face the last time he had gone out to fight. He hadn't wanted to leave them.

As soon as her mother had disappeared, Erin put on her shoes, tying them painstakingly. The Lady of all Elliath would be there herself, and Erin didn't want to look bad. She waited for a few moments more, then timidly pushed the front door of her house open and took her first step onto the well-trodden path.

She knew the way to the Great Hall; she'd been there many times, with many different people. It felt strange to be going there alone. Everything seemed quiet, as if the trees, sky, and wind were watching her and listening.

What if the doors are closed?

She tried not to think about it. If they were, she would have to go home without seeing her father; they were too large and heavy for her to open.

She walked more quickly. What if he left before she got there? The Great Hall seemed suddenly too far away, and she ended up running the rest of the way.

The path curved gently beneath her racing feet, but her eyes sought the height of the Great Hall's large dome. It stood mute beneath the pale gray sky, a work of stone with hints of gold along its ribs. It was huge—easily ten times the size of the build-

ing that she called home—and it towered above Elliath like a
watchful guardian.

Lungs heaving, she reached the doors and froze. The wooden,
peaked doors were open; people—adults—were entering quietly
in ones and twos beneath the petaled arch of the inner hall. Like
the breeze, they were silent.

She forgot about catching her breath because she was holding
it. She stood very still, hoping not to be noticed. When the last
of the people had entered, she slid between the large doors and
into the hall itself. She had never felt so small as she looked up,
and up, and up to the center point of the vaulted ceiling. At
twelve points of the circle, the Twelve Servants of God, carved
in marble, watched down upon her. She looked away then, to
the crowd ahead.

All she could see were the backs of the line members that
crowded into the hall. They were pressed together in the shape
of a human wall. There were almost too many for the silver
circle along the ground to contain.

After a minute, she began to sidle along the wall, traveling
the arc of the chamber until she could see the front of the room
more clearly. No one seemed to notice her; all eyes were upon
the Lady of Elliath.

Erin found herself staring at the Lady as well. She had forgotten—she always forgot—just how beautiful the Lady was, all
ringed in bright, soft light. The Lady was speaking, but Erin
could not hear the words. She inched along the wall, coming
closer to where the Lady stood.

In front of the Lady, in a half circle, stood several of the
warrior-priests, those like her father, who fought the enemy with
sword and blood. They wore their full uniforms, chain mail
beneath silver-bordered gray surcoats that seemed to melt into
gorges, and they held unsheathed blades rigidly forward. One
of them, the youngest, was crying. The tears ran down his
cheeks, but he kept his position. In the center of the half circle
was Telvar. Anyone, child or adult, recognized him on sight—
he was the finest warrior in the Line Elliath, perhaps in all of
the rest of the lines as well.

Today he looked old, his face more dour and grim than ever.
Erin stopped moving, afraid to attract his attention; he always
noticed everything.

She relaxed as she realized that he, too, stood rigid and unmoving. She could not see what this half circle of warriors stood

guard over, but she could guess. Now she had no choice but to edge through the crowd as quickly as possible and hope that no one tried to stop her.

She plunged between two of the line members, brushing against the stiff gray of their robes without stopping to see who they were. Behind her, she heard a brief murmur of shock or surprise, and it made her move more quickly.

Daddy!

The commotion that she caused rippled outward through the crowd.

Now Telvar will *see me.*

But it didn't matter, as long as she made her way to the front of the room where the guards stood with their naked blades, where the Lady of Elliath watched.

Maybe it was because they were surprised. Maybe they were too wrapped in their sorrow to react quickly. Maybe they could not deny Cordan's child this last sight of her father. For whatever reason, none of the priests or priestesses of the line saw fit to stop or catch Erin as she frantically made her way to the front of the room.

"Daddy!" Erin broke through the last rank of the gathering and ran forward, arms outstretched.

"Erin!"

She turned automatically at the sound of her mother's voice. People moved out of the way as Kerlinda separated herself from the gathered mourners.

Erin took a step toward her mother as Kerlinda knelt to the ground and opened her arms.

"Erin, please," she said, more softly. Her voice was shaking.

Erin almost went to her mother.

Then she turned around again, to face Telvar and his warriors. In front of them, on a table that was half Erin's height, rested a large, dark box. It was wood, dark wood, and well oiled; it gleamed in the torchlight like a marvelous new thing. Her brow furrowed slightly in confusion, and then she darted forward.

"Erin!"

She reached the table and, placing her hands on the edge of the box, pulled herself to her toes.

She stopped moving then. "Daddy?"

Her father lay in the box. His eyes were closed, but even Erin could not mistake this rest for sleep. A bloodless cut ran across half of his face. His jaw was slightly open, his face shrunk inward. His arms, always open to catch her or hug her, were crossed over his motionless chest. Some of his fingers were just not there.

"Daddy?" She reached out to touch one of his hands, and felt it, slack and cold beneath her small fingers.

No. No no no.

"Daddy? See—I have something to show you."

She shook him a little.

"Watch, Daddy. Watch what I learned to do. I'm—I'm the first."

He still wouldn't move.

In a panic, she let go of his hand and raised her arms in a small circle. She had to show him this, had to make him *see* it.

With ferocious determination, she concentrated, and the syllables fell trembling out of her young mouth. If she could show him this—if he really saw it—everything would be all right. Everything would have to be all right.

Light, pale and green, encircled her father's still face.

"See? See, Daddy?" He was blurry now, and she struggled to stay on her toes. It was very important not to lose sight of him. "See what I can do?"

She felt arms around her waist, drawing her away. Angry and afraid, she kicked outward.

"No! No, he has to see! He has to!"

"Erin."

The voice stopped her. It was the Lady's.

"Hush, child."

She turned around, struggling against the strength of immortal arms and losing. She was lifted off her feet. The Lady's sober eyes met hers.

"He cannot hear you, although he would be proud of what you have shown."

"He has to—"

The Lady's arms drew tight. Over her shoulder, Erin could see her mother's pale face.

"He can't, Erin. He's dead."

Dead.

For the first time, the word had a meaning.

Wordlessly, the Lady set her down, and she walked silently to her mother. Kerlinda gathered her into stiff arms.

"Come, child and grandchild. This is the ceremony of departure. The spirit of husband and father has not been trapped by the malice of the Enemy; it has gone beyond. The circle has opened to free it."

Kerlinda had hoped to spare her daughter sight of her husband's diminished body. Now she must do what she could to soften the blow.

"Erin," she said softly, as she made her way to the coffin and its honor guard. "We wear clothing. The body, yours and mine, is just a larger, deeper layer. But the spirit—you remember the spirit? That goes on to freedom and peace."

Her daughter was weeping now, her face buried into Kerlinda's strong shoulder. Erin would not look at the corpse again, nor would Kerlinda force her to.

But Kerlinda was an adult. A widow, one of too many. She looked at the lifeless body, her eyes glassy and hard.

Does the spirit go on, Cordan?

Bitterly she placed the fingers of her right hand against the cold lips of the corpse.

Is there truly peace beyond?

The Lady of Elliath watched her, torn between different pains. *Daughter,* she thought, *your child is our hope. She can be spared nothing. I pray that she learns your strength and mine, for it is on her shoulders that everything will rest.*

She raised her arms, calling for the light that signaled the midpoint of the ceremonies.

And you, my youngest—you will be with your husband soon.

These thoughts, these pains, she kept to herself. But it was hard; it had never been the way of Elliath to stand alone among its brethren.

It was many months before Kerlinda's strength broke enough to allow for tears. Erin heard them as she lay awake in the darkness of night. She stayed in her bed, unable to comfort her mother's pain; she knew how hard her mother tried to keep it hidden from her.

But Erin cried freely. Every time the door of the house opened, she would hold her breath and turn, half expecting to see her father's smile. She spoke to him every night at first, but when he didn't answer, she slowly stopped. Now she left him to Lady Death.

Nothing came to fill the hollowness that his death left. But she swore two things: She would become a warrior-priest, like her father, and make the Enemy pay. And she would protect her mother from the death that had stolen the father she loved.

chapter
two

"I don't see why you get to train with Telvar." The boy who was speaking appeared to be concentrating intensely upon the fascinations of the market path, although he knew every twist and turn it took quite well.

His companion's gaze was firmly fixed on him. "I don't know either. Besides, it isn't like it's that special." She ducked her head, nearly knocking the brim of her sunhat askew in an attempt to get a clearer look at his face.

"Come on, you know he's the *best*." Belfas gave her shoulder a little shove. "And it's not like you're better than any of the rest of us." He kicked at a stone with his foot.

"Belfas—" Erin closed her eyes as Belfas yelped in pain. "Belf, you're wearing sandals." Sometimes it was hard to believe that he'd been born nearly a whole year before she had. She'd seen ten summers, he eleven. She shook her head as he bent down to examine his toenails. Not hard—it was impossible.

"Besides," she said, to soothe the red from his face, "Telvar isn't easy. He's the best, but he thinks all his students should be better. You remember Carla?" She lowered her voice.

Belfas nodded quietly, foot momentarily forgotten. Carla was ten years adult, and Erin's cousin besides. She was one of Telvar's prize pupils, and she looked it—her face all grim and hard, her cheek scarred from "carelessness" in her first battle.

"He still drills her, you know. I can tell when she's been with him—her arms and legs are always black." She gave a shudder that was only part theatrical. "And you *want* to train with him?"

Belfas's eyes were wide. "I didn't know about that." He frowned for a moment. "But I'd train with him. I mean, if you have to."

"That's 'cause you're stupid." She started to walk again.

14

"We're supposed to do things together—we're year-mates, remember?"

She smiled. "How could I forget?" One hand touched his shoulder. "We promised."

He smiled in return.

"Besides, I'll teach you everything he teaches me, all right?"

He thought about it for a minute. "Except the bruises."

"Well, maybe." She looked down the road to the sloping hill. The market flags were flying full mast in their triangular greens and blues and golds.

Belfas knew her well enough to know what she was thinking. "Erin, we can't. We've got our lessons."

"Not for a quarter hour at least."

He looked to the Great Hall. Five minutes to walk there from the market, if they were quick. He shook his head.

"Erin? Erin!"

To his great surprise, she stopped only ten feet in front of him. She fished around in the pockets of her student's browns, then sighed.

"Belf, do you have any coin?"

"We're going to be late for lessons, and it's Cartannis today."

She thought on it for a moment; Cartannis was one of the few instructors who taught the lines without being born of the blood. It didn't, however, make him any more friendly or any less severe when it came to the "important" matters of history.

"After class?"

"Kerlinda."

"Grandfather." Kerlinda bowed and stepped out of the rectangular door to allow him to enter. She held the bow a moment longer than strictly necessary while she tried to gather her thoughts. Serdon's office and title kept him busy, and he rarely had time for visits that were merely social in nature. No one wondered why; as the Grandfather, Patriarch of Elliath, he was heir to the responsibility of leading and guiding all of the Lernari of his line. So had Helmi been in her time as the Grandmother before him.

"What brings you here?"

"Is Erin about?"

She shook her head, compressing her lips. "Out with one of her year-mates. Belfas, I think. She's managed the Greater Ward, you know. She's trying to make sure he learns it 'properly.' "

She shook her head, her voice completely free of any trace of parental pride.

The Grandfather looked at her carefully.

"Good; young Belfas seems to be the only one of her year-mates that she's easy around." He rolled back the gray sleeve of the summer robe; it was a matter of habit with him when he had something unpleasant to say. "I've come to speak to you about Erin."

"Is she causing difficulty?"

"No." He sighed. "And it's a rare child that doesn't at one point or another. But that's what I've come to speak about.

"Over the last four years she's learned to control most of our blood-linked abilities. Light, direction, the Lesser Ward, and the Greater. She can also handle minor healing—"

Kerlinda's eyebrows went up.

"I hadn't heard that," she said, frankly and softly.

"No, she probably isn't aware of it. You know as well as I that it isn't something we attempt to teach until perhaps the first year of adulthood. But she has it; I've seen her use it to calm physical—and emotional—pain." He allowed himself a wry smile. "Mostly for Belfas; if she won't get into the difficulties we associate with childhood, he seems determined to make up for it. When she is adult and can walk in the hand of God, she will be a healer such as the lines have never seen. I think only the instant touch of Lady Death will be able to stop her."

The smile vanished. "But it disturbs me. Your daughter is very powerful. She's aware of it, which is fine. And she takes pride in it, which is also understandable. But it's the type of pride that makes me uneasy, Kerlinda. It's too bitter, too angry."

Kerlinda turned away, a shadow crossing her face.

"I, too, see what you speak of, Grandfather. But she shows no interest in anything other than her studies.

"I keep wondering if it's my fault. I didn't handle Cordan's death well; I'm not sure I handle it well now, and it's been six years. Maybe this grimness is something she's learned from me. But what can I do? I try to interest her in games—do you know that she doesn't even know the rules of squares?—but she's always too impatient. Too directed. She'll be adult soon, one way or the other."

"I see." He bowed his head. "And Telvar?"

With a slight compression of lips, Kerlinda wrapped her arms around her shoulders.

"That was not my idea, but Erin seems enthusiastic enough—God alone knows why. And Telvar drives her; not since Carla or Tedrin have I seen a student so pushed."

"If it helps, Kerlinda, it was not my suggestion either. Nor would I have recommended it." He sighed. "Continue to do what you can for her. Keep trying to involve her in activities that do not directly affect line training."

"I—I think I will have to trust that to you."

"Pardon?"

She faced him squarely. "I'm due out in the field in six weeks."

"I haven't heard!" He took a seat in the simple wood chair that Cordan had made ten years previously. His shoulders began to sag, lending age to his carriage. It didn't often show, but Serdon was not a young man, not even by line standards.

Kerlinda saw the creases in his forehead deepen, and she swallowed. Unconsciously she began to knead the folds of her robe. "It hasn't been approved yet. I'm sure it will be."

"You've spoken with the Lady, then."

She nodded.

"I see." Now he had two worries instead of the one he had come with. "Kera," he said, a name that he had used only rarely since her childhood had ended, "you aren't warrior-trained."

"Not with Telvar, no. But Kaymar taught me use of sword and crossbow. And I'm healer-trained. At that, I'm the best the line has. You know it."

It was true, but irrelevant. "You agreed to—"

"That was three years ago!" She stopped, forcing her voice down. "Three years, Grandfather. Three years, and more deaths than we've suffered in the ten previous to it. I cannot stay here; every time the bodies come back I think of how I could have done something had I been there."

"Daughter." His stern voice stemmed the angry flow of her words. "You take too much upon yourself."

"Maybe." The word was a concession that the voice held no hint of at all. "But the Lady herself has granted my request."

And I will speak to the Lady about it. It's patently ridiculous, daughter. In only one thing have you been right: You do not, even now, handle the loss of Cordan well.

He stood slowly.

She watched him, willing his departure. The gentleness in his eyes was an accusation she could not bear for much longer.

Yes, she knew that Erin was too serious, too bent on revenge. But how could she fault the child? Was it not a desire that festered in her even now?

As if he could read her thoughts, he stepped forward, resting one hand on her shoulder. The hand was large and steady; for a moment she wanted to sink back into childhood and be comforted.

Instead she retreated, tossing the hand away in anger.

"Damn you! *I saw his wounds!* I know what killed him."

He saw the flush of her cheeks, the angry glint of gray-flecked green eyes. *Ah, daughter* . . .

"Do you know what it's like? I could have *saved* his life! I could have—" She broke off; there were no tears. She felt shame at her outburst and struggled to control herself.

"I'm sorry, Grandfather. You do know what it's like." She shut her eyes too tightly. "But I'm not as strong as you are. I don't have to be." She took a deep breath. "I just know that if I don't go out to the front, I'll wither here. I should have gone years ago."

"And what of your daughter?"

"She's safe here." But she cringed. The soft-spoken question had found its mark.

He knew her well enough to know that she would not reconsider the decision, so he left his questions unasked.

Erin was at the Lady's pavilion to see her mother off. A large troop of armed Lernari waited in the southern fields beyond Elliath, in full view of the circular platform that had been raised so the Lady might speak to her warrior line-children. Surcoats, gray and silver, matched the hue of the sky. Soon they would not look so fine or so clean, but at least here, in the processional before the Lady, the warriors would stand at their best. They were grim and silent as they readied their equipment and mounts, but no more grim and silent than Erin herself.

A warrior must be prepared to leave all behind in defense of his or her land.

Erin nodded at the echo of Telvar's words. These were no teaching homilies, uttered in the safety of the Great Hall. They were real. Telvar's scar-worn face attested to it.

What else had he said? That all of the line's warriors were adult. When—if—she attained this, she would understand better what war was about.

She looked for him; saw him standing in his position beside

the Lady of Elliath. He, too, wore the dress uniform of the warriors, but on his shoulder glinted three concentric circles. He was once unit leader and he still looked every inch of it.

The Lady stood robed in white to see her line-children off. It was her custom to do so. Erin continued to watch the crowd, searching for sight of her mother. She felt worried and knew it showed, so she kept out of sight of Telvar as much as possible. He never approved of any obvious display of emotion.

The warrior-priests began to fall in behind their various commanders. Their swords, sheathed, hung slack at their armored sides.

Telvar glanced at the Lady, who nodded. He faced the crowd, nodding in turn, and one by one the warriors began to approach. Each unsheathed his or her sword and laid it, briefly, at the Lady's feet. The Lady gestured over each in turn, speaking low, formal words that were not meant for Erin's ears.

Erin recognized some of the warriors. There, Carla, the only student that Telvar had ever spoken of with anything other than disparagement. Two behind her, Keldani, the quirky, likable man that everyone younger knew as "Uncle," and everyone older knew as trouble. He smiled broadly, ignoring Telvar's ferocious expression, as he laid his sword down with a flourish. The Lady even touched his face.

Then, at the back of the third unit, Erin caught sight of Kerlinda. Robed in gray, a short sword at her side, she waited in silence, her crossed arms indicating either annoyance or worry. She had no mail, no gorge, no helm, but her hair was drawn back in a warrior's braid, her lips in a warrior's silence. Erin began to move toward her.

The Lady was aware of her daughter as well. But she continued to give her blessing to these too-young warriors of the line that she had mothered. She could count the faces that she would never see alive again; could count on one hand the number that her blessing might save. It was hard. Not for the first time did she wish that she had never sought the path the future would take.

But the worst—the worst—

"Kerlinda."

"Lady." Kerlinda bowed stiffly. Her sword she placed at the feet of the line's blood. It was small but finely crafted, and she'd been practicing with it to try to achieve a better level of competence. Never mind; it was not for the use of the sword that she traveled to the front. Her weapon against the enemy was the blood that carried her ability to heal.

"So formal, daughter?"

Kerlinda smiled stiffly. "Mother," she said at last. "I give you the warrior's pledge—it is not as daughter that I've come."

"No. But warrior or healer, you are still my child. My youngest. Come." She held out her arms, and, after a moment of hesitation, Kerlinda embraced her mother.

"What's wrong?"

"Wrong? Child, are you still determined to walk this road you have chosen?"

Kerlinda stiffened again, and the Lady released her with great reluctance. She studied her daughter's face as if memorizing every detail: the hard set of her mouth, the dark rings beneath her eyes, the way her chin tilted slightly up in defiance. The Lady's emerald eyes snapped shut.

"I cannot do this."

"What?"

"I cannot do this. Kerlinda—"

"Mother!" They both turned as the young voice rang out, turned in time to catch Erin's hurtling body. Kerlinda kneeled to lift her only child and hold her tightly.

"Erin," she said softly, but with no anger, "we said our good-byes. This is not— Never mind." She breathed in the fragrance of soap and sweat, thinking, *Will I see you again?*

Perhaps this was what her mother felt. She turned. "Mother?"

But the Lady's gaze was now upon Erin. "It is nothing." Her voice was faint. "Come, warrior child. Take the meager blessing that the Lady of Elliath offers. Fight well." But she made no move as Kerlinda put an arm around her shoulder, catching her in the same embrace that held her child.

They stood there for a few minutes, grandmother, mother, and child.

Then the moment was lost as Telvar gestured.

Kerlinda kissed her daughter a last time, setting her down. She bowed formally and joined the ranks of the army.

Erin watched her go. Determined to be brave—to be the sort of warrior that Telvar often spoke of—she swallowed her tears. But her mother was going to the front, as her father had gone so many years ago. She bit her lip, her resolve weakening. A hand touched her shoulder, and she started guiltily, thinking it to be Telvar's.

It was the Lady's.

"Erin, stay with me. Help me give the line's blessing."

Erin, tears forming in her eyes, nodded at the Lady's request. She bent at shaking knees and touched her forehead once.

"Elliath." Line name; the name that warrior, healer, and teacher alike called their own.

She bowed and touched her forehead for the second time, unintentionally scraping the silvered carpet that rested beneath the Lady's feet.

"Lernan." The name of God, the brighter of the Twin Hearts locked in eternal conflict.

Only on the third did she falter, although she knew the benediction well. Her eyes saw the world through a film of water.

"Erin." Her own name, so small, so insignificant compared to the value and worth of the two previous. But one day that would be different. One day, Erin of Elliath would serve Lernan in a way that all would note. She swore it silently, as she had done for so many years.

The Lady nodded and turned stiffly to face the rest of the warriors of Line Elliath.

Erin stood on the lawn and looked at the white face of her house. It seemed, as it cast its afternoon shadow, suddenly large and empty. She had argued, alongside her mother, to be able to stay in it alone; now she wasn't so certain it had been a good idea. The Grandfather had allowed their request, with the provision that he come to check in on her in the evenings.

Evening was still hours off.

Her head turned to look at the smooth market path, and she dug deep into her pockets before giving a little sigh; there were coins there.

Her mother had gone with the warriors to the front.

She couldn't follow; no one would allow that. And she'd been excused from class for the day to attend the ceremony.

Her mother was gone.

Shaking her head to clear her eyes, she began to march down the path, keeping her eyes on it. Her fists were clenched in her student robe so no one could see them. Even if she had seen only ten summers, she was still of the lines, and war was the way of life. She wasn't going to embarrass her mother by crying.

The flags were flying in the circle; she searched their colored triangles until she caught sight of the brown and green of Katalaan the baker.

Katalaan had been part of the market circle for as long as Erin could remember; longer, as she'd come to Elliath on merchant caravans years before Erin's birthing. She was a short, plump woman whose hair had grown grayer as the seasons passed. Sight of her, covered nearly from head to toe in the colors she'd chosen, was always welcome, especially to the children of the village, whether Lernari or not.

Erin wanted to see the old woman now, even if the pastries had already been sold or given away. She began to hurry, hiking the folds of her robe well over her knees.

The market square was almost empty, as the remaining shoppers packed up their purchases and made their way to their various homes. Erin drew a deep breath and looked up at the flagpoles to see that Katalaan's still flew full mast. They hadn't packed up yet; there was still time.

She followed the perimeter of the circle until she hit its northern edge. There she stopped, her hands touching the counter of the baker's stall.

Korfel came out from the back, holding a towel that looked as if it needed several good poundings. He worked with Katalaan, as he had done for years, yet he still wore initiate's gray and silver. No greens and browns for a warrior, not even if that warrior had retired.

"Erin," he said, raising an eyebrow. "What brings you here?"

"I've come to see Katalaan."

"Class is out early today." He stopped for a moment, and his eyes narrowed. "Today was the day the warriors left for the front."

She nodded.

"Did Kerlinda leave with them after all?"

She nodded again, bowing her head. It wasn't Korfel that she wanted to see.

"Erin." He leaned over the counter, carefully balancing himself. "You understand about the warrior's duty?"

"Y-yes." She looked at her feet. "Is Kat gone for the day?"

"Not quite." Korfel reached out to touch her chin. "But don't change the subject, Erin."

She wanted to tell him that he was the one who was changing it, but years of respect held her tongue. That and the knowledge that he was many years adult, and had done all he could in the Bright Heart's name to combat the Darkness.

"Everyone's parents must go to the front, sooner or later. The war is important, if all of this—" Here he swept one sturdy hand to encompass the market circle. "—is to continue. Do you understand?"

Yes, she understood. Hadn't her mother left?

"We have to be strong, Erin, we of the lines. We have to be stronger than any other mortals. Let's keep the tears to ourselves, shall we? I know it isn't easy, but we have to keep a good face to let those we defend know that the war goes well for the Light."

It was easy for him to say. He wasn't the one who was crying. Mortified, Erin nodded and turned blindly away from the refuge of Katalaan's stall.

"That's the most preposterous garbage I've ever heard."

Erin stopped at the sound of Katalaan's angry voice. She brought her hands to her cheeks and tried to smooth away the tears. They only smeared.

"Katalaan, I—"

"Can shut up any time now." The hatch to the stall was lifted, and Erin heard the bustle of brown and green from behind her back.

"Katalaan—"

"Didn't you hear me, Korfel?"

No one talked like that, not to Korfel. Erin turned around to see Katalaan's distinctly red face.

"Erin?"

She nodded dumbly, partly from shock, and partly because her throat felt too swollen for words.

"Don't you listen to him, dear. You didn't come to see him, after all." She reached out and gripped both of Erin's shoulders tightly. "We're not all so stupid, and we're not all so weak that we need to be lied to."

"Katalaan, I've not lied. This is the route the Lernari take to deal with their own troubles. We do not seek to burden others."

"For the Bright Heart's sake, Korfel!" If Erin thought Katalaan had sounded angry before, she was mistaken. "Even the Lernari don't demand that their children go out to the front! You've obviously never lost a child yourself—or never had to leave one—" She caught herself almost grimly. "Why don't you pack up and go."

Korfel nodded, equally grim, and disappeared from view.

"I don't understand that man sometimes. Says this life is a better one—but still can't shake his training. Don't you ever be like that, Erin. We're all people, and this is all our war, no matter what anyone says. We've come from different places to be in Elliath, and we may not be perfect, we may not pick up swords, but we're willing to help.''

Erin nodded quietly.

"Come on, dear.'' She cast a backward glance at the stall. "I've not much left to sell or eat, but I'm just as good a cook when I'm not in the circle. Where are you staying?''

"At home.''

"With whom?''

She shook her head.

Katalaan nearly lost her eyebrows. "By *yourself*?'' Without waiting on a reply, she took Erin firmly by the hand. "Korfel!'' she shouted over her shoulder. "Close up here. I have to speak with someone. Come along, dear.''

"Are we going home?''

"Not quite yet.''

The knock that sounded at Serdon's study door was singularly unwelcome. He was tired; the ceremony often had that effect. He knew that many of his line-children, armed and armored, had marched to the front to die there, and there was nothing any Lernari could do to prevent those deaths. Worse still, Kerlinda had gone: Kerlinda, the healer; Kerlinda, the Lady's youngest daughter; Kerlinda, who had not been trained well enough to know how to die the warrior's death.

He chose to remain silent and hoped that the person on the other side of the closed door would accept this; whoever it was should well know that at this moment he needed his privacy. He bowed his forehead into his gray sleeve.

The knock grew louder and more distinct.

He waited a few moments more, then rose, scraping the hardwood legs of his chair against the carpet.

"What is it?'' he called as he opened the door.

To his surprise, no initiate grays greeted him; instead he saw the colorful brown and green that could only be market wear. And he knew the face well, if not the expression.

"Katalaan!''

"Don't you 'Katalaan' me, Serdon,'' the baker said, barging past him and into the room.

"Is there some problem?''

"I'll say there is.'' She looked at the chair for a moment and decided that she didn't want to sit. Her plump hands met her hips with a decided thump. "What by the Hearts do you think you're doing?''

"Pardon?"

"Leaving young Erin to live on her own, without even another Lernari for company?"

"Erin?" His blue eyes widened then. "Ah, Erin."

"She didn't lose her father that long ago, and her mother's gone the same route. Where is your brain?"

"Katalaan, she isn't just a village child, she's—"

"She's still a child, even if she's of the lines."

"She's not your concern. Her mother and I have arranged for her care between us." Serdon's words had grown distinctly more clipped.

"Is that what you call it?"

Swords could not have been as sharp as the glare that passed between them.

"Very well, Kat." The Grandfather's voice said no such thing. "What would you have us do? The child wishes to remain at home. She approaches her adulthood quickly; we cannot just disregard her wishes."

The baker's snort told him what she thought of that.

"Enough, Kat. If you have a better idea, I'd be pleased to hear it. If you don't, I have pressing matters here that require my attention."

"All right then." Katalaan headed toward the door. "I'll stay with her."

"Pardon?"

"You want her to stay with the line, and the line lives in the northern village. I live in the southern village, so she can't stay with me." She stopped, framed by the door. "I'll move in."

"You're going to live with *me*?"

"If you'll have me." Katalaan looked at the open sky that the cloister walls framed. "I've been living on my own these past few years, since Gerris died. I'd be happy for company."

Erin bit her lip, not sure of what to say.

"I asked the Grandfather, dear, if that's what's worrying you."

"Oh." The wrinkles in her forehead deepened for a moment. "What did he say?"

Trust her to ask. Katalaan smiled. "He said if I'd a good idea, I was welcome to it."

"So he thinks it's a good idea?" She smiled almost shyly and looked at the crimson splash of sun. "Then we'd better go; dinner's really late."

Katalaan took her hand firmly. "Yes, we had. You'll have to lead the way from here."

Erin smiled. "There's not much to eat. But we—I have plenty of room."

"Children!" The word slammed into the four stone walls of the east courtyard. Telvar frowned in disgust as Kredan limped out of the drill circle. "All of you!" He drove the point of wooden sword into the packed dirt. Erin was surprised it didn't splinter even though the ground was "soft" in the lesson area. "Time and again you forget yourselves. You let words interfere with your abilities!" Not that he thought much of the ability, either.

Kredan was in tears. His left leg pained him; he knew well from his two years with Telvar that it would already be purple and swollen. He felt the sympathy of his classmates as he bowed his head under the open blue of the sky.

"Well? What do you have to say for yourself?"

Kredan said nothing. The sting of Telvar's tongue was legendary—it hurt more than any injury the weaponsmaster might inflict.

Today he was worse than usual. Everyone knew why. He had spent the last three days standing honor guard at the ceremonies of departure.

He wants to be out on the front, but he's too valuable here. He may be the best warrior, but he's also the best weaponsmaster.

Erin grimaced; she bore her own set of bruises from the day's exercise, and Telvar's grim fury showed no sign of abating. She smiled wryly; compared to Telvar, the enemy was going to be utter joy and ease.

"You! Is there something amusing about this?"

Bright Heart, Erin prayed—her own was sinking rapidly.

"No sir."

"Good," He gestured. "Maybe you'd care to take your turn at the sword again."

But I just did! Nonetheless she hefted her practice blade. Everyone in the class knew better than to question one of Telvar's orders, no matter how indirectly given. Erin had always learned quickly. She walked away from the safety of cobbled stone onto grass, and then onto the dirt of the circle itself, until she stood five feet away from the master.

"Stance." Telvar barked.

The word was irrelevant; Erin had fallen into proper stance the moment she'd lifted the sword. On occasion this would elicit an approving nod from the weaponsmaster—but not, it appeared, on this one.

She kept the stance, but Telvar had apparently forgotten her for the moment. The sun beat down on her; she thought her hair was burning, because he didn't allow the use of a sunhat. The padded jerkin and leggings that she wore didn't help either. But at least they were near white so they didn't absorb extra heat—as if that were possible.

"Today we start on the most important aspect of the warrior-priest." He glared at the class, waiting for some response. Everyone listened attentively, not wanting to interrupt Telvar's lecture with the extraneous questions he disliked so much.

It was a no-win day.

"I see that you all know well what it is from your lack of questions. Kredan, since you were so hapless at arms, perhaps you can redeem yourself by explaining it to me."

Kredan wished, very briefly, that the enemy could arrange its attacks at a time when they didn't have lessons. He let his head dip in guilt; the thought was in poor taste.

"No, sir."

"No?"

"I don't know what it is, sir."

"I see. Well then, perhaps Korallis."

"No, sir."

"Anyone?" He snorted in disgust. "Very well. Skill at arms is important in defense of the line. I shall take that as the given in the hopes that even one of you will attain some skill in the future." He lowered his weapon.

Erin relaxed slightly, but she still kept her stance.

"There will be times when this skill avails you nothing." He looked up for a moment, beyond their youthful heads, and closed his eyes—as much a sign of sorrow as he permitted himself. "The enemy may have greater numbers than our scouts could see. A nightwalker may roam abroad among the corps of the Malanthi fighters. You do know what a nightwalker is?" A child barely able to talk could answer that question, but Telvar's glare made it clear where he placed the intelligence of his students.

"A Servant of the Enemy," Korallis volunteered.

"True." Clearly Telvar was not impressed. "And why do you call them nightwalkers?"

"'Cause they walk at night," Allantir broke in. "They can't

walk during the day. And when they're walking, they're feeding on the death-pain and unwillingly given lifeblood of those that they kill. I hear it takes a long time for their victims to die, worse than in blood ceremonies of the Enemy.''

"Well, it appears you can learn something after all. You had better listen to what I say now. You *will* learn this.

"Against such a power, you cannot prevail. Do you understand this? Only on two occasions have the Servants of the Enemy ever been caught by Lernari fire, and on each, they were feeding on the lifeblood of the taken. They will not feed among our warriors; the cost and risk is too high. Do not attempt to be heroic should you see or sense a nightwalker. Understood?''

Nods all around.

He closed his eyes again. Shook his head wearily.

"If you can escape, you are to do so. But if you cannot . . . that is what we begin to learn today.''

He wheeled suddenly, lunging at Erin.

She blocked, dodging to the side as he had taught her; taking advantage of size and speed rather than brute strength.

This time, when he met her eyes, he nodded briefly. One never let one's guard down around Telvar. Never.

"Erin. You have some skill in blood-power. Call forth light.''

She frowned, an expression not lost on her master.

"You can call forth light at your age, can't you?''

Bristling, she bent to put the sword down.

He attacked, the ferocity of the strike forcing a whistle from the breeze. She had enough time for a feeble block, but the impact tossed her off her feet. By luck alone, she managed to keep her grip on her sword.

"Again.'' But this time he began to circle her, his intent clear.

This isn't fair! She watched him warily, her concentration on his attack alone. She had managed, over the years, to call light without the necessity of broad gestures, exchanging the width of full circle for the dance of two fingers. But she still had to clear her mind and *think* on it.

"Light, Erin. Now.'' On the last word, he swung.

She leaped lightly off the ground, avoiding the sweep of his left foot. Her blade forced his own to the side.

In anger, she returned his attack, desperately searching for an opening. Unlike Telvar, she was indirect in her attempts, dancing to the side and feinting, striking for lower thigh or upper shoulder cuts. He warded off each attack very coolly.

It was hard not to succumb to the same trap that had taken Kredan. She ignored his taunting command to summon forth power and poured her energy into thoughtful attack.

Then, out of nowhere, a brilliant light flared in the quad. It took her by surprise; it was strong enough to be almost white. Normal eyes could have seen it. She backed away to the periphery of the fighting circle, her sword at an awkward angle—but still in her hands.

A muted exclamation of surprise touched the air.

"You see, Erin. It can be done. You may rejoin the class."

Feeling humiliated, she put her sword away and stood stiffly behind most of her line-mates.

"This, this is what you must learn: the ability to use your blood-power when it appears that you are unable to concentrate. There is a risk; when fighting an opponent of greater skill, you will most certainly be killed."

Kredan raised a hand; Telvar nodded.

"Then why take the risk, sir?"

Telvar smiled bitterly. "There are times when no risk is involved." He saw the quizzical looks on their faces as they watched him. He had seen it many times, on faces that now lay beneath the shallow earth.

"If you are taken, or captured. If you fall into the hands of the Malanthi or the nightwalkers."

Someone else raised a hand.

"You just said that we can't hope to win against a walker, sir."

"No. All you can hope for is a clean death."

Silence. Always this uneasy silence. Telvar dearly wished that his pupils were adult, but at that age there was too little he could teach them in skill at arms.

Clearing his throat, he continued.

"I will teach you how to summon a clean death for yourself if the need arises. You will feel no pain, or little of it, should any attempt to use you for the dark ceremonies. Nightwalkers will have little or no satisfaction should they personally destroy you; there will be no pain to feed on; no fear."

May you learn this well, students. May you keep enough wit to use it. Unbidden, his dead returned to haunt him, their faces frozen in the rictus of agony. *The Servants walk. You will learn.*

"This is the warrior-gift. This is what all warriors must know."

* * *

"Where on Earth did you get that bruise?"

Erin reached gingerly for the milk jug. "Lesson," she murmured.

"Lesson?" Katalaan placed a large, covered dish on the center of the table. Her hands, callused and strong, apparently didn't notice how hot it was. Erin wondered if *she'd* feel the scorching heat less as she got older. She doubted it.

She placed the jug on the table and went back to the kitchen for plates and cutlery.

"What kind of lesson?" Kat's question followed her.

"Sword." Erin smiled tentatively, although her jaw hurt. "I relaxed too much."

"And that's how they discipline relaxation? No wonder I've trouble tearing you away from your books!" This time Katalaan chuckled, although her eyes never left the purpled side of Erin's face. "I'd have been happy if my own son had half your determination."

Erin nodded. She'd heard this many times, but had discovered that Katalaan didn't like to be asked about this son. Instead, she began to talk about history lessons, as Kat was happy with those. They sat and began to eat, after Kat had said a "proper" thanks.

It was nice to have her there. She wasn't a mother, true, and she wasn't of the lines, but she was a friend.

Not as good a friend as Belf, of course, but pretty close.

"Ow!"

"Belfas, you let your guard down again!"

"Sorry." He clearly wasn't. He limped, with exaggeration, to one side of the grassy slope near the quiet market circle and sat down heavily, tossing the sword from one sweaty palm to the other.

"Belf, it's important. Do you think the enemy is going to care—"

"We've got enough real enemies. We don't need to pretend. Can't we practice something else?"

"You said you wanted me to teach you what Telvar's teaching us." Erin sighed. At times Belfas was fast, and his parrying better than hers.

"I said no bruises."

"All right." She put the weapon down.

"It isn't like I'm not already taking lessons."

"Not from Telvar."

He grimaced. *And I used to want to. Thank the Bright Heart*

I wasn't chosen. He put his sword down happily and sank into the grass.

"Belfas!"

"Erin!" He looked up, shading his eyes from the sun. "This *is* supposed to be a day of rest."

"We agreed."

He groaned and forced himself into a sitting position. "Erin, I can summon light. I can perform the Lesser Ward and the Greater Ward. I can find my way back home from anywhere blindfolded. What else do you want?"

"I—"

Half-maliciously, he added, "And I can also walk memory."

"Your father's blood." But she frowned; she'd tried it secretly several times, but her memory wasn't any better than one without the blood. In fact, if you asked most people, they often said it was worse.

"Sorry. I didn't mean that." And he genuinely was sorry. Erin could be impossible, but she was still his best friend. He just couldn't understand why she always had to be so perfect— and worse still, why she always tried to make him perfect.

"Doesn't matter. You've got it, I don't." Her eyes became quite businesslike, and Belfas groaned. She'd thought of something else.

"Fire."

This time he did sit up. "Fire? *White-fire?* Are you crazy? That's war-skill, Erin. They don't teach that until we become adult."

"They don't teach us enough until we become adult. But I'm sure we can learn it. I mean, you've started memory walking, and they don't really teach that until we're adult. Besides, I'm eleven summers, you're twelve. We're bound to be adult soon. We can just start early."

He hated that phrase.

As he watched her brow pucker in concentration, he wondered briefly why he hadn't found a more sensible best friend yet.

"Word from the front?" Serdon, Grandfather of Line Elliath, looked up from a desk littered with papers—each important, each urgent, and most unanswered as of yet. The windows of his study showed sundown was near, but years of discipline kept him at a pretense of work, even when his mind wasn't on it.

Latham nodded quietly, walking into the study itself to take one of four vacant seats. He looked up at the flat, plain ceiling and stretched his neck, pushing his cowl aside. "Pallen's just arrived, Grandfather. He's taking a moment with his daughter; he'll be in shortly."

The Grandfather smiled and shuffled his chair around to face his visitor's. "Not if I know his daughter. But come, what word?"

"As much as we may both have disagreed with Kerlinda, she seems to be doing her work well; our casualties on the front have lessened dramatically, although apparently she's ridden three horses into ground. She's been traveling with the companies, but she goes where she's needed."

"Worried?"

Latham nodded. "But I do that frequently."

The Grandfather frowned.

We both worry, Latham, and we both have good reason. She drives herself harshly. I wonder if she sees the faces of the saved at all—or if she dwells only on the dead. But even that was not the greatest worry. He ran a gray-sleeved arm over his forehead and closed his eyes a moment.

"She isn't warrior-trained. Not truly."

Latham was grateful to the Grandfather for putting into words the fear that not even he would voice. But having said it, what else was left?

"The Lady will be pleased."

Latham watched the Grandfather closely for a moment.

Will she? He wondered. *Kerlinda is her youngest.*

Telvar swung low, pulling his shield back.

Erin jumped up, feeling the wood of the blade skim the bottom of her boots. She landed to the side as his shield came forward, missing her.

They had been fighting for fifteen minutes—each one, like this, strenuous and exhausting. He was pleased; she could tell this because he drew the energy—from where, she didn't know—to step up his attack. He'd not yet managed to connect.

She parried well, but dodging was more effective; twice the sheer strength of his blow had almost unbalanced her. Unfortunately, dodging required more energy. She bit her lower lip. She was going to lose this one. Then again, she always did against Telvar.

He feinted low; she began to jump to the side when he shifted the direction of his sword in midswing.

The sound of wood against bone was unmistakable.

Against any other opponent, she would have cried out in pain. This was Telvar. She bit her tongue, tasting the tang of salt in her mouth.

She kept fighting, but less smoothly now, and much more defensively. The pain was bad.

She tried to concentrate around it, adjusting her movement to favor her injured side. Just as she would have to do if she fought a real enemy.

Real enemy? The strength of Telvar's continued attack made her wonder. But not for long; just as she favored her side, he did, striking or feinting for her injuries.

It wasn't fair; they both knew it—but they both knew that their enemies would not be fair in battle.

She concentrated, defending against his attack. His sword hit her side again, less easily and less viciously than before, but no less painfully.

For a second she wanted to call it—but only for a second. Then she clamped her jaw shut.

No. Let him call it when he's finished. She pushed the pain back with the force of her will, raw and angry.

The pain diminished. Not immediately, but quickly enough that she noticed it. She had no time to wonder; instead she took advantage of her renewed freedom of motion.

And for the first time, she managed to land a blow. A feeble one, but it didn't matter.

Telvar raised his right hand.

"Hold."

He was smiling.

Erin couldn't recall a time when she had seen him smile before, not even outside of the circle.

She began to back away to the edge of the green.

Still smiling, he saluted her. "Congratulations, Erin. You've managed to achieve power-use and continue to fight." He frowned as he met her confused stare. "You did that on purpose, didn't you?"

Did what? She shook her head. It was the only time that she had ever done well enough to receive Telvar's praise—and she had no idea what he was talking about.

"Bright Heart, girl. You've a power, then." His frown deepened. He'd seen the pale green glow that had briefly touched her—the signature of Lernari magic. And he could guess at its use. But if she'd summoned it unknowing . . . *She must be very*

much her mother's child. Healing blood; Lernan's truest legacy.
Why do they train her in warrior arts? He paused a moment.
Kerlinda is at the front.

"Erin!"

Both the master and his student turned at the sound of the
familiar voice. Surprise kept Telvar's customary—legendary—
reaction to interruption of his lessons at bay. He even managed
not to frown as Erin threw down her weapon and leaped out of
the drill circle.

"Mother!"

Kerlinda was already kneeling, arms spread wide to catch her
daughter in midflight. She was dirt-stained, the edge of her cloak
as muddy as her booted feet. Her hair, once long and glorious,
was now cropped closely about her ears for practicality's sake.
Even so, there was no mistaking who she was. She felt her
daughter's thin arms close tightly around her neck and smiled
breathlessly over Erin's shoulder at any who cared to watch their
reunion.

Telvar was one. He knew well what Kerlinda was feeling, and
the fact that she was still alive to feel it almost brought a smile
to his lips. Almost—he was, after all, still in the middle of a
lesson.

"Kredan."

The entire class turned back to the drill circle at the clipped
word.

"I see that you've learned enough to be able to ignore what's
being done. Come. Enter the circle."

Kredan groaned wordlessly. If he could ever manage to school
his facial expression, he'd be set.

Only Telvar watched Kerlinda and Erin depart. Arm in arm,
heads bent together in quiet whispering that even his ears could
not catch all of, they made their way home.

But it was different having her mother's quiet presence instead
of Katalaan's noisy one. Kerlinda had invited Katalaan to stay,
but the older woman had demurred, wanting Erin to have the
chance to be alone with her mother.

And that's how Erin felt—alone.

The moment they entered their house together her mother had
gone strange and silent, as if the walls were too small, too tight.

"Mother?"

"Hmmm? Oh, Erin." Kerlinda smiled dimly. She turned

away, running her hands along the rail of the stairs. "Have you changed the house around?"

"No!"

"I'm sorry, I didn't mean to criticize." She brushed her fingers through her short hair and began to pull her boots off. "I just wondered."

Erin said nothing.

After a moment, Kerlinda looked up. "Erin, I didn't mean anything by it." She was pale, and the rings under her eyes were dark. "I'm fine; it's good to be home."

Erin wanted it to be true, but her mother looked so different. Thinner. Harsher.

"Can I—can I get you something?"

"No. Not for the moment. I'll take care of it myself." Her mother paused. "Is everything in the same place?"

Katalaan had rearranged much of the kitchen with Erin's help, but Erin still nodded. She wanted her mother to feel at home.

But although her mother stayed for two weeks, she never seemed as if she truly belonged there. And Erin didn't know how to ask her why.

chapter
three

"Belf, why were they made?"

Belfas looked up to see Erin as she paced across the lawn. This was the second time in his life that Erin had allowed him to just relax; he should have known that it was too good to be true. He pulled at a piece of grass, inspected its end, and inserted it between his lips.

"They?"

"The Light and the Dark."

He shrugged. "Don't know. Why not ask Kedry?"

"Kedry doesn't know either."

"Well, if she's adult, and a teacher, and she doesn't know, how should I?"

Erin sighed.

"But someone—something—must have made them. I mean, everything has a beginning."

"Erin—" He cut back the sentence and picked another piece of grass. "No one knows that, not even the Lady herself." He propped himself up on one elbow, shielding his eyes from the sun. He watched her for a moment, then frowned.

"You're thinking about the dead again." It wasn't a question.

She nodded, biting her lower lip gingerly between her teeth. Her mother had been at the front for nine months—no, ten now. And the attacks along the front had shifted the line of defense; the Enemy and his cursed Servants had once again gained ground.

We believe that the spirit goes beyond, into peace and a different life—one free of our eternal conflict.

Believe. She snorted. Why didn't anyone *know*?

She walked over to the edge of the lawn, where a small row of flowers had been planted by Belfas's mother. She stared at

36

their brightly colored faces without really seeing them—she often didn't notice the outside world when she was thinking.

If someone or something had created this Light and this Dark—this endless conflict—why had they bothered? Why not just create something peaceful and whole to begin with?

Then her father would be alive. Her mother would be happy. And they wouldn't have to say so many good-byes to so many of their line-mates. She ground her teeth.

"C'mon, Belf. Let's go down to the Gifting."

"What, *now*?"

"Yes, now. I'm not going to use it; I'd never be that stupid."

"I didn't think you—"

"Then stop being so lazy."

"Lazy? Erin, it's five miles. We might miss dinner."

She brushed her robe clean. "Well, I'm going."

Belfas grumbled. He stood, looked at the plain front of his house, and thought about what his mother would say if he told her where they were going. It wasn't good. But he followed Erin; he almost always did.

Erin kicked at a dry branch. Birds fluttered away at the noise. Thoughts about the histories still held her fast; she could hear the din of battle and the cries of the dying more clearly than the twittering of the birds.

She kicked another branch, noticing the shadow it cast as it flew. Belfas was right; they would definitely miss dinner. Never mind; they were almost there. The dense forest had opened up slightly around the gentle depression of the footpath that arrowed into the Gifting. The Gifting of God; the wound from which the blood of the Bright Heart flowed freely, to aid His followers in their battle against the Servants of the Dark Heart, grim nightwalkers who cast a shadow of death wherever they chose to walk.

They hated life. Erin remembered that most clearly when she thought of her father. Their hate for life was their power, for in destroying it they grew stronger.

And God, they were so strong right now . . .

She shook her head; beyond the last uneven row of trees, she could see the Gifting of Lernan. Even Belfas stopped grumbling as they entered the well-kept clearing. No eyes had ever seen the keeper of it, but no eyes could doubt that he or she existed; the flowers and grass, the wild weeds and stones, seemed placed perfectly to highlight the nature and strength of the well.

It didn't look like much to human eyes. A large, stone well, surrounded by pretty white flowers—flowers that remained in bloom no matter what the season. The water was clear; it glinted with sunlight and reflected the green of leaves.

But both Belfas and Erin were of the blood. And they saw, in the water, a green that radiated so strongly they would have seen it in the darkest of nights. This was the blood of God; his gift of succor to those who fought their uneven battle against the Enemy.

Very quietly, as was their right, they approached the sparkling font of water, passing around the stand of the Lady's trees, where small golden petals flittered to the ground. Erin dipped her hands into soothing cool liquid. She lifted hands to face; felt a familiar refreshing tingle along her cheeks. This little gesture cost the Bright Heart nothing, but it comforted his descendants.

Belfas did the same, content to rest for a moment in the warmth of the Gifting of God. This well, this clear pure water— this was the very blood of the Bright Heart. It could lend its healing to any who came for His aid; could comfort the weary or broken.

For as time passed, Lernan realized that too many of His followers fell, sacrificing their lives to touch His power. Many times He tried to reach them, but their very life was alien; only by blood, lifeblood, could He be reached at all. Long He thought, and hard, and then one day He summoned His Servants to Him. And with their aid, He returned sacrifice for sacrifice, blood for blood. He opened up His own body in two places and offered it to his children.

And thus the Gifting.

Erin sighed, letting rivulets of water run down the contours of her face. The Gift of God. Even without mingling her blood with His, she could feel a hint of His comfort.

She had often wondered what it would feel like to let her blood run freely with God's—but anyone of the lines knew better than to satisfy that curiosity, for the mingling of the blood brought the power of God to mortal man. It diminished God in small measure for a time, and it was never a thing used lightly.

Even now, with the battle constantly raging, Erin could not recall the last time that an initiate had come to the well to draw upon God's power so fully. Most of the adults chose to rely instead on the smaller amount of power the True Ward could bring them.

Erin sighed.

"The thing I understand least—" She glanced at Belfas in time to catch his grimace. "—is why life only started when the Light and the Dark touched for the first time. They were so different; they hated each other so much."

"Life?"

"Well, the Servants are alive."

"Some of them." But he smiled. It wasn't often that he could answer any of Erin's questions.

She caught the smile and returned a frown. "Tell me."

"Sure. Kedry started it a month ago. You'll get to it soon enough, so I don't suppose it'll hurt.

"The important thing to remember about the Light and the Dark is that they weren't really alive—and they weren't at all human. I mean, sure we say they 'hated' each other, but Kedry says it's only so we can relate to it—what they really felt is both older and stronger."

"What's that got to do with life?"

"I'm getting to it." He didn't want to get to it too quickly, though. If he was going to miss dinner, he wanted something to savor. "The Light was light, but more than that. It was . . . possibilities. I mean, everything that we are came out of the Light. The Dark was darkness, but it was more, too." He frowned. "And part of all of us came out of the Dark as well." That part he still had trouble accepting. He shook his head. "But the important thing is that they both were unchanging. They each had everything they needed."

Erin didn't have to prod him now; she began to understand what he was saying.

"And when they touched, they both saw all the things that they weren't, and where they touched, their nature changed."

"Changed?"

He shrugged. "I'm not clear about it. But they changed—and the change was life. Something that had the ability to be anything."

"Anything?" She frowned again. "But the Servants were first. And the Lady could never be the First of the Enemy."

"I didn't think so either," Belfas confessed. "But Kedry says that perhaps the Lady could choose to be—it would just be really hard for her, because there's so much of the Light in her."

"Maybe that's why they call themselves the Sundered. They aren't all of Light or of Dark."

"I didn't think of that."

"You never think unless you're forced to."

"You never give me enough time." But he smiled, letting his fingers dance over the surface of the Gifting. "Does it make sense?"

"Sort of."

"People—like us—came after, when the Light and the Dark were more tightly bound. More change. More growth."

"But—" She stopped, cupped a handful of Lernan's blood, and swallowed it thoughtfully. "But that means that we'll always be fighting. I mean, because there's Light and Dark in all of us."

"Maybe. Dannen asked Kedry about it. Kedry said, 'Yes and no.' "

Erin nodded; it sounded like Kedry.

"She says the important thing is choice. Either of us could choose to be like the Malanthi. And we don't. So Lernan touches us and wins a little more of the Light. If all our battles, Light or Dark, were so easy . . .' "

"But they aren't." She looked up at the pink sky. "We'd better be getting back."

But she was disappointed. If the Light and the Dark were so absolute, why couldn't they give her absolute answers? Why did everything have to be so confused?

Why? She stretched her face into the hushed velvet of moonlight and stars; the breeze of a gentle night wind; the hint of trees that stood, like Earth's fingers, unmoving. None of these held her answers.

"Lady?"

She turned, all flowing regal light, knowing who she would see. Of all her line, Latham was the one who came closest to offering her comfort. Still, she had thought that this far from her hall, this far from the line, she might have the peace of privacy.

But any could find her who had the motive and the blood, both. Even here, where the outermost edge of Elliath met her forest.

In the darkness, she saw that his chin, smooth and rounded, was edged toward his chest. And she knew why, but let him speak his piece.

The night made his robes, silver and gray, take on the likeness of black.

"I've come with news. A rider just arrived from the meadow. Trist and Hayworth have fallen."

She was silent, absorbing the news that was no news to her.

The possibilities had now become fixed; she had raised no hand to change their outcome.

"The villages were razed; the fields burned down. Much of our supplies have been lost. The Grandfather is sending supply wagons into Hillrock."

"Hillrock?" She knew the word, knew the small, isolated village well. "Ah. Yes."

Latham watched her near-expressionless face, seeing for a moment the majesty of mountains, of tall, endless rock, white-peaked even this far south. He wondered then, as he had often wondered in the last few years, how much she knew from her dangerous vision quest. She could not be moved to speak of it. But it troubled him more as time passed; the shadows evident in her face never left.

"It is not often, Lady, that you walk so openly among us." *Not often that you walk in darkness.* For she was as true to blood as any could be, and the dark diminished her.

She looked up at flickering starlight and moved her face to catch the hint of gentle breeze.

"No," she answered. "Not often."

He stood a few feet away, his distance respectful as always. She studied his shadowed countenance carefully.

"But at times, Latham, the dark has its comfort."

She stretched her arms out, as if to touch the brightest star that glistened so impossibly far away. "Once, once I might have wandered there. Once I might have touched the fire and felt cleansed."

She was weary. She knew she would never do so again.

"Lady." Latham took a step forward and raised an arm. He lowered it without touching her, and she moved away.

"But the dark. Sometimes the dark can give me a hint of what mortality feels like."

Latham was concerned. For the last two months, the Lady of Elliath had been somber. Watching her, he saw she looked almost translucent; as if the light could cut right through her and leave nothing behind—no shadow, no outline. He had never seen her so.

If she felt his worry—and she must have—she did not let it trouble her.

"I walked the skies before you were born."

He knew she spoke not of him alone, but of the mortal race.

"Centuries passed, with the touch of nothing beneath my feet. All was Light, Dark, or the Servants that followed their closest parent. And we fought, Latham. Many of the Sundered fell in ways that you cannot conceive of. But then we felt no sorrow. Can you imagine that? No sorrow, no pain. There was Light; there was Dark. And each, unalloyed, can blind.

"And then you were born, the world was born. The Twin Hearts awoke by the touch of Gallin Bright Sword. And I have walked this world since, following Lernan.

"Lernan is not the Light. Malthan is not the Dark. Not as they were."

She was silent a moment. More than at any other time, she wanted to tell Latham all: the loss of the lines; the destruction of her child; and the fate of her grandchild—the darkest and direst of all paths of the possible that she had walked.

It is the way of Lernan to share all, she thought. But she did not tell him. Instead she yearned for the past in a way that she could not explain. All had been simple, clean, elegant. There had been only one Enemy—the Dark—and only one way to fight Him. But then came the world and the mortal creatures. She remembered how much she had pitied them, despising their taint, their grayness. She had forced herself, at the beginning, to find Light in them.

How, she thought, as she turned to Latham in silence, *how did you come to mean so much to me? Your lives are so short— without the wars, we would lose you all, should we wander again. How is it that your loss grieves me, who felt no loss at the fall of my brethren?*

She kept the thought to herself, but she could not contain all of the emotion. Of a sudden, she thrust her thin, long arms outward. Fire flared, white and hot, brilliant even in the darkness. Thus had she fought her ancient enemies; thus had darkness been consumed and forgotten.

The fire flickered and dimmed. Not so easily now could the light prevail.

"I am sorry," she said to a quietly startled Latham. "It is . . . dark tonight. Come, let us return to the hall."

But it was hard, this night, to turn her back on memory. The Dark that so many had fallen to had never been able to hurt her so.

It was the only time in her long existence that she had ever yearned for the Dark, and that troubled her.

"Lady?"
"Latham."

He walked down the length of the conservatory, his steps measured and slow.

"What news brings you?"

"No news, Lady. But I have been asked to deliver this to you personally." His lips lifted a little; something amused him. She liked to see him smile. It happened rarely these days.

"Who uses you as a messenger?"

"The Lady's granddaughter."

It was a measure of her strength that she did not freeze. Instead, she held out one graceful hand for the letter that he carried.

"She is much like her mother. Little consideration for age or authority, but no knowledge whatsoever that she's flouting it."

"Thank you, Latham." She nodded without breaking the uneven seal.

He was surprised, but he knew a dismissal when it was given. Bowing, he left her standing amid the exotic plants that lived in perpetual summer.

Only then did she lift the letter in trembling hands, gripping it as if it were a viper.

So soon?

With Latham gone, the need to appear completely strong deserted her. Her strongest desire was to destroy the letter, innocuous and innocent, in flame. Instead, she opened it.

"Grandfather." Telvar substituted a nod for the more formal bow he might have given in other circumstances—any other circumstance, in fact, than lessons in the drill circle.

The Grandfather smiled quietly. It still unsettled him, at times, to receive such a gesture from Telvar; Telvar was by a good many years the elder of the two—and in his youth, the Grandfather had been one of his students.

He felt a little like one now, as he stood by the weaponsmaster's side and watched his line-children in the drill circle.

"Erin," Telvar said, before the Grandfather could ask. "And Dannen. The two best in my class. You chose a good moment to come." He frowned. "Dannen is more solidly grounded than Erin, but Erin's fast. Light."

The Grandfather nodded.

"And it's strange, Grandfather," Telvar continued, folding his arms behind his back, "Erin is Kerlinda's child in more ways than one."

"Yes," the younger man replied quietly. "She has the

strongest healing blood the line has seen—or will see, if I guess correctly.''

"Healers aren't usually sent to me."

"No."

Telvar heard more in the one word than the Grandfather cared to speak. He nodded brusquely, which was the way he did everything. "You wish to speak with her?"

"If I'm not interrupting anything."

"Erin!"

The smaller figure in the circle dodged, leaped, and rolled in one smooth motion that brought her outside of the drill range. Dannen's blade skittered off the periphery.

"Telvar," the Grandfather said, before Erin reached them, "is she good?"

"Very. But she isn't adult yet, Serdon."

"I know." The lines of his face etched themselves into a smile.

"Grandfather?" Erin gave a sweaty bow. Telvar held out a hand, and she gave him her sword almost thankfully.

"Erin. I see you've taken well to lessons with the weapons-master."

She glanced around quickly to see if Telvar was still listening. Apparently not; he had already started his long stride to where Dannen stood panting.

"As well as anyone who hasn't had an arm or leg broken here can." She grimaced.

The smile on his face became genuine; it was a sentiment that any of Telvar's students, no matter how long ago they graduated, could appreciate.

"Good. I want to speak with you."

Her face paled. "Is it—is it my mother?"

"She is well, but yes, it's about your mother." He watched her relax. "I'm not sure how much you know about the action on our borders."

"A bit," she replied cautiously.

"Two of our villages have fallen, and with them much of the supplies for our companies. Two separate wagons are to be sent out, under guard, to Hillrock."

"That's in our borders."

He nodded. "A good forty miles."

"And?"

"Your mother is in Hillrock; she's due to return for a few weeks." He slipped a hand into the inner pocket of his robes and pulled out a folded piece of paper. When she didn't react, he unfolded it.

She had the grace to blush.

"You know 'a bit'?" He smiled. "I imagine Telvar has been talking, but no harm done. The Lady has approved your request, Erin; you may ride with the caravan to Hillrock."

The smile that spread across her face was a delight to behold.

"But child, the next time you have such an unusual request, please forward it through *me*."

"Yes, Grandfather," she replied demurely. But they both knew she was lying.

"I don't believe it. You had the cheek to go 'round the Grand-father's back and you still get to go with the wagons." Belfas was hopping from one foot to the other, partly because he was angry, and partly to keep himself awake. It was early enough that the trek to Erin's house hadn't managed to drive all the sleep from his eyes.

Erin folded down the flap of her small pack and tied it with jubilant authority.

"The rest of us try to be polite and proper about it, and we're told we have to stay here."

She picked her weapon up off the bed. It was a short sword of less than perfect craftsmanship, but she loved it nonetheless; it was Telvar's gift to her.

Not, he had added severely as he'd dropped it in her hands, *that I expect you to have* any *use of it. Understood?*

"Erin!"

"Hmmm?"

"I'm talking to you!"

"At me." She looped the sword around her hips and fastened the belt. "*To* me is when I answer."

"Very funny. It isn't fair, that's all." He shoved his hands roughly into his pockets.

"It isn't like I'm going to war or anything."

"Then why're you taking the sword?"

"In case."

"I just don't understand it. You aren't even adult yet!"

"I will be soon enough."

He sighed. He knew she was right. She'd become adult prob-ably years before he did; and she'd be out fighting battles and becoming a hero long before he'd manage to shed lifeblood and call God in True Ward. He could barely manage the Greater Ward even now.

She threw on her jacket and lifted the backpack. He automatically caught it and held it out, waiting for her to slip her arms into its straps.

"It's because you're one of Telvar's students, isn't it?"

"No, Belf, it isn't."

"Then why?"

"Because I asked the right person first." She walked toward the door. "Are you coming to see me off?"

"I didn't wake at four in the morning just to talk."

"You wouldn't know it."

In the fading darkness, she could still see the flush that took his face. "Sorry," she murmured, letting her hand fall away from the door. "I didn't mean that."

He shrugged. "Yes, you did. But I guess I deserve it. I just want—I want to be able to go with you. I mean, we do almost everything together. That's what year-mates are for."

She nodded. "I asked the Grandfather. He said no."

"You could have asked the Lady."

She nodded again apologetically. "I didn't—I didn't think about it."

"I would have."

Which was undeniably true. She let her head hang for a moment. Sometimes she wondered why Belfas put up with her.

"All right, all right. I didn't mean it, Erin. Come on. You'll miss the wagons."

She looked up and smiled as if testing the water.

He smiled in return—with less effort than he would have thought it would take. "Can I carry anything?"

She shook her head, but held out her hand.

He accepted the peace offering, and together they walked the path to where the wagons were already loading. It was market center, the only place in Elliath with enough room for the impressive number of horses and covered wagons.

"Just be careful, Erin. Okay?"

"I will be. But I won't be fighting, Belfas. I won't be anywhere near the front."

He snorted. "If anyone can find a way, you can. Just don't go adult on me when I'm not even around to appreciate it."

She hugged him, a brief, hard hug that surprised them both. "I won't. Swear it."

"And you'll hug that one, but you've nothing for me?"

They both gave a little jump.

"Kat!" Erin was already halfway across the green.

Katalaan smiled and held her arms out as Erin ran into them. "Thought you'd sneak off and leave, did you?"

"I didn't want to wake you."

"That's no excuse." She gave her almost-daughter a very tight hug. "You be careful, all right?"

Erin nodded.

"And come back to me. I've gotten used to living with another person; it wouldn't be nice to make me live alone again."

Erin shook her head and smiled. "Everything'll be fine."

From the Woodhall, the Lady watched the wagons leave. She was alone; she had insisted on being left alone. If it had been within her power to curse, she might have done so; but there was nothing to curse but the evil of choice.

Lernan. She longed to rest a moment in the hand of God as only true Servants could do. But she could not leave; the dread and anticipation of what was almost the present caught her in its ugly web and pinned her to Earth.

Why? Why is there no other way?

The drivers mounted their wagons, and the surrounding Lernari guards took up their positions. She searched for a glimpse of her granddaughter. Ah. There, sitting on the coach seat beside the driver. Talking. Erin so rarely talked, and never quite this cheerfully.

As the wagons began to roll, she started to her feet, then forced herself to be still.

Choice. Lernan's hope.

For the sake of certainty, she would have willingly borne all. But Lernan's hope was only that: hope—hope of an end to Darkness, to the Enemy and his schemes for all life; hope that rested not only on her choices, but on all the choices she could not influence and could not predict.

And for this she must sacrifice kin? For this she must forsake daughter and send granddaughter into a darkness that had no escape?

Yes. Because there is only one hope.

But not all of the choices that must be made are mine to make.

Oh, grandchild, as I must be strong, so must you be.

She let her head drop into her hands and began her endless wait.

chapter
four

"Well, Erin, you've certainly taken well to the traveling life."
Gordaris's fingers were tangled in the red-gold of his beard. Just
as well the lines wore gray—his hair was so striking, it didn't
blend well with most bright tones. It was pulled back in the
warrior braid and bound with what looked like copper. At this
time of day, it looked as if the sunset had reached through the
trees to touch and color him. *"Where on Earth did you learn to
pitch a tent so quickly?"*

Erin smiled almost shyly at the compliment. Rain and the
unusual chill of the past four nights hadn't managed to dampen
her spirit. She watched Gordaris as he inspected her tent pegs;
he'd done it every night since they'd left Elliath. And he always
said the same thing, too; sort of like Belfas.

"Telvar," she answered, as she straightened out her bed roll,
taking care to see that it rested against the oiled tarp and not the
sodden ground.

"That's right. You mentioned that."

She sighed. It was her first real hint that becoming adult didn't
necessarily mean being adult. Belf would, no doubt, be something like Gordaris. It could be worse; he could somehow grow
up to be Telvar. The thought made her want to giggle—but not
in front of adults.

"Well, I imagine you'll be happy enough when we arrive.
Hillrock's a few hours away yet, but we should hit it by midday
tomorrow. I hear your mother's out that way."

She nodded, catching his momentary frown. Everyone
seemed to react that way to the news that her mother was near
the border. She couldn't understand it.

"Still, it's quiet enough now. The last attack may have cost
us—but it cost the Enemy as well."

She nodded; it was something that everyone hoped for. But she didn't really believe it. "Gordaris?"

"Hmmm," he answered as he sat on a large rock, carefully avoided its sharper edges.

"Is the Sarillar going to be there?"

"The Sarillar? No." He scratched his jaw thoughtfully. "Not unless things have changed quite a bit since we left. Andin's out on the northern flank. Fighting's worst there, and his power's needed."

She hadn't heard much about the news from the north, but the Sarillar always went where the battle was fiercest.

She poked at the ground with her toes. The Sarillar was special; out of all priests, he was chosen by the Lady to be a vessel for a part of her power. The white-fire he could call at will was one example of that; he didn't need to complete the True Ward to do it. She envied him.

Of the seven lines, only Elliath had chosen—could choose—to invest so much of its power into a living being. But Elliath was special in other ways: Only Elliath, of all the seven lines, had been founded by a Servant of Lernan. The other six had been started by mortal followers of Lernan, their strength of blood the heritage of other Servants—Gallin of Meron, Bethany of Culverne, Gareth of Destarre, Curranen of Lovar, Marellesit of Laneth, and Guerdan of Cormont: the greater circle of initiates. They had all commanded great power in their day, and to guarantee that their power did not die with their mortal selves, they had vested it in various items: crown, staff, and ring.

Only the Lady of Elliath could be assured that the death of the Sarillar—or, of course, if it were a woman, the Sarillorn—did not mean an end to her power, for it flowed back into her to wait again upon her choice for a vessel.

And among the initiates of Elliath, there was no greater honor, and no greater responsibility to the line.

At least the enemy Malanthi and Servants didn't part from their power for any common good. It was one of the few advantages the Lernari had in their long fight.

"Don't look disappointed, Erin. If I'm not mistaken, you'll be adult soon enough. And if you're one of Telvar's, the border's where they'll send you. You'll see the Sarillar—and more of battle than you could possibly want to see. They sort of go together." He stood with a soft smile. "He's a sight when he calls the line power. Almost like the Lady—a little piece of God on Earth.

"Now come on, I smell what passes for food in these parts and I'm not going to trust my share of it to these wolves."

Erin smiled and joined him.

They were almost at Hillrock.

The road was rugged and hilly, twisting ever upward through dense thickets or scraping close under low-lying branches. The wagons, with their great wheels, had been built for it, though, and the horses seemed not to notice. Hillrock was aptly named, for it rested at the summit of a steady incline. Farms were there, but the ground was meant for mining, and the people of Hillrock split their time between these occupations.

Before the caravan entered Hillrock they saw the first wave of people from the village. A group of children, too young to be useful in the fields, caught sight of the wagons and came running. Erin watched them from the cab of the wagon, noting the way that their clothing fit—or didn't; Hillrock was not on an easy route for Elliath merchants, and clothing supplies were limited.

The children stopped about ten yards away; she could see the older ones craning to catch a glimpse of the wagons that followed hers. The little ones all shouted, waved frenetically, then turned heel and ran toward the farmhouses that were coming into view.

Gordaris smiled broadly.

"This is why we fight, Erin," he said as he urged the horses on. "Don't forget it. No cause, no deep ideal, can possibly mean more than this." His face hardened. "And this," he added softly, "is what we stand to lose. But that part you'd do best not to remember." He caught the curious look on her face. "War is a mass of contradictions and carefully acknowledged truths."

Maybe, she thought, as the wagons rolled onward, Gordaris was more of an adult than he first appeared. The brief pain that showed on his face was only the barest hint of what he had suddenly reminded himself of. Without thinking, she reached out and clutched one of the hands that held the reins. She felt a warmth swell briefly in her and flow out through her hands.

The tight grip relaxing was barely noticeable. But it was there, and it made her feel better.

As the fields came into sight, Erin sat forward in her seat, precariously balancing on her hands.

"Back, Erin," Gordaris said. But he smiled; she reminded him—for the first time—of his own young children, curiosity evident in every move she made. Not that she would be a child for much longer. He sighed, letting his glance stray from the road for a short while.

There are so many of you that we cannot protect.

It was the hardest lesson of adulthood to accept. Even accepting it, no Lernari could dwell on it for long—leave that to the Lady and the other Servants of the Bright Heart.

The wagon rolled noisily into the village center, toward a series of large tents. It was obvious that they were not a permanent part of the village. They were gray, bearing the circle proudly atop their peaks, but they had also been decorated with ribbons of red and yellow—Hillrock's colors.

Erin's eyes widened.

"Yes." He nodded at the silvered circle on the tent flap. "But wait until we stop. You didn't come this far just to break an arm or leg."

She was so excited she didn't resent his comment, although it was obvious he was talking to her as if she were a young child. Instead she waited for the wheels of the wagon to grind to a halt.

Before that happened, the flap of the tent lifted and someone peered out. He disappeared too quickly to be identified, but Erin heard the happy shout that came from behind the cover of gray canvas.

She clambered down the side of the wagon, adjusting the hilt of her sword. For a brief moment she wished that she had waited until she'd achieved her True Ward—she could see clearly just what her mother's silent expression would say.

Then she had no time to wish at all—her mother walked into the open. Erin's small feet nearly flew off the ground in her attempt to bridge the distance.

Kerlinda had barely enough time to recognize the hurtling figure before it was around her. And then her eyes widened; she disentangled herself just long enough to free her arms, then scooped her daughter into them. Only the care that she took to make sure that Erin's sword hilt didn't jab into her spoke of her experience with the warriors.

Later, Gordaris thought, as he took a moment to watch them, *later you'll wonder what she's doing here.* But it was the now that warmed him. He'd been fighting for long enough to take joy in any reunion, however brief or unusual. It was the one thing that all hoped for and too many never saw; no one here could take it for granted.

God, will this fighting never cease?

* * *

Kerlinda watched her daughter sleep on one of the makeshift cots that had served the injured so well. It was obvious that she was one of Telvar's young—and eager—students; even in sleep she didn't let the sword stray from hand's reach.

But this sleep, untroubled and gentle, made of the sword something of a stuffed animal; Erin's hands curled around it and drew it in.

Well, Erin, you may be a fine swordsman, but you are *still a child.* The thought gave her comfort; it meant that among the faces of the wounded and dying that drifted through her life, Kerlinda would not yet have to dread seeing Erin's. She felt guilty at the thought and wondered if all mothers of Lernari warriors felt thus when their children chose to take to the sword.

Very gently she leaned down and smoothed out Erin's hair. The darkness of it glistened with hints of deep red; Cordan's heritage. She hesitated, not wishing to wake her child. It had been years since she could sit so.

Nor would she have too much time to enjoy it; in a few hours she would have to see to the rationing of supplies and make sure that those who carried them knew their routes well enough to take alternates in case of trouble.

But then, finally, she would have a few weeks, sandwiched between the comfort of daughter and mother—the Lady of El-liath.

It was from you, Lady, that I gained my power. She sighed, letting rings of light cascade idly down her fingers. *But from father all else.*

I used to think you so cold, so distant. She cocked an ear, listened carefully, then turned back to her thoughts. *Maybe I didn't understand. Maybe distance is what you need if you have to live forever in this world.*

Instead of distance, Kerlinda had been forced to cultivate a peculiar numbness; to continue to heal the injured solely to send them, armed and ready, to the waiting fields. The deaths didn't hurt her as much now as they had when she'd lived at home in Elliath. There, life was almost normal, and what you lost to war was so clear and so blindingly sharp. But here, amid the noise and pain, it was easy to forget that death was loss.

Cordan, she thought, *was this the life you knew? Perhaps there is peace, not in dying, but in death.*

She leaned down once again, hovering over her daughter like shadow.

"Kerlinda."

She smiled up at the familiar face framed in its golden red. "I'm almost ready."

"You've been saying that for well over an hour now. You've got a few minutes more, but the last of the wagons is nearly loaded." He put an arm out and tapped her gently on the shoulder. "They'll survive well enough without you for a few weeks. They've done it before."

She nodded, a gesture that had no force behind it.

They shouldn't have sent you out here without training you first. Gordaris frowned. It wasn't the first time he'd thought it. *The whole world is too large a burden for any one of us to try to bear.*

Erin quietly carried what her mother had given her, slipping into the wagon she thought of as hers. Between bedrolls and supplies, she put down her mother's clothing. Maybe, if the Bright Heart smiled on her, she wouldn't have to watch her mother leave again. If she could somehow attain her True Ward, she would be adult—she could go with her mother back to the front to fight in the cause of God. Everybody told her she'd be adult soon.

She straightened the bedrolls, calling light to alleviate the darkness of the enclosed wagon.

The Lady of Elliath stood at the edge of line holdings. The grass, broken by the shadowed outlines of scrub, wavered inches below her feet. No building, no Great Hall, touched the horizon; no people, and no sound. Only here could she feel certain that Latham's power would not find her before she had proper warning.

It was dark.

She held herself very still, felt the breeze touch and gently lift her pale hair.

Once . . . once I would have walked . . .

But she did not look up at the stars; she did not seek the face of the helpless moon.

Is it darkness alone that I yearn for?

Her fingers bit bloodlessly into her palms. It helped to still their shaking.

It has not happened. She looked up now, seeing in the night sky all that she had seen in her five-year trance. *It has not hap-*

pened yet. Her feet suddenly touched the ground as she spun around to look almost wildly at her woods. She took a step forward and then let her knees collapse.

Yes, she was alone here, and the better for it. It would do no good to let Latham find her in such a state. Although her actions were rarely futile, she allowed herself this one indulgence: She covered her face with her cold, cold hands, feeling them as slim, ivory bars.

She waited. It was the most horrible thing that she had ever been called upon to do.

Time ends the burden of all mortals. I envy you.

It had not happened yet; she knew it because she knew the exact position of the moon in the clear sky. But it would happen; she would do nothing to prevent it.

The wait, the interminable, terrible wait, was almost over. She counted the minutes. She saw again the darkness, the flash of red-fire. She heard the terror and pain of Lernari screams.

She made no move to rise. This decision had been made almost fifteen years ago, and the cost had been accepted then. But she shook as she waited, curled against the living grass.

And when she raised her white face, her eyes were dark.

Kerlinda . . .

It was dark; in the years to follow, Erin would remember this clearly. Their camp fires burned cheerfully, lighting rock and leaves alike. They sat around them, playing with the images that each could find out of the burning of the wood. It was pleasant; a cool wind blew gently through the air, moving the low flicker of firelight as it pleased.

She sat beside her mother, too old to huddle in the curve of her arms, but too young to need to sit at a distance to prove her age. Gordaris and Trevor were there as well, resting their arms on their knees and conversing quietly.

All around the camp fires the wagons were huddled like walls, and between these, tents housed their weary travelers.

"Kerlinda."

Her mother looked up, eyes drawn away from the fire that seemed to hypnotize her.

Gordaris gave a tired smile. "To bed, I think."

"Bed?" She stretched, feeling almost idle. Leather chafed slightly at her arms, but it was a familiar feeling; no warrior went without armor except in the home of his line. "I've not had this much sleep since . . . since . . ."

"Since the last time you traveled with me, I'll warrant." He stood, stretching his arms. "But you'll have it now, Erin."

She stood up before her mother did; four weeks of traveling with Gordaris made his friendly tone impossible not to obey.

"Leaving me already?" Kerlinda smiled wistfully. "You've grown so much. I'm not sure I should let you out of my—what was that?"

The smile that had warmed her face fell away, and Erin saw clearly for the first time how lean her mother had become. Firelight shadowed the hollows of her cheeks as she spun around, her head tilted upward.

"Kerlinda?"

She stood thus a few moments as if listening, and then her face paled. Wheeling, she grabbed her daughter by the shoulders.

"Go," she said, her voice brooking no argument. "Not the tent. The second wagon. Go now." *Not here, Bright Heart!* Her daughter's face loomed before her like an accusation. *Not now!*

But power recognized power; this rule she understood clearly. And somehow—Bright Heart's blood, somehow—seventy miles from enemy lines, red-fire was burning.

Erin stumbled forward at the force of her mother's push. She righted herself and turned to see that her mother had already unsheathed the small sword she carried.

"Gordaris, call the alarm!"

Gordaris's sword already glinted in the darkness, his face the mirror of Kerlinda's. He nodded, and the sharp bark of his voice filled the clearing. Nothing remained of the friendly, absentminded driver that Erin had come to know so well.

Red-fire, Kerlinda thought. *The taint of the Dark Heart.*

But it's strong—it's never been so strong before. Without thinking, she blooded her blade, her finger skimming along its edge. *Why is it so strong when they aren't among us yet?*

And then she knew.

"Erin!"

Erin had been watching in confusion. She fumbled with her sword a moment, her hands shaking. Her fingers would not cooperate for long enough to release the sword from the scabbard. In frustration, she called forth light.

Nothing happened.

Biting her lip, she closed her eyes and began to concentrate.

Someone slapped her. Her eyes flew open and she saw her mother's face, white with either fury or fear.

"Go!"

This time she obeyed, her legs shaking even as they carried her into the covered wagon. Her mouth was dry as she shook her head; no words spilled out. She stumbled across the open ground, scraping her leg against a rock. The wagon was close.

Hide.

She stumbled into the wagon and stopped, her knees bent against the wooden boards. In the darkness she could make out very little, but her hands told her where she was; spare bedding was kept here, and tents.

Hide.

She scrambled beneath bedrolls, pulling them above her head. Her breath came in short, shallow gasps. God, something was *very* wrong.

She could smell the sweat of horses and hear them begin to trumpet the same panic that now gripped her. Her face was all but crushed into the wagon floor; the scent of aged wood clogged her nostrils.

Death—there was death in the clearing. And it would be her death, if she didn't stay very, very still. She tried to hold her breath and failed.

She was curled up as tightly as one her size could be—and for the first time in years, she felt her smallness and was glad. The Lernari hearing that she had always been so proud of caught each supernatural crackle of red and white meeting in the air above the ground; she could hear the screams, the shouts, and the rasping clang of metal against metal. The hands, her hands, over her ears could not prevent that.

Worse, though, was the sudden silence that followed. And much worse, the muffled screams.

She felt she would never be free of the physical feel of fear: the way her heart drummed so loudly against her chest, and the way her breath cut in and out so sharply it hurt. She grabbed a handful of bedding and tried to cram it into her ears, but her hands were numb and shaking. The screams—dear God, the screams—twisted into her body while she lay still and hidden, too paralyzed even to cry.

Then the screams stopped. She knew a moment of relief before they started again. She could not help but recognize whose throat they were torn from, no matter how distorted by pain the voice was.

And she could not move. She lay silent, writhing in darkness.

There was the taste of blood in her mouth from where she had bitten through her lip.

Bright Heart let it stop please let it stop!

And then, for a moment, it did. There was a silence so total it was almost deafening. And Erin saw, for the very first time, the shadowy visage of Lady Death, with her long white hands and her ebony nails. It might have been delirium, it might have been vision, but whatever it was, it was clear.

It struck her like a dull sword.

Lady Death had come for her mother. And she, cowering in the wagon, hoping—praying—not to be noticed, had done nothing, nothing at all, to prevent it. She was a warrior—she was warrior-trained . . . *She* was warrior trained.

What had Telvar said? That the warrior, the true warrior, knew how to die. Die a clean death.

Her fear sharpened unbearably and shifted.

Her mother was going to die if Lady Death couldn't be prevented from speaking her name, because Erin had done *nothing*. Her mother was going to die—her mother, no warrior.

The bedding toppled away as she jerked up, her hands finding the sword that Telvar had given to her. She stumbled over the disordered tents and bedrolls to reach the wagon's closed flap.

With a wild, incoherent shriek, Erin stumbled out of the wagon onto the dry grass. It was dark, Bright Heart—and the light wouldn't come.

But the moon glared balefully down until her eyes could clearly see the wreckage of her mother's body. Surrounding it there were four: three armored figures and one—one . . .

"No!"

They turned at once to see her. She stood, raised sword in hand, shaking with shame and fury. One of the four said something and stepped forward. He was pale and cloaked in a shadow that was stronger than night.

It was the first time in her life that she had seen a Servant of the Enemy. *Nightwalker.* He was tall, too tall, and ice seemed to form in the shadows he cast upon the still ground. Not even the firelight touched his blackness.

Telvar's words echoed dimly in her mind.

Against a nightwalker of the Enemy you stand no chance. You are overmatched by the power of his Servants; if you see one, and it is walking—flee.

And it didn't matter. For the sake of her cowardice she had sacrificed her mother. Because of her fear she had lost, in a few moments, the one thing her life had centered around. What if the walker hurt her, made her scream, made her suffer what her mother had suffered? What if he chose to feed on her lifeblood; to play with her spirit in an endless game of agony while he slaked his endless hunger? She deserved it.

The Servant came forward as she stood, feet planted firmly on the ground, arm raised to strike. She could not see any expression on his face; the shadow he wore obscured it. Nonetheless, she knew what was there.

"You are the last."

She did not reply.

"We felt your power, little one. It is almost as strong as hers was." He stepped closer still and lifted one hand. "It will never be used against us."

There was death in the clearing.

Erin saw his hand draw closer, but before she could move, she was surrounded by a nimbus of brilliant, glowing white. Her brown tunic, her pale leggings, seemed somehow transformed as the light flared like a wall.

The walker screamed, a signal to all of the enemy that the lines had come.

Erin screamed as well. The sound contained everything that words or tears could not. Almost crazy, she lunged forward at the retreating figure of the Servant of the Enemy. He didn't even notice her; his attention was drawn to the sight of Kandor—Servant as well, but of the Bright Heart.

Kandor of Lernan, followed by warrior-priests, came into the clearing. As the nightwalker wore his shadow, so Kandor wore his light; it was all the armor and all the weapon that he needed. Those warrior-priests wore the light as well—too bright and powerful to be their own. They had touched the Gifting, then. But they also wore armor that glinted beneath surcoat and helms that obscured their faces. Their weapons were drawn as they followed in Kandor's wake to step into the ruined campsite. Two of the wagons were on their sides, their canvas torn and shredded. The horses were lumps that rested upon the ground in stillness and silence. And the Malanthi were there, dressed in like armor, covered in dark surcoats. The blood-shadows surrounded them; they had pulled their power from the dying and wore it well. Already some carried the items that the Lernari dead had worn, but these they dropped at once.

Kandor barely paused to survey the surroundings before battle was joined anew. But this time the odds were even. The

Lernari warriors began their wards and attacks against the invading Malanthi, and Kandor began to circle his chosen foe.

"Valeth."

"Kandor." The Servant rose slowly. The white-fire of Lernan had left its mark.

They spoke no other words, but they had no need to. They were Servant of Light against Servant of Dark—an echo of the battles that had once existed before the birth of the world. What words were necessary?

Erin walked in a daze through her first battlefield. If any saw her at all, they didn't seem to pay her much attention, and she was hardly aware of them in her turn. One foot followed another in a seemingly endless path to the deserted corpse of her mother. Only once before had she seen such a corpse—and then she had turned away into the comfort of shoulders that would never catch her tears again. This time she did not balk at the sight. She had to see and to memorize the exact price paid for her fear.

She had to swear, though no one would hear the blood-oath, that she would never, *never* pay that price again.

Tears would not come, but she didn't deserve them. Let the sounds of renewed battle be her mother's farewell; Erin knew she didn't have the right to speak.

But she could not stop herself from caressing the still, torn face, or trying to embrace what was left.

She felt, rather than saw, Kandor's approach. She heard his words, Servant-sure and calm, echo in the emptiness that was left her. He had led them to victory.

"Come, child. This is no place for you. You are safe now."

She turned to him, eyes glinting like steel, knowing—hoping—that she would never be safe again.

"She's dead."

He watched her still, pale face, his eyes darkening. "Yes," he said, bowing to the inevitable. He reached out for her with one hand. "Come, little one. There is nothing to fear, not any longer. You are safe."

"I'm not afraid of dying," she replied, limply following where he led. "And I never will be again."

Kandor's arm encircled her shoulders; she felt the faint pulse of his power ebbing into her and yanked herself away to continue walking with him at more of a distance.

"Child . . ."

She turned only once, to look again upon the body of the

woman who had given so much to the warriors on the fields of battles such as this one.

"It should have been me." Her voice was ash.

Kandor said nothing, and once again she felt his power come into her to try to soothe the loss she felt.

But it was all she had left and she would not release it.

The trunk of the Lady's tree shimmered as Latham walked into it. The disorientation that he normally felt upon entering the Woodhall meant little to him now; it paled to insignificance beside the weight he carried.

The long hall was completely still; no hint of fragrant breeze showed evidence of the Lady's power. His steps, quiet as they were, echoed down the length of marble corridor.

He could see, as he approached the conservatory, that even the plants looked wilted.

Bright Heart, he thought as he walked past them, *is all the news I bear to be bad?* He ran a tired hand over his face. Only then did he realize that he was crying. *Only a Servant of the Enemy could have done this to you, Kera. The best of the Malanthi would not have had the power. Only a nightwalker.* He wiped his cheeks clean.

Almost no healer died such a terrible death; the very act of injuring them allowed them to reach their power more fully. The Malanthi—the half-human, half-Servant priests of the Enemy—hadn't the power to stop a healer from touching the Bright Heart's blood. But a true Servant's power would be enough.

Ah Kera, Kera—you must have helped the war more than we knew to draw such attention to yourself. Rest in the peace of the beyond.

The sound of his footsteps stopped completely as he struggled to compose himself. Later, much later, he would allow himself the luxury of feeling this loss.

But now . . .

He began to walk again, taking slow, deep breaths. He had his duty to perform. At least he was not the one to bear the news to the Grandfather, or to Telvar.

"Lady?" He called her name once before he turned the last corner. His voice was quiet but solid.

"Latham."

He took the last step and saw her back.

"What news?"

He opened his mouth, and for the first time in years, the words failed him completely.

She turned then. And her expression destroyed the last vestige of control that he'd maintained.

For her face was old, tired, and terribly vulnerable. It seemed, for an instant, that the Light of God had never graced it; that the Blood of the Bright Heart had never flowed through it. And her eyes, which were always living emeralds, were now only cold, large stones. She stared almost helplessly at him, her arms spun tightly around her like translucent web.

She knows, he thought. *Somehow, she knows.* And for the first time in his life, as he looked at her, he saw her as Servant of the Light—ageless and immortal. It was odd to think of her so only now that she displayed a weakness that might barely have been hinted at.

He felt a cold anguish well up in him.

She knows. He let those words sink in, but this time, instead of turning away from them as he had for fifteen years, he pushed them forward that one logical step—he was, after all, line scholar.

She knew.

Five years she had spent in spell trance. Five years, following futures that only she could follow; pushing aside a veil that only the Servants dared touch.

How many other deaths did you see, Lady? How many other lives might we have saved?

How could you sacrifice your own daughter?

And watching him, the Lady of Elliath saw that he knew. She drew herself up, calling upon the remnants of her power to provide her with some ragged comfort and some hint of the glory that the Lernari had always associated with her.

It would not come.

Lernan, God, I have given you everything. Do not desert me now.

And a hint of His light, a finger of His power, reached out to embrace her.

She faced Latham squarely.

"Latham. What brings you?"

He heard her words, but could not answer her. Instead he turned, showing her the circle that emblazoned the gray of his back.

The Lady of Elliath watched him walk away.

Is this all? she thought bitterly. She was too tired to panic.

Have I revealed what I dare not reveal? Have I spoken wordlessly of what I dared not speak? Is all my pain to serve no point?

She called him again, but he did not halt.

She set her power aside wearily and began to follow. *So be it, then. Did I show no grief or pain in the future?*

"Latham!" The voice that came from her throat startled her. It was a human voice, mortal.

Where the Light could not touch him, this simple thing could. He stopped and, after a shaky second, turned to face her.

She spoke no words as she approached him. She made no plea, not even to ask for his trust or his silence.

And because she did not, he knew he would give her both. For she was the Lady of Elliath, the strongest of all Servants of the Light. Darkness did not—could not—mar her.

He had only part of her blood—the barest hint of Light. He was mortal and caught by mortal traps. If for Lernan's sake she had done nothing, there had to be a reason for it. If she had forced herself to be silent all this time, it was for the good of the Bright Heart.

It had to be.

"Lady," he said softly.

She shook her head in denial—of what he could never be certain.

There was so much that he wanted to ask her.

She shook her head again, forestalling him.

"Latham, what if you knew that there was only one hope to end this eternal war? What would you give up for that hope?"

"Anything," he said automatically. But the word hung tautly between them, and he stiffened as if feeling its significance truly for the first time.

"And what if you knew that that hope was no certainty, that you were grasping at a slim chance that you could not control? What would you give up then?"

This time he did not answer. Instead he stared across at her bowed head.

"And what if you knew all this, but knew also that to speak of it fully would doom the hope?"

He was scholar, master scholar of Elliath. The questions that he longed to ask still swirled around his mind chaotically. He contained them, for he knew what his answer to her question must be.

"Lady, I would want to take that hope if that was all I would be given. At any price." He took a deep breath and released it shakily, thinking of Kerlinda. Thinking of the manner of the death she had gone to, untrained. "But I would not have the strength. I am mortal, with all that condition entails."

She looked up, and he saw the blackness of despair shroud her features with loss and guilt.

"I do not believe I will ever be truly immortal again."

Without knowing why, he reached for her, his arms the stronger of the two for the first time in any memory. He held her, and she allowed herself to mourn as a mother does for the death of a child.

This time, Erin was allowed to be present at the ceremony of departure in the somber circle of the vaulted Great Hall. Adults stood on all sides, wearing their grays and their circles and their sorrow equally. Belfas stood beside her and cried all the tears that he knew she would not.

Instead of sneaking into the hall as she had for the other ceremony, she had walked to the front of the gathering. No gray for her, no silver, just the plain brown robes of a student in training. She had never felt so out of place. People made way for her, their expressions a mingling of bitter grief and sympathy.

Kerlinda was given the warrior's departure; her coffin was surrounded by warrior-priests, arms held at ready.

Telvar had asked Erin if she would like to stand. She had refused. If she had not had the strength to stand by her mother when her mother was alive, she had no right to stand by her corpse in any position of honor.

The Lady of Elliath presided over this departure, as she had done over all. But the words that were spoken by her and the Grandfather flitted by Erin's ears without ever touching them. Everything was a dim, gray blur.

She approached the coffin once and looked at what remained of her mother in cold, stiff silence.

I will never forget you.

She did not touch the body.

After the ceremony many people, some that she recognized vaguely and some that she knew well, came up to her to offer her their sympathy. They couldn't know that each word they spoke cut her sharply.

Only the Lady of Elliath seemed to understand, and for this one thing, Erin was grateful.

* * *

"Erin." Katalaan wiped her hands on her apron although they'd been dry since the fourth time she'd done it.

Erin continued to wash the plate, each movement of the rag slow and methodical. Her eyes, wide and glassy, stared into the cooling water.

The baker wondered what she saw there. For three years they had lived together. Not one day in all that time had prepared Kat for this silence, the wall of it cold and hard. Korfel would have been proud of the stoic Lernari spirit that Erin showed. Katalaan hated it.

"Erin?"

"Yes, Kat?"

"If we've finished here, I think I could use your help setting up in the circle for tomorrow." She began to remove her apron.

"I—I have a lot of studying to do."

She always had. If it weren't for Belfas, her studying would have been a mausoleum.

Why hasn't she cried? The older woman shook her head. *It isn't natural.* Then again, by all accounts neither was her mother's death. What had happened to kill the special hesitancy that was Erin's childhood?

She shook her head again. Better not to know. What mattered now was bringing that back, if it was possible.

"Study can wait. I'm not as young as I used to be and I could use the help."

They both knew it wasn't strictly true, but Erin nodded listlessly. She removed her own apron—brown and green at Kat's insistence—and set it aside on a chair.

The circle was quiet, the flagpoles naked in the evening breeze. Katalaan approached her stall and set the boards up so she could enter. Erin trailed behind, a quiet ghost. Even her feet made no sound.

On impulse, Kat said, "Why don't you set the flag to fly?"

Erin looked mostly confused as Kat deposited the carefully curled flag into her vacant arms. "Now?"

"We're here. Might as well let people know it."

"But you've nothing to sell."

"Erin, when you came three years ago, I'd nothing left to sell either."

Erin swallowed. "Oh, Kat—" Her eyes glimmered for a moment as Kat held her breath. Then Erin shook herself and bolted to the pole, her student browns flying at her sandaled feet.

Damn, Kat thought. But she let her almost-child flee.

The ropes and pulleys of the pole were stiff; if not for Telvar's training, Erin doubted she'd have had the strength to put up the flag on her own. She carefully tied the flag into place and, once she was sure it was secured, began to pull for all she was worth.

She stopped when something began to tug at her dress. The flag was at half height.

A young child, fist attached to her robes, looked up at her. "Is that Kat'laan's?"

"Yes," Erin said quietly.

"I've got something to show her." The young boy looked at his stomach. He had pale, gold hair that was already browning at the roots. His clothing, bright blue and red, marked him as the smith's son.

"What is that?" Without thinking, Erin lowered herself until their eyes were level. Talking with a child was better than thinking about her mother.

For a moment the boy looked suspicious. Then he nodded as if to himself and opened up his shirt. Curled against his ivory stomach was a small kitten, fast asleep.

"I got it off Kerris's mom," the boy whispered. "She says it's part of old Mag's litter. Says there were five." His brow puckered. "Don't know how five fit into old Mag's stomach."

The little white ball of fur shifted suddenly and the boy gritted his teeth. Between them he hissed, "He does it all the time. These little ones got claws."

Erin nodded slowly.

"You all right?"

"Yes." Her lips hardly moved.

Very gingerly, he shifted the kitten between his hands and held it out. "You want to hold him?"

"Could I?"

He nodded. "You're okay. Jimmison's stupid; he almost strangled it. But you'll be fine." There was a world of trust in those words.

Erin took the kitten. It was warm and soft; it moved as she began to scratch its ears. It had a little, rough tongue that darted hesitantly out.

"He's pretty, isn't he?"

Erin nodded.

"Hey!" The voice was high. "Are you all right?"

She nodded dumbly. Then she began to cry. She lifted the kitten, felt its claws scrape her cheeks, and felt its tongue take her tears.

She heard the boy's footsteps, heard him shouting for Kat, and heard Kat's low mumble—words that didn't mean anything to her. She didn't know why she was crying, but she held the kitten that much closer.

Hours later, Katalaan took her home. Erin leaned into her friend's shoulder in silence. She didn't speak about her mother's death, and Kat didn't ask, but they both felt better for the visit to the circle.

And very often, when Erin was tired or frightened or lonely, she returned to the circle, looking for the smith's son and his friends. And in time they came, to show her things and share with her their little secrets and complaints. And their trust grew to mean a lot to her, because she trusted herself so little.

chapter
five

"Erin! Erin!"

Erin rolled her eyes. Belfas was a full seventeen summers and a bit, but he still had not learned to keep his voice down in the cloisters. Her name, cushioned and hallowed by the ancient stone walls, rang loudly for a while. She glanced around quickly to make sure that he had disturbed no one before turning to look at him.

It's a good thing Kedry isn't here to see you, Belf.

She would have said it aloud, but he wasn't close enough to hear her. She watched him run—run!—down the long, open walkway. His hair was flying in fourteen different directions, but even at this distance she could see the sparkle in his eyes.

Before she could think of anything to say, he was upon her, arms stretched wide to catch her in a bear hug.

"I did it!" he shouted, as he nearly knocked them both over.

She disentangled herself in some annoyance; even this close he was still shouting. "Belf, we're in the cloisters."

"In the—oh." He lowered his voice, but only a little. Given his state of excitement, Erin knew that was the best anyone could ask for. "I did it, Erin."

She looked at him quizzically.

"I made my True Ward! I did it!" He looked down at his feet. "I'll have my robe in a ten-day."

She stood almost stunned as the words sank in. Belfas had made his True Ward, had touched the hand of the Bright Heart. He had become adult.

Belfas's smile dimmed suddenly and he turned an awkward shade of red. He started to speak, then stopped himself before he could add to the damage.

Erin shook herself and forced her lips upward in a semblance of a smile. It wouldn't fool Belfas, but would have to do.

"I'm really happy for you, Belf." She hugged him weakly. She meant it, though; attaining the rank of initiate was something that every child coveted and looked forward to. It was the one thing that separated the adult from the child in the eyes of the community. "I—have you told Taya yet?"

"No. I wanted—" *to tell you first.* He looked away and Erin could almost hear him thinking, *Idiot. Think about how she feels!*

"Go and tell her. She'll be so happy for you." Erin made her voice light, knowing that wouldn't fool Belfas either. At least it salved her pride somewhat.

"Erin, I—it doesn't really mean any—"

"Belfas—just, please . . ."

He knew she was deadly serious because she rarely used his full name. "I'm sorry, Erin."

"Sorry? Why? You're an adult now, and you should be—be proud of it. Now, please . . ."

He nodded and turned quickly to leave her standing alone in the cloisters.

She watched his back, trying to control the horrible envy she felt and failing miserably.

I'm sorry, Belf, she thought, knowing that she'd probably crushed any real enjoyment he would feel for the next few days. She knew she should go after him, but she just couldn't force herself to do it. *I know you'd have been happy for me.*

Only when he was gone did she relax completely, even though she knew he wouldn't look back.

It doesn't matter, she told herself firmly as she turned and made her way toward the Great Hall. *When I—when I finally make my ward, I'll be the best initiate here.* The thought was hollow, and she knew it, so she walked more quickly, entering the rounded double doors of the north hall.

But what of now? *Nearly all of my year-mates—and even some a year below—are adult. Am I going to be a child forever?*

It seemed so unfair. She knew her blood was strong—out of all of the line's adults, there were maybe five who could claim a more powerful lineage—and of those five, not one was less than sixty.

So why had everyone else passed the testing?

A hint of guilt and fear welled up, and she swamped it with anger.

Knowing that she was being childish, she walked briskly to the Great Hall. It would be empty now, and she could find solace there, through prayer—although that had stopped being even remotely useful six months ago, when Rein had become initiate.

The hall was quiet, almost soothing. She walked over to the altar and bowed her head.

Lernan, why, why, why?

She started to cry and was instantly ashamed of herself.

Tears are for children. She drew a deep breath and straightened out. Then she let herself curl up again, resting her head against the cold stone in front of her. *So what? I* am *a child.*

She sat alone for a while, easing her frustration and her sense of humiliation. And then, to make matters worse, she felt a hand on her shoulder. Her tears stopped immediately.

"Child, why are you crying?"

She turned around to face the Grandfather. She started to set her face, saw the gentle concern in his, and closed her eyes. One could never lie to the Grandfather, and it had been four years since she'd been naïve enough to try.

"Belfas made his True Ward." She began to speak in a rush. "It isn't that I'm not happy for him—I am. It's just that I've tried, Grandfather; I've tried with the priests, I've tried when the circle doesn't watch me, I've tried in my sleep—and I can't call His power."

Very gently he lifted her into his arms.

"When you are ready, you will be able to do so. Why are you trying to rush so quickly out of your childhood?" He closed his eyes a moment, knowing the sentiment to be misplaced, but unable to put a voice to his concern. In any way but this, Erin had ceased to be a child four years past. And try as he might, he would never be able to quite forget this.

Erin hated his question. She'd heard it often; each of the eighteen times she had appeared before a gathering of the elders and failed, yet again, to draw the power of God in the True Ward.

"Youth," "childhood," treasure it while you can. She felt a loathing for these sentiments that went beyond words. *What good did that do for my*— She cut off the thought, suddenly too raw and hurt.

"What good is youth? Can it go out and fight the enemies of our people? Can it stand against the—the priests of the Enemy? Can it save the lives of the villagers who die every day on the blooded altars?"

He looked down at her, his face creased, hearing the words that she did not speak, would never willingly speak. And once again, he tried to address them. "Erin, your mother—"

Erin yanked herself away from him and ran down the hall, only to stop as the large doors swung shut. Spinning around, her face white and pale, she shouted, "Don't talk about my mother! You weren't there! You didn't see what happened!" The vaulted ceiling caught her words, spinning them about the room in a weblike echo. She turned again, unwilling to face him in her anger and guilt, and began to pull ineffectively at the handles of the large doors.

He came up behind her and took her into his arms, but this time to keep her there for a while. Of all the things he had expected, this was not one—he had never seen her so openly expose her pain, and he was unwilling to allow her to mask it again.

She screamed at him, all of her precious control gone.

He held her until she had quieted, more from exhaustion than from any sense of peace. "Erin," he said in a gentle voice, "your mother was an adult. An adult fears death but accepts it."

She wanted to shout, but her voice came out weakly. "She didn't. She wasn't warrior-trained. I could hear her—" She brought her hands up automatically to cover her ears as she had done for so many sleepless nights. She could still hear the screams echoing down the years. "She—it was—she wanted to die."

The Grandfather tensed slightly, knowing the truth of her words. It was his greatest guilt—to let one not warrior-trained go to the fields of battle and to the hands of a Servant of the Enemy unprepared. Slowly he forced his hands to resume stroking the back of her head.

He did not tell her that there was nothing she could have done, but only because he knew she had heard it many, many times, and that she could not, would not, believe it.

As if she heard his thought, she said, "And if I'd been adult, if I'd had my full power, I could have stopped them. I would have—"

"You would have died."

"It doesn't matter!" She balled her hands into fists. "She was stronger of blood than me! She was important!" Her voice petered away into sobs, but he caught the words that came between them. "And—and He didn't come to her either. He didn't listen."

"He couldn't." How could he explain clearly enough for her to understand? "The Enemy's Servant bound her power too closely to her."

She didn't seem to hear him, lost—as she had been for so many years—in her own silence. Then, unexpectedly, and in a tone of voice that tore into the Grandfather, she asked, "Is it because I didn't save her? Is it because I didn't help? Is that why

He won't let me touch His power?" She tried to pull back and failed.

"No, never think that. Our God could never be so cruel."

"Then *why*, Grandfather? Why can't I ward?"

He pressed her close. *How do I tell you?* Gently he said, "God is not of the living."

"I know that."

"Then you must know the story of Gallin Bright Sword."

She nodded into his chest.

"And you know that our connection—unlike that of the Servants—to God is a very fragile thing, for we are of the living.

"Very well," he added, as he felt her nod again, "there are two things that separate an adult from a child. We do not normally speak of them. They must come on their own." Holding her, he understood the truth of his own words completely. "This knowledge is a sign of . . . of maturity." He stopped, struggling with his better judgment. At length, he spoke again, choosing his awkward words with what care he could.

"This is something that each of us realized in time, and in private.

"Child, your blood is strong. It is true. I've seen you with the younger ones, and I see in you both the desire to help, to protect—and the desire for vengeance. The latter troubles me greatly, but I believe that your blood, and our teachings, will soothe the desire for revenge." *Bright Heart, let it be so.* "So I will tell you what you should have come to on your own."

"Three things brought Gallin close to God. His fear of death—which was very strong. His acceptance of death. And the fact that he was physically dying. Of these three, the third is strongest, but it is not necessary—else the lines would have perished at the beginning of our long war.

"Those of us who are initiates have realized the first two: That death is real, and that we fear it. For by it, we lose the life that we love—and it is that life that is all that we are, all that we know." He looked down at her bowed head and shook his head slightly, knowing that the importance of the last sentence had made no impression. Sighing, he continued.

"Fear is one of the strongest emotions engendered in man, and we use that fear to become more open, or more vulnerable, to the hand of God. Only by rising above the fear—and the fear *must* exist—are we . . . purified enough to be almost beyond life."

"I know that death is real," Erin said quietly. "My mother is dead."

"You know that *loss* is real. But death?" His grip on her tightened. "Kandor of Lernan stopped you from effectively killing yourself when you tried to save Kerlinda."

Fear? She thought on his words, trying for the first time to remember, rather than forget, the incident that had hurt her so much. *I was afraid.*

The screams returned to her, echoing through her body until she shook.

The Grandfather tightened his grip, knowing what it was that she felt. She had been all of twelve years; one year, perhaps, from attaining adulthood; one year away from being able to put herself between her enemies and their victims—or so she thought.

She pulled back. Now she was sixteen, almost seventeen, and still no closer to the goal that was all that she lived for. The Grandfather's words, meant to calm or instruct her, had only put that goal at such a distance that she was certain she would never reach it. The despair that had taken root years ago bloomed strongly within her as she looked up for the first time.

"Grandfather."

"Yes?"

"When we make a vow, we must keep it."

He thought her words odd and looked long at her pale face, so calm that if it were not for his blood-sense he would have thought the storm over. She looked so impossibly grave that she reminded him briefly of her younger self.

"Yes." He stroked her hair. "We ask you to break no vows."

"Lernan's power does." She drew a deep breath and pulled away from him so gently that he had no choice but to allow it. "I will not fear death. I'm sorry. I can accept mine. I can accept that if I join the border patrols I might die in combat. But I won't fear it."

He sighed. "When you are older, you will."

She gripped his bent hands in hers. "No."

He heard the age in her voice, saw the surety and the bitterness of it in the green sheen of her eyes. Suddenly he knew what she would say next, and regretted it.

"But you spoke of another way. Not *fear* of dying, but dying itself.

"Grandfather, you've seen me in the training ground. Talk to Telvar. I can fight, and fight well. Let me join the patrols. Please?

If it must be, I'll earn my circle on the field, near death at the hands of our enemies.

"Please."

"Erin, to call upon the power of God so close to the edge— it is . . . difficult. You must be able to concentrate, ignoring pain or—"

"I'm warrior-trained—unlike my mother." She said the last three words, knowing that they would hurt him and unable to stop.

The quick breath he drew was sharp. "Erin, you'll make your ward in your own time and—"

"Then what use am I now?" She caught the note of hysteria in her voice and clamped down on it. "Please."

"If you have not completed the True Ward once, you will almost certainly fail."

"Then I'll die. But I might as well be dead now, for all the good any of you will let me do!" She wanted to turn and walk out but subdued the urge, willing the child in her to leave instead. She met his eyes squarely.

It was he, at last, who turned away.

"I will talk to the Lady."

The Lady of Elliath stared into the waters of her marbled fountain. Although magical sunlight glimmered off the rippling water, her eyes saw clearly what moved beneath the surface: the image of the outside world.

The view in the wavelets was of Erin's brown-robed back. Her long hair was drawn back and bound with copper in an imitation of a warrior's braid. She sat beneath the shade of the trees at the periphery of the wood. No one interrupted her as she forced her hands into the fluid motion of the full circle that opened the True Ward.

The frustration that radiated from the young woman could be felt in the Lady's Woodhall; the Lady didn't have to use her power to touch outward.

Granddaughter. She straightened as the water shimmered into playful rippling.

Footsteps echoed down the long hall. She had a visitor. She knew who it was.

"Serdon."

Although he heard her call him, he waited until he could see her before he made his reply; he was dignified and old enough to feel no need to shout.

He approached her and, when he was a few feet away, bowed deeply. "Lady."

"What brings you? Is there more trouble on the front?"

"As much as there has been these last few years since . . . these last few years." He sighed at the near slip of the tongue; even now Kerlinda's death was not spoken of in the presence of the Lady. "But no, it is not about the battle that I've come to speak."

"Another matter of concern? Come, Serdon."

She turned and he followed her, leaving the garden for an alcove in which there were two chairs. He took one, but the Lady remained standing; she rarely felt any need to be seated.

"Speak, then. Tell me what troubles you."

"Erin."

"Ah."

Their silence acknowledged the truth of what they both knew. The Lady turned away, staring for a moment into the green of the large trees that grew in her eternal and isolated world.

"You've spoken with her?"

He nodded. "Again. But today—today she was more open. I think that if you were willing, you might be able to touch the anger and guilt that she feels. Might be able to soothe it enough to—"

"I cannot, Serdon. Were I to try this, she would resist even my power." It was true, but it was not all of the truth. She was doomed to keep all of the truth in silence to herself.

The Grandfather sagged a little into his chair. If not the Lady, then no one. Erin had been to the three remaining healers of the Line Elliath—and five others from the various lines whose holdings were closest. Each time she had forced their power away. And without healing the bitterness that had so deeply scarred her, he knew that she would not—as she had vowed—be able to touch the Hand of God.

As if reading his thoughts, the Lady said, "Serdon, she will not touch the Bright Heart, not in the way that the lines are accustomed to. I have seen it once or twice before, but never so strongly. She has much of the blood."

"Then what are we to do with her, Lady? She obeys our commands to stay here, but she will not do so forever." He touched his forehead wearily, brushing back silvered strands of black.

The Lady turned again to face him.

"Send her, then. Send her to the front. Let her try to walk the path of Gallin."

The Grandfather rose to his feet; the chair could not contain the sudden surprise that he felt.

"The front?" he said incredulously. "But she is not yet adult."

The Lady's green eyes glowed brilliantly a moment. Slowly, the Grandfather resumed his seat.

"She is adult by the standards of the mortal world—and that is the world we have fought so long to protect. If we cannot have her power as healer, let her exercise her skill as warrior. It is great."

He heard what lay behind the Lady's words. Even so, he had his own determination. The anger in his voice reflected it. "Lady, Line Elliath does not send children into battle."

"By mortal standards, Serdon, we have done exactly that. Kredan joined the front when he reached his thirteenth year."

"Kredan was not a child. He touched the Hand of God. He proved that he understood what death is, what it means. Erin has not done that."

"No." Her eyes never wavered. "But it was the battlefield that wounded her, not the lines. It may be that on the fields of battle, she will learn to heal herself."

The Grandfather knew, from the feelings that the Lady projected so strongly, that Erin would be sent to war. But he stayed an hour to argue against it. He was the patriarch of the line, and upon him fell the duty of protecting his line-children.

"Erin, don't fuss so." Kat's words came from around the pins in her mouth. She looked up at Erin, who was doing her best to stand straight on the stool as Kat pinned the hem into place.

"I just want to make sure I look all right."

Katalaan rolled her eyes. "This is the first time you've ever done any such thing."

"Kat—"

"I know, I know. It's Belfas's celebration."

Erin nodded.

"Don't jump about like that, I'm almost finished." Kat drove the last pin into the green velvet skirt and stepped back to admire her work. "Looks a sight better on you than on me, at least at my age." It was a joke; Katalaan hadn't worn this dress in over thirty years.

"I just want to look good, that's all. I—I want to make it up to him."

"Make up what, dear?"

"Haven't you been listening?"

"Hmmm. Step down now, and you can look at yourself in the glass. But be careful, or you'll prick yourself."

Erin jumped down lightly, strode across the room to the oval mirror, looked at herself, and frowned. "It doesn't look much like me, does it?"

She saw Katalaan's reflection come to stand behind hers and fiddle with the laces at the bodice.

"It looks fine. You look like a regular lady."

"You mean that people in the cities do this all the time?"

Kat sighed as she tried to fasten Erin's hair with an old jade comb. "More than once in a lifetime at any rate. Hold still. I never realized how fidgety you could be!"

Erin tried to hide her nerves and failed utterly.

"Erin, dear, you look lovely. Don't be so nervous. There, that's done it. Now look at yourself." Kat smiled broadly. It was obvious that she was very happy to see her charge in the dress that she herself had worn for her marriage years ago.

Erin was speechless. She put up her hand to touch her hair and Katalaan caught it gently. "No, dear, don't touch it."

"I can't go like this."

"Why on Earth not?"

"I look like—I don't look like me."

"Well, I think you do. Come on, you'll be late." She hustled Erin down the stairs. "Remember what I've told you about table manners, all right?"

"Right."

Katalaan laughed, kissed Erin on the forehead, and opened the front door. "Go on, dear."

Erin felt stupid. The skirt was all right, but the bodice—how did anyone breathe in something like this? She would have loosened it, but was afraid of unlacing it completely. The sun was setting on the path to the Great Hall, and she stopped fretfully. Maybe she just should have worn her student's browns.

But then she'd be the only one who wore them.

She lifted her chin slightly. At least if she was going to stand out, she'd do it right. Or so she hoped.

She reached the Great Hall and headed for the west wing,

where long tables had already been set up for the celebration. Belfas was not the only one to become an initiate of the circle in the last three months, but he was the only one that she really cared about.

Maybe she should have worn the browns. She knew she'd already hurt his feelings once and she didn't want him to feel like an idiot—he'd already gone out on a limb by insisting that she be allowed to attend.

People bustled by as the halls grew more crowded. That they stopped to stare at her didn't help at all; she wasn't used to being stared at. The ceilings, already vaulted archways double her height, seemed to loom taller as she walked.

No. She was going to go home and change. She turned around abruptly and ran into someone. She stopped, started to apologize, then heard an astonished squeak that could only belong to one person.

"Erin?" Belfas was either in shock or doing a good imitation of a fish out of water.

Erin felt her cheeks grow hot.

"Is that you?"

A number of silver-gray robes seemed to gather around them as they blocked the hall.

"Yes," she hissed. "It's me. Can we go now?"

"The hall's behind you."

She turned around and sighed.

"Can I, uh, offer you my arm?"

She smiled then, her cheeks still red. "Okay." The brown velvet of her sleeve brushed against the new gray of his robe as their arms locked.

And the dinner went very well. Erin remembered everything that Katalaan had taught her, and ate, in her opinion, like a lady. Belfas—well, he was still Belfas. Every time he went to touch a fork, he'd look at her to see if she nodded or shook her head. Any time he wanted to reach for something, he'd do the same.

It made her happy to know that he was still Belfas and, even if he'd gone adult, he still needed her.

And Belfas was happy to have her back. So happy, in fact, that he didn't bother to feel guilty about becoming adult before she did. She was still Erin; of course she'd follow. They did everything together, didn't they?

He had almost finished his second dessert, filched from Erin's plate when both were sure no one was watching them, when the door to the east hall flew open. The congenial chatter died away into the silence of four stone walls.

"Grandfather, initiates." The silver-haired master scholar gave a low bow. "I'm afraid that the festivities for the evening are over."

Murmurs began as Latham paused to draw breath.

"The Lady of Elliath summons you to a council of the full circle in the Great Hall. Immediately." He bowed again, obviously out of breath. "If Erin is among you, she, too, is to attend. Else, she is to be summoned."

Erin stood, the brown and green of velvet marking her clearly. "I'm here."

Latham nodded. Chairs scraped along the floor as the hall emptied.

The Great Hall was already crowded when they arrived. Erin caught sight of Elise, an older woman of the lines, wrapping her arms around a thin blue nightdress. Further into the crowd, she caught sight of Kredan's back. He'd only come from the front last eve. He caught sight of her—it was hard not to—and whispered, "Up to Telvar."

She nodded and caught Belfas by the hand.

Just before they broke through the last rank of people, Erin heard the creaking of the great doors as they closed. Light, so pale a green it was almost white, flooded the hall, chasing the shadows away from even the arches that towered so high above them.

She stopped a moment, inhaling sharply. Belfas squeezed her hand. "Over here." He used as quiet a voice as he could manage, but at least a dozen people heard him because the hall had suddenly become so quiet.

Erin nodded and allowed him to drag her the rest of the way. She managed to maneuver skillfully enough that she only bumped into one more person. But she recognized that person even before he turned to stare down at her.

Thanks, Belf. A blush started to rise in her cheeks. Why did it have to be Telvar? She was on the verge of stammering out an apology when he nodded sharply. "You're here. Good." He turned to face the altar, and Erin was forced to do the same; one didn't question Telvar when he was this curt and businesslike.

But she was curious. After taking a moment to catch her breath, she looked around at the gathering. Hundreds of people thronged the room in various states of dress. Almost all of them were familiar to her in one way or another. But why had they been summoned?

She turned back to the empty altar and then craned her neck around again. Belfas was beside her, as usual. Kredan, she'd seen. Deirdre, still rubbing sleep out of her eyes, was four rows behind. Carla, war-scarred and wary even now, was standing silent toward the back.

They were all adult.

A flush of excitement reddened her cheeks, adding color that had been missing there for months. Daring Telvar's impatience, she began to search every face she could see.

All adult.

Belfas tapped her urgently on the shoulder, and she spun around again, half-rocking on her toes.

She wasn't adult yet, and as far as she could see she was the only child that had been summoned. It gave her a hope that she had thought she would never have again. The smile she turned on her best friend was both anxious and warm.

He returned it with a confused glance. The whole of the line in the holding had been summoned—undoubtedly for a very good reason. Why on Earth was Erin smiling like that?

Erin wanted to hug him and laugh out loud. If Telvar hadn't been standing beside her, she might have done it. Of course he couldn't understand why she was suddenly so happy—he didn't really comprehend how significant his becoming adult was to both of them; he had never really thought of her as a child.

A movement from behind the altar caught her attention, and she schooled her face carefully.

The Lady of Elliath entered the Great Hall, sweeping through the open arch, her arms held out to either side as if in welcome. She entered the edge of the inscribed circle and came to stand before the altar.

Sight of the Lady was not unusual. But the light that she brought with her was; it glowed brilliant white, casting aside the previous green as if it were shadow or darkness. She was limned with it; her hair seemed to dance to invisible wind like strands of diamonds.

So magnificent was the Lady that Erin did not immediately notice the man who followed her. He was not a familiar face or figure, but it was obvious that he held great power—one of the twelve, perhaps. He was tall, his hair was pale and fair, his skin almost translucent. She started to glance at the Lady again, then suddenly stared at the man. For although he carried the white-fire, his eyes, at this distance, were blue—not the emerald green that so clearly marked the Servants. She noticed then that he wore the surcoat of the line, and that it was not for dress; it was dirty and torn. In one arm he held a dented helm.

There were only two things that could explain this. Either he had visited the Gifting of the Bright Heart and had truly mingled with the blood of God, or he was the Sarillar of Elliath—the single Lernari warrior-priest chosen to be the vessel for a part of the Lady's power, her presence on the field of battle. And either of these things boded ill for the line.

"Line-children." The Lady bowed her head gravely in the man's direction. "Andin has returned from Karana recently."

Erin gave a small start at the man's name. It was truly Andin, Sarillar of Elliath. She found herself holding her breath, and tried to relax, as did everyone in the audience.

The Lady did nothing to still the disquiet of the Lernari. Instead, she stepped to one side, and Andin strode forward.

This close, Erin could see his expression. Beneath the light, there were scars across his face and brow—healed but nonetheless visible. The lines around his face were the only things that spoke of his age.

"Line-mates." He bowed. "I will—I must—be brief. Karana has fallen."

There was a ripple that passed through the audience, wordless but audible. Karana was the major trade city closest to the border. But it was not that close; a hundred miles or more from the fighting. At least it had been.

He allowed the information to sink in before continuing.

"A full four of the Twelve of the Enemy were present at the fall." He closed his eyes. "And some six hundred of the Malanthi as well. Their exact numbers are unknown; Corvan was the only one among us who could memory-walk, and he perished. The enemy army has also availed itself of the nonblooded. Much planning has gone into this.

"The Ninth of the Bright Heart fell in battle; the Twelfth of the Enemy preceded him. But our losses were great."

He seemed to slump for a moment and looked toward the Lady of Elliath.

"Yes," she said softly, the thrum of her power touching everyone. "Karana was in Elliath territory. This night, I must touch the Gifting of God and I must travel to the ruins of that city."

Again a rustle went through the Great Hall. The Lady of

Elliath—First of the Twelve of Lernan—had not taken to the field since the days of Gallin Bright Sword—the days of legend.

"The Sarillar will travel with me."

Almost everyone in the crowd nodded; Erin felt herself doing the same.

"I will take some ten others. The cost to the Bright Heart will be high—but we cannot wait; behold."

And she cast her arms wide. Power crackled down the thin bareness of her hands. Above her head an image began to coalesce beneath the beamed ceiling. It was white and formless at first, like clouds too thin to block all sunlight. But this mist drew slowly back into the blackness of night, punctuated by glimmering starlight.

Black against even the darkness were three of the four that the Sarillar had spoken of.

Erin froze. *Bright Heart . . . not again . . .*

Surrounded by shadow, they stood tall. Only their backs could be seen, but there was no mistaking them—or what they were doing.

Walking.

There was no sound; the Lady had spared them that. But jutting out at odd angles from the closest Servant's back were two flailing arms. The Servants, the nightwalkers of the Enemy, were feeding.

Erin's hand flew to her sword and smacked uselessly against her unadorned hip. She opened her mouth, but like the Lady's image, she, too, was silent, unable to voice what she felt.

The flailing arms fell into shadow even as she took her first step forward.

Two hands gripped her, one on either shoulder. The light, sure touch on her right she recognized as Belfas. But the other—she turned to her left to see Telvar's face. His lips were drawn back tightly and she wondered if she only imagined the tremor of his hand.

"Not yet, little warrior. But soon." There was something strange about his tone of voice; it contained disapproval—with which she was only too familiar—but approval as well. She was not surprised to see that his hand rested squarely on the hilt of his sword. She couldn't think of a time when she had seen him walk unarmed, and this was no exception.

The image crumbled into light.

"The Grandfather of the line will travel with us. Katri, come forward."

An older woman came quickly through the crowd at the Lady's command. Erin could see the likeness between the set of lines of her face and the familiar face of the Grandfather.

"Lady." She bowed, looking completely formal although she was not dressed for the occasion.

"You will preside in the Grandfather's place, as is your duty and right. Guard your line-children well and see to the front—if I am not mistaken, there will be much activity there, and much loss."

"Will you take Karana back, Lady?" someone asked from the audience. It was a male voice, one that Erin didn't immediately recognize.

"There is little enough to take," she replied. "It is the Servants of the Enemy that are my concern; they must not walk further into Elliath lands. We will do what we can to succor those that survive."

There were no more questions.

Telvar stepped forward.

"It will be some moments before your guard is ready, Lady." He bowed once to her and then turned to the Sarillar. "Sarillar."

Andin nodded.

"Lady," Telvar said as he straightened out, "your guard?"

"Yes, weaponsmaster. You shall accompany me."

A look of relief flittered across his scarred face. "The others?"

"Only two here can memory-walk; the others are at the front." Her eyes turned to rest upon Belfas, and Erin felt her heart sinking. To see him go out with the units in the long line that had taken her mother the first time was going to be difficult enough. To know that he was going into the lands that the Servants occupied was worse than anything else she could have imagined.

Not him, not Belf. Please, Lady, not him.

But of course the Lady couldn't hear her thoughts.

"Latham is completely untrained. He is master scholar; he must remain."

Telvar turned to look at the newly adult Belfas, who was standing speechless beneath their gaze.

"Who did you train under, Belfas?"

"Carne."

Telvar nodded. "He'll manage."

The Lady looked out into the audience again.

"Kredan is one of yours, is he not?"

Telvar nodded. "He's returned from the front, Lady, but he's relatively uninjured."

Kredan stepped forward. He, too, was armed; Erin could see this clearly.

"Carla."

Carla stepped forward, grim-faced and sure; every inch Telvar's prize pupil. She came to stand beside her master. She, too, was armed.

"Evanyiri."

Another woman came to the front, one that Erin didn't recognize. She was older, but her face attested to experience in battle, most of it hard. Like Carla, she nodded once to Telvar to show clearly whose pupil she had been.

"Anders."

This time a man stepped forward and paused at a respectful distance from Telvar.

"Rodry trained me," he said.

Telvar frowned for a moment, noticing the man's lack of weaponry, then nodded almost bitterly. "You'll do."

"Dorse."

Another man, this one maybe seven years older than Erin or Belfas. She recognized him and smiled to herself. He was a part of Kredan's unit and had just returned from the front. He, too, gave Telvar the name of the master who had taught him arms, and Telvar once again grunted assent.

"Dannen."

Erin took a deep breath and struggled to remain standing at proud attention. Dannen nodded at her as she walked past; they had drilled together for several years, and while Dannen was larger and stronger, Erin knew that in a short bout, she had the advantage.

Eight, Erin thought to herself as she counted the assembly over and over. *Eight, and the Grandfather makes nine.*

"The Lady said she would take ten."

She forced herself not to speak, but it was very, very hard. She had to avoid looking at Belfas.

The choice of the tenth seemed to trouble the Lady as well, for no name came immediately from her. Instead she gazed outward, into the audience, and beyond. Her wide, green eyes seemed to see something that troubled her greatly, for they closed and she seemed to shrink inward momentarily. Then the Lady straightened out, light pulsing from her thin body as if it were a beacon. She was strong, she was powerful, she walked with the power of God. Erin wondered then if the doubt she thought she had seen was merely a reflection of the way she herself felt.

"Erin."

Erin froze for the second time in the evening.

This was what she had prayed for; this was what she had pleaded and argued for; this was what she had existed for all these many years. But now that it had come, she didn't quite know what to do.

Her wide gaze met the Lady's, and for a moment she stared into endless green light, mesmerized like a moth.

Again the Lady seemed to hesitate, and this time Erin thought she knew why. Fear of losing her one chance to prove herself moved her, where the Lady's choice had not. She walked over to stand in front of Telvar.

He looked down at her, tight-lipped and silent. Then he looked up beyond her head to meet the Lady's eyes.

"It is unusual, Telvar, but these are darker times. You yourself have said that Erin may soon be Carla's equal."

He said nothing, but Erin knew what he was thinking: she was only a child; she did not belong on the field of battle yet. As the rest of the audience caught sight of her, a murmur rose at her back; they did not approve of the choice, for they knew she was no adult.

The Lady knew it as well.

"Telvar, in the days of Gallin Bright Sword, almost all were children. I would choose another, but most of yours are already fighting for their lives far from here."

He looked down at Erin again, his dark eyes searching the green eyes that she turned, fearlessly, to meet his.

"Serdon?" he murmured quietly, never taking his eyes from hers.

"It is in the Lady's hands, Telvar," the Grandfather replied.

The weaponsmaster put one hand on either of Erin's shoulders. "Well, Erin? Will you fight?"

He knew what she would say; child or no she was still one of the best of his students. But the radiant smile she gave him as she nodded still cut him deeply with its double edge; pride in and fear of her determination.

chapter
six

"You're going where*?" Katalaan was white as a sheet. Her* night robe was crumpled from sleep and drawn tightly around her wide girth. The shadows that followed her down the stairs flickered in lamplight.

"To Karana," Erin said. Her sword was already at her waist. Gone now were green and brown; the baker's colors had been exchanged for the student browns that Telvar trained with. "I go with the Lady."

Kat was confused, but all she could see was the sword that hung by Erin's side. Gone was the young lady who had left in such a nervous rush. In her place, this lean young fighter that the lines had trained stared back at her.

What had happened?

"What are you going to do?"

"Fight. Fight them."

Katalaan shook her head. "Erin, you—you can't."

Erin straightened herself out. "This is important, Kat. The nightwalkers are out there killing people like you and like me. I have a chance of stopping them. How can I stay?"

"Nightwalkers? Bright Heart's blood." Katalaan sat down heavily on the steps, her white hand still clutching the banister. "Erin, only the Lady can stand against a walker."

"The Sarillar is going, too. And we have the Gifting of God." She picked up her pack and turned to the door. "I have to go—time is too important."

"Erin?"

The young woman turned back.

"Is this so important to you?"

"Yes." Her green eyes were preternaturally bright. In a lower

85

voice, she added, "They killed my mother." She had never spoken of it before, but she owed Kat at least this much.

Katalaan bowed her head. "Come back to me, Erin. Don't be only a warrior."

But Erin was already gone.

Belfas intercepted Erin on the way to the Great Hall. Apparently he had more faith in providence than she did, for he carried no pack, although he was properly armed. She stopped for a minute to inspect him and nodded.

"I'm glad," he struggled to get out, as he followed her forced jog, "that you're coming with us." He didn't really have the energy or opportunity to say it shyly.

"So am I," Erin said, without looking back. "Someone has to keep you out of trouble."

"Erin!"

"Besides, we always said we'd go to war together. We were right."

She didn't need to look back to know that his smile was the twin of hers.

They weren't the last to arrive at the Great Hall, although they weren't the first, either. The Lady, all willowy white light, stood silently apart from the rest of the gathering as they clustered beneath the southern arch. Carla, the Sarillar, the Grandfather, Telvar, and Kredan were speaking among themselves. Horses had already been saddled and looked as if they were only waiting for riders.

"Look at Telvar!" Erin whispered to Belfas.

"Where'd he get that armor?"

Erin turned to give Belfas the look he was most familiar with.

"What? What did I say?"

"It isn't the armor. Look at his face."

"What about it? Looks like Telvar to me."

"Belf." Erin shook her head. "You're the memory-walker. You tell me the last time you saw him smile like that."

"What, now?"

"Well, you're going to be called upon to use your talent sometime soon—otherwise you wouldn't be going."

Belfas grimaced and closed his eyes. "I'm going to have to walk a lot for this."

"Don't be so lazy."

But Belfas couldn't hear her. He had already called upon the strength of the line-power and let it swirl through his blood. The whole of his body was tingling with a faint, green light.

Human memory was not a linear thing, with one image following another in logical order. Rather, memories were interlinked, with one image as the key for any number of others in a loose, disorganized sequence. Belfas began to shuffle through his memories, searching for Telvar and comparing the images of years ago with the one of seconds past. Thus had Latham taught him.

At length he opened his eyes. "Never," he admitted. "I've never seen him smile like that."

Erin shook her head. "It's a good thing you can memory-walk, Belf, because you've no normal memory of your own."

They turned back to look at Telvar. The smile was gone from his face, but Erin could see the differences that lingered in his familiar countenance. He looked lean, as always, but there was an aura of danger about him, an aura of the predator. She shivered as he showed a quick flash of teeth and let his fingers linger over his sword hilt. For the first time in her life, Erin realized that Telvar's bouts in the drill circle were in no way in earnest—not like this.

As if aware of their observance, Telvar looked up.

"Erin, Belfas." He nodded, indicating that they should join the larger group. He watched them as they made their way across the courtyard. "Are you ready?"

Erin nodded as Telvar inspected her, his eyes taking in the fitted browns, the scabbard, and the back straps. He nodded in return and turned to Belfas. Only newly an adult, Belfas also wore his browns; no grays had yet been made for him, and no armor had been fitted.

Evanyiri, Dorse, Dannen, and Anders joined them soon, and the Grandfather gave the signal to mount.

"Lady?"

She shook her head. "I will walk; it will be easier to create a path for the horses."

They began to move into the night. The Lady's light was dim in the darkness, but evident nonetheless. She walked swiftly before them from the Great Hall to the edge of Elliath.

As they made their way toward the Gifting of Lernan, Erin saw, for the first time, the power of the Lady at work. She had wondered, briefly, how the horses were to carry them the last three miles through dense forest to the well; she did not wonder further. The Lady stopped at the outskirts of her forest and raised her arms, making a crossed circle in the air. A trail of light followed her hands, marking the pattern clearly into the eyes of those who watched. She spoke but few words, then brought her hands down. The light about her dimmed.

Very slowly, the trees began to move, sidling in a rustle of leaves as far back as they could.

Erin shook her head in disbelief, knowing it to be no dream.

"Come. It will last only long enough for our passage."

The Sarillar, who was in the lead, spurred his horse forward, instructing the others to follow single file.

The forest swallowed them as they made their way toward the Gifting.

Only when they reached the sparkling water of the well did Erin breathe a sigh of relief. Green, pale light robbed the clearing of the shadows of nightfall.

"Dismount," the Grandfather said, even as he left his horse. "Form the circle."

Kredan, Dannen, Belfas, and Erin looked at him in some confusion.

"Do not worry." The Lady's voice came to them alone. "Here we form the circle of initiates—and it is just that: a circle. Come, Erin. Take my hand."

Erin did as the Lady ordered and, after a minute, felt Belfas take her other hand. One hand was warm, one almost icy.

"In time you would have been shown this, but you are all too newly adult, and there has been little need of it."

Dannen and Kredan formed up on the other side of the Lady, until the group formed a circle facing inward. All eyes settled on the rippling surface of the living blood of God.

"Lernan, God." The Lady spoke. "We ask for your aid in this darkness. Three of the Enemy walk abroad, and without your power we cannot hope to face them all."

Once or twice before in her life, Erin had spoken to the waters of the well, but never with such an effect as this: the water bubbled upward, forming an irregular column. She felt the tension of Belfas's hand in hers as he took a step backward.

"Erin."

Erin dragged her eyes away from the Gifting of God.

"As I have asked, so now must you, and all of this circle."

"Lernan, God," she whispered, in a voice so low she could feel it more than she could hear it. "The Servants of the Enemy are walking. Grant us the power to—to save those that we must protect."

"Good, Erin." The Lady's hand squeezed briefly and coolly into her granddaughter's. "Belfas."

Belfas repeated the Lady's words perfectly, and then, in sequence, every member of the circle did.

"Now you may release hands," the Lady instructed them quietly. "Now those of us with the experience to do so must draw upon the power of the blood of God."

So saying, she pulled her own hand back. She drew out a small knife, one that glittered with the reflected light of the column. Without effort or pain, she slid the knife along her palm.

Only Erin was close enough to see that the color of the Lady's blood was not a mortal color. Before she could look more closely, the Lady lifted her palm and laid it gently against the living pillar. A flash of light struck the Lady, and she absorbed its brilliance, slowly drawing her hand away.

Erin began to pull her sword; it was the only edged knife that she had. She felt the warmth of the Lady's hand upon her own.

"Not you, child. You do not know the way of it, and I fear we have not the time to teach you. Untaught, you would draw more from the Hand of God than your mortal body could contain. You would be consumed by the living Light."

Before Erin could think on it, the Lady also ordered Belfas, Kredan, Dannen, Dorse, and even Evanyiri away from the blood of God.

The Grandfather was the next to step forward. He, too, cut his palm to mingle his blood with God's. But he barely touched the light that grew in front of him. The Sarillar, Carla, Anders, and finally Telvar repeated this process.

The column of water lingered in the air another moment as if saying a muted farewell. The Lady bowed low to something that no other ears could hear, and the blood of God once again became a sprinkling well of water touched by light.

"When I give you my word, step forward quickly. I cannot hold this gate for long without losing the power we will require later."

Gate? Erin's brow creased, but she didn't ask.

The Lady lifted her arms in an arch that ended with the tips of her fingers. For the second time that evening she called upon her line-power, and white light—visible even to normal vision—flooded the clearing. Erin shaded her eyes and, squinting, caught a glimpse of the haloed statue the Lady made as she focused her magic outward.

Then the ground seemed to give way in the clearing, shifting rapidly between orvas flowers and cracked stone over dirt. A mist of beaded light took the air, surrounding them all in a halo of the Bright Heart's power. Erin held her breath, waiting shakily for the Lady's command. Only the very greatest of powers had the ability to affect the physical world so obviously.

The mist grew dense, obscuring the sight of Lernan's Gifting. And then, as if it were glass, it shattered, and Erin found herself gazing at the remains of a wall; shattered stone and rubble lay all around. In the moonlight, the temple spire could be seen; a dark ghost of Karana.

"Now." The Lady's voice came, softer than usual, but much more urgent. "Step forward quickly."

Erin swiveled around, searching for Belfas. She couldn't see him. After that tiny hesitation, she took a firm step forward. Belfas appeared, as if magically, at one side. The Grandfather caught her arm at the other.

In silence she looked around at the ruined wall of Karana. She had never been to the city, but the extent of the destruction was obvious. She could barely imagine what the dim outline of ruined buildings might once have looked like. Nowhere was any movement evident. How had so much been destroyed so quickly? Shadows, completely hidden from moonlight or starlight, grew at the base of the wall, devouring rubble and grass alike.

"Be at ready."

All faces turned to see the Lady of Elliath, hovering a foot above the ground. Her hair was shot through with brilliance. A breeze blew through the open sky, but it was not the same as the one that touched her. Her garments swirled about her bare feet in an eddy of light.

This, Erin realized, *is what she must have looked like in the days before Gallin. Beautiful.*

Beautiful and terrible.

For the first time in centuries, the warriors of Line Elliath saw the unveiled glory of their founder upon the field of battle that she had chosen to take. Even Telvar's face was touched by awe at the wild beauty, the cold grace of the Lady.

"They are here still; they know that *I* have come." She called upon her power yet again, and a grim, harsh daylight destroyed the darkness. "And they will not touch the Dark Heart this night.

"Be prepared now, warriors of Lernan. The Light has sounded its call to the Darkness." So saying, she lifted her arms, fingers pointing outward. Thus had she fought her enemies before the birth of the world.

White-fire flared in the darkness, tracing its path across Erin's vision. She unsheathed her sword and followed its flight across the empty field.

After a moment, a deep ugly red flared to life, not far from where they stood. The remains of the wall provided little cover against the red-fire that must surely follow.

"Break away from the Lady!" Telvar barked, and began to run to the west along the periphery of the wall.

The Sarillar nodded and began to run in the opposite direction. Dannen followed him, as did Evanyiri, Dorse, and Anders.

After a moment, Erin followed her teacher, pausing only long enough to grab the front of Belfas's tunic. Telvar ducked into an open section of the wall, motioning for his line-mates to do the same. The stone was rough and unevenly broken, and even the standing wall was cracked.

"Belfas." Belfas nodded in silence, amazed that Telvar could find words after all that had transpired. "Watch with me."

Erin started forward as well, and Telvar shook his head sharply.

"We'll not be here long." His own sword he kept parallel to the matted sheen of his armor. "Let the Lady draw them out if they dare to come."

Clamping her jaw in frustration, Erin stepped aside. But she kept as close to Belfas as she could, just in case she had to yank him back into the cover of the wall.

Belfas knelt carefully by one side of the ruins and craned his head forward to catch sight of the Lady of Elliath. She still stood above the ground, as if her feet, immortal and eternal, would find no purchase there. From this distance, he swore that he could clearly see the emerald brilliance of her gaze.

Then he heard it, a sound that no one alive save the Servants could boast of hearing; the battle cry of the Servants of the Dark Heart. The white brilliance of sky was split by bands of crimson, the bitter blood of the Dark Heart. Darkness grayed the edge of the Lady's day and began to push it inward, reasserting natural order.

Red-fire flared like a javelin thrown unerringly toward its target: the Lady herself.

Only her hand moved, but white-fire spread outward to meet the enemy charge. A thunderclap split the air.

If the Gods ever fought, this is what it must have been like.

Belfas's eyes scanned the area he could see, trying to make out the three that he knew were in waiting. *There,* he thought. *One.* He glanced up at Telvar.

"I see him," the weaponsmaster said. "Keep watching."

Belfas nodded, but he could only make out the one.

"Belf!"

Erin's voice caught his attention, and he turned, as did Telvar. The weaponsmaster's frown faded as he followed the direction of Erin's shaking finger.

She had found the second of the three.

Like the Lady, he hovered—but this time many feet above the ground.

"Bright Heart," Telvar swore softly. "He dares." For the second of the Servants stood atop the smoldering wreckage of the Temple of Lernan's highest spire. His arms were spread wide, limbs of shadow around which brilliant red entwined like serpents.

"The third must be beyond the walls, closer to Andin," Telvar said quietly. "A triangle around the Lady's center. I do not believe they notice us." He frowned and corrected himself. "Or that they think us a threat." He began to move forward, leaving the wall for the blackened buildings of the inner city. "Their mistake, then. Come. Let the Lady hold their attention a while longer." He picked Belfas up by the shoulder. "Are you prepared to remain here?"

Belfas nodded, his eyes transfixed by the Lady. She was a sight given to few to see, and of these few, he alone would truly be able to remember the glory of it.

"Erin, come."

Erin stared at Belfas's bent back and hesitated.

"Erin."

Shaking her head, she whispered, "Keep safe."

If Belfas heard her, he didn't acknowledge it, and she turned to follow Telvar.

He moved with the grace and confidence of a cat stalking its small, helpless prey. Erin followed directly behind, trying to mimic the fluidity and speed of his movements. Her training held sway; she was silent, her feet barely disturbing the rubble, dirt, and timber that they passed over. Behind her came the Grandfather, but she didn't take the time to see in what order the others ran. It was hard enough to keep her eyes upon the ground; everything in her screamed a silent warning as the ruins of the Temple of Lernan came ever closer and the creature on the smoldering spire loomed ever higher.

There was little grass on the route they took; the ground was hard and felt uneven. Stones, flattened, carried the sound of her feet. What remained of the buildings was a chaos that she could not understand; they were packed too close together, and there were so many of them. They were tall, most at least twice the height of her home.

She was looking up when she ran into Telvar's outstretched arm. It took her by surprise, and she gasped before she could quiet herself.

Without speaking, Telvar pointed.

A large, dark chasm ran across the breadth of the city streets. This, then, was what had destroyed so much. Erin shuddered.

"Telvar." The Grandfather spoke above her head. She turned, caught Kredan's astonished stare, and heard Carla's single syllable.

Telvar looked back at the Grandfather, shaking his head. "Too wide to cross." His face was grim. "The three have done their work."

The Grandfather looked up at the sudden flare of red across the gray sky.

"Serdon?"

The Grandfather looked back at Telvar. "Only three of us now," he muttered. "It will have to be me, I think. I am not so fast as either you or Carla."

Telvar looked at Carla, who nodded her assent.

Erin glanced at Kredan, but the significance of the exchange had apparently bypassed him as well, though not for long.

The Grandfather raised his arms, a shadow of the Lady's movement, and spread them wide. His hands traced twin circles in the air, and he spoke three words; words that Erin would not later recall no matter how hard she tried.

Light flared around him, light pale but pure—the Gifting of God's blood. It flowed outward in a rush to the ground, taking sluggish root there.

The Grandfather closed his eyes, bowed his head, but continued to force power outward.

And the ground began to *move*.

Erin had heard all the teaching stories about the Gifting of God, but never before had she understood it so completely. None of the Lernari alone, past or present, could have achieved this miracle; even the strongest could only affect the living. In awe she watched as the Lady's meaning became clear: No one untrained could possibly hope to contain this much of the living light and survive.

The rock struggled outward, swaying and leaning as it reached for the other edge of the chasm. When it connected, it made its purchase, and the light ebbed away from it.

Telvar caught the Grandfather as he fell to one knee.

"Serdon?"

"I am . . . fine."

The weaponsmaster nodded and ran lightly across the new bridge. Erin hesitated for a moment before she felt the Grandfather's hand upon her back.

"Look at Telvar," he said softly, "and only at Telvar. The bridge is solid rock; it will carry you and hold you if you follow it quickly."

She inhaled, forcing her eyes away from the yawning darkness.

"Erin, please."

Nodding, she bit her lip and stared at Telvar's retreating back. She put one foot upon the uneven stone and followed it quickly, trying not to look down. Only when she reached the far side did she breathe again; she could not even imagine having to go back.

The temple pulled at her attention; the temple and the darkness that defiled it. She stared upward as her feet began their steady pace across the rubble once again. They were almost upon it when red-fire launched outward, traveling high above their upturned faces. If the Servant was aware of them, he still did not condescend to notice their existence.

Telvar reached the base of the tower and looked up, shaking his head. In the pale, unnatural light, Erin could see that only the shell of the spire remained intact. Large, gaping holes darkened its sides.

Carla cursed again, and Telvar touched her shoulder.

"Serdon?"

The Grandfather shook his head. "I've nothing left."

The weaponsmaster nodded in grim agreement. "Let us hope that Andin is not in the same straits." He took a deep breath and readied his weapon. "We will have to call it down, then. We cannot afford to go upward to greet it.

"Erin, Kredan, stay with the Grandfather until the nightwalker touches ground."

"If," Carla added darkly. She looked at Telvar.

"On my count," the older man whispered.

The Grandfather touched Erin and Kredan, pulling them into the cover of the tower's base. Two bodies lay there, naked and broken.

"Not now, Erin." The Grandfather's voice was sharp.

She swallowed and turned away from the corpses.

"Watch."

She nodded; she still couldn't speak.

Carla and Telvar stared up for a moment. Then each in turn slid the edges of their blades deftly across their left palms. They lifted their arms, mirroring each other's gestures almost precisely. But for all that their movements were graceful and fluid, neither relinquished weapons. Flashing steel formed the periphery of two small circles; battle circles, if one could see it.

And Erin could see it clearly. They seemed consumed in the same radiance that had touched the Grandfather at the chasm. But instead of pulsing outward, the light remained contained by their bodies, growing stronger and more brilliant as the seconds passed.

The Grandfather's hand tightened upon Erin's shoulder as she tensed. She watched as the impossible happened; the light grew stronger still. Her eyes narrowed, but she could not look away.

Telvar nodded once, briefly, at Carla. Then the Bright Heart's power exploded up from the ground, crossing the length of the tower in an eye blink. White-fire cut the sky.

Erin didn't have time to watch it connect, but she heard the sudden chill scream that seemed to come from everywhere.

"Now!" the Grandfather said.

Erin's sword was already in the air.

Kredan paused for only a moment, and Erin saw the now-familiar, painful sight of blade against skin. He closed his eyes briefly and then started toward Carla and Telvar.

The light had gone out of them completely.

Erin and the Grandfather watched, tense and ready, as the shadow began to descend. The red lines that coursed through it were much weaker, but no Lernari could doubt they were there.

Remember this, Erin heard Telvar say from the distance of years. *You cannot hope to defeat a nightwalker; it can ward easily and quickly against* anything *you can attack it with.*

Not anything, she thought, as she followed on Kredan's heels. *We may not have destroyed it, but we* have *weakened it.*

Carla and Telvar were already gesturing as red-fire flashed in the air to collide sharply with the sudden periphery of the True

Ward's circle. Kredan joined it with his own ward, and the red-fire crackled against the sudden barrier. Even the Grandfather, weakened as he was, added his blood to theirs.

Only Erin, not truly adult, was unable to come to their aid, at least not that way.

The red-fire held, but it gained ground slowly through the barrier as Erin breathed a sigh of relief. It was true; the power of the Servant had indeed been drained by whatever damage Telvar and Carla had done.

But not enough; the red-fire moved slowly, but it moved nonetheless—moved toward the nonhuman blood of Line Elliath, to consume it, to destroy it.

Four against one, they waged their motionless battle, with one lone person on the periphery of their tableau.

She noted the straining, pale faces of her line-mates, but the face of the enemy was obscured by darkness, the same darkness that had shrouded the face and form of the one other Servant of Darkness she had ever seen.

She froze for a moment, her grip on her sword so tight that it hurt. *Was it you? Was it* you?

She knew that she couldn't afford to let the sudden rage that she felt take her completely. Knew it, but couldn't stop it. Nor could her companions, too caught in the battle for their lives to notice her fleeting form as it circumvented them in the shadows.

Fear? She felt none.

She saw only the darkness, felt only the black, bitter anger that had come to replace *her.*

I'm *warrior trained. I* know *how to die.*

I know how to kill.

She raised her double-edged sword as she approached the shadow. Raised it high above her head, as she had done one other time, in defiance of the darkness, in the wake of the dead.

If she could not have the True Ward, she would have the Greater. One hand danced a stilted jitter across the air. If she could not have God's power, she would have her own. Light—pale green, but nonetheless bright—cascaded up her sword. And Bright Heart, if she could not have her mother, she would have this, the arc of her glowing blade, its whistle keening through the suddenly stifling air.

Not from this quarter did the enemy perceive a threat. But still a claw of darkness, much like a badly burned hand, shot through the air, flying upward to meet the solid steel of Erin's sword.

For a moment she was twelve again, but this time there was no Kandor, no warrior-priests with the strength of their True Wards, no rescue. There was a death here, a better death than her mother had died.

The truth of Telvar's many words was proven as the night-walker's hand slashed the blade down to one side and rose for Erin's throat. But even the touch of the meager light she had summoned seemed to anger it.

"Your blood, half-breed," it demanded.

Erin only smiled. "Take it." She wrenched back, using the distance as the only leverage she had. "Take it, then!" She raised her sword.

And then Telvar's keening blade also came in. The hand that had reached for Erin swung round to fend off Telvar. The darkness that shrouded the face glowed suddenly red, and the weaponsmaster bit back a cry and stumbled, gesturing.

But it had been only a flicker; the Servant had not the time for much more, and the cost of his fire was high.

Carla danced in, her speed the equal of Erin's, but her strength the greater. No green fire touched her blade, but rather a white one; the purity of the power of adulthood. The Bright Heart, weakened by his Gifting, had nonetheless come to her call.

And this strike found its mark even as the Servant's eyes flared in shadow again. Carla felt the red-power that swirled around her like a whip, but she held herself in, her hand not leaving the blade that was buried in the nightwalker's dark side.

Erin struck, also, as she had been denied the chance to do once before. She felt her sword connect and nearly dropped it as darkness crawled up to meet her hands.

There was another white flash as Kredan found room to enter the fray; yet another as Telvar found his feet and battled on in spite of his injury. His face would bear a new scar from this battle; it was bleeding profusely.

The Servant's cries grew louder and more frenzied as it parried those blows it could, but each contact with the wards affected it. It began to move more slowly, and the red stopped flashing from its eyes. The warriors of Elliath attacked the more intently for their renewed hope.

Silver and gray encircled the darkness, driving light to the shadow that had blistered the ground. At the last that darkness uttered one long howl, staggered back, and . . . unraveled.

A chill lingered in the air as they stared at their blades, but the winds soon blew it away.

"Well done, Erin," Telvar said softly, as he sheathed his sword. He looked up at the Grandfather wearily. "Did you feel it, Serdon?"

The Grandfather nodded quietly. "The Lady must have drawn more power from the Gifting than we thought possible; our wards have never been so weak."

"Let us hope, then, that Andin has been as successful as we have. Come; we must return to the Lady."

He turned and walked away, and after a few moments, his line-mates followed, each in the privacy of his or her own silence.

Erin felt drained. For the second time in her life she had come face to face with the death a nightwalker offered; for the second time she could walk away. Even the bridge across the still chasm couldn't wake her fear; the darkness of the depths paled beside that of the Servant. As if in a dream, her feet padded lightly across it.

"Erin," she heard the Grandfather say.

She looked at him blankly.

"The Servant will not walk again in these lands. Perhaps I have been wrong; perhaps there is a place for you on the field of battle."

The light in the sky had dimmed much during their encounter; either the Lady had triumphed, or her power was weakening. Erin saw the dull glow of red across the horizon, and a shudder returned her fully to reality. The Lady's power was waning.

By silent consensus, they ran the rest of the way to the broken wall.

Only when they were near it did Erin hear the familiar sound of hoofbeats. Her eyes widened and she looked across at Telvar.

"What is it?" he asked.

"Horses," she whispered. "Many."

"Serdon?"

The Grandfather shook his head. "I can't hear them yet, but Erin is—no, wait." He closed his eyes and then his head sank. "Horses."

Telvar listened, and after a few seconds the sound became clear to his ears as well. "Damn them," he said softly as he estimated numbers. "We've been here too long."

He strode along the ruins of the wall until he found Belfas, still crouched partially behind cover, still watching.

"We did it, Belf," Erin told him.

Belfas looked back, breaking his concentration for the first time. He smiled, but wearily. "I think the Lady is getting tired," he told her softly. "But so is the enemy."

"Not all of the enemy," Telvar replied. From his back he took a simple longbow and busied himself stringing it.

"What do you—"

"There are horses coming," Erin answered before he could finish asking his question.

The Grandfather nodded. "Malanthi."

"Let us hope it is only Malanthi," Telvar added as he pulled an arrow. "Andin can deal with the half-blooded."

"And if they are nonblooded?"

Silence.

Erin stood stiffly, her hand upon her sword. To fight normal humans, she could count on sword skill and speed alone. Only now did she *feel* the truth of all the lessons she had been taught; Light affected the Dark; Dark the Light. In the gray nonblooded, the normal mortals, there was not enough Darkness for her meager light to touch and affect. She was faster, yes; she healed more quickly, saw more keenly, heard more clearly, and aged more slowly—but her power was not enough to hurt them. Only the Lady and the Sarillar carried enough of the Light within them to affect the minor Darkness inherent in the gray.

Belfas stretched and began to reach for his weapon.

"Not yet, Belfas," Telvar told him. "Even in this, we need you to watch; we must identify those on the field if we survive it. If I'm to guess, I would say that the Malanthi here rank high, both in power and station."

So saying, he stepped out.

The Lady of Elliath still hovered above the ground and, seeing her, it was impossible to believe that her power waned.

"She fights the Third of the Enemy," the Grandfather said softly. "We know where the First is, and the Second comes to the mortal lands but seldom. No other could stand so long against her."

He brushed a hand across his forehead. "Come, Carla, Kredan, be ready. The horses are driven at a gallop; they will be upon us soon.

"Do not look yet for help from the Lady's quarter."

Then he, too, stepped out. Once again he called upon his ward, and once again the light of the Bright Heart filled him.

Erin bit her lip. In the distance she could see clearly the first rank of riders. There were perhaps forty, but they were armored well; glinting gorges stood above dark surcoats. She could make out the flag of the Enemy; red against the blackness. They were the priests and Swords of the Dark Heart. A low, loud sound came rushing toward the walls of Karana: the horns of the Enemy.

If there were foot soldiers, they came at too great a distance to be seen by even her eyes.

She pulled her shield from across her back and gripped it tightly.

Carla, longbow readied, went to stand behind Telvar. Once again, she mirrored the master's stance perfectly; it was easy to see why she had long been considered the best of his students.

Erin had not had the strength to wield the longbow; she had no way of taking advantage of the distance that lay between the Malanthi and her line-mates. She had to wait until the charge came to them, so she lingered near the wall.

A crackle split the air.

Red-fire sprang to life around the Lady's feet as Erin gave a muffled gasp.

From where she stood, she could see the highest tongues of flame make contact with the Lady's unadorned feet. She watched as the Lady's head shot back, revealing the tight arch of her pale throat. There should have been screaming, but the Lady was eerily silent.

Something hurtled past Erin, nearly knocking her over. As she regained her balance, she caught a glimpse of student browns and heard a raw shout.

"No!"

The Grandfather's hand caught her shoulder as she started to lunge forward after the running figure.

"No," he said tersely, then shouted, "Belfas!"

But Belfas didn't appear to hear the Grandfather's call. He ran, unerring, to where the Lady twisted in pain, his arms already outstretched as if to pull her from the grip of the fire.

Shaking her head slowly from side to side, Erin watched him. Ten feet from the Lady. Five.

His hands stretched upward to try to catch the Lady's. They never made it. The red-fire that hovered upon the ground turned suddenly toward him and flared up. Student browns were consumed by the Dark Heart's fire. Belfas screamed, dragging his hands downward, as if to put it out.

"Ward!" Erin screamed. "Ward, damn you!"

The fire burned upward to lick at the twisted visage of Belfas's face.

Erin tore herself free of the Grandfather's grip and began to run forward as well. She heard his shout and ignored it, just as Belfas had, and for just the same reason.

No! She saw the fire suddenly stretch out a finger toward her, and she kept on running. *No! You've taken everything else—you won't have him!* She barely had time to see the flame coil like a serpent and spring up.

Contact.

Later she would understand why Belfas, nearly consumed, was unable to make his ward to stave off the fire. But at the time, all she could feel was the pain that seared the *insides* of her skin. Momentum carried her forward when nothing else could, as she grabbed at her arms, trying ineffectively to put the fire out.

She tried to open her eyes and realized that they were open. She felt a scream tear itself out of her throat; all she could hear was the sharp hiss and crackle of the red-fire that sought to burn her very blood away.

Of the two encircled by fire, Erin was the more powerful—and therefore the more vulnerable. Her knees gave way beneath her and she collapsed entirely into the fire's embrace.

But she felt no fear, perhaps because the pain was too overwhelming, or perhaps because a part of her knew that even this was less horrible than what her mother had suffered.

Her mother. By a Servant's hand her mother had taken so long to retreat into death. By a Servant's hand, so would she.

And so would Belfas.

"Belfas!" She screamed as she remembered why she had walked into this terrible redness. She tried to struggle upward, but she could not move; the memory had come too late. Too late.

I've failed, she thought wildly. *I've failed again.*

Bright Heart, why? Lernan!

The name echoed in her mind as she called it. But instead of growing weaker, it took on strength until her entire body seemed to resound with the feel of its urgency and its despair. And as it did, the pain within her retreated like a wave on the shore of her body. In its place came a gentle warmth that would not be denied. She opened her eyes and struggled to her knees even as the feeling built.

Looking down at her shaking hands, she saw a pale light that brightened as she watched. The red-fire still surrounded her, still touched her pale skin—but it caused no pain as it crashed against the barrier of white and fell away.

In wild desperation she lurched to her feet. Only three steps and she could touch the prone body that lay in an eddy of flame. Two. One.

Her hands, shaking, plunged into the fire that covered Belfas's back. With a strength that she never guessed she could have, she yanked him to his feet, wrapping her arms around him and holding him as tightly against her light as she could.

Come on. Come on, Belf. He felt so still and hot. She drew upon the light within her, pushing it out to envelop her line-mate.

"Belf," she whispered. "Please."

The light grew, encircling him in bands so brilliant that she had to close her eyes yet again.

He moved.

She bit her lip, praying that it was his motion, and not her trembling, that she felt. "Belf?"

He moved again, this time planting his elbow feebly into her side. Light or no, her eyes flew open. Even the tears that started to slide down her cheeks were glowing.

She turned him around, supporting less and less of his weight as the power built in him as well.

"You idiot." She half shouted into his ear. "You b-bloody i-idiot."

She felt his lips move against her hair, and although she couldn't hear a word he said, she knew it was an apology.

Beyond the fire that still tried to cage them she could see the Lady of Elliath. Although the fire around her feet had not grown much closer, it still bit into her ankle. And if it caused Erin pain, who had only half the blood . . .

Clutching Belfas tightly by the shoulder, she walked the last few steps and reached out to touch the Lady's taut hand. She felt pain shoot into her palm for a moment, and then she dispelled it, as if it were a careless word that a friend had said in a moment of anger. She was glowing, she could see this beyond the red of the enemy light. Glowing, yet casting no shadow, she stood in the Hand of God. In that moment, although she could not see it, her eyes flashed the deep, living green of the Lady; and of the two, she was momentarily the stronger. No eye, mortal or blooded, would have easily been able to tell the two apart.

This blood, this power, this was God's—and wrapped in its warmth and its strength, there was nothing that she felt she could not do, nothing. She turned to look for a moment at Belfas and met his wide-eyed stare; she saw a reflection in his eyes of her face surrounded by strands of glowing hair that blazed a trail that the red-fire could not follow. Then she turned to look back at the Lady of Elliath, standing free now of the pain that had gripped her only moments before. The slim, immortal hand felt cool to the touch. If not for the pale color of the Lady's hair, they might have been sisters at the dawn of the Awakening.

And the Lady of Elliath knew fully, for the first time, Lernan's Hope as it stood before her, cloaked in his fires.

Standing in red-fire, with one hand on Belfas, and one hand on the Lady, Erin looked ahead into the dark horizon.

The shadow was there, closer and larger than it had been. She smiled as the Lady suddenly returned her grip. From somewhere, she heard the faintest whisper touch her mind. *Great-grandchild* . . . But it was not the Lady's voice; it was both deeper and stronger, for all its faintness, than Erin had ever heard before. She shook her head, and it was gone.

A pillar of white fire rose from the ground, utterly destroying the red.

The Lady of Elliath slid her hand free of her granddaughter's.

"Enough!" A ball of white-fire raced outward. It touched a red wall; touched it and crumbled it almost at the same moment.

Erin had barely time to shout, "The horsemen!" at Belfas. He swiveled his head around, caught a glimpse of the cavalry, and lost it again as the white-fire spread out like a tidal wave.

"Come to me, line-children! Come, and quickly!"

From the left came Telvar, Kredan, Carla, and the Grandfather. From the right came the Sarillar, Evanyiri, Dannen, and Dorse.

"Anders?" the Grandfather shouted.

The Sarillar shook his head sharply.

"Now," the Lady said. "Step forward; we have done what we must."

She looked once, briefly, at her granddaughter before the scene shifted and the Gifting of Lernan once again sparkled dimly in an open clearing.

They returned to the Great Hall in silence. Anders had fallen; a victim of the nightwalker that the Sarillar and his warriors had struggled to destroy. All others who had been chosen still walked—all but the Lady, who lay in a slumber from which none could wake her. Andin, the Sarillar, was the only one who had power enough to try, and when he failed, they carried her gently homeward.

"She sleeps," the Grandfather told the younger line-mates. "Were she . . . dead, she would not remain; she would pass from us like sunrise. Do not grieve."

He turned to look at Erin.

"And you, Erin." He bowed formally. "Your childhood is past; you have touched the Bright Heart's hand and He has welcomed you."

He waited for Erin's reaction, but she stood staring blankly past him. Shaking his head a little, he turned to leave.

"Grandfather."

He stopped walking, but did not look back.

"I touched the Bright Heart. I think I heard His voice."

His eyes widened, but she couldn't know that, couldn't know that the power of the Servants alone was strong enough to *hear* the words of the Bright Heart.

"Why—why did he come to me?"

"You were dying," the Grandfather replied, thinking, *you heard the voice of God, child. No, not truly child any longer.* He saw again the image of her face as it had been just an hour ago, alive with the light of God. It was a wild thing, a terrible thing, and a sight of incredible beauty. *I have presided over the initiation ceremonies many, many times. Never have I seen such power.* No, not even in the days of his youth, so very long past. If only Erin could have made her ward in the natural way . . . He shook his head; best not to think on it too much. "You were dying," he repeated softly.

"So was my—so was she."

"Erin," he said, turning to face her, "God comes as He is able; He listens for any sign from His children that He can hear. He came to you because your death-voice could reach Him. He did not aid your mother because hers couldn't."

"But she—"

"She faced a Servant of the Enemy, one who could afford to turn all his power against that communication. We faced three, true—but those three could not silence us all because they had to contend with the Lady herself."

"Why didn't the Lady—"

"It wasn't known until it was too late. And had it been . . .

you have not touched God's power before; you can not know how much our use of the Gifting weakened Him.

"Erin, any adult faces death and accepts it when it comes to *any* warrior. You *must* learn to do this. Not all life can be the responsibility of any single man or woman."

He left her then, not wanting to diminish her achievement, but fearing his expression could do nothing else.

Katalaan was waiting for her. Light flickered from beneath the curtains of the house they shared. It was near dawn, which meant that the baker's stall would be empty for at least the half day. Erin was weary.

She had left as a child. She returned now as a warrior, an adult.

But as she opened the door to the house and its luminous shadows, she wondered for the first time if that would mean as much to Katalaan as it did to the lines.

"Kat?" she whispered as she stood hesitantly in the entrance-way.

Lights touched the ceiling and flickered there as Katalaan stepped out of the small fire-room holding a lamp aloft. She closed her eyes for a moment and sagged against a wall.

"Erin."

"I've made my ward, Kat," Erin began. She could think of nothing else to say. "I'm an adult now."

The lamp was deposited on the stairs as Kat took two steps forward and put her arms tightly around Erin.

"Blessed Bright Heart," she whispered. "Thank you." She stood there, shaking a moment. "Thank you for sending my daughter back."

"Kat?" Erin whispered.

Katalaan only shook her head.

"You've never called me that before."

"I never had to, Erin." Tears streaked the old woman's face; old tears, covered now by newer ones. "I don't know how they can take this. I don't know how the lines can send their children to war."

Because they're all warriors. Erin had heard it many times before, but couldn't bring herself to say it. Instead she held on to Kat tightly. For she realized that sometime soon, there would be no Kat to come home to at the end of the day. The war had called, and she had proved she could answer it.

That morning, she left off class and went with Kat to the market square.

Although Erin was acknowledged from that point on as adult, it was a full month before she was granted the robes of her office at her ceremony of initiation.

For that month, the Lady of Elliath lay suspended in a healing trance, her body seeking to recover the power that she had spent in the final moments of the confrontation. The ceremonies were never done without her presence.

The information that Belfas was able to provide from his brief glimpse of the cavalry charge enabled the strategists of the line to identify the Malanthi that had been present, and for some time Elliath knew a measure of relief, for the high priest, foremost of the Karnari, had indeed been upon the field, and had almost certainly perished under the last great wave of the Lady's light.

The deep blue sky was tinged with the faint red of sunset, but even that hated light vanished as the clouds began to roll in.

The First of Malthan stood upon the highest spire of his palace and looked westward. The shadows of his fingers pressed into the buttressed cut stone.

"Three."

The priest in attendance bowed yet again to control his shaking. His black robes fluttered above the stone as if they, too, feared his Lord.

"Yes, Lord."

The fingers upon the wall bit deeply into precisely cut stone, leaving their mark.

"The high priest?"

"Yes, Lord," the man stammered. "And the—and the commander of the Swords." He did not mention the twenty others who had died in the charge; these he knew his Lord would deem inconsequential. Although he stood in the center of the platform, he could still see over the edge; the fall was said to be near endless. He did not want to find the truth of that, not this eve.

"I see." The First Servant turned, a swirl of midnight velvet. Of all of the nightwalkers, fell Servants of God, only this one chose to maintain a semblance of human appearance. But it was far from a comfort for those of the Malanthi that had to work under him, for each expression was crystal clear and unveiled by shadow. Between the shadow and the sudden red glint in the Servant's eyes, the shadow was by far the better option.

Nevertheless, the Malanthi priest struggled to hide any sign of fear. It was the one thing that was certain doom when the Lord was in this frame of mind.

"How?"

"The First of the Enemy, Lord. She came to Karana short days after it had fallen. We believe that the Sarillar of her line was also present." As the priest watched the First Servant, he relaxed. Although he did not know what he had said, something in his words calmed his Lord.

"The Lady herself," Stefanos said softly, turning away. "We drew the Lady to the fields she had forsaken." He was silent a moment, but the priest did not move—he had not yet been dismissed.

"Any other news?"

"Yes, Lord. We believe that an army composed of three lines will reach Karana within a week. At this time, our own army is not capable of holding the city; the nonblooded are leaving in spite of the incentive to remain."

"Very well. You may go."

The priest nodded and began to retreat.

"One more thing."

"Lord?"

"There were a number of prisoners taken for the altars."

"Yes."

"When the new leader of the Greater Cabal is chosen, have him perform his ceremonies along the broken walls. Tell him he is to leave the bodies there when he retreats."

The priest smiled softly.

"As you command, Lord."

In silence and privacy, the First Servant drew strength from the coming of the night.

"First of Lernan," he whispered softly. "When we meet, you will rue this."

So saying, he took a step over the edge and descended from the spire. The night had come, and he would take time for the luxury and necessity of walking.

chapter
seven

Erin lay back against her bedroll, forcefully massaging her sword arm. She was tired—no, exhausted—but she'd gotten thoroughly accustomed to that state during her four years at the front. She'd almost gotten used to four small walls of canvas, to rain, heat, and insects as well. And trees. She had never thought to be so weary of forests. It made her appreciate her leave and her visits with Kat. But even at the end of those weeks she longed for this. Bright Heart, she was stupid sometimes.

The thin flap of canvas couldn't block out Telvar's angry shouting. It was a wonder that at the end of day he had the voice left to berate the newer fighters. She smiled, remembering her own first days under his command. But the smile was half wince; many of his words still had the power to sting over time—even at almost four years' distance.

The next few weeks looked to be peaceful ones—at least as peaceful as the front ever got. Tomorrow—or more likely the next day—they would begin their twenty-mile march to the Vale, where Korinn's unit was fighting.

She rolled over onto her stomach, letting the ache of the day settle into her back.

In four years, they had lost about fifty miles and gained back ten. In four years, the Lady had traveled out to the front another six times to stand against powers assembled that were too great for her warrior line-children. And it wasn't enough.

Stop it, Erin, she told herself firmly.

Twice the unit had been forced to retreat, and only due to Telvar's harsh and complete authority had the unit survived. It was only two battles, compared to any number won—but Telvar had the highest success rate of anyone fighting on the front.

She closed her eyes.

The field is not the place to grieve for the dead.

But all of the dead returned to her. Yesterday she alone had prepared fifteen bodies, and each of the fifteen had been comrades. Ten were newly ranked; sixths. But two had been experienced thirds; it had been a vicious, bloody fight. The bodies would return to the holdings now that the battle was over, and there the living could mourn and mark their passage into the beyond. Erin tried to think instead of the lives that she had managed to save with her healing skill—a skill that had been trained to its height, even if she couldn't touch the Bright Heart at will. But this didn't help, precisely because she *couldn't* touch the Bright Heart as her mother had done before her. Mortal wounds were mortal wounds, and she was a glorified field surgeon, no more.

Even wrapped up in the shadows of such musing, she still did not fail to hear a lone horse as it approached the encampment.

Her hand was on her sword before she found her feet. She rolled out of her tent lightly, as she had no time to armor up, and began to move toward Telvar's when she saw him emerge from it. He nodded at her, noting the readiness with which she approached him.

"I heard it as well," he replied, his own blade readied.

In a matter of minutes, so did everyone else that was there.

Erin heard the challenge of the watch, as the horse stopped its frenzied pace a moment. She also heard the watch let the rider by, and she relaxed—as much as she ever did.

Only when she saw for herself the shining circle upon gray surcoat did she sheathe her weapon.

The man looked vaguely familiar, but he was not of Line Elliath; his markings were of Cormont, the line that had the troops to spare to send to the Elliath front.

When the horse came to a stop in front of Telvar's tent, the man nearly fell off. Erin stepped forward immediately to steady him, letting a hint of her power out to ease his exhaustion.

"First," he said, inclining his head sharply—the salute of a near equal.

Telvar returned it. "What news?" he asked grimly, ignoring the formality of rank and name.

The man handed Telvar a sealed scroll.

Telvar didn't read it immediately; he didn't need to.

"Carla!"

His second in command came apparently out of nowhere.

"Ready the unit; we're to march south tonight." He closed his eyes. "Have the initiates bury our dead before we leave; they won't be going home."

She nodded briskly and left to carry out his orders.

"Erin, see to the horse; find water and food for the third." He eyed the man's uniform and nodded. "Must you carry our reply ahead of the unit?"

"No."

"Rest, then. We march in two hours."

Erin nodded briskly and turned away shaking; no one in Elliath's force could fail to recognize the seal that she had just caught a glimpse of.

All told, there were sixty able-bodied people who could respond to the urgent request of the Sarillar of Elliath.

The third of Darek of Cormont, as he had named himself, did not seem surprised that the number was low; it was not, perhaps, the sixths, fifths, fourths, or thirds that he was counting on. The first was Telvar, and even among the other lines, Telvar was near-legendary. Of the three seconds, Carla and Marek were also well known.

Telvar did not address his warriors, but this was common; he was accustomed to leading, and they were accustomed to trust that lead. Their lives depended on it.

Unlike warriors outside of the circle, however, they had the freedom to speak about it if words didn't interrupt their duty.

And even Telvar's sixths had the uncanny ability to think on at least two levels.

"Which part of the front do we march to?" Belfas asked as he ducked below an overlying branch and narrowly missed tripping over a flat stone ledge. His fighting ability had kept him solidly in the fifth rank. Erin was certain he'd survived the four years at the front because he was seldom called upon to join battle. His ability to memory-walk was his true weapon against the Enemy, and no one risked it needlessly. Having fought in chaos, noise, and tumult, she knew how important it was to have someone who could be trusted to have clearly seen and heard all that took place.

Erin's own circle was underlined three times—a good showing for four years. But although her skill with a sword was respectable—admirable, really, given her relative strength and size—it was not for frontline combat that she had earned third.

It was for her sight and her hearing. All Lernari had, by nature of blood, better hearing or sight than the nonblooded; it came from the parentage of Servants of the Bright Heart. Of all members of the unit, Telvar notwithstanding, Erin could see the farthest and with the best degree of certainty; and she could hear even the more subtle sounds that signaled something wrong.

Telvar always utilized these abilities to their full potential. In any battle that she had fought in after achieving fifth, she had been sent to scout. Sometimes with Dannen as backup, but more recently with Carla.

She was good at it.

She could move nearly silently; when she was at her best, Telvar swore that only a Servant could possibly detect her presence—and then, by blood-power alone. It wasn't true, and they both knew it, but Erin treasured the compliment. It was one of maybe three that she had received from the first.

"Erin?"

"I'm still thinking."

She caught Belfas's nod out of the corner of one eye.

Where was the Sarillar?

If they hadn't been marching, she would have asked Belfas to memory-walk. Instead she had to rely on her own recollections.

"Beryon Valley," she said at length. "I think we're going to Beryon."

"Isn't the Sarillar there?"

She looked up; occasionally Belfas could still surprise her. "Yes."

"It's bad, then."

"Belf, we'd hardly be on a forced march if it weren't." But the friendly exasperation that usually marked any sentence that began with "Belf . . ." was missing.

It was the first time that either of them could remember the Sarillar sending for help.

Beryon Valley was a good twenty-seven miles away by the straightest path, and Telvar pushed them all, setting a pace that they could follow at some cost. Words drifted away into silence and the occasional snap of dry twig beneath booted foot.

Ahead and behind Erin could see the faint green glow that each line-member carried instead of a torch; the power of blood to light the path that must be traveled. She had seen it many times, but it never failed to strengthen her. Sixty people, each carrying an emblem of the Bright Heart and His Servants that nothing but Lady Death herself could dim, marched on toward morning.

They stopped once, taking no more than an hour to massage their legs and refresh themselves. Many of the unit insisted that they were fit to carry on, Erin among them. But it was Telvar's command, and no one seriously considered disobeying it.

Still, it was obvious that Telvar was worried; he was grim and silent, instead of grim and verbal. His mood lent an edge to his followers; and when they at last moved on, they, too, walked in the cloud of silence.

When they stopped for a second time, Telvar called for Erin and Carla. Belfas touched Erin's shoulder quickly as she left the ranks, and she caught his hand in a firm grip.

"I'll be okay," she whispered.

"You'd better."

She walked away to join the first and second.

Telvar nodded. "Do you hear anything?"

She shook her head.

"Good. How far have we traveled?"

"Twenty-six miles, sir." She thought for a moment. "And some hundred yards."

He smiled briefly. "Very good. Andin—the Sarillar—has been fighting alongside three of our units and two of Cormont, these past three days.

"Losses to the lines have been high, but losses to the Malanthi higher still."

Erin nodded; this was common enough on a field where either side rarely retreated.

"Yesterday, word came to him that a larger group—composed primarily of the nonblooded—were coming to Beryon to aid the Malanthi."

The nonblooded. The familiar anger that she felt at this momentarily rippled across her face. How could the nonblooded join the enemy ranks? Was it not for their sake that so much of this fighting took place? And worse, far worse, the Lernari effectiveness against the nonblooded was poor unless excessive amounts of power could be called.

"Andin believes that they will be led by the high priest of the Enemy with a number of his Swords. He has called in Tara's unit and Shorla's unit as well. We may not have arrived in good time.

"Be back in an hour and a half. If you aren't, we'll move on in defensive formation."

She nodded.

"If the numbers are too large, we will retreat."

She nodded again.

"Carla?"

"Ready as well, sir." She saluted, although a salute was, strictly speaking, unnecessary, Carla never failed to produce one.

Ahead, the forest waited to give them the cover they would need. Erin listened for a moment and then began to walk toward it, her feet no longer making the firm, hard step of the march. Indeed, to those watching her progress into darkness, it seemed that she must be almost dancing just a hair's breadth above the ground, her movements were that sure and that silent.

Carla followed a few feet behind, walking just as swiftly as Erin did, but much less gracefully. Both women kept their swords sheathed.

Nor did either speak. By signals that they had worked out before their first mission together, they allowed the other to know where they intended to move, how far and how fast. These signals—the way a hand brushed a shoulder or touched a cheek or arm—were second nature to them, and they moved quickly and confidently forward.

Only when the ground began to slope downward did Erin pause; they were at the peak of the valley now. Beryon Valley, or Beryon's valley as it had once been called, was the final resting place of an army, remembered in children's stories and in bardic verse.

Carla tapped her shoulder twice in quick succession; Erin signaled a stop. She tilted her head to one side, listening. Leaves rustled by; a breeze blew through shadowed trees. Ahead a small stream trickled past. Crickets, frogs, and the occasional dart of feet too small to be dangerous added their rhythm to the night.

But beyond these comforting sounds, something else moved. Something . . .

Erin shook her head, touching Carla's open palm with two fingers, then three. Carla nodded and they began to make their way down.

Beryon's valley lay in wait. Erin had seen it once, maybe three years past. She and Belfas had gone exploring to try to learn the truth about the legend of the buried army. They had found nothing: no markers, no stone, no emblem to suggest that important battle at the dawn of the world.

But they had gone in daylight, and the night was always different. The darkness, natural or not, held a hidden world with a secret language of its own. As she walked forward, she could dimly make out the occasional fallen log or boulder jutting from the forest floor like some forgotten tombstone.

She could almost hear the sounding of the horns and the charge of foot soldiers making their desperate last stand because they had nowhere to retreat. She could almost hear the whistle of the archers, and the twang of greatbows releasing a hail of arrows; could almost hear the clash of metal against metal, and the screams of the dying.

The clash and the screams . . .

She stopped suddenly in her tracks. Carla was good enough that she could mirror Erin's quick reaction. She pulled up, touched Erin's shoulder, and knew that it was shaking. But although she listened, she could not hear what Erin heard.

Trembling, Erin moved forward. Every step she took brought the noise closer.

Maybe, she thought, *it's just imagination. Maybe I've been thinking on Beryon Valley too long.*

Then Carla stopped, and Erin felt three fingertips across the back of her neck. Not imagination, no.

She nodded grimly.

Go back? Carla's fingers signaled.

Not yet, Erin's replied. *Numbers.*

She picked up her pace, knowing that she would lose the silence that she was known for, but knowing that it wouldn't make any difference.

Carla stopped only once more, and Erin waited as the older woman strung her bow and pulled an arrow from her quiver. Then they advanced again, seeking the source of the growing sound, moving this time with more caution toward those that might see than those that might hear.

They quickly reached the outer edge of the valley and, through the last of the trees, saw what they most feared seeing.

Beryon Field was on fire—and no normal fire, either.

Some five feet from the last of the trees, they knelt with their eyes above tall brush that tickled their cheeks. Neither noticed.

Backs of warriors lined the edge of the gray rocky fields that stretched out for some miles. Some were wounded; Erin feared mortally so from the quantity of blood. Links of chain showed through torn strips of gray—and glinting in green light, Erin could see the circles.

It was obvious that they were fighting a defensive battle, but

Erin couldn't name the position. Still, she thought she recognized the insignia of at least one fighter. These were Elliath warriors; Shorla's unit.

The attackers wore uniforms that Erin was also familiar with: the black of the Swords of Malthan. Limned in red, they moved forward, striking their way into the retreating wall of Lernari.

Numbers? Carla signaled.

They were high. At best guess, Erin thought three hundred, maybe three hundred and twenty-five, at least two to one in enemy favor.

She considered the odds carefully and started to turn toward Carla when a flash of light caught her attention.

Not green light, this, but white. She heard a chorus of screams, and for an instant saw the banner of Darek of Cormont's unit outlined in the glow.

That light heralded the presence of the Sarillar of Elliath, caught in the midst of enemy soldiers.

The import of greater numbers fell away as Erin responded to the call of the blood, light against the darkness. Raising her own arms high, she summoned almost all of her personal power. It shot upward in a flare of light that sent a ripple through the enemy, so bright was its call.

Carla caught her arm as the last of the power left her. "What have you done? Our unit can't hope to win against these numbers. You've cut off a safe retreat!"

"What choice do we have?" Erin shouted over the clashing of swords and the crackle of magic. "The Sarillar is cornered on the field!" In a single, clean motion she was on her feet, blade out and readied.

Carla released her and unsheathed her own sword. There was nothing to be gained now in argument—Telvar would see the light and he would know what it meant; he would lead the unit to the battle without further delay. She opened her mouth to order Erin to stay, then clamped it shut before the words had started to form.

Blood-call. Light-call. Damn you, Erin. Later she might remember how little choice the inexperienced had against the Sarillar's call—if she survived. Her sword came out as she watched Erin.

Already the power that had not gone into the flare gathered round the younger woman like a mantle. Carla had seen the flare—it was more than she herself could have called. And Erin still had the power to cloak herself so. The older woman shook her head.

If only she could ward . . . Carla followed Erin onto the field, leaving the sparse shield wall of tangled growth and shadow behind her. Four years had not been enough to dim the memory of Erin's display at Karana.

Erin raised her sword and ran to join Shorla's unit.

"Elliath!" she cried, in a voice so loud that it might have been the call of the horns.

She fought like one frenzied. She had always been known for her speed, but no one, not even Telvar, could have predicted just how devastating that speed could be.

Light flashed anew on the field, the Sarillar's call. Erin began to cut a path toward it. She felt the way her sword swept cleanly through living—and dying—flesh, felt the pain that she caused come echoing to the part of her that was healer and not warrior. It was not as strong as the urgency that drove her to try to reach Line Cormont's unit.

She whirled around to see those fighting by her side continue their retreat and she almost snarled.

"The Sarillar!" she shouted, whirling her blade.

She heard another voice bark an order, and the unit continued to retreat.

She could not.

No warrior, no matter how good, can face five to one odds. And the good warrior values prudence.

Her thought, but Telvar's words, as she saw the line pull further back. She took a step toward them without dropping her defense, and the Sarillar's light flared again.

This time she could see the angry crackle of red that followed it.

The field seemed to melt away. She could see the Sarillar clearly; he was bleeding from multiple wounds but still stood tall, facing his *true* adversaries: five men, dressed not in armor, but long, black robes, red arms stretched toward the Sarillar.

She knew she should follow the defensive line of retreat. She knew it, but could not do it. Telvar's voice faded into the whisper of an unimportant past as she raised her blade anew. Light danced down it, swirling in the marks of its maker and the blood of her enemies.

And she fought as she had never fought, stumbling over stones and bodies alike, the landscape unfamiliar. Fought as the Sarillar's light grew weaker, and weaker again. Fought as the sea of enemy troops, with their faint taint of darkness, closed in around her.

Here she learned the truth of Telvar's words. The light armor she wore was no match for the blades that struck against her body, leaving their signature in her flesh. As soon as one man fell, another stepped in to take his place.

She cried out once in fury as the light of the Sarillar—the light of Elliath—burned into the night sky. And once, in pain, as steel found her forearm. Her blade fell away from her as she dropped to her knees, automatically clutching the nearly severed limb.

Frantically she brought forth her power to try to still the bleeding, but even as the green warmth touched her, she felt the point of a sword enter her back.

In agony, she staggered forward; saw another sword raised to strike.

No!

No!

Lernan!

For the second time in her life, Erin touched the Hand of God.

Power flowed into her, a power so sudden and so brilliant that even the nonblooded could see it.

The second sword never found its mark.

Great-grandchild.

Bright Heart. She shut her eyes as the wound that marred her body began to close.

You stand too close to Lady Death. You have called; I have come.

Her eyes snapped open as she stood once again, reborn in the fires of God, mortality overshadowed by the Light.

She could sense the presence of her line-mates as the ragged retreat of Shorla's unit suddenly halted. Such was the strength of her contact with God, that she could wake the sleeping fires in even the weakest of the Lernari, where the Sarillar's power alone could not.

She called upon the white-fire, and it swept across the field like a wave, bringing succor to the Lernari, and pain—or death— to the Malanthi.

It wasn't enough. Over the screams she could hear the shouts of surprise melt into shouts of determination. The nonblooded were, indeed, upon the field of battle. They could see her power; they could feel the fan of warmth the Light provided—but it couldn't burn at a darkness that was not part of their blood.

Still she retrieved her sword and walked forward, wielding it as a brand of light. It swung without hesitation, leaving an afterimage where it cut through the air.

An arrow struck her, and she removed it even as the wound began to close. Shorla's unit surged forward behind the path she had cut. She nodded and forgot them; at this moment there were only two things on the field that she was fully aware of: the Sarillar and the priests. And the Sarillar's light was waning beneath the storm of red.

"Sarillar!" she cried, and he turned.

His robes were red, the circle that adorned them only a broken line. Something struck him, and he staggered.

"Elliath!" he shouted, but his voice was weak, an echo of its former strength. His light flared again, surrounding his body like a halo, or a shroud.

Erin began to run forward. He fell to one knee, righted himself, and looked across at her, blue eyes dimming in the ragged scars of his face.

"No!"

Even as she shouted, she saw his form begin to alter. She knew she couldn't reach him in time—all the power in the world couldn't give her that skill. And she knew the ward he made with God; it was the same, measure for measure, as the one she herself had made.

But Andin the Sarillar was not a healer; not in that did the strength of his blood lie. The power that he called now could not be used to save him. He had chosen—could still choose—Gallin's death. The power that gathered in his fallen body burned away what little life remained; and for an instant, no more, Andin was as the First: an imperfect vessel for pure Light.

"Elliath!" he cried anew.

And the very land rose up in response, breaking beneath the feet of the nonblooded to form the perfect grave.

She drew upon her own power then, drew it and aimed it outward at the priests. She was shaking with anger, and the anger gave her purpose; if the ward with God could not save the Sarillar, she could at least make the priests of the Enemy pay for his loss.

Her fire stretched out across the sky, a lethal, gleaming bridge. It left her empty, only Erin, third of Telvar of Elliath, without the hand of God beneath her.

But that was enough to hear the screaming; enough to see the red wards splinter like glass beneath the sudden onslaught of the Bright Heart.

And when she finally turned away, the field was no longer a field—but it was silent.

Telvar's unit arrived a few minutes later, to walk carefully across the newly turned earth, clearing away what little of the enemy force remained.

It was Telvar himself who found his scout as she knelt beside the lifeless body of the Sarillar of Elliath. She had done what she could to lay him out in a semblance of rest or sleep, with grass as a pallet, stones as a pillow.

"Erin," he said, and she looked up. "There is still work to do yet; this is not the time for tears."

She shook her head, unable to stop them.

"What better time?" she asked, the warmth of tears sliding hopelessly down her cheeks. "I—"

"At the ceremony." His voice was grim. "If at all."

Carla came to stand beside him.

"I won't be back for the ceremonies." Erin's hand gripped the Sarillar's more tightly. "This is all the good-bye I get."

"Then do not waste it weeping. The Sarillar died a good death." He looked out at the field, saw the bodies, half buried in the teeth of the ground, broken by rock and rubble. "And he made our enemies pay."

Belfas seemed to appear out of nowhere; he knelt beside Erin and slipped an awkward arm around her shoulder.

"Erin?"

She shook her head. "I tried. I tried, but I couldn't save him. I had so much power, Belf." She looked down at her hands. "I had so *much* power. But it wasn't enough."

Carla whispered something to Telvar, and he looked down at Erin again, his expression softer.

"I see," he whispered back to his second. He shook his head and turned away. He, too, remembered Karana; he remembered the amount of raw power that Erin could contain, and use, without destroying herself.

"The call of the blood, then." He turned back to Erin and touched her almost gently on the shoulder. "We assemble the units in an hour, Erin. Meet us then."

She didn't hear him, but Belfas nodded quietly. Telvar left them there together; he knew that Belfas wouldn't be parted from his line-mate.

chapter
eight

"What is going on?" Telvar's fingers rapped against the sur-
face of his desk gently—always a bad sign.

Jethren shook his dark head, allowing his angular face to
show his own confusion. That was often a dangerous thing when
dealing with Telvar, but less dangerous than an out-and-out lie.
At least, that was the wisdom of the temple initiates, and although Jethren wore the armor and surcoat of the unit, he would
have been happier with the simple gray robes that he was used
to.

Telvar snorted and laid the dispatch down, where it curled
above the small stack of papers that had already been placed
there. Had any other hand signed it, he might have been tempted
to ignore it altogether.

"What is she thinking?"

Jethren shook his head again.

This time Telvar looked up, and his eyes locked with the
younger man's. "Tell me. Tell me what has happened in the last
four weeks."

Although he suspected that Telvar already knew, he complied.

"The Lady of Elliath began to conduct her interviews after
the ceremonies of departure."

"I'm aware of this," Telvar replied crisply. He had been
pulled from his unit for two weeks of travel as one of the three
candidates for the position of Sarillar and had only just arrived
back at the front himself.

"The three that she interviewed, she did not choose."

"None of the three?"

"No, sir." He hoped that Telvar was not one to covet such a
title, as there was no arguing with the Lady.

Telvar looked down at the document again. "And so she turns from the most experienced warriors of the line to one who is only a third? There is no precedent for this in line history. None."

Jethren sighed. "Telvar, we understand it no better than you do, yourself. But the tales of Karana, and if you must know, the battle of Beryon Field, have reached even our ears in the temple. Shorla herself said that she found it difficult to resist the call to battle that Erin, unknowing, invoked; Shorla fought. What Erin lacks in experience, she makes up for in her ability to wield God's power."

Telvar smiled grimly. "She has to walk onto the end of a pointed sword to reach it. Do you understand? Her power may be great, but it cannot be counted on. In both of the cases mentioned she was lucky." His fingers drummed against the makeshift table. "What is the Lady thinking?"

"Who can know? But she hears the voice of God Himself, and we cannot question her word."

"Not and receive any answers, no." He shrugged as Jethren's jaw dropped two inches. "If she's called for Erin, she'll have Erin, then. Is she to travel with you?"

Jethren nodded. "I have six others with me for guard. But Telvar, remember that it is only an interview. It need not be said that most of the temple initiates do not believe that Erin's experience will prove up to the office."

"There's that." Telvar nodded gruffly. But there were so many strange circumstances connected with Erin that he took little comfort in Jethren's words. *Lady,* he thought to himself, *may you indeed know what you are doing.*

He sent for Erin.

"But I don't understand!" Erin said, as she crammed her belongings haphazardly into her pack. Her cheeks were flushed almost crimson against the white of tightened lips.

Belfas pulled her spare suit out again and began to roll it up; from experience he knew that economy of size was an absolute necessity. That Erin had forgotten it spoke volumes.

"She's only requested an audience," he said mildly as he tied the pack.

"But why now?"

"I don't know." He handed the pack to her and she yanked it onto her shoulders. "Why don't you ask?"

"Thanks a lot, Belf." She loosened the straps, tightened them, then loosened them yet again—an awkward maneuver given that the pack was still attached to her shoulders. "I already did."

"And?"

"What do you think?" She snorted as she readjusted her sword. "They won't tell me a thing!"

"Maybe you don't need to know. Maybe it's information that could be used against us if you were ambushed."

"I hardly think we'll be ambushed now. The office of the high priest of Malthan isn't filled at the moment, and they usually don't move without one."

It was true, which was why Belfas wasn't too worried.

"I just don't understand why they're calling me in. I mean, we don't have a Sarillar—the front *needs* all the fighters it has! I should just refuse to go, that's what I should do." Her voice quavered on the last few words.

"Erin."

"What?"

"You're one of the best in the unit; no one would argue that. Turn around." She did, and he adjusted the straps of her pack so it hung properly. "But you *are* only one fighter. We'll be fine."

She knew it was true—just one more fighter. She shook her head angrily to clear her eyes.

"Come on. Telvar was back in sixteen days; I imagine you'll be back in the same." He hugged her, ignoring the fact that she kept herself quite stiff. "Don't worry, okay?"

She sighed and forced herself to relax. "All right. It's just that—"

"It doesn't matter. The Lady's called you home, and you have to go."

"It's just that Telvar didn't look pleased about it, either. I just keep wondering if I've done something wrong. Maybe he told her that I called in the unit at Beryon when I knew the numbers and odds were off. Maybe she'll pull me from the front for it."

"Erin." He gave her a gentle tug in the direction of the waiting horsemen. "The numbers and odds didn't matter—you saw to that."

"Well, maybe it's—"

"Come on."

She sighed again, loudly, and let him drag her along. He was probably right; on things like this he often was.

Jethren was waiting with his escort, six armored and armed men astride Lernari riding horses in silence. He looked tired but alert as he stood by the only two riderless horses, and he offered her a leg up.

She accepted his help; although she loved riding, it was seldom that she got an opportunity. Maybe if she thought of this trip as riding practice, she might get through it. Maybe.

"Erin!"

She turned her head and caught sight of Belfas.

"Best of luck!"

She waved once and then they rode out of camp.

Only the Grandfather was there to greet them when they finally rode into the Great Hall's courtyard, covered with the dust and sweat of the journey. He nodded to Jethren and his escort.

"There is word for you at the temple, Jethren. Thank you for carrying the Lady's message."

Jethren nodded. "Erin?"

She looked at him solemnly—as she had done for most of the journey.

"I'll see to the horse."

She nodded, dismounting. "Grandfather?"

He reached out and pulled her slowly into his arms. "Thank you for returning."

"I—I didn't want to."

He smiled. "I know. I don't suppose you've made this trip an easy one on Jethren, either." She started to flush and he shook his head. "If it helps, know that Telvar was far, far worse. We expect this from any student of his. Bright Heart help us if we ever call Carla before her time.

"Come; it's nearing dinner and I'd be honored if you'd join me."

For the first time in a week, Erin smiled.

"Tell me," he said softly, as they walked into the Great Hall, "about Beryon Field."

She looked up at the arches as they entered the Great Hall, at the familiar tapestries and the wide, simple altar. "Beryon?"

He nodded as he led her to his quarters.

She began to recount events that had already blurred into a haze. He only interrupted her once.

"You heard the voice of the Bright Heart?"

"Yes," she said softly. Her eyes were glowing faintly as she looked straight ahead.

He nodded almost to himself and urged her to continue, although he paid little attention to the rest of what she said.

Lernan, God. She touched enough of Your power to fully hear Your voice.

The next morning, Erin was to meet Latham, who would lead her to the Lady's Woodhall. She knew the master scholar by sight—all of the children did; they were taught several of their history classes by none other. But his appearance surprised her. His hair was streaked white, and the lines across his forehead were more prominent than they had ever been.

"Are you ready, Erin?"

She nodded.

"Then come. The Lady has been awaiting your arrival." He held out a hand, but let it drop when she ignored it. "Child," he said, seemingly unaware of how the word made her bristle, "you have nothing to fear from the Lady. She wishes to see you, that is all."

His eyes caught all the nuances of her expression, and after a few minutes of walking she turned her intent, green stare upon him, ignoring the sun-tinted green of the hushed forest.

He smiled, not at all self-conscious. "I am the memory-walker of the line at the holdings," he explained. He ducked beneath the low branch of a nearby tree, his movement a contrast to the warriors of the march. "And I always watch carefully."

"Oh." She walked ahead a bit; after her years on the front, the majesty of the forest was lost to her. "Latham?"

"Yes?"

"Do you know what she wants?"

Latham continued to watch her, even as he followed the path that led from the holdings to the old forest.

Child, he thought, for everyone that he had ever taught was still a child in his mind, *if I knew, truthfully, all that the Lady requires from you, I might tell you.* He shook his head. *But I believe that all that has been done leads somehow to this, and I, too, would like to know the truth of it.* But he knew, as she did not, that that truth might never be given to him.

"Here. We are coming upon it."

Erin nodded automatically, then looked around. No entrance lay in sight, just large, tall trees that seemed to reach endlessly upward.

"You will have to follow me; do not be surprised at where I will lead, but rather have faith in the Lady."

So saying he took her hand, and this time she allowed it. He walked through the maze of trees until he reached the largest of them. Here he stopped and bowed a moment while Erin watched in confusion.

"Did you think," he said, as he stepped directly toward the huge trunk, "that we call it the Woodhall without reason?"

Before she could answer he had disappeared into it—only the hand that held hers could still be seen, jutting as it did from the craggy, silvered bark. She had the time to gasp before that hand dragged her forward. A light flashed all around her, blinding in its intensity.

Shaking her head, she pulled away from Latham and brought her hands automatically to her face.

"Erin," she heard him say, and she looked up.

For the first time in her life, she stood inside the Woodhall of the Lady Elliath. Beyond Latham, she could see the beginnings of an arched hall; similar in style to the Great Hall, but narrower and somehow more majestic. The walls, or as much of them as she could see, were tall, blank, and white as they stretched forward into one long corridor.

She met Latham's eyes, all anger with him forgotten.

He smiled. "I know," he said softly, turning to look down the expanse of hall. "I felt the same when first I entered here. "This is the Lady's hall. This is her home."

"But we—we walked through—"

"The tree? Yes. But this is old—older, I think, than the tree itself, the work of the Lady when first she walked the world. It is not altogether real, in the way that we understand it." He held out an arm in the direction of the hall. With a tinge of regret, he said, "But go ahead. The Lady waits within; you will see her when you reach the hall's end. She has made it clear that this appointment is to be private; I will go no further."

"Will you—will you wait for me?"

At this he smiled. "If you request it, Erin, I will be happy to wait."

"Please?"

He nodded and stepped aside as she stared down the hall that suddenly seemed endless.

She took a deep breath and stepped forward, wishing, although she didn't know why, that Belfas were here. The sound of her step echoed down the hall. It was the only noise; even her breathing was too shallow to break the silence.

Step after step she walked, as if remembering how for the

first time in her life. She could see a hint of green that slowly became the leaves and flowers of the Lady's conservatory.

Lady, she thought as she glanced at the comfort of her very normal feet, *what do you want from me?*

As if in answer to her question, there was a flash of light, and she looked up. The Lady of Elliath stood at the far end of the hall.

"L-Lady?"

Deep, green eyes searched Erin's upturned face. It was the only motion the Lady made. She might have been a statue, pale and still, that marked the entrance to the life of her garden.

After a moment, Erin began to walk toward her, her steps smaller and quieter.

The Lady held out one hand, much as Latham had done earlier. Erin glanced down at the long, smooth fingers, and then looked at her own, now short and stubby by comparison.

She did not know why, but she couldn't quite bring herself to accept the Lady's hand. After another silent moment, it was withdrawn.

Then the Lady turned and walked into her garden. Erin followed, finding in the chaotic greenery a warmth and a life that was welcome. For the Lady, her grandmother, seemed like the moon, a welcome light, but distant and immovable.

Although Erin had learned something of flora in her earlier years, most of the plants that grew here were unfamiliar to her. Some had leaves—leaves?—that were thicker than her fingers; some sprouted spines along bulbous, irregular bodies; some had brilliant, delicate blossoms that stretched toward the sunlight in splashes of crimson, gold, and azure. Sunlight? Walking along, Erin looked up and searched the large, domed roof for any sign of a window. Nor was she particularly surprised to find none; this was the Lady's domain, after all.

Latham would not have been familiar with the direction that the Lady took, but he, like Erin, would have followed her without question.

Thus the silent companions came to the very heart of the Lady's garden. It opened onto a large circular fountain from which clear water, dappled with light, splashed outward into a pale basin.

At the center of the fountain stood a large, alabaster figure, casting a moving shadow over rippling water. Its hands reached upward and its face looked into the nonexistent sky.

The Lady gestured toward it, and Erin stepped hesitantly forward until she stood at the lip of the basin. From here she could see that the statue's features were subtle and smooth. It had no real definition, no real expression, but she thought it must be a woman, surrounded by water and a wall of flowers and trees.

"It is."

She stiffened at the sound of the Lady's voice.

"No, do not turn. Look at my fountain, granddaughter. Tell me what you see there."

"A statue."

"Yes."

"I think—I think it must be alabaster; it's too pale for anything else."

"Yes." She was clearly waiting for something more.

"But I don't know who it's supposed to be." She had an idea, as she looked at it. "Maybe—maybe it isn't finished yet?"

"No, it is not."

"Oh."

"It is not old; thirty of your years, no more. I started it the day I returned."

"Returned?" Erin glanced back to see that the Lady's eyes were not on her, but on the fountain itself. "Returned from where?" She tried to remember any stories of the Lady traveling, but the only ones she could think of were centuries old.

A faint light gathered in the stone of the statue, as if its heart were suddenly laid bare for observers to see.

"From dark lands, Erin." The Lady closed her eyes. "Dark lands and darker time." She turned, suddenly, and caught Erin's shoulders in her hands.

"Erin, child, what would you give if you could end our eternal war? Answer me carefully. Take what time you need to consider my question."

"Anything," Erin replied. She didn't need the time to think about it. She was a third, but one day she would be first, and one day she would lead her people to their last confrontation with the Enemy.

The Lady's eyes searched hers for a moment, and her grip slackened.

"Anything. Such an answer I would expect from a warrior of the line." She turned to look at the statue again. As if musing to herself, she continued to speak. "I returned from the darkness. And to the darkness I must yet again travel. Do you ever fear it, Erin?"

"No. I hate it and I will destroy it. But I don't fear it. What can it bring me but death?"

"If you could live centuries such as I have lived, I fear you would come to know the answer to your question better than even I."

Then she turned yet again, and the look on her face was one that Erin would never forget. For Lady Death had such a face: old, like mountains, like the elements, like nothing that knows life truly. In spite of herself, she was frightened.

And the Lady said, "If you will accept the position, initiate, you will be the new Sarillorn of Elliath."

Just like that, each word a splinter of something so shattered that one could not tell what the whole had been.

Before Erin could force herself to speak, the Lady continued.

"I have walked between the present and the future, the many futures. I have chosen the path and the price for viewing it. I have seen the Heart of the Enemy.

"I know of your weakness. It has troubled the line greatly, for you know as well as we that could you but touch the full extent of your power, you would be the greatest healer any of the lines have ever seen. But I have also seen Karana; I felt the touch of God through you on the field, and I know the power you wield, even if you do not.

"Perhaps, in time, you will find that your weakness contains a hidden strength; this I do not know.

"But this road, this road that I have walked, you, too, must walk, Sarillorn or no."

"What road, Lady?"

"The road between Dark and Light. And you, of the Light, must take that path, knowing that light casts its shadows, and that they lie at times in places that no eyes can see."

She stopped then, closing her eyes again. *How much can I tell you, child?* For Erin was, truly, a child in the eyes of the eldest.

"If you become the Sarillorn of Line Elliath, all the responsibility of the field will be yours. Your friend and line-mate must remain with his unit, but you will belong to all. You will go where you are needed and will lend my power—your power— to all of your kin.

"You will see death, child, and more; your gift, your talent, is the talent of your mother. You are a healer by birth and warrior by choice, but when I grant you a part of my power, it is the healer that will often dominate. When you fight on the field, you will fight two battles: the one against the enemy, and the other against your need to ease the pain that will surround you.''

Erin nodded. "I already do," she whispered.

"It will be worse.

"Will you become Sarillorn?''

Erin took a deep breath, weighing the responsibility. Becoming Sarillorn was a dream—a hope—that was never talked about. No honor was higher, no position more respected. But it required so much knowledge, so much skill . . . She swallowed.

"I—I can't, Lady. I don't have half the skill the Sarillorn—or Sarillar—would need.'' It wasn't easy to say the words, but she took comfort in knowing that somehow, Belfas would be proud of her.

The Lady seemed to shrink slightly.

"Erin. This thing that I ask of you—I ask it with reason. For although I may not speak of all I have seen, I have seen this: That you, and you alone of all the lines, may one day pull from the darkness a lasting light. If the Bright Heart has a hope, it is this: the end of the war that destroys so many, blooded and gray.

"And thus I name you Lernan's Hope.

"Yet even where you walk, more than hope must sustain you. For the good of the future, you must allow the line to risk some of the present. If you are not yet qualified to be Sarillorn, have faith that you will become the greatest that the line has ever honored.

"Will you become Sarillorn?''

Of all the things that she had imagined, this was not among them. She wanted to say no.

And she wanted to say yes. To say yes, and become the strongest single force that the Enemy would have to deal with. She looked at the Lady as if for guidance and found her answer there.

But she could not speak it. Instead she nodded quietly.

"Go, then. Latham still awaits you. Ready yourself and return to me on the morrow.''

Erin walked away from the fountain, following the green path until she could once again see the long, pale hall that she had come through. She looked down its length to see one man standing against a blank wall.

Latham.

Wordless, she went to meet him.

And wordless, he offered her his hand. He thought, this time, that she would accept it completely. Nor was he wrong; even those very strong of blood who spent too much time in the Lady's presence yearned for the familiar sight and touch of an-other—mortal—being.

Bright Heart help me to live up to my line.

She touched the cool stone altar with her forehead and rose. Latham was waiting outside of the Great Hall; waiting to take her back to the Lady. She belted her robe tightly, feeling a chill in the autumn air.

Hunger gnawed at her, and she ignored it to the best of her ability; she'd not been able to eat at all either the previous night or this morning.

"Lernan," she whispered, near silent, as she passed through the doors. "Guide me."

Latham bowed as she entered the day. He noted that she was wearing the simple gray robe of the initiate that had been given to her four years ago. Her hair, unbound, fell loose around her face like an auburn wimple. Only the sword that she wore at her side separated her from the other temple initiates.

"The Lady waits," he murmured.

She looked beyond him to the very edge of the woods. "I know."

He knew that she was frightened; she held herself, in fear, the way the young do—tense and withdrawn, as if to avoid the notice of danger or threat. But it was a different fear than the previous day's. The unknown had been replaced by the known. And the known was no less terrible.

"Child," he said softly.

This time, Erin didn't bridle. For the first time, she heard the warmth and concern in the word instead of condescension. She looked up at him almost gratefully, holding out a barely steady hand.

He took it.

"Come." He began to walk. "If I am to judge, this day will be the end of it, one way or another."

She didn't ask him what he meant.

The forest swallowed them both in its shadows and shade. She heard the muted whisper of birds and the patter of small animals as if from a great distance.

She paused only once, at the foot of the tree that marked the entrance to the Lady's hall. Eyes wide, she turned to Latham.

"I'm not ready yet." She was ashamed of the words almost

before they left her mouth, but that shame couldn't stop her from speaking them.

"No one ever is, Erin." His grip on her hand tightened reassuringly. "If you wish time, you have it."

She rushed on, her eyes imploring. "What if I'm never ready?"

Very gently he shook his head. "You know yourself, and you must be the only judge of that. I cannot help you.

"But know this: Of all Elliath, the Lady was first; she is eldest and wisest among us. For centuries Elliath has taken counsel with her and trusted her guidance. She makes no decision lightly, nor are her choices foolish even if we cannot always see the end of them." His voice dropped a little over the last words.

"Come, Erin, will you enter?"

She nodded almost timidly and stepped into the tree, into the flash of light, and into the Lady's Woodhall.

"Will you wait for me?"

"If you wish it."

"Please."

He smiled. "Go, then. I will be here." And he watched as she walked down the hall, dwarfed by the grandeur of height and marble.

The Lady was waiting for her. Erin could almost feel her presence as she stepped once again into the garden. She tilted her face toward the light, but felt no warmth from it. The breeze that touched her cheek was cool.

Come on, Erin, she told herself as she took a step forward. *You already made your choice.*

But it isn't too late to unmake it.

Go ahead. Then the Lady will know you for the coward you really are.

No. No, I'm not afraid of this.

But it wasn't true; she was afraid, afraid of failing the line in such a crucial position. The power of the Lady was invested in one man or woman until the end of that person's life—and once given, only death could call it back.

But death was common in war.

No. She had made her choice. She would not turn back from it now. She lifted her trembling chin and walked toward the center of the garden.

The Lady sat, cross-legged, directly in front of the fountain.

The alabaster statue looked like a white shadow of her out-stretched face and arms.

But where the statue held trickling water, the Lady held a dagger that caught the light, inner and outer, and kept it there.

"Lady," Erin said, surprised at how steady her own voice sounded. "I am ready."

"Erin. So soon?" But she rose, looming above her mortal grandchild. "Very well. I, too, am ready."

In one swift moment, she laid the dagger's edge across her palm, then handed the golden-edged blade to Erin.

Erin duplicated the motion, although she wondered at it; the Lady must know that it held no power for her.

"No," the Lady said, as if reading her thoughts, "we do not ward here; it is not required. The power that passes into you is not Lernan's, but Elliath's. Lift your hand."

Erin complied, watching beads of blood run into the lines of her palm.

"Will you be Sarillorn?"

"Yes."

The Lady nodded and raised her own palm. Slender, ageless hand touched callused, mortal one as blood met blood. The Lady's fingers closed around Erin's like iron clamps.

Erin cried out. Her hand jerked back automatically, but with no success; the Lady's hold was sure. She shouted yet again, giving release to a pain too sharp for words.

She was on fire. Heat burned up through open palm, scorching her arm and spreading across all of her body. Only once in her life had she felt anything akin to it. Her left hand shot up toward her right one as she struggled, ineffectively, to free herself.

Then, in the midst of the heat, she felt something cool and comforting.

"What is mortal in you denies this. But what is Light within you will not. Hold fast."

Her knees gave way; if not for the Lady's terrible strength, she would have fallen. Suspended by one hand, she bit her lip, trying to contain her cry.

The fire continued to burn until the only thing she could see was the merciless glare of white behind her eyelids. Then she tumbled to the ground.

"It is done."

Done? She knew, from the feel of moss beneath her cheek, that the Lady had released her—but the pain continued. She bit her lip, drawing and tasting blood, as her body curled into a tight little ball.

"Erin. Remember your training. Remember what you are."

Pain. Pain? She could almost see Telvar in the drill circle. Could almost hear him shouting when she had failed, again, to summon the power necessary to continue the fight—power that she alone had.

Desperately she called to it. Wounds, fractures, burns—these were things beyond her. But pain was a known: she had quieted or destroyed it for many of her line-mates over her four years of frontline service.

A faint green glow struggled to surround her body. It was cool, like the waters of the Gifting, and like those waters it began to put the fires out.

But something was different. Something felt strange. Before she had truly even begun to pull power, she felt a distinct *snap*. Where there had been pain just seconds before there was a dull warmth that grew and spread.

She opened her eyes in surprise and moved her hands away from her face. Both were unscarred.

She unfurled her legs hesitantly, but they, too, were free from any pain.

"Erin?"

She looked up, through drying tears, to see that the Lady of Elliath knelt beside her on the ground.

"L-Lady." She couldn't stop herself from adding, "You should have warned me."

"I am sorry. Can you stand?"

"I—I think so." Once again she was surprised. She gained her feet with no difficulty. "Thank you for helping me."

"I did nothing, Erin. It was your power."

"My—but I—" Her eyes grew wide, and she looked once again at her hands. There was no cut. "I?"

For the first time in two days, the Lady smiled. "Yes. You are Sarillorn. You have more power now than you did before—and that power answers to your call."

"I can do this?"

The Lady nodded again, but this time more soberly. "Remember my warning, warrior. On the field, you must protect yourself against the call of pain—for you will feel it now more strongly than you have ever felt it. If you are not cautious, it will draw you as surely as Andin's white-fire did, and you will expend what you have in healing and not in battle."

Erin nodded. Her eyes, as she met the Lady's, were glistening, not with pain but with hope. Now she could truly fight; she need not fear her own inability. She called forth light, and the room suddenly paled in the blaze of it.

"Yes. Much that you have done before will be easier now. But it is not the power of the ward; it is not the power that you have found in the Hand of God."

Erin didn't hear her.

I can heal! She looked at her wounded hand. *I can really heal now! I can fight—I'm good, even Telvar has said so.* She wanted to be on the field; wanted to test her blade and the strength of this power against the Enemy's minions.

"Sarillorn."

She looked up.

"I see the warrior's light in your eyes. Let the Malanthi beware. But even in battle, you must remember this: nothing is unalloyed. In you, there is hatred, chaos, and some small measure of darkness."

Erin was silent.

"In a like wise, the Malanthi have their love, their order, and their light. It is peculiar and dim; it does not affect the whole—but never doubt that it is there.

"This is the fruit of the Awakening, and the heritage of the Sundered, that everything but the Bright Heart and the Dark Heart must bear the taint of his enemy. Even I, First Sundered, First of Lernan, must acknowledge the truth of this. So it is with the First of the Dark Heart as well, although he denies it."

Although she understood what the Lady was saying, Erin was confused. Why was she telling her this? Why did she think it important? No trace of darkness could ever sway the Lady from the Bright Heart, just as no trace of light could ever move the Servants of the Dark one.

The Lady stared at her intently.

"Lady, I don't understand. Are you saying that the Malanthi or the Lernari might change somehow? Do you think that even though we aren't as strong of blood as our founders that either of us might falter from our course?"

"No, Sarillorn." But the reply was a weary one. "In the end you will prove true to your heritage. But I ask this of you, if you will grant it. Remember that in change, no matter how strange or slight the chance, all hope lies." She turned suddenly, unwilling to share the expression that caught her face.

"If there were no darkness, no Dark Heart, we—none of us—

would exist. Try to see this when you walk in darkness. Try to forgive it, though you walk with light." The straight, rigid line of her back sagged slightly.

"Do what I cannot do, child. Hope that in touching the darkness you can change it instead of destroying it. For if you have no such hope, you will in time become as we—hard, cold, a weapon for which war has use, and peace none. Our warriors are thus, but for a healer it is a kind of death that I do not wish you to die."

Erin caught a hint of pain in the Lady's words, but it was nothing compared to what she felt beneath them.

She stepped forward and rested one hand against a stiff, white shoulder. She couldn't help it; her feet had moved before she could consider what she was doing.

Gently and surely she summoned her power, spinning it about the Lady like a gossamer web of green warmth.

"I will try," she heard herself say.

The Lady only nodded. "She was my daughter. I never thought it would be so hard. Forgive me."

Erin wondered if she would ever understand the Lady's words.

Latham watched as Erin made her way toward him. She walked in the exact center of the hall, as if following a path visible to her eyes alone.

Ah, he thought. He stared at her more closely, knowing what he would see beyond the strained pale face of youth.

When she reached him, he dropped to one knee and bowed his head. "Sarillorn," he whispered softly.

She started in confusion and then smiled weakly. "Yes."

This time, when they left the hall, he did not offer her his hand or his support. And she missed it.

interlude

The sounds of screaming filtered out into the cold stone halls and shattered against the beamed arches of the ceiling.

The priest frowned a moment and then schooled his face more carefully. *How long will this go on?* He turned, an impatient swirl of red-tinted black, and crossed his arms.

He did not speak aloud, however, or touch the closed door that stopped him from carrying his message to Lord Stefanos. He doubted whether God Himself would dare to interrupt the First of His Servants when he was feeding.

The screams stopped abruptly, but it gave the priest no hope; he could surmise, from their tenor, that they would begin again in a few minutes when the Lord was ready to resume.

Annoyed, he stalked down the hall to glance out of the one large window there. Beyond it, the city lay shadowed, and the moon was high. His reflection came back at him, the narrowed point of his jaw convoluted by colorless glass.

At least two hours had passed. Were the moon full, he might be able to make a better estimate; but were it full, his Lord would be more available.

Screams.

He walked back to the door, his hands clenching and unclenching. There was nowhere to sit, something the priest felt ambivalent about. Were there a chair, he might be tempted to take it.

No one sat in the presence of the First of Malthan, not in his private quarters.

To still his annoyance, he caught the strangled web of screams and folded them into private fantasy. Although he knew well that the victim was one of the villagers they had taken two months ago, he spun a picture of a different body dying so slowly under the Servant's hunger—the new Sarillorn of God-cursed Elliath.

If it were possible, he could almost regret the death of the

Sarillar. The man, older and perhaps less tainted, had not the effect the young woman managed to achieve.

Who could possibly imagine that the trait of healing, a lowly and insipid use of true power, could have such an effect? He almost reached for the report again, before he stilled his hands. He had verified the numbers himself.

It is the nonblooded among us.

For where the Sarillar had routed the nonblooded who served with the Malanthi, the Sarillorn used a different—and unpredictable—approach. She did not use her granted power to destroy or kill—he suspected she did not have the ability—but rather to heal. To *heal*!

He looked down at his fists and forced his hands to relax.

Because of the Sarillorn, many of the nonblooded soldiers left the army. This was natural, although the priests and Swords made sure that any who were caught served God in one way when they would not serve Him properly on the field. What was unnatural was that they often chose treason instead of flight. They served *her*.

And she accepted them, although the lines had never before employed the nonblooded in their battles.

Another advantage lost.

He had not, himself, seen her on the field and was grateful for it; too many of the Malanthi perished at her touch. This at least he understood; the white-fire ate away at the glory of the red. But still, some stories were circulating of her first appearance on the field. After the victory, she had wandered among the fallen, *healing* those that had dared to raise arms against her. Healing her enemies! And while the Swords and the priests could be counted on to see this as the infirmity that it was, it had a different effect on some of the nonblooded.

He wanted to spit, but refrained from doing so.

The screams showed no signs of abating, and he continued to wait.

Granddaughter.

The Lady gestured once, an elegant, subtle movement, and the waters of her fountain stilled. She gazed into them, brushing the strands of her hair from her cheeks.

Erin was sleeping.

Of course. It was night, after all, but the front had been quiet. The Lady hesitated a moment and then continued to watch the even rise and fall of Erin's chest.

Do you dream, child? she thought. *Do you dream of the future that I have set upon you?*

The tiny smile that tugged at the corners of Erin's mouth gave the Lady her answer.

You have done well, better than any expected. You still have not learned to control the pain-call, but this weakness has served the line well.

It was true. For three years now, Erin had been the talk of the council when it met. The Grandfather and Latham followed closely all of her battles and the outcomes of them. Only once had voices been raised, and that over the question of allowing the nonblooded to join in the fight against the Enemy.

Erin had not been present at any of these meetings, of course. Her place was on the field. And it was on the field that she won her point. Many of the nonblooded now joined the Elliath front.

They could not be relied upon as surely as the Lernari, but they did not flee nearly as often as the Grandfather had feared. Indeed, twice they had been instrumental in saving the Sarillorn's life.

The Lady gestured, the equivalent of the sigh she would not express, and the image vanished.

The Sarillorn's life would not have been in danger had the call to heal not been so strong. Not without reason had she refrained from choosing a healer as Sarillar or Sarillorn in the past.

She rose; it was night and she felt a sudden yearning for the open sky.

Stefanos looked up, his face a careful study of controlled annoyance. Beneath him, the glowing contours of the continent twisted midway between the smooth, polished marble of floor and the hewn wood and stone of rounded ceiling. He saw a man, robed head to toe in the dark night of the Karnari colors. Only one of those would dare to disturb him here.

The high priest bowed deferentially, but without the fear that the lesser Malanthi always felt in the presence of the First. His dark head was still a moment before he raised his face to meet his Lord's gaze.

"You interrupt me."

"At your order, Lord." He stepped forward. "I have ridden these past three weeks with news."

"And it could not wait?"

"If you wish it, although you asked that I report in person when I arrived."

"I see. The information?"

"Three of the Elliath units and one of Cormont have been destroyed."

Stefanos looked down at his map. "Where?"

"Along the northern front. We have advanced some thirty miles; four of the Lernari villages are now ours."

"The northern front?" The First Servant smiled. "That is Telvar of Elliath's domain."

"It was."

The map twisted again and red lines slashed through white ones.

"The news is good."

The high priest nodded.

"And Telvar of Elliath?"

"Dead," the man replied, but with less satisfaction.

"Is there more?"

"Yes." The high priest bowed. "The news is not mine; I was not present for it."

Stefanos looked up once again. He did not like the tone that the priest chose to use. "And?"

"The army in the east is gone."

"Gone?" He crossed the room, the map forgotten. Shadow curled around his silent feet. *"Gone?"*

The high priest nodded. He had elected to present this news to the First Servant; too many of the priests had been destroyed in the last year as it was.

"How?"

"The Sarillorn took to the field. Stanthos's division made the mistake of wounding her fatally in some way that allowed her to touch the Bright Heart.

"Shortly after this, the command structure of the army was destroyed."

"White-fire."

The high priest nodded.

"The nonblooded?"

"They broke, for the most part. But again, we lost a number to the Lernari, and not through their deaths."

"And our Swords cannot deal with one who is nearly a child?"

"It is an unusual case, my Lord. While the Sarillorn does not choose to use the Bright Heart's power on the field proper, she will call it when mortal injury is done to her.'' He shrugged.

"That makes no sense.''

"No, Lord. We have tried to make sense of it, with little luck. The Lernari are strange. But she is one of the healers of the line; they are few. The last one died some years ago—but you will recall that the Servant Valeth was sent against her.''

"Yes.'' He looked once more at the map that showed the struggling birth of his empire, stared at the throbbing lines that were unfraying in the east. "Dismissed,'' he said, but softly.

The high priest did not linger; like any of the Malanthi, he had no desire to remain in the presence of one whose power was greater than his own.

"It has been long,'' the Servant said. He walked once again to his customary position, looked at the map his power had laid out, and watched its glimmering lines.

"Long.'' He raised one arm and shadow swirled around it like a dark mist. His skin grayed and paled until he no longer wore the semblance of a mortal. Red eyes flashed in a face that knew no life.

One delicate claw tore the map asunder.

"First of Lernan,'' he whispered. "First of the Light.'' The darkness about him grew blacker still. "You send a healer against us as a vessel of your power.''

His power filled the room until no light existed within it at all. For a moment he could see the void again, the darkness of the all that existed before the coming of the world. And he could see the First of Lernan, cloaked in a light that matched his darkness, calling a power that matched his power.

"We were well matched then. But you have squandered much for the tainted.

"I will take to the field against your vessel.

"I will break it, Lady, and return it to you. Only your full power has any chance against all that I can summon.''

And then he began to concentrate, calling his power to search the continent for this Sarillorn. It was not easy; the Lernari had their own methods of guarding against this detection. Nor would his answer be quickly gained; but to the Servants, even the least of them, time was of no concern.

"Lady.'' Words accompanied the rustle of grass and dry leaves.

"Latham." Once again she stood under open starlight, a pale beacon in the shadow of the night.

"What brings you here?"

As if she had not heard the question, she raised one arm and pointed between the crook of two large branches. "What do you see there?"

"The southern circle, Lady." He began to search the sky for other constellations.

It did not matter; the Lady was no longer attending to him. Instead she saw the village of Colmen with its outlying fields and flat rectangular buildings, surrounded by a deep, red shield as it lay in slumber. Saw the army, priests, Swords, and the nonblooded approaching it under the grim command of the First of Malthan.

It was not a sight she could close her eyes against, so she gazed at the stars that Latham sought.

Beneath the southern circle, the guards of the fourth watch were being slaughtered.

". . . and that, that one is Beryon himself, before the battle of field and valley . . ."

Under Beryon's eyes, Erin lay sleeping on a thin bed in the rooms built onto the small village temple. Sleeping peacefully, perhaps for the last time, in the small village that she had made her home when the road didn't force her to march. It was closer than Elliath, as Erin had explained to the council on one of her rare visits, nearer to the front.

Farther from the line.

She wanted to understand these people by living among them as one of their own. The Lady might have told her the falseness of that hope.

". . . and there—there, the sky is clear enough, I see the sword of Gallin."

It was raised; the Lady could see it clearly fixed above Colmen like a doom. She could see the fires starting, their red glow forcing screams from dying bodies. She could see the Sarillorn of Elliath, torn from sleep in the middle of the night, sword already in hand as she leaped to answer the call of war in an unexpected place. No time here for the warrior braid; her hair swung about her wild eyes like a dark net.

And clearly, so clearly the distance made no difference at all, she could see the enemy that Erin could not see: the First of Malthan, as he had walked the skies eons past, cloaked in the thick, immutable darkness of the beginning. Only great age and accumulated wisdom allowed her to ignore the ancient call to battle.

As the village dissolved into chaos, she turned to Latham.

"What do you see there?"

And if there was a note of fear in her voice, he could not hear it—but unknowing, he answered her plea, eyes touching the stars that his comforting, familiar voice then named, while the battle, unknowable to him, raged on.

She listened, paying a little more of the price that Lernan's Hope exacted.

chapter
nine

Antel, you can't be dead. But the peculiar stillness of the blistered chest beneath her hands told her otherwise. Denial dissolved as her fingers searched his neck for a pulse and found nothing but slackness and silence. Around her the clamor and clash of fighting tried to catch her attention. The screams of the dying told her firmly that he was only one among many, and the number would grow before the hour was out.

"Antel." She shook her head, a wavering smile already dying on her lips. "Can't you wait for your ability to catch up to your courage?"

He was the first of the nonblooded that she had raised on the field of battle; he had carried the enemy banner into the field with no true idea of how to protect it. He was young then, perhaps that was why she had saved him; his age in his terms had been no different from her own when she had first encountered the wars. But she had been with friends, fighting for a cause that she believed in with absolute certainty. He had not had those comforts.

But the truth was that she hadn't had any choice. The Lady's warning hadn't been given without cause, and Antel's nearworship of her was given solely because she hadn't either the Lady's, or her own mother's, self-control.

She shook her head as the red outline of empty buildings at the nearest edge of the village grew brighter. Shadows crisscrossed the trampled grass; swords rose and fell. These grew fewer with each passing moment.

She had tried, after the day of healing, to tell him that she wasn't going to serve as the cause for a young man's death; had even gone so far as to criticize his technique—a generous term—in battle. But his eyes had followed her, perhaps the same way

143

hers had once followed the Lady, and she found herself unable to get rid of him. And so he had stayed, no matter where the war took her. And now . . .

"You just can't wait, can you?"

She imagined the grave lines of his face folding into an embarrassed blush at the tone of her voice, the way Belf's once had. Imagined it, but not strongly enough to erase the look of hurt surprise that tightened his frozen lips. There was so much she wanted to say.

Instead she bent over him almost protectively and closed his eyelids with the tips of her fingers. She kissed his forehead, tasting the salt of tears that had splashed his brow.

In the distance she imagined the low thread of a familiar voice. "There is no place for tears on the battlefield. After all is over, you may mourn in pride—but never show that weakness to the enemy."

Telvar, can you never leave me alone? Perhaps it's true for the Lernari—but the nonblooded, no. Let me mourn, damn you, as I see fit.

"No, Sarillorn. The enemy understands suffering. They know that they've caused it and are satisfied."

Does it matter what you think?

She could see Telvar's stiff, brittle frown. Not that it mattered; he was dead these many months and only his words remained with her, a gift from her very first battle upon attaining her rank.

He was dead.

If the war had permitted, she would have gone to his ceremony and stood guard by his coffin, as he had stood by so many others. But perhaps it was better this way; his death was still just a story, and he lived in some way within her.

It doesn't matter anyway, Telvar. The battle is over. Her tears continued to fall.

Already the sounds of metal against metal had faded; the smoke that lingered from the fire-strike wafted wayward in the strong breeze, obscuring the corpses of Malanthi and human alike. It billowed like a ghost in a night punctuated by the glare of red flames.

The village had fallen.

She was weary. Loss of blood and the endless stream of enchantment that she had called forth had taken a heavy toll. She stood, forcing her knees not to buckle beneath her, almost giddy with apprehension. There had been Malanthi here, and in great numbers, but her blood was stronger than theirs—her own power should have been able to hold or drive them back in time to evacuate the village. She had done it countless times before.

No. It was not the Malanthi that had buckled her shields, allowing the enemy free passage, and not the Malanthi alone that had slaughtered so many of her people.

I should have been watching. I should have felt something. She shook her head bitterly. *This isn't the first time they've struck so far within our lines. Damn, I should know it's never safe!*

She straightened her clothing and looked around quickly. Her armor was lost; there had been no time or help to don it. Never mind. Word must be sent, and quickly.

A Servant of Malthan walked the lands.

She was bitterly thankful for the fact that she was almost exhausted—only the depletion of her blood-power allowed her to walk away from the pain of the dying villagers.

Swaying, she turned her back on the fire and began to walk toward the forest, knowing it would be easy to lose pursuit there if she could make it. She was dizzy, and twice stumbled as her legs rebelled against carrying her weight that far. Gritting her teeth she moved forward, listening for any sound from behind. Nothing but distant screams; no footsteps, no shouts. The soft unevenness of turned earth gave way to forest—she had reached the first line of trees. She stopped to brace herself against a maple, faced away from the village.

I'm sorry. I know I've deserted you, but the lines must have word of this. The Lady must have a chance to meet this threat. Please, please forgive me. Rough, old bark scraped against the back of her neck. Time to start moving in a darkness that she dared not alleviate with Lernari light.

Twenty feet of tree cover was behind her when she halted abruptly.

In the shadowed light that breached the leaves a figure had emerged. It stood very still, dark against darkness. A cold finger traced Erin's spine, and she snapped her hands upward, tracing the sigil of the Greater Ward. The black outline of hands moved languidly in the air, mirroring her gestures and mocking them with a ward of their own. Her teeth clamped down as she repeated the ward, her hands and body tense with a concentration that was almost physical. The tingle at the base of her spine eased slightly, but she could still feel it. She gave ground slowly, stepping back as a foreign power pushed at her defense.

"You are very powerful." The voice was casual. "I can almost feel your ward."

She did not waste the energy or concentration necessary to respond.

"Sarillar? Ah, no. I see that you are female." Light, the voice, and mocking. It told her that he knew full well who she was. "Sarillorn, then. I am not feeding, and I am therefore not open to any of your little wards. I suggest that you stop wasting energy on them; if you do not, you will not last for long. And that would be a pity."

Only her hands moved. Every bit of a reserve that she did not know she had fueled the gestures. *You may be powerful, but I've noticed that you aren't breaching the ward.*

An edge slipped into the velvet of the voice. "Very well. I grow quite bored of this."

At his words, Erin threw the last of her flagging strength into the Greater Ward. She thought that she had long since recovered from her inability to draw a true one, but she suddenly knew that she had never wanted the hand of God so badly.

Her opponent stepped forward, then staggered back with a soft curse. A small, tight smile caught Erin's lips. It vanished as her enemy gestured in a single, sweeping motion, one too wide, too deep. A red-fire flared in the darkness, crackling through Erin's barriers as if they were kindling. A tongue of flame swirled round her, unable to quite reach her pale skin. It didn't matter; Erin screamed in agony, and the color of her pain was red. She dropped to the ground, her body curling in on itself. Let the fire touch her, and she would have her God. But it didn't; it lingered so close to her skin that it was almost clothing, but it did not push further.

"Come, little half human. The time for defiance is long over."

Hands pulled Erin's head up by the hair.

"Can you not stand?" He shook her sharply, but she remained limp. Exhaustion held her immobile. "A lesson, Sarillorn. One should never overextend one's abilities in battle. As you shall see, it bodes ill for survival."

Strong hands pulled her to her feet and kept her there. Slowly they turned her until she faced the village. It was almost more than she could bear.

"Walk."

She was shoved forward. Her feet took a hesitant, automatic step before she crumpled. Again she was lifted.

"Your value as amusement is diminishing. If I have to carry you to the village, you will pay for the effort before you die."

Erin said nothing. She closed her eyes, drawing deep, even breaths. She was very cold. A Servant walked her lands; she was powerless to stop his progress; she could get no word out; and in a short while she would be dead.

Just as her mother had died.

The Servant carried her back to the village. The noise of fading screams grew louder; the smell of burning wood and flesh clogged her nostrils and mouth. Involuntarily her eyes fluttered open to see what they had not seen since she had become Sarillorn: loss in war.

"You are conscious. Impressive. You!"

A figure separated from a crowd of armored men that had clustered in front of the ruins of the mayor's home. It had once been grand—the only two-level home in the village. Now it was no more than broken glass and charred wood—an empty shell. The man who approached wore the red and black surcoat of the blooded—one of the Swords. His face shone with the glisten of sweat and blood, his eyes with feral triumph. He gave a low bow.

"Tend to her. She is the Lernari that has caused so much trouble with our borders. Bring her to the center of the village when the other survivors have been gathered."

Erin was set down on shaky feet. Resolute, she met the eyes of the Malanthi, not flinching at what she saw in them. This was the way of war, and the death that warriors had faced from the dawn of time. He smiled and grabbed her, the grip of mailed fingers bruising her arm.

"And Damar—she is mine. Tell the others."

The light in the eyes of the Malanthi guttered at the chill in the Servant's words. He nodded briskly and began to drag Erin along what was left of the village road. She walked with as much dignity as she could muster—in this, at least, she showed herself to be Telvar's pupil.

But she could not help but see the caved-in sides of the small homes that the elderly chose to live in; the peaked wooden fences that lay in pieces against the winding dirt road; the empty, silent streets. The tiny market circle of Colmen was just ahead. The Sword turned off abruptly before they reached it. But she could see the flagpoles—wood, these, not steel—as they lay splintered on the ground, and she could see the bodies beneath them.

With little ceremony she was thrown into a dark, crowded

hut. Meryman's home, close as it was to the market circle. She wondered if the old man was still alive.

The door slammed shut behind her, although there was no longer any lock to secure it with. She leaned against the wall, allowing her eyes to accustom themselves to the gloom. Slowly the outline of huddled bodies made itself visible. The stench didn't take nearly as long. Her throat was dry and tight; it caught as she gagged slightly.

I don't have the power for this.

But it wasn't quite true. What she didn't have was the power to deny pain. She stumbled forward, her hands already outstretched and shaking. Beneath her fingers she felt the wrinkled visage of an old man. He groaned.

The voice was not Meryman's; it was Gordan's. There was fear in it, but little strength.

"Shhh. It is the Sarillorn. I will try to help you."

The man's tension eased as Erin sent a small part of herself outward to gather his pain. She cried out then, all of her body writhing with the sudden contact that swamped her—but her hand remained in place, unmoved by the other's agony.

From out of the darkness, another voice spoke up. It was hoarse. "Sarillorn. We thought you dead."

"Not yet."

"It would have gone easier for you; you would have been spared much. There is a nightwalker here."

"I know. But maybe it is better this way. I can ease your pain before the end." Weakly she withdrew her hand from the old man's face. She did not allow herself to think on the extent of his injuries; instead she concentrated on sleep, and as the last tendril of his thought merged with hers, he drifted off.

She moved on, her hand cupping the cheek of a young girl. The child did not move when Erin touched her, although Erin knew her to be awake. Gritting her teeth, she pushed herself outward. The physical injuries the child had suffered were minimal. Erin calmed the pain of them easily, but the girl did not even react. Shuddering, Erin brought her other hand up.

No, she thought. *I am already too tired.*

Shaking the thought away, she steeled herself and merged with the girl's mind, praying for the strength she did not feel she had.

At first she felt only the darkness of oblivion. To one less experienced it might have passed for sleep. But Erin had been a healer for years, the brightest of her number. For her the black she encountered was a hard, icy barrier, devoid of the nebulous currents of sleep patterns—catatonia.

She traveled along the seamless wall, looking for some crack, some chink of light, that held the identity of the child. The search yielded nothing; no part of the girl faced the real world.

"Sarillorn."

Shaky hands touched her shoulder, pulling Erin momentarily out of her link. "Yes?"

"Leave her. It will do her no good to be awakened."

"What do you mean?"

"She's suffered much for a child of her age. If you bring her back to the world, she will only suffer that much more. I've seen the state before; in other circumstances yours might be a worthy endeavor. But not here, not now."

"But—"

"There are others you may be able to help more."

"I can't just leave her like this, she's—"

"She's somewhere where pain doesn't touch her. Not all of us are so lucky."

Lucky? Erin thought bitterly. Words rose, but she caught them in her throat and held them there. Dully she acknowledged that what she was doing might indeed be just another form of cruelty. "Maybe you're right."

A rasping sigh answered her, and she reached toward it almost eagerly. Her hands fumbled blindly in the air before lighting on an arm.

Contact. Almost automatically she flowed outward, with less energy than before. Heat rose in her palms and traveled to her fingertips, where it rested between her skin and her patient's. It left her with a jolt, drunk in greedily by the demands of a body's pain. Twining around broken ribs, it formed a cocoon that radiated gentle light, visible only to Erin's eyes. She let the contact fade and turned, already stumbling toward another person.

A small voice in her mind told her to lie down and acknowledge defeat. But she was too close to those surrounding her, and their pain jerked her to her feet and called her to their injuries.

In all there were thirty people in the hut, some ten of them minorly injured. Of the remaining twenty, fifteen had been hurt in ways that time and rest might heal, and five were already dead, but had not yet acknowledged the fact. Erin touched all of them, absorbing their pain and returning an unnatural calm in its place. She did not ask how they had come by their injuries, and no one volunteered the information; they sheltered it the way one shelters a secret that words alone cannot describe.

When she had finished, she curled up in the corner of the hut farthest from the door, her body pressed against the many that lay on the packed dirt floor. Sleep took her then, and she welcomed the gray neutrality of its touch. She had done all that she possibly could.

She was not allowed to sleep for long, but the few hours she did rest refreshed her; she found she could stand and walk easily enough when she was forced to do so by the armed Swords that entered the hut. One by one the surviving villagers were paraded out; those that could not walk were dragged. Erin gritted her teeth at the sight of them, but said nothing. Flanked by two guards, she came out into the near-moonless night.

They were taken to what remained of the village circle. Once the center of judgment, joining, and artisans' displays, it was surrounded on all sides by gutted buildings and corpses left for carrion. Small torches ringed the square, held by people intent on the upcoming spectacle.

One thing stood out in the bleak landscape, a richly upholstered chair with an engraved back and thick arms. In that chair the Servant sat, watching the arrivals. Erin could see the faint glow of wards surrounding him; she knew that none of Lernan's fire would touch him this night. Worse still, the power that it cost him to maintain those protections would be replenished by the people she had failed.

That failure weighed heavily on her. Any success she had won upon the field seemed to dissipate. She had failed, as she had always done when it was most important.

Two of the villagers died before they could be brought forward; their bodies were thrown to the side. The others were pressed together in front of the Servant. Erin came through to stand at their head.

The nightwalker smiled.

"Sarillorn. I see your captivity agrees with you. Do come a little closer."

"You can see well enough where you are."

The Servant's smile grew broader.

"As you will. Swords, kill one of them."

"Any particular one?"

"Any but the Sarillorn."

"No!" Erin started forward and a guard cut her short with a

shield block. She staggered back as one of the villagers was pulled from the crowd by four men. In the scant light, Erin could see the taut face of a young woman. Her lips were set against her mouth almost ferociously; no pleas for mercy would escape them if her will held out. Each of her limbs was secured by one of the guards; she struggled futilely, still maintaining her silence.

"A good choice." A new voice entered the square as a man in dark robes stepped between the guards that ringed it. He nodded at someone—Erin could not tell whom—and a Sword entered the square holding a gold-leafed box. With consummate care the box was opened, and the man in dark robes lifted something out of it. He held it high, and his eyes found Erin's. She saw the glint of red in them and paled.

With a very formal bow he said, "I am Talon, Karnar of Malthan. You've troubled us, Sarillorn; you've gathered debts that must be paid."

Erin tried to push forward and again ran into a shield.

"Attend to this, if it will not be too much trouble." He brought a hand up and slid it gracefully along the jagged edge of the knife that Erin now knew he carried. She could not see it clearly, but memory supplied detail—it was perhaps seven inches of toothed steel, with an irregularly shaped obsidian handle.

Talon turned toward his intended sacrifice, paused, and pivoted neatly on one foot.

"Oh, and Sarillorn?"

Erin met his eyes.

"Something for you to think on in case the entertainment is not enough for you." Deftly, and with surprising speed, he raised his arm and pointed. Erin managed to dodge in time to catch a flare of red with only her shoulder. She bit back a cry as she brought her hands up, too late to ward.

"Talon, you go too far." The Servant leaned slightly forward in his chair, his hands clenching the armrests.

"Really, Stefanos? A pity. I'd forgotten your claim." Without waiting for a reply, he turned back to the business of his God. He nodded to the Swords.

"I think you may start by breaking her legs."

In a very short time the silence was shattered by the low, hoarse sound of sustained screams. The high priest watched as his men worked, his red eyes a gleam of his God's love of pain.

Erin tensed visibly when the screaming began. For a moment she was shrouded by darkness, her legs folded beneath her shaking body under the cover of bedrolls, the smell of horses in her nostrils. The cries that rent the air were familiar ones. This death was familiar. Her throat closed, she felt an old fear begin to paralyze her.

No. I am adult *now. I am not what I was!*

The ache of tension was solid; she let it bind her to the present. She watched the man set to guard her as he, in turn, observed Malthan's ceremony. A sheen of sweat touched his face, and it grew pale. He was not Malanthi, then; against him her weakened white-fire would have no effect. It was not easy to bide her time. Her fingernails cut small crescents into the palms of her hands. But the waiting had its effect; the guard blanched at last and looked away. Erin caught one glimpse of his face as he turned, enough to wonder at the profession he had chosen and the God that he served. Then her hand lashed out, followed quickly by a sharp strike from her leg. The man toppled with a surprised grunt. She did not wait for reprisals; instead she lunged for the group of Swords that surrounded the Karnar and his chosen victim. Both of her hands shot out, connecting with the unhelmed heads of two Malanthi; they fell back, reeling at the unexpected strength of her blow. The priest whirled to face her; his knife glistened wet and black in the poor light like a little tendril of the shadow.

She did not stop to think; she raised her hands and called on the white-fire. It exploded outward over what remained of the girl, detailing her ravaged features in an incandescent flash. The priest and his Swords cried out, their voices an eerie harmony as they fell away, cringing.

Without pausing, Erin knelt, her hands gently touching the girl's chest. She could feel the ragged rise and fall of it; somehow this young woman had survived. A wave of nausea almost overwhelmed Erin as the cost of the white-fire made itself clear. She ignored it and pushed herself out into the roiling agony of a fragmented mind. Erin had never seen a victim of Malthan's ceremony; nothing in her experience prepared her for it. To soothe such injury would take hours, if it could be calmed at all. She had seconds.

Lernan, guide me. I cannot save your child's life—but I can save her from being Malthan's tool.

Her power bent outward, radiating a forced calm, a forced peace. Like a drug it spread into the woman's mind, seeking out the core of her identity. Amid the pain and terror that twisted everything into ugly chaos, a small spark flickered. Erin arrowed toward it, disregarding all else. As she touched that single spark, it skittered away, the need for escape from torment fueling it. Erin followed and gently, carefully, pulled it in.

Hush, little one.

Only a whimper returned to her. She wanted more; permission for what she had chosen to do. But though she pulled and coaxed, the mind yielded nothing. There was nothing left to give. Nevertheless, she had to try.

Little one, I can send you to where there is no pain, no fear. Would you like that?

Another whimper.

She closed her eyes. *Then sleep. Sleep the last sleep and wake in the peace of the beyond.*

Erin's power shuddered, snapped, and flowed back into her, severely depleted. The chest beneath her hand rattled once and then stilled. It was done.

Looking up, Erin could see three of the Swords struggling to their feet; the fourth lay where he had fallen, his face a twisted husk of agony. A movement at her back alerted her; she twisted around, bringing her hands up. There was a flash in the dark as a knife was raised. Erin rolled awkwardly to one side of the body as the blade plunged downward with a piercing whistle.

"Talon. That is enough." The Servant's eyes glowed, and the knife stopped in midair. The hand that still held it was shaking with the effort to bring it down.

The priest whirled toward the nightwalker. Erin could not see his face, but his words painted a clear picture of what his expression must be.

"You saw what she did and you allowed it! Let her pay in blood for the blood she's denied to God!" His face, fine-boned and sharp, was twisted into a snarl.

The Servant's face flickered spasmodically—an expression that looked suspiciously like laughter deprived of sound.

"Oh, really? You wish to give the blood of a Lernari to our God? I think it would be unpalatable, at best."

"That is not for you to decide; I am the high priest here, and the decision is mine alone."

"Dear Talon," the Servant said, rising from his seat, "you and your minions would not be here at all if I had not chosen to intervene. Do not make me regret the generosity of that decision."

With two long strides he bridged the gap between himself and the Karnar. Erin noted that his feet never touched the ground.

''If you were too careless to ward yourself against the Sarillorn's strike, that is your problem. It changes nothing, not even my opinion of you.''

Talon was silent for a few minutes. When he spoke again, his voice was smooth and even. ''Lord Stefanos, let me make it clear that the Malanthi value and respect the abilities that you have proven here; in no way do I wish to suggest otherwise. But this woman has proven herself in every way our enemy, and as she has demonstrated, she still has power here. I believe it would be expedient to dispatch her immediately.''

With equal smoothness the Servant replied, ''And I do not. I did not bring her back for your amusement, but for my own.''

''Nevertheless, Lord, I must do as—'' The words were cut off as the Servant leaned forward and casually grabbed the collars of the priest's robe. With contemptuous ease he lifted Talon off the ground and let him dangle there.

''Half blood, you will do nothing.'' The mockery was gone from his voice. ''This night's effort has cost me much that I will have to spend the time to replenish. Another word from you, and you will be my first.'' He jerked his arm and threw the man aside without further comment. Then he walked quietly to where Erin crouched.

She felt his shadow spread across her upturned face and knew the meaning of the word *enemy* more clearly than she ever had before. The hair on the back of her neck rose as she met the red flash of his eyes. If the Lady had eyes of emerald, this Servant's were living ruby. It surprised her; she thought they should be cold.

He held out a hand, which also surprised her; it was almost human in appearance, but longer and finer. She ignored it and rose to face him. The Karnar had named him Lord Stefanos, and she knew the name: He was First of the Twelve of the Enemy, with a power equaled only by the Lady's. There was death here.

At last, there was a death.

''You did very well, Sarillorn. Very well indeed. Walk with me.''

This time she did as she was bidden, the shock of his shadow surrounding her. So great was his power that she hardly noticed his height—it was too, too insubstantial.

''You do not cooperate here,'' she noted.

He didn't bother to look at the high priest, who was already rising from the blackened earth.

"No." He stopped in front of his makeshift throne and smiled. "Perhaps the Lernari have learned to respect their superiors in a way the Malanthi have not. Perhaps not; the light must give way to the darkness, and the beginning to an end. I shall teach you respect of that darkness and that end, Sarillorn."

"Perhaps not," she replied, her mimicry soft but evident. "For the darkness gives way to the light; the end to a new beginning."

He smiled. "Well said. But look around you and look well. For you and your people, dawn is a scant few hours away, but it may as well be centuries. None of you will see it."

Erin went cold; her muscles clenched tight, stifling breath. Tilting her chin, she said, "No. If our eyes cannot see it, our memories will hold it before you like a shield. We carry the light within us; you may dim it, but you will never destroy it. That is our nature."

"No, little Sarillorn. That is *your* nature. And if I gave you all to the Karnar, you know that you alone would prove true to it. I offer you, as proof, the human you have just killed."

Erin shuddered inwardly, and the Servant sank back into his chair, his fingers forming a steeple beneath his chin.

"But other things interest me; other things motivate me. Do you know," he said conversationally, "that none of my number has ever devoured one of yours? The Lernari are protected against us in ways that are not easily broken, and they die so quickly. If I had a few days with you, Sarillorn, I would attempt it. And I would succeed."

She stiffened, waiting for him to finish.

"But such is the nature of time; when I am here it affects me as any mortal. Already your people will be on the move against us—Kandor of Lernan will know I am present, although he will not be in time to move against me if my business here is short." Leaning forward, he motioned to two soldiers. They quickly separated from the crowd. "Take another. There, the boy. If the mother tries to stop you, hold her and kill the child slowly."

They nodded curtly and did as he commanded. The woman allowed them to remove her young son from the dubious safety of her arms. He was perhaps five; certainly old enough to know the caution of fear. Although he trembled in the mail of the arms that held him, he made no sound or struggle.

"Very good." His eyes returned to Erin. "Now, Sarillorn, I have a choice to offer you. You are intelligent; I assume you know what it is."

She had already turned away from him to stare dully at the boy. They had disarmed her, else she might have considered dealing herself a death-wound. It would not save the villagers, nor would it destroy the Servant—but the Malanthi here would suffer before she died.

"I wish to destroy you, painfully and slowly, in the fashion of my . . . kindred. It has never been done before because my brethren are less subtle than I am known to be; they believe they can beat down the will of Lernari blood by force alone. I am willing to grant you more strength than that during the short term and, as I have already said, I do not have the long term to look forward to where you are concerned."

Erin looked carefully at the soldiers; their faces were guarded but she could detect the strain beneath their careful neutrality. They were not Swords, then. Her eyes scanned the crowd, squinting in the sparse light. She sent out a hesitant probe— the smallest spark of light—but it failed before it could reach the first rank. The Servant had stopped it.

With a soft smile she turned back to him.

He returned a brittle, edged version of her expression.

"Yes, Sarillorn, your little ploy has incapacitated most of the Malanthi available. I will give you the respect that is your due. I make no attempt to convince you that the human soldiers here would willingly carry out the service of Malthan on so young and so helpless a crowd of civilians.

"But there is still the priest."

She nodded, waiting.

"For reasons that do not concern you, I wish to deny him that pleasure. Which is a pity—" He stood. "—for that leaves me."

His smile was wide and genuine; that was the horror of it. "It is the blood of the Sundered that allows the Malanthi to be what they are; to convey the sensations of pain and terror that come from a shattered human mind. Their mortal blood limits them, but even with this limitation they are easily up to their work.

"Can you bear to imagine what I can do? I am the eldest of my kind; no mortal taint inhibits me." He gestured, beckoning the guards. They carried the child to him. Gingerly he encircled the boy with his arms.

"Can you?" His arms tightened around a sturdy linen smock. The child stiffened, his pupils dilating. A low, strangled moan slid out of his mouth, and he slumped back to rest against the shadow. The Servant casually let the child fall to the ground, his eyes never leaving his true prey.

Erin started forward, reaching for the child. No one interfered as her hands sought and found his skin. She went outward, catching the injuries inflicted by the nightwalker's embrace. To her great relief they were only physical; a few ribs were snapped but had not pierced the lungs. She soothed the confusion in the boy's half-conscious mind as she dulled his pain. Then, although she knew it would make no difference in the end, she healed the cracks in the ribs themselves.

"As you see, I can choose to be merciful. I seldom do so without good reason."

Erin walked quietly past him. He made no move to stop her. With quick, flat steps she approached the boy's mother.

"Here," she said, handing the child over with great care. "Take him. Hold him carefully." Without another word she turned back to the Servant.

He watched her as she approached, aware of the odd light that suddenly glinted in her eyes. She stared at him as if seeing him for the first time.

"Your decision?"

She held out a hand and flinched as he took it. And she gazed down at the red lines of it, a pale fascination in her eyes. "I can give you what you wish for—but not 'without good reason.' " Her imitation was bitter and failed on the last word. "If my people are to perish at your hands or the hands of the Karnar, there is no reason to submit to you."

"You will not be forced to observe it."

"Don't insult me. If you think that squeamishness is the driving force behind the Lernari, you're wrong."

"Very well. Guards—"

"And if you kill or injure another one of my people, I swear blood-oath that you will never accomplish your desire. Not with me."

"Ah. Very good. Very, very good." He made a gesture of dismissal with his left hand. Lazily he said, "If I promise that your people will receive a clean death—"

She shook her head. "I want their freedom."

He darkened slightly. "Sarillorn, what I do, I do for amusement only. Insolence never amuses me."

In a low voice she said, "Let them go. Without my protection they have little chance against your forces—but it is that chance alone that I will bargain for."

"And if I give you my word?" He laughed. "What is the worth of the word of a Servant of Malthan?"

"Maybe nothing."

"Indeed. And for risk of that you give the word of a Sarillorn of Elliath." His hand tightened around hers, cutting off her circulation. His robes swirled in the windless night, lapping at her ankles. "I accept."

She pulled away, her free hand tracing the least of the wards. "My people first."

He laughed openly. "It has been a long time since I have encountered one of your number. Too long, perhaps." He turned to the men that ringed the square. "Release them."

A look of confusion washed across the ranks like a wave, but no one put this into words. Moving forward, they surrounded the villagers and began to push them out. Erin thought she could see one or two of the soldiers sigh with relief, and it warmed her a little.

"Gently."

Only one of the villagers stopped to look back. He was an older man wearing a makeshift bandage that obscured a third of his face—the schoolmaster, Dorcas. His familiar, bloused shirt was stained red and plastered against his chest. "Sarillorn, we—"

"You must leave. Remember your vows of trust and faith. Let me invoke them now; one life is in the balance against many." She could hear the tremor of fear and hope in his voice, but knew that his concern transcended them. The knowledge of what it must have cost him to turn back warmed all of her; she accepted it as the tribute it was. In a quiet voice, she said, "Thank you."

He nodded gruffly and began to move along with the rest of the people, her people. They were taken by the night.

And Erin was alone with death. She felt an odd sort of peace envelop her fully as she stared at the Servant. She watched, half adult and half the child that she had been the night her mother died. Her memories blurred, spilling forth into the imperative of now.

My word. She faced the Servant, her expression remote. *Lernan, help me prove true to it.* There were ways to distance oneself from pain. She could see Telvar, or the ghost of Telvar, instructing her yet again in their uses. She could remember the struggle to call them forth in his drill circle. She touched on them briefly, then cast them aside; their power was derived from the complexity of her blood, so the use of them would break her vow.

He brought his hands up to either side of her face, and she watched him, mesmerized. Contact. She cried out at the shock of it. Her hands shot up and she forced them down. Through clenched teeth, she said, "Do it quickly."

"That, Sarillorn, was no part of our bargain." His fingers slid across her cheek, peeling it open. When she jerked back and the sensation vanished, she knew it for a game. Flinching, she forced herself to be still.

This, this was the death that she had earned for herself nearly thirteen years ago.

The game stopped; the pain began in earnest.

He closed his eyes and lifted his head to savor this dark communion. His smile grew, transforming the lines of his face, pulling the corners of his mouth over sharp, angular teeth. For a moment the lines of his face flickered in shadow; half the human he chose to appear, and half the Servant he was.

Yes. Take my lifeblood. Take it, freely offered, freely given. She called no God; her word—and her desire—prevented it. But she was dying. *Take it.*

He tried, but more than her life passed into his hands. Something strange, something new, something brilliant; it was pure and clean. A soft glow, a hard light—it somehow embodied the essence of the unknown. It overwhelmed him with the strangeness of its taste and texture; he pulled it in as quickly as it was offered, but instead of dimming, it grew stronger, brighter, hovering above the shell of the life that was ebbing.

It hurt him, but not enough to stop him from marveling; he was curious for the first time in millennia. Pain, suffering, disintegration—these were familiar, these were expected. But this half mortal gave him more than this. It was almost as if she yearned for the touch that life itself fled from.

He let the thread of her life slip away, choosing instead to coil himself around this other sensation before it vanished. He called to it, drinking it in, and it came. He could not analyze it; could not dissect it; could not sever it from its source. He hurt her, clinically and deliberately, but though the life faltered, this thing did not; like a beacon too high to touch it shone on, disregarding him. He pulled at it—minutes, maybe hours passed. They were of no matter.

Light. But it was surely not a light with which he was familiar. It was not solid enough to strike, and if he cast a shadow in its glow, it was insignificant, unnoticeable.

After a while, standing on its edge was not enough—if she was the source of it, he would break her to reach its center. He threw himself into the fragments of her mind, tearing them open. Methodically he sifted through her memories, discarding all that seemed irrelevant. He stripped her carefully of experience, peeling away the layers of years and identity until something beneath that stood revealed—a spark in the chaos. Hard and clear, it hung suspended by thin strands, waiting for him.

He went to it, unerring, wrapped it in the velvet of his night, and began to feed on it—or tried to. But the warm light of it washed over him like a wave; he could not hold it long enough to consume it. It pushed outward, beyond his night, his darkness. He struggled with it futilely, unwilling to admit that its very nature defied his hunger.

It began to recede as he fought with it; it pulled farther and farther away from the iron of his grip. He cried out once in frustration—and once in pain.

Sunlight began to make its hold on the world felt; it streaked across the horizon in a pale, red blanket. Stefanos lost his grip on the Sarillorn and she crumpled to the ground. He looked up once at the eye of morning before turning his back on the pain it caused. Grimly he knelt beside Erin. His hands, deprived of their ability to absorb, only touched the surface of her throat. There, insistent and faint, he felt the throb of a pulse. It amazed him.

"Perhaps," he said, stroking her skin, "it was not lack of subtlety on our part, but rather some subtlety on yours. There is still no Servant who can claim to have fed on Lernari life."

Life. I'm alive. She thought it almost bitterly, but the words would not make their way through the parched tunnel of her throat. Self-awareness flooded back to her, dimming the light of her earlier determination. She knew she was cold, hungry, and tired—but she would give in to none of these things. Not yet.

"And still conscious." The sunlight had not yet deprived him of strength, although he could feel it blistering his back. Sliding his arms around her, he lifted her quickly and glanced around.

"Stefanos."

He stiffened and turned his head slightly into the sun.

Talon stood a few feet away. Without bothering to reply, Stefanos started toward the encampment; in a few moments day would be too close and too dangerous. He ignored the footsteps that dogged his retreat.

He stopped at the entrance of the tent. Six men, armored and armed with crossbows, barred his way. The bows were not pointed at him; as weapons they would have little effect. He looked carefully at the men, engraving their faces into his perfect Servant's memory. He moved forward, and one of the six stepped toward him. His words were apologetic and shaky.

"I'm sorry, Lord." He was very pale—a rare sight among the Swords. "You may not enter with the Sarillorn."

"Get out of my way." Each word, measured and calm, had the force of a blade.

Talon's voice came from directly behind. "I'm afraid, Stefanos, that the men here are under *my* orders. Hand the Sarillorn to me and you may enter or leave as you wish. My business is not with you, but with her."

"Talon, I begin to find you annoying."

"And that is, I'm sure, quite unfortunate. Nonetheless, you will do as I ask."

Stefanos placed Erin very carefully on the ground and turned to face the priest. The sun was rising; he could feel its nails across even his unexposed skin. He gritted his teeth against the pain.

"Yes, the sun is out, isn't it?" Talon said casually. "Rather careless of you. It's good to know that we now share similar opinions of each other."

Stefanos had never liked Talon, although their paths had crossed only briefly. This time he would be sure that he would not endure another such meeting. The sun was on him; with each passing minute it grew more acerbic. Talon's smile acknowledged the fact that he also knew it.

"Captain, take the Sarillorn."

Stefanos spun around and the soldiers drew back, their hesitance painting a clear picture of their fear.

"Stefanos, do not force a confrontation here; it would be most unpleasant for me." Talon's tone belied his words.

"It will be." With a swift, sudden lunge, Stefanos moved forward, his left hand swinging in a clear, wide arc. Talon's eyes widened in surprise as the fist smashed into his neck. Choking, he bent over. The Servant was not finished. His hands rose again, twice, each movement precise and economical. Talon jerked forward and fell prone in the trampled grass.

Leaning over, Stefanos picked the priest up by the back of

the robe. He ordered the men to one side and this time they did not refuse him—a good thing for all concerned. If the sunlight had taken its toll of flesh a moment longer, Stefanos was determined to exact no less a price from the Swords. They knew it.

The tent flaps slid open and the Karnar was thrown to one side. Stefanos glared balefully up at the sunlight. Baring his teeth he returned for the Sarillorn. She gave a low moan as he lifted her.

"I see you are still awake." The guards noticed the way his grip altered to become at once more secure and less painful—something he himself was barely aware of. "Come, Sarillorn." He carried her into the cool darkness of the tent. After looking around for a few minutes, he lifted the flap and barked out an order. Almost immediately two men entered in, carrying a small cot. They set it up in the middle of the room, their hands unsteady. The Servant ignored the smell of their fear; they did not hold his interest at the moment. He waited until they had gone before laying Erin down between rough wool blankets. Smiling, he watched her feeble efforts to throw them off.

"Now, Sarillorn, I have a task to attend to. Sleep; I will be with you shortly."

The "task" lay in a fetal curl on the canvas floor, dark robes askew as it gasped for breath. With an unseen smile, Stefanos walked over to where it lay.

chapter
ten

I'm very tired. *Numbly Erin tried to move her fingers; they trem-*
bled in response, but refused more. She could hear, as if from
a great distance, the sound of cloth shuffling. Rest would come
soon, and sleep. It was cool and dry, and the sounds of the
dying were mercifully absent for the first time in hours.

Sleep? Erin, there's a Servant here. What are you thinking?
Hysterical laughter welled up but she hadn't the strength to release it. She could feel the trickle of tears along the side of her
face and wondered absently who they were for. Her eyes closed
over them, forcing the last few out, and the shadows that flickered at the edge of her mind dimmed. *At least I'm still alive.*

The thought brought her no peace.

Sleep curled tentatively around her and she let it pull her
further away from awareness. Floating, she felt the lull of its
eddies as they carried her away . . .

A scream dragged her back abruptly. It was high, almost
mindless in its intensity. Although it was cut short, the shock of
it lingered like echoes.

Instinct shored her up. Instinct gave her the strength to stumble out of bed—bed?—in the direction the cry had come from.
Almost immediately she collapsed. The rough touch of canvas
slapped her skin as she dragged her head up.

Ican'tseeyouIcan'tgetoutfromunderthese—

No, Erin. You are in a dark tent.

The scream came again, weaker in volume, stronger in intensity. Taking a deep breath, she crawled; the pain that called her
would not let her rest. Her hands reached out toward a patch of
something that seemed darker than the rest of the tent. She felt
cloth beneath her fingers and weakly pulled at it. It moved; it
gave a sharp intake of breath as if it were alive. A whisper of a

163

sigh came from her mouth; this was not what called her. She moved beyond it and felt a hand at her back, pushing her down.

"Where are you going, Sarillorn?"

The words made no sense to her. She hadn't the energy to shake her head, but her sense of frustration grew. Her knees moved, but she could go no farther; the hand still held her down. Almost inarticulately she mouthed two words: "It hurts." It was the only explanation she had the strength to offer, but it seemed to appease the darkness; the hand lifted and her knees began to inch her forward.

Her arms were already stretched out to their full length along the floor. She lifted them and stretched her fingers out.

Contact. This was it.

Something shuddered at the touch, writhing as if to avoid it. Surprised, she pulled her fingers away, but they were called back, to rest against warmth and pain. The struggle against her grew feeble; Erin felt an unfamiliar barrier touch her hand—an unpleasant sensation that reminded her of the color red. She withdrew her hand once more, and again it returned, called to the pain. So she kept it there and pushed outward against the barrier to the thing that called to her so strongly. Like a poorly made tapestry, it began to fray under the tips of her fingers. It throbbed as if unwilling to grant her entry, but she could sense it grow weaker as the call grew stronger. Then the barrier broke; attacked from within and without, it fell away in shards.

It took most of what she had left to open the channel between herself and this other. She couldn't have broken the contact even if she'd wanted to, but the thought didn't occur to her; she had gone too far. All that was left her went out through it, out to the one who was hurting so very badly.

Like a blanket, she wrapped herself around it, absorbed what she could of it, and comforted what she could not. She sensed a terrible, lost confusion and, as if it were a child, she eased it, rocked it, and cradled it—all without a single motion. She was the Sarillorn of Elliath; what else could she do?

And through it all, the darkness was laughing.

"Ah, Sarillorn—I do not believe you even know who it is you are trying to help."

Words. More words. She ignored them; the other was almost asleep, its pain dormant. She could rest soon.

"Mercy, little one? Mercy to the Karnar? No one of your people would grant it."

Again the laugh, like the buzzing of an insect, sounded

through the tent. Then hands tugged on her shoulders. Hurriedly she pulled herself out before the contact was broken. She allowed herself a weak smile.

"Sarillorn, do you realize what you've done?" He shook her, and her head snapped back to loll against the air. She didn't answer and was shaken again.

Stop it! She wanted to scream. She had done her best—why could she not rest? But the hands and the voice troubled her too much, and she forced herself to acknowledge them.

"Sarillorn, this man is Karnari. You have just granted him a peaceful, painless death. Why?"

Slowly the words twisted into her, piercing the gray that clouded her conscious thought.

The Karnar? I saved the Karnar?

Images of his interrupted ceremony filled her mind's eye in the darkness. The feel of the ruined flesh of his victim came back to trouble her shaking hands.

Why? He's everything we fight against, everything we die to prevent. No death at his hands was ever painless—he deserved a hideous, endless torment. Why? Why did I do it?

The answer returned to her as quickly as the question left. The bitterness of the truth of the Lady's warning, offered years ago in the quiet and peace of the Woodhall, struck her sharply.

She opened her mouth. Her voice, when it came, was dry and rasping. "It's what I am. He called me; I had to come." And she wept, although she had little energy for it.

"Yes, Sarillorn. Yes, you did." His voice was almost hushed. "He is half blood no longer."

What do you want from me? Erin glanced from side to side at the escort she had been given: six soldiers, all without the taint of blood that marked the Malanthi. Their black surcoats were torn and dirty, but no hint of red embroidery scarred their surface. They would not meet her eyes. The day the march began, one had leered at her, fondling her right breast between callused fingers. He was no longer with her, nor with the army at all. She shuddered, remembering the haze of shadow that had torn through him before she could even react. At least there had been no pain-call.

No one bothered her now.

During the day the troops slept, and during the night they marched. These were the orders of the nightwalker and none sought to disobey them. It lengthened the march, but their lives were worth the extra time.

What do you want?

Two days had passed, but she was still not used to walking like this, a refugee in the shadows of tree, stone, and night.

She thought of her failure, and it hurt. *Is that what this is about? Am I not even enough of a threat to merit death?*

But she walked free.

Every so often she would look at the pale thinness of her wrists and wonder. No other prisoners had been taken by this army.

She walked free, under oath.

She walked under moontouch and starlight, discovering the way darkness transformed the landscape; she walked behind a rank of torches that flickered over helmed and unhelmed head alike, bringing into relief the traces of sweat and dirt that lingered on grim faces. She walked with her own thoughts as company, conversing with voices of people that she had not touched for years; advised by the dead.

She walked free, and this simple fact confused her.

I don't understand it. She sent out a glimmer of white-fire; the smallest trace of her renewed power. It danced a small spiral before dimming, and she watched it, bemused. *He didn't bind me.*

You gave him your oath, Erin; until you reach the capital, you can do nothing to escape. He knows what the word of a Lernari is worth.

Yes. But I don't understand why it matters. He could have killed the soldier . . .

She could still see the outline of the Servant's body against the flat horizon; knife poised, eyes glinting steel. And beneath him, secured by Malanthi, a member of his army, a victim of his ceremony. A "deserter," or so the hushed whisper of grim troops said.

She could feel the smoothness of his robe beneath her fingers as she gripped his cloak, could see the dimming of his eyes as he looked down at her. All around her was sharp intake of breath followed by the tension of sudden silence and the vague hint of relief.

"Please. Please don't do this."

"I must, little Sarillorn. I need his blood to bind your power. My own I will not spend."

And she could see again, clearly, the odd stillness of his face as the words left his mouth, the way he looked down at her as the dagger came to rest at his side.

She said, "Please, you don't need to do this, not because of me."

He said, "The blood of this 'innocent' will not stain your hands." Speaking, he reached over and grasped the hands he mentioned in one of his own. They were stiff and cold to the touch. "It is not your doing, if that is what troubles you. Leave, now." He had released her, assured of her compliance. She had stumbled back, but not far enough.

"No." It was important to her, more so because she was surrounded by her enemies.

"Sarillorn—"

"No. Please, if it's my power you're afraid of, I won't use it. If it's a life you want, take mine."

"You have already bargained your life to me; it is no longer yours to offer." But he made no move to continue. He stood, unnaturally still, his eyes opaque. It was odd; she had expected always to see the redness burning in them.

"I—I will give you my word, as the Sarillorn of Elliath of Lernan. I will bind myself as effectively as you could bind my power." She knew none of the fear that the others knew; she was not afraid of the death he could offer. Reaching out, her hands had found his cloak, her fingers grasping it as if to shake his implacability.

And she was left with the feel of the dagger as he placed it, handle first, in the palm he pulled loose from his cloak.

"I accept."

It still surprised her as she dwelled on it. She had been speechless with a peculiar shock, unable to say anything as he had walked away from her, leaving her free.

Free.

She had helped the shaking man to his feet, but her eyes had followed only the Servant's departure.

Why am I still alive? What game are you playing?

"Does something trouble you, Sarillorn?" His voice, as always, came out of the night with no warning.

She started slightly before glancing at him from the corner of her eye. "No."

He fell into step beside her, his feet avoiding the missteps that she made. "You are very quiet."

She said nothing.

He looked down at her. Even though she kept her word and

used none of her power, he could see the faint glimmer of light that surrounded her face and hair.

She was his enemy, by birth and by taint.

He knew a moment's urge to destroy her completely, but he fought it. Her destruction would tell him nothing at all about the strange quality that imbued her life, the odd light that had so captivated him that she had survived his touch till morning.

For a moment, as he contemplated her silent profile, he saw that light again, and he called it beautiful.

What have you done to me, Sarillorn? Almost, he reached out to touch her, but he knew that she would start or shy away, so he kept his hand still. Even this was strange, stranger than she could know, for anything that he wanted had always been his.

Perhaps that was because his desires had always been simple ones, and his strength alone enough to grant them.

She was not afraid of him. He, the greatest of her enemies but one, engendered no fear. How odd.

He knew that he should leave, but could not bring himself to do it. *What have you done?*

We are enemies, yes. But still . . .

He gave an elegant shrug and continued to walk by her side as the army moved on its rough path through forested hills in a procession of torchlight and heavy-footed silence. He found himself asking of her life in Elliath—questions that no Lernari would ever answer. Nor did she prove an exception. Still he could not leave.

Instead, he began to tell her of Rennath, the heart of the empire that he was building. He described its spirals and towers; its streets and the way they looked when shrouded with evening mist; its dark cathedrals, and the worshipers they gathered when the moon waned. He spoke of the shadows that it housed when day lingered, and the way those shadows traced their graying fingers over the landscape. He told her how he closed those fingers when he walked the streets of the city—*his* city.

In confusion, Erin listened to the rise and fall of his voice. She would not look at him, but she could not look completely away, nor stop his words from touching her. She heard beneath them a cold and deathly silence, and beneath that something she did not want to identify. It was as if he spoke a eulogy over the corpse of a worthy enemy at last defeated in battle; it had the same exultation of victory, the same emptiness of purpose, that the born warrior knew.

He watched her as he played with the words, awaiting a response that never came. He could see the lines of her face; they spoke of confusion and weariness beneath the invisible cage that she had chosen to wear. He continued to speak.

She listened, losing the thread of his words to their smooth cadence. She tried to capture the spirit behind them; to appreciate for an instant the beauty of the icy, chill world he described. For a moment she stood on the outer edge of Rennath, a distant observer. The twin spires of the city cast their delicate shadows along her face, and she could nearly feel the gentle way they called her into the twilight. She could almost understand his dark pride then, for she could perceive beauty in the cold elegance of his words: the beauty of frost on windows in winter. She turned to face him for the first time in the evening, half wanting to share her thought.

Then he began to speak of something else. The words penetrated the shroud of fragile image Erin had constructed, shattering it.

For he spoke of the subjugation and enslavement of the people of Kerwin, the small kingdom the Malanthi had conquered a decade ago. In a voice full of the same pride with which he had spoken of Rennath, he described the conditions of their life and the reasons he believed they would never break free of them. As if unfolding the technique behind a much-loved piece of art, he spoke of their fragmentation and the way they had been thinly spread across the country to labor for the rest of their lives without glint of hope at the whim of the church-born nobility. He told her of how the use of their language had been made a crime punishable by death, most often the slow death of close relatives or friends. In time, without language or countrymen, they would forget that they had ever known a different life. They would be completely his.

And as Erin listened, each word formed the link of a familiar chain. A wave of revulsion and anger welled up from her and she grasped it gratefully. She cast off the confusion that had accompanied her for the last few days, remembering clearly who she was, and who he was.

He did not notice. In the same tone, the same voice, he continued to speak, only this time more theoretically. Like a surgeon, he described the fragile points of a culture—a king, the church, or the popular heroes; how, if careful, one could apply specific pressure, or pain, and the whole structure would collapse. He smiled quietly as he spoke of how those who remained would seek out some inspiration, some guidance, some God when the strongest among them had failed; or better, how many would feel, without knowing how it ran their lives, that they somehow merited the treatment they received after their defeat.

Under the hail of his words, the night grew darker and grimmer. Erin walked under the slowly rising heat of anger; her eyes followed the road a few inches away from the tips of her feet. He talked on; and this time, when his words ran together and she lost the text of their meaning, she felt overwhelmed by the destruction inherent in the quiet pride of his voice. For that was all she could feel: his quiet, strong confidence. There was no gloating, no intent to cause her added pain—this she would have understood and, in some perverse way, readily accepted.

He was speaking to her as if she understood the enjoyment he had at the fruits of his labor, as if she were his equal.

Unaccountably she was reminded of the way children would often come to her with things they found joy in: a kitten, a painted toy, or a new story. They would carry these things in their hearts or hands, their eyes shining with a shy pride and an open desire to share them.

Her head snapped up and glanced off the endless line of men before her. She could see in them all that the Servant had spoken of: the fear they fought for, or because of, and the way the night gathered them up and held them out in the palm of the Servant's hand.

With a small, inarticulate cry she stopped short and swung round, bringing her hand up quickly enough to slap the side of the Servant's face. The words stopped; that was good. Without waiting for a response, she turned and darted off the road, into the waiting darkness of trees.

Low branches stung her cheek and brow as she ran through them; they clung to her hair and the collar of her robe as if animated with a desire to stop her. The moon, a pale sliver of silver on black, wavered before her in an odd sort of dance. She blinked, and its glow became static as tears slid down her cheeks.

Her fingers came up to touch them.

I'm crying, she thought, numbly. *Why?*

The hint of an answer formed at the back of her mind, and she began to run again. Running was good; the shock of her feet hitting the ground kept thought at bay. She fought to keep her breathing clean and even.

* * *

How far can you run, Sarillorn?

The Servant stood out of the reach of the light, in the cover of a large tree. The road was some distance behind—not that it mattered; the army had stopped to wait for his return. He was slightly vexed; the nature of her sudden departure had surprised him. The touch of her hand on his cheek lingered—an insult that no other mortal would survive. But the Sarillorn . . .

He could not see her, but the sound of her progress was clear; in the distance she was snapping dry branches. He followed her, keeping a constant distance between them. Twice she slowed, but as he approached, she began to surge forward again. The third time she slowed he could hear the halting shuffle of her feet as she came, at last, to a stop. He walked silently, feet barely touching the ground, until he could see her.

She sat curled against the side of a tree, head buried in the arms she had wrapped around her shoulders. Too tired for tears, but not for thought; her body's momentary stillness let thought have free rein.

He had spoken to her of the empire he was building, of people as the mortar that held it together, crushed between different deaths. His voice had held such pride, such quiet pleasure—as if he were a child, his dream clutched in deathly, orphan hands, the mask of his face revealing death, the destruction of her village, the corpses of her people strewn along the streets beneath his watchful eye.

His eyes.

They should have been red; they should have contained the horror of red-fire and malice.

She began to shake, and her hands lost their grip on her shoulders and came to lie in weak fists on her lap. How dare he? How dare he come to her, to share the evil that he had done and would continue to do? How dare he remind her of—

"Sarillorn?"

Her head shot up. In the distance, deprived of even meager torchlight, she could discern his outline, nothing more.

And in the darkness, with the night so clear and so strong, he could make out the throbbing pulse of her lifeblood, and the frail chain of light that bound it. He was surprised; he recognized the light easily and knew that it should not have been visible to him, not when he was separate. He started forward, drawn to it, but stopped as it began to dim.

Erin stood in one fluid motion. Her face, every detail plain to his eyes, was a mixture of rage and guilt. A familiar look, but one he'd not yet seen her features take. He took a step back. She stood very still; only her hands trembled.

Very stiffly he said, "I meant you no harm." Involuntarily he reached out as the light in her began to gray.

Erin stepped forward, neatly avoiding his outstretched arm. Her mouth opened silently as she stared at him, unseeing. Her fist rose in an awkward swing and crashed into his waiting hands. What started as a snarl in the back of her throat came out a whimper; she pulled against the vise that held her. Her foot lashed out, connecting with his shins. He lifted her off the ground by the arms, reducing the force her legs could muster. She met his eyes, expecting them to be red, hoping for rage or anger at the least, and, beyond that, hoping for victory, threat, or death. She looked to see the familiar image that had haunted her dreams, that had come so close to touching her the night that her mother had died. She hoped finally to see the curved claw, free from Kandor's undeserved restraint.

He did not give her what she wanted. There was no death in the eyes that met hers; just a blackness that held some hint of confusion. He shook her, but not roughly, as she dangled in the sight of his hollow eyes.

"Why are you looking at me like that? What do you want?" The blows of her feet grew weaker, as her voice rose. *"What do you want from me?"*

He watched her face as she walked the thin line between rage and sorrow. Both were familiar; he'd seen them, caused them, many times. But from her they suddenly felt wrong.

His answer returned in a cold whisper.

"The light, Sarillorn. The light that grows dim."

His answer was wrong. She felt confusion begin to take hold of her and cast it off, shoring herself up with the full force of her fury. In a low, deep voice, she said, "You'll never, never do it. You'll never have your empire, or spread the disease of your city into *my* lands. The Lernari are ranged against you; the Servants of Lernan stand with us. We'll never rest while you rule a single life!"

He laughed. His hands bit into her flesh.

Now. Now . . . She pulled her head around and down to meet his eyes. The laugh died—and so did a part of Erin.

"Little Sarillorn, what do *you* want from me?"

Shaking, she replied, "Your death." But her words were empty, the rage that should have been in them misplaced. He set her down on legs that would not hold her. They crumpled, and she felt the touch of solid earth beneath her hands and the touch of tears that Telvar would have despised on her cheeks.

His fingers pulled her chin up as he knelt beside her on the ground. "Sarillorn. I meant you no harm."

"Don't."

He did not release her, nor did his words. "I meant only for you to understand the things I wish to create out of the pain and bloodshed you have been party to. I meant for you to see that there is, in my goal, more than just chaos and death, more than the darkness of the first Awakening."

"Don't!"

She pulled her chin away and he felt the touch of water. He lifted his fingers briefly to his mouth, stopped, and looked down at her more closely. In a voice that held wonder, he said, "Sarillorn? Sarillorn, I have hurt you."

Like a child. She tried to stop the tears before his hand could catch them, before he could drink them in like the lifeblood they were.

Oh, Telvar, you never warned me of this.

The Lady's Woodhall echoed the Lady of Elliath's words. *Nothing is unalloyed, Sarillorn.*

Stefanos lifted her gently off the ground. She tried once, feebly, to release herself from the tangle of his arms.

But he would not let go; for watching her he had seen some subtle change. Rage had fled, and beneath the pain she expressed, the bands of her light were glowing faintly but surely. As he held her, as she pressed against him, tears mingled with the silk of his clothing, he reached out to touch them, to marvel anew at the foreign feel of them and the way they slipped so easily from his grasp.

He held her, his fingers trailing through her hair. After a time, he began to walk back to the road. She had fallen asleep.

How . . . human. How fragile.

"Sarillorn."

Erin looked up. For three days she'd seen nothing but the backs or profiles of soldiers in the darkness. No one spoke to her; even those that offered her food did so in stiff-lipped silence. She wondered, often, what Belfas was doing, but was glad that he was not present to share the march; bad enough to have failed her friends in the village.

By the third day, she was almost willing to help with the

injured men, but no one in the army would acknowledge her—no one but him.

"You travel well."

She nodded. She wanted desperately to know where she was being taken, and what awaited her, but she didn't want to give him the satisfaction of a reply.

"Sarillorn, are you troubled?"

Troubled? Her eyes widened and she opened her mouth, whether to laugh or cry, not even she was sure. Her jaw clamped shut and she looked away.

Why does he have to look so human? For it was hard to look at him; hard to see what in any other eyes would have been curiosity, even gentle curiosity, and remember whose eyes they were.

"Do you mind if I walk with you?"

She heard his words, looked up at him again, and said, "Yes."

"Ah."

And he was gone.

It wasn't a reaction she'd expected. Nothing he did was predictable. She tried to tell herself that she was glad of her isolation as she continued to march toward dawn.

"Sarillorn."

A shadow cut the glow of torchlight as it lay upon the ground. Erin looked up, surprised. The First Servant stood before her, a small tray in his hands. In silent grace he placed it down before her and stood.

"You—you don't normally bring me food."

She thought she could see a hint of a smile in the shadows of his lips.

"No." He took a step forward. "I do not usually . . . serve another."

Hands shaking, she reached for the knife on the tray. Her eyes widened slightly.

"The army is eating better than it has been."

"Not the army, Sarillorn. Would it trouble you if I remained?"

She closed her eyes, seeing for a moment the silent, voiceless backs of the soldiers.

"No," she said, but softly.

She ate while he watched.

"Would you—would you like to—" She gestured at the plate.

"No." After a moment, he took a seat beside her. "It is not yet time for me to feed."

A hint of a smile again. The food turned to ash in her mouth and she set the knife to one side. She wanted to tell him to leave, to go, to kill her—to do something that made any *sense*.

"Sarillorn?"

"Why do you keep coming to me?" Her hands were clenched and shaking, but she kept them at her side. "Why do you bring me this—" She waved at the food.

"It is better than the food you have been eating, and you have grown weaker this past week."

She hadn't seen him for a week; it was too much to hope that he hadn't seen her, either.

"Why does that make any difference?"

Why? His eyes grew remote and dark, as if the shadow that he would not wear in front of her dwelled entirely within them.

"Why do you choose to look like—like that?"

"Would you prefer the darkness? Do you desire the shadow?" His fingers began to pale into gray as his eyes flashed red.

"Don't—that doesn't answer my question. Why are you doing this?"

The emerald green of her eyes flashed, not with magic but with mortal emotion. And it would be easy to gutter them. Fingers became claws. Easy. Claws became nails. His hands fell, once again under a mortal seeming.

"Why, Sarillorn?" He stood and began to walk away. "I do not know."

She did not know what it cost him to say it; she heard only the words that drifted from his retreating back. But the words were enough to leave her staring helplessly into the small fire.

He came to her the next night, again bearing his gift of food. It was venison, surrounded by greens—fresh and lightly cooked.

"Would it trouble you if I remained?"

"No." She took the food from his hands, setting it aside for the moment, although she was hungry.

"Servant," she began, her voice almost formal.

"Stefanos," he said quietly. "Although I am often called 'First' as well."

Whatever she had hoped to say vanished. "You—"

"If it makes you uncomfortable, do not call me anything."

Fire and food were the only two things that Erin could focus her attention on. She chose the food.

As she ate in silence, he watched her. Frustration was not a thing he was familiar with, but now he felt it keenly. Somehow, in a way that he could not understand, he had once again said or done the wrong thing.

The third night that he brought her dinner, she once again accepted it. Chicken this time, with corn and peas. She shook her head, wondering how on Earth he had found such food; to the best of her knowledge they had not come through any villages. She smiled almost hesitantly as she began to eat.

"Would it trouble you if I remained?"

"No," she replied, around a mouthful of chicken.

He took his accustomed seat to her left, but said nothing.

"Do you want any of this?"

"No," he answered gravely. "I do not normally eat this mortal fare."

"You should try it." She stopped, trying to remember if she had ever seen the Lady of Elliath eat anything. Her memory wasn't up to it. She doubted if anyone's was—with the possible exception of Latham or Belfas.

Stefanos watched as the fork fell slowly away from her mouth. He saw her face lengthen and felt his hand clenching once again into a fist. This time he felt he knew what he had done.

"Sarillorn," he said, almost quickly, "if you wish, I will try what you are eating."

She started and then looked up. "Pardon?"

"I will have some—chicken?"

The plate stared up at her as if it had become a living entity. Very slowly she cut a piece of her dinner and handed him her fork. Her hands were trembling.

He looked at it, his expression no less grave than it was when he asked if he might remain each evening. Then he took it and raised it to his mouth.

Erin watched as he chewed, each movement precise and almost meticulously timed. She counted to five and then watched him swallow.

He turned to meet her wide stare.

"It is—interesting," he said, still grave. "Perhaps I will join you in more of this—" He gave a controlled gesture. "—at another time."

Erin laughed.

The sound seemed to come from everywhere, enclosing him as her light had once done.

"You, you're the most powerful force the Enemy has—and you've never lifted a fork!"

He was torn then, torn between pleasure at this strange laugh and anger at being the cause of it. No mortal had ever laughed at him before.

But unlike other laughter, this held a sense of wonder in it. It puzzled him; he listened.

"Tomorrow," Erin said, a smile lingering, "we can try vegetables."

She began to laugh anew, but he did not ask why.

In the month that followed, he kept his word. He brought dinner and joined her in the eating of it. She showed him how to look "normal"—as she put it—while chewing and swallowing and how to make proper use of a knife and fork. When she laughed, she told him of her childhood, of how she, too, had needed to be civilized into eating like an adult.

In fact, as the time wore on, she talked of other things: her lessons in the drill circle, her life with Katalaan, or her attempts, failed, at the use of the longbow. But she did not talk of the war, of battle, or of the losses she had suffered there. Likewise, he did not talk of battle, or his empire, or the Dark Heart.

He learned of things human, things mundane, and she of the stretch of infinity that lay beyond the body of the Twin Hearts.

Only one thing marred the strange friendship that they struggled to share: She asked him, once, if he might let her go. And he answered.

But even then, when he came, Erin could force herself to forget that he was a Servant; she could look at the human façade that he presented, to speak and laugh with it.

When he was not there, she would think of the Lady and wonder whether or not the Lady had taken the time to learn about the things that the First of Malthan did: human things, trivial, common, and precious.

Maybe, just maybe, there was a hope to be found in the time that he spent with her; maybe there was a light, as the Lady had once said, in the darkness.

Erin waited as the day faded. It was one month into her travels; two weeks from the Rennath that the Servant had once talked of so proudly. She knew she was to be delivered there, but not to what. Nor did she care to question her only companion about it; she wanted, in some way, to preserve the illusion of his humanity.

She watched as the torches were lit, listened as the night came down. The Servant did not arrive. She felt an odd disappointment then and wondered at it as she made ready to march. Twice she scanned the ranks of the men before and behind her, but no hint of the Servant's shadowy presence was evident.

Maybe he would join her on the walk.

But he did not. And as she looked around at the tense, silent legion of men, she felt her heart sink.

Don't be silly, Erin, she told herself as she shivered. *Just because he doesn't come for one night doesn't mean that he's— he's . . .*

No. The month of evenings shattered into painful, brittle fragments.

Her hands folded into themselves and grew taut; the edge of her nails bit into her skin. Before a scream cut the silence, she knew what he must be doing, and when the cry came she knew where.

No!

The ranks buzzed with a sudden relief; the tension that she'd been peripherally aware of faded into grim acceptance in everyone present—everyone but Erin.

No man made move to stop her as she pushed by them, her sense of direction and place honed by blood-power. Only three present could see how she smoldered with white-light in the darkness and they also let her pass, satisfied that at last she would meet the death due to her.

Your word, Erin. Remember you gave him your word not to break the binding. She kept her flame contained, but barely, barely. She flew across the rocky terrain, her footing sure for the first time in weeks. Her eyes were blazing with the power that she had vowed not to release. *No—I only promised not to try to escape with it.*

She saw him, bent over a body that shuddered in a silence near death.

He saw her, a living pillar of fire that cut through the night.

Their eyes met, red and green, over the distance that Erin had not yet covered.

She began to walk slowly, hands at her side. The man beneath the Servant gurgled once as the grip that clenched his face went slack. Erin could see the glinting white of the man's eyes before they rolled shut.

Just as slowly as she approached, the Servant assumed his full height, as if they moved to the beat of the Twin Hearts. His eyes narrowed at the brilliance she held within; he could not make out the details of her face. Nor could she clearly see his; even to the whiteness of her power he was shadowed and gray. There was nothing remotely human about him.

It was Erin who spoke first. She was shining. "Don't do this." She lifted one hand, palm up. In it, a haze of white stirred.

"Sarillorn, I hoped to spare you this." He raised his own hand, red claws that glowed gently. "But this is what I am."

She shook her head once, side to side, the movement slow and deliberate.

He offered her a smile he knew she could not see. "Lady, while I might force you to do other than you desire, I know I could not force you to be other than what you are—except in death. This—" He gestured at the man on the ground. "—is part of what I am. You have only two choices. Accept it, or try to banish me with the fire you hold, as all others of your lines would do."

Again she shook her head, but this time the motion was sharp.

"I gave you my word."

His smile dimmed. "The word of a Lernari. Yes. And I accepted." From the corner of his eye, he could see the man inch his way across the dirt toward Erin. Reaching down, he lifted the man up by the neck, dangling him to one side as he continued to watch the Sarillorn of Elliath. He knew that this glowing, dangerous light was the light that his army had met on the fields.

She flinched and took a few steps forward.

"Your word . . . Then you have only one choice." He readied his own ward to counter her attack. But it felt wrong to him.

"No." Quickly, lightly, she walked over to where he stood. "I have others."

He gestured briefly with his free hand and was surrounded by a dark red halo. Her face, closer and clearer, was odd; he saw a trace of hesitation in it, fear in the eyes that would not waver from his. But it was not the fear he was accustomed to seeing, for it was not directed at him.

"Are you frightened, Sarillorn?" His voice was calm; he might have been asking her what a word meant, or a gesture.

"Yes."

Her answer surprised him with its stark simplicity. He looked down at her for a time before replying.

"You have nothing to fear from me. It is not your life that I have chosen this night.'' He knew what she would say; she did not disappoint him.

"It isn't for my life that I fear."

"This one's?'' He held up his victim.

Again she surprised him, reaching into herself for an answer that she could never have given him at any other time.

"No.''

"Then what?''

"I'm afraid that I won't be able to stop you.'' She said each syllable slowly.

A touch of frustration showed in the furrow of his brow—and this, although his brow was ash-gray and shadowed, was also familiar to her.

"Sarillorn, this man is a soldier. Many must have died trying to kill him. Had you won, he would no doubt be dead at the hands of your people. How is my action different?''

How? "I am not afraid of his death. Only the manner of it.''

"What does it matter? In the end the result is the same.''

Those claws had held cutlery. She had shown him how to do it. "No.''

"And if I chose to break his neck instead?''

She shook her head.

"Sarillorn?''

Softly, she repeated, "I'm only afraid that I will not be able to stop you.'' Then, reaching out, she touched the arm that held the man.

Both Erin and the Servant flinched at the same instant that red met white. The air crackled sharply. Neither recoiled.

I am afraid, she said, silently, *of hope.*

Then this is your chance, Erin. Let him feed. *Get rid of any hope permanently. Let him do what he has done for millennia; watch it, feel it, and see it. Accept the truth of what he says.*

I am afraid, she replied, *of the death of hope.*

Or the true birth of it? For what is the Enemy if you can stop him? What are you really afraid of?

I'm afraid that I will *be able to stop him.*

She cringed at the mental dialogue, her eyes going through the Servant. Seeing, beyond the shadow, the emergence of a man.

"But I have to try.''

"Sarillorn?''

"Stefanos.''

The shadow flickered as the name slowly drifted away on the night air.

"I cannot force you to be other than what you are. But nonetheless, I ask it of you."

"You are very formal tonight, little Sarillorn. It is—unusual." His hunger was forgotten for a moment.

Her hands curled lightly around his arm, sending a shock of pain through her body, and his. She tried to push the whitefire back, to absorb it into her core. It was hard; it was not the way of the Bright Heart's power.

He raised his free hand and brought it to rest a hair's breadth from her chin.

"I do not believe that you have been entirely honest with me."

She said nothing.

"Or perhaps with yourself; I know little of humanity's more subtle emotion. You are afraid, yes, but it is not—" It was not a fear that roused his ancient hunger, not a fear she offered to him. He had never felt its like.

Gently she touched the hand that clutched the man's neck. As she did, she met the nameless man's eyes. She felt his call and let her hands cup his sweaty face. "Please, Stefanos. Please put hunger aside for now."

Then she went out, washing over the terror and agony that wracked the body of the Servant's victim. Dimly she heard laughter, cold and chill, permeating the air around her. It didn't matter; fingers of her comfort picked up the fragments of a mind almost lost to the nightwalker's hunger, pulling them together and binding them beneath a fragile peace, a fragile sleep.

And when she looked up, she saw that the soldier lay stretched out along the cold ground. A few feet away the Servant stood, arms crossed, as he watched her.

She rose, the light of her power dimmed by her effort.

She was weary, too weary to be surprised or afraid. She walked over to the Servant, to Stefanos, a sad, bitter smile touching her lips and eyes. She wanted to weep and hated herself for the desire.

He reached out to catch her hands and felt the heat that they still radiated.

"Why?" she whispered, making no move to free herself.

He touched her face, his expression distant and grim.

He would not answer that question—not for her, and never for himself.

"Come, Sarillorn. You have far to walk this night."

He turned, but she made no move to follow him. And when he turned back, he could see her lingering like shadow, pale and white, where he had left her. Almost as if he had somehow broken her. He felt a distant satisfaction, but it was hollow; when he touched it, it vanished.

He walked back, and she looked up almost blindly, her eyes again focused at a point beyond him. When her voice came, it sounded very young.

"Lady, I'm afraid. Choose another road for me. I don't have the strength to follow this one."

She started to sway, and he caught her at once, moving quickly enough to stop her knees from hitting the ground as she buckled. Whatever had kept her steady this far had snapped. He lifted her and carried her back to the troops, knowing that they would be in some disorder. He caught a glimpse of one priest, noting the almost comical look of disbelief on his face.

As he slid his arms around her back, Erin looked up, her eyes windows into a landscape that he himself had never walked. He saw the light in her—so different from the white-fire that had burned there minutes earlier—pulsing softly, beautifully. When she shut her eyes, he could still see it. She tucked her chin into her neck.

He thought she slept, as she had done a month earlier, and was surprised to hear the soft whisper of her voice, almost inaudible even to his hearing.

"I'm afraid."

"There is nothing to fear, Sarillorn. The man will survive for tonight."

And for the third time that night she surprised him. She curled up against his chest, bringing her hands up to touch him. As she did, he saw the bands of her light come up and pass through and around him.

"There is nothing—to fear," he repeated.

But he wondered, as her breathing became deep and more regular.

What are you doing, Sarillorn? What is being done here?

chapter
eleven

Sarillorn, Rennath does not agree with you.

Stefanos turned away from the map he had created, and it vanished. At this moment it could not hold his consideration. He glanced out through windows that stretched from high ceiling to floor, opening like an eye into the night. Thick, red velvet had been pulled and bound by gold rope to allow the darkness to enter, or to watch.

For one week the Sarillorn had been in his palace. At the expense of great power, he had renewed the northern wing of the palace proper for her—not one of the lesser outbuildings—removing the frescoes and tapestries that he knew she would find disquieting. He had provided her with slaves, young and unbroken for the most part, and had given her more freedom in his domain than any mortal had ever dreamed of having.

He had not expected her to like Rennath overmuch, not to begin with. But he hoped, in time, that she would see the inevitable beauty of the city that he had built. He glanced up, and up again, to see the twin domes that had been carved and painted in the stone of this chamber. Beauty?

His feet made no sound as he turned and walked slowly to his throne, his human conceit. Five long, marble steps led up to it, and no other ever stood on the gold inlay of patterned floor that it crowned.

The priests were not happy about her presence; two had even gone so far as to question his command. He smiled grimly. Only two.

The smile vanished.

What he had done for her did not matter; he could almost wish that the trip to his capital had taken many months instead

183

of two. She would no longer eat with him and would speak very little when he arrived.

Almost wearily he sat in the contours of velvet, gold, and wood, his elbows touching smooth, hard armrests, his fingers making a steeple beneath his chin. He had thought long on these things, and no answers had come. He hated to be in ignorance.

He heard the rapping at the double doors that the priests used to enter and twisted his hand viciously. They swung open, revealing three people at the head of the hall that stretched into torchlit darkness.

Erin stared at him, tremulous and defiant, flanked on either side by priests. She was bleeding, the white of her dress already a deep, gorgeous crimson.

The sight of the blood as it trailed down her arm and side enraged him. The sight of the Malanthi, holding the chains that bound her wrists, filled him with a cold, wordless fury that even she could feel. She took an involuntary step back and the chains at her wrists grew taut.

The priests dragged her into the room.

"Lord." One of the men gave a deferential bow. Coppery thread winked in the light, revealing his rank. "This guest tried to interrupt the ceremony in the palace temple."

"Did interrupt it." Erin's voice, slightly shaky, carried an immeasurable wealth of satisfaction and pain. "Just not as much as I'd—"

The man who had not stepped forward slapped her almost casually, wiping the smile away. His face was red, the only trace of that color he wore. Acolyte, then.

The priest who had spoken looked down at his captive with a flash of annoyance before continuing. Stefanos recognized him: Derlac, one of the junior priests in the palace. The other man did not merit recognition.

"As she wears your mark, Lord, we thought it best to inform you of her crime before meting out the punishment it has earned."

One week. One week, Sarillorn, and you have already brought battle to my home.

"Continue."

Derlac looked carefully at the neutral mask of the Servant he addressed, then turned and whispered a few words to the acolyte. The younger man dragged Erin to her feet, where she swayed slightly before gritting her teeth. She would not meet the Servant's eyes.

"I see that my mark did not prevent you from damaging her."

"I regret to say, Lord, that we did not cause her wounds. We did manage to interrupt her before she could call full ward against us."

Almost perceptibly the tension ebbed out of the Servant. *True Wards in Rennath, Sarillorn?*

"I see."

A trace of relief crossed Derlac's face. "I have come to request your permission to continue the ceremony with the help of this young woman."

"Denied."

"But Lord, she's Lernari—" the acolyte began, outrage twisting his features.

"Craden!" Derlac hissed. The acolyte fell silent, his eyes smoldering with anger and confusion. He yanked at the chains and Erin nearly fell forward.

"I might add, Lord, that two of the Swords are near death— or dead."

"Denied."

"As you command, Lord."

Stefanos smiled slightly. Derlac was ambitious, but also perceptive. That was not uncommon among the half bloods. But he was cautious without being cowed, and this was rare. *A pity that he is not a more senior member of the Church. I shall have to alter that state of affairs.*

His gaze, as it touched the acolyte, was glacial. This man, on the other hand, was a fool; the type of fool that he tired of seeing make its way into the hierarchy.

"The worshipers, Derlac?"

"Under control, Lord. But it would be best to continue the ceremonies as soon as possible."

"Agreed. You acted with considerable circumspection and speed. Preside over the ceremony."

Derlac showed no hint of the pleasure that the Servant's command had given him. His face, smooth and placid, gave little away.

"As you command."

"Tell Geslik that it is a personal request of mine; I'm sure the high priest will understand."

At this the faint trace of a smile did touch Derlac's lips; it was gone before it became substantial.

"He will understand that it is your desire, Lord."

"Very good."

"And the woman, Lord?"

"Leave her with me. I shall make sure that she does not interrupt your mass in the future."

The priest bowed again, a low, crisp salute. As he turned to leave, Stefanos smiled softly. "Your acolyte did not have the wisdom not to restrain his hand when he knew she bore my colors. I am certain he would nonetheless be happy to grace the altars of the God he serves."

Guards had to be called to escort the acolyte out. Stefanos oversaw the proceedings with a cold amusement. It was a fitting fate for one who, in his presence, had dared lift a hand against one who was under his protection.

Erin kept her head bowed in her hands until the door closed on the pitiful sounds of the young man's pleas. She was tired of tears; it seemed to her that she had done nothing but shed them since her arrival in Rennath, this ugly, dark city. Nonetheless, tears trailed down her cheeks. She had not had any sleep in the past two days; the sounds of screaming echoed through her as if the ceremonies were being performed at the foot of her bed. And the slaves were afraid of her, and that hurt. In the heart of the Enemy's empire, everything she could do caused death, and yet to do nothing—to do nothing was worse.

She looked up to meet the unwavering eyes of the Servant.

"Come here, Sarillorn."

Wordless, she walked to the dais. Maybe this time he would be angry enough to call an end to it. Maybe she had done enough with her attempted ward to make him realize that she was, irrevocably, his enemy.

Stefanos's throne seemed impossibly high and far, but she forced her feet to cover the cold, hard marble as she mounted the steps. He did not rise to offer aid; waiting in his impeccable black robes, he was every inch the king. He waited. She came.

Inches away from the throne itself, she paused, numb with hope and fear as he reached out to touch the steel that bound her wrists.

The manacles snapped audibly and fell away in his hands.

"Your freedom."

She looked down at the rawness of skin that showed that she had struggled too hard against her chains. He caught her chin, forcing her to meet his eyes.

"Can you not leave well enough alone?"

She wanted to be angry; to feel again the righteous wrath that had been hers from the time of her investiture. She pulled weakly away from him, and he let her go in search of the fire that had vanished. She took a breath, then another, deeper one, and began to speak. She would not look back at him.

"Stefanos, Servant, nightwalker—whatever you are." The words trembled out of her lips; try as she might, she could not give them the force they merited. "Were it well, I would leave it, and gladly. But I cannot walk these halls without knowing that by night people die—people whom I might save with the blood of my birth. I'm the Sarillorn of Elliath."

"You are the Sarillorn, yes. But you are lost to Elliath now, and those that die are not numbered among your people. Do not let them concern you. There is nothing you can do."

Just as, she thought bitterly, *I could do nothing for my mother.* And it was worse here. The screaming never stopped. Late at night, she could no longer tell the difference between reality and memory.

"Power such as mine is only granted for one reason—to protect those with less, against yours."

"Power such as yours? Sarillorn, if the power that you wield is too great a responsibility, I will take it from you; you may then have peace, knowing that there is nothing at all that you can do."

She wheeled then, her hands coming up automatically between them, fingers awkwardly beginning their inimical dance in the air. Less frantically, but no less quickly, he mirrored her gestures. Still, he did not rise.

"Why will you not just accept what is? You have done as you will in my domain. I have exacted no price for actions that would be the death of any other."

"Why? I *am* your enemy here!"

"It does little harm."

She was speechless for a few moments; the color drained out of her face and returned as a darker red. Her hands flew up and a stream of blinding light flashed forward, unerring, to where he stood. Just as quickly his hands came up; the white-fire slid off a shield of faintly glowing red.

He thought her odd in anger; there was nothing cold in it. Take this strike: He was sure that if he allowed it to touch him, her anger would vanish completely. Not that he would take the chance, but still . . .

"Why?"

He sighed as she stood trembling with contained fury. Fury,

yes, but his blood-sense lingered over the familiar taste of despair and guilt as well. It was heady.

"Stefanos, please, finish this! Let me go to my people, or let me die—I don't care if it's a clean death anymore; I don't care if it's on your damned altars."

"Is it only death that you seek, Lady?"

"I don't have to seek it," was her bitter reply. "It comes all around me." All around, yes, but never did it come *to* her.

He watched her stiffen. Why not have an end? Why not kill her now, or lay her out on the altar of Malthan and set the minds of the priests at rest? Why not remove from himself all trace of the ambiguity that she evoked by presence alone?

Indeed.

But when he spoke, all he said was. "No. I will never release you. You will never leave."

He was not prepared for the speed of her answer, unaware until the moment the steel touched her flesh of the desperation behind the set of her lips. He did not pause to wonder where she had gotten a knife; if she had asked for it, it would not have been denied her. With a wordless cry of frustration he leaped to catch her as she crumpled. His hands on her shoulders were rough, but after a few seconds he became aware that he could not shake life into her on command. His hands curled around the handle of the knife and pulled it out, calling on power to hold her blood in—a particularly difficult task for a nightwalker. The knife had missed being fatal by very little.

"It hurts." Her eyes were wide, young eyes. They cut him, as the knife had cut her, but less cleanly. Her pain was subtle and beautiful, but he still did not desire her death.

He swept her up and headed into the hall. The irony of the situation was bitter. His power was not of the kind that encompassed healing; that was the domain of the Lernari and the Servants of the Bright Heart. Any such who might once have existed in his domains were long dead.

"This will please the Karnari, Sarillorn," he said through gritted teeth. "But I have already given you my word. I will not release you."

He looked at her as he walked, flinching at the shadows in her eyes. On impulse, his fingers stroked her brow gently, too gently for Erin to bear. She had never felt so helpless, never felt so lost or so trapped. She retreated into the black of unconsciousness.

* * *

Physicians saved Erin's life, thereby guaranteeing their own for a time.

She woke to spare, curtained twilight in a large, empty room. The ceilings were flat and plain, unlike the broad, wood beams and vaulted domes of her own quarters. The walls were gray rock, unadorned by windows, fireplace, or color. A man stood over her. She was momentarily confused, but disorientation gave way to memory.

"You're the Sarillorn of Elliath." His brows, as they drew together, were a winter frost with large streaks of black that hovered over his pale, brown eyes.

With a wan, cautious smile, she nodded.

The man ignored the offering of her smile. "I'm the former royal physician of Kerwin."

Her look cooled in response to his.

"They don't make you Sarillorn for nothing—or so I've been led to believe." There was an edge of anger in his words that Erin didn't understand. He waited for a response, but realizing that none was forthcoming, he went on. "Are you proud of that?" He gestured to the ugly welt below her breast, and she suddenly realized that she was unclothed. Blushing, she pulled up the thin covers. He gave the action a bitter smile. "Are you?"

Numbly she stared at him, her confusion evident.

He was not impressed. His broad arms covered the front of the large white apron he wore over a stiff, red tunic.

"If you're going to play stupid," he said cuttingly, "I'll be more specific. Are you proud of the fact that you tried to kill yourself?"

She balled her hands into the bed covers.

As if reading her mind, he continued. "You failed. And before you go off wailing in self-pity, I want you to know what your success would have cost: my life, the lives of my four assistants, and quite probably the lives of our families. And our deaths wouldn't have been nearly as clean or painless as yours." He paused again, waiting.

Erin closed her eyes. *More death. Lernan, everything I do in this cursed empire causes nothing but death. When will I be free of it?*

She was unprepared for the strength of the large, rough hands that gripped her shoulders, shaking her eyes open.

"Damn you! If he'd wanted you for the blood ceremonies, we would have let you die. We'd have accepted our fate in exchange for yours—the lines are our only hope and we owe them that much! But it isn't your death the Servant wants. The priests have demanded it, but he has refused."

"Leave me alone!"

"No!" But when he saw the flicker of response that broke through her numb silence, he let his hands fall away and stepped back to look at her.

"Sarillorn, how old are you?"

Dimly she replied, "I'm an adult of seven years."

He shook his head and brought a trembling hand up to massage his wrinkled temple. He walked the length of the room, his steps, like his words, terse and pointed.

"You're very young, then." He spoke as if to himself. "But you've been in battle?"

She nodded.

"Often?"

"Yes."

"And won." It was not a question.

She looked away. "Yes. You only fail once."

"Usually that means death?"

"Yes."

He hated the passivity of her answer.

"Then why aren't you already dead? Why are you trying to take your own life like this?"

"I don't know!"

"You're lying." He'd seen enough of people to know that much. He walked back to the foot of the bed. "Sarillorn, if you aren't the rescue we've been praying for, you owe us at least an answer. Why?"

She looked up to see the long brand on his right forearm. Like the rest, he was a slave. And he was right.

But it wasn't easy to give voice to her fears.

"I've been Sarillorn for three years now."

He was quiet.

"I've fought so many battles—I've always been so proud of that, of being able to defeat the enemy on any field that I could reach." She cast back. "I remember—I remember my first battle. I wasn't as sure of myself as I am . . .

"If you could have seen all the death—if you could have seen what had been done with the two villages that had tried to stand in the way of their army—"

Bitterly, but no more softly, the physician said, "I have."

She looked up at him then, as if clearly seeing him for the

first time. She held out one hand, and after a brief hesitation he took it.

"I was only a third. A good fighter, but not strong enough, not large enough. And too inexperienced. I got better over four years, but not enough. And the Lady of Elliath chose me to be Sarillorn."

He said nothing.

"I wanted her to choose someone else. I asked her why—why she wanted me."

Erin's voice trailed off. *Why? Why choose the only one of us who could never harness the power of God when it's needed—never except to save my own life.*

"What did she say?"

"She didn't answer directly. Instead she talked of Lernan's Hope, of the first Awakening—I don't think you know much of that. The gist of it is this: That in all darkness that exists now, there is some element of the light, and in the light, darkness." With a sharp, sudden motion, she freed her hand and brought it up to her cheek. Face beneath her hand, she stopped speaking for a moment.

She saw again the radiance of the Lady's face; the distant look of pity and some other thing unnamed and unknown.

"And she talked of the road walked between the dark and light, of the shadow that all light casts. I didn't understand her then—I was too new from battle, and the images of blood and death that came with Malanthi were close. Too close."

The physician rose and took a step back, turning his face to a blank wall. Erin didn't notice.

"But she said the road walked would be hard, harder than anything I could ever imagine. And I didn't understand.

"I only understood her when she spoke of necessity. When she told me that I alone of all her line could face the task that lay ahead, I was afraid and I was proud. I wanted to believe that I could be as good as other initiates, just once. That I could finally prove worthy of being adult."

"Sarillorn, what did she say?"

"She said that she had looked into the future; that she had seen a time when one of her line might pull, from darkness, a lasting light. She said that this was Lernan's Hope. And I thought she meant that through the light, through the Lernari, all darkness might finally die. I thought . . ." She stopped.

Gently, without looking at her, he spoke. "Sarillorn, what is your fear?"

"I know—I know what she meant now. I don't want to know it, but I do. You see, for some reason I don't understand, the Servant—Stefanos—listens to me. I can sometimes ask him for mercy, and he'll grant it. Not always." Her voice fell again. "On the march here, he never fed."

The physician's eyes widened with a wonder and a fear that he kept from the Sarillorn.

"So, for no reason, I have an effect. And I'm afraid that if the light can truly touch, truly change the darkness, then what can this darkness, stronger and older, do to the light?"

"And death is easier than facing the answer to that question?" His voice was harsh, but he kept his face turned away so that she would not see what was upon it.

In a simple, stark voice, she said, "I thought so."

"And now?"

"I don't know. Can you understand that? *I don't know.* What if I stay here, as he wants me to, and I grow numb enough, or changed enough, to hear the cries and the screams of the blood ceremonies without flinching—without even caring? What if I lose my sense of what I am and feel only relief that the victims on the altars aren't me? Can't you see how that's worse than any physical death, no matter how long or painful?

"And there's more." Now that she had started, she couldn't stop. "What if, by drawing out some semblance of humanity from a Servant of the Enemy, I lose sight of the evil beneath the façade? What if I learn to . . ."

"What?"

She started, choked, stopped, and with great care began again. "What if *I'm* the one who changes?"

He turned to her then, hearing the end of the sentence that she had not completed. "Sarillorn, you must be stronger than you know for the Lady of Elliath to make the choice that she did. Have you no faith in the head of your line?"

"It isn't—"

"It is. Sometimes hope is the refuge of fools and those who won't face reality. Sometimes hope is more than that—but the cost is high. When you became Sarillorn, you accepted the price for the power you were given. Don't prove false to your rank."

He could see tears begin to trace her cheeks, and he could see by the light of her eyes that she was fighting to contain them. He watched her a few moments, then began again, taking a different tack.

"Sarillorn, do this, not for yourself, not for us; we're lost and we know it. Do this for the future; do this knowing that you will be the hope of those yet unborn or untouched by the Enemy's hand. For hope we will risk much, but consider this: If you succeed, we have gained more than either of us can know.

"Sarillorn, we will rely on you."

The tears came freely as Erin cursed them. *I don't deserve the luxury of tears. I haven't earned them.* There was so much that she hadn't earned. But they fell anyway, and with them, resistance. She curled her arms around her body, bending forward into the sheets.

The physician watched her, torn. Silently he moved over to where she sat and reached out to touch her shoulder.

She didn't hear him move, too wrapped in her own care and fear to notice his. In turn, touched by her misery, he did not hear the door open, unaware when someone entered the room until hands gripped his neck. He was hauled backward and off his feet, then turned around to face the First Servant. The grip on his throat was too tight to allow for words; his eyes bulged slightly as his breath was cut off.

"What do you think you are doing, physician?"

The man's lips moved silently. His hands ineffectually struggled with the Servant's grip.

"You were brought to save the Sarillorn's life. You were not required to add to her pain." The Servant's hands tightened almost casually around the physician's neck. His eyes were a deep, livid red. "A pity that one so skilled at his allotted task should prove so unfortunately—"

"Stefanos."

Slowly, without releasing his victim, the Servant met Erin's gaze. The cold taste of anger faded as he read the rimmed green of her eyes.

"Sarillorn," he said gravely. "This man has obviously caused you distress."

"No."

"No?"

She smiled wanly. "Your hearing isn't as good as it was on our march here."

The look her comment evoked was a mixture of curiosity and, oddly, pleasure. Not since her arrival in Rennath had she even attempted to speak with humor. He was surprised to note that he'd almost missed it.

"No, then. But if not this slave, then what?"

In a clear, quiet voice, she said, "Rennath."

The physician fell to the ground. He brought shaking hands up to massage the five red lines that circled his throat.

The sound of his rasping breath brought a strange feeling to Erin. He was alive; she had asked for that.

You've saved his life, Erin, but for what? For the altars of the Enemy? For some painful servitude under a twisted noble? For a long, lingering, echo of life?

She pushed the bitter thought away firmly.

No. He said it for himself: I saved his life for the hope of a better one—for hope.

At what cost? Will you risk all you've been and believed in for something so nebulous?

Yes. Fully, completely, finally, Yes. I'll be the glimmer of light in the darkness of this empire. I'll do what I can, as I can, to alleviate the suffering I see around me. I'll be cruel enough to keep hope alive.

"Sarillorn?"

"Yes?"

"Would it trouble you if I remained?"

"No."

He started to speak, but Erin interrupted him. "Doctor?"

"Sarillorn?" His voice was still weak.

"Thank you."

The doctor gave her a very shaky bow. *I hope that I've done right by you, Sarillorn. You're very young.* But he felt, as he watched her, the faintest glimmer of pride.

The Servant's curt dismissal did nothing to alter the warmth he felt as he hurriedly left the room.

A Sarillorn of the lines walks among us yet.

chapter
twelve

"What is this?" The staccato beat of the words crackled through the still air. These chambers were second in importance only to the Lord's own, but they were much more finely appointed. Gold glimmered everywhere, on floor, wall, fireplace, and furniture. The inlay had been most costly; the rooms were not small.

Derlac bowed as the high priest, Geslik, looked up from his duties. He was a fastidious man, but during the more energetic activities performed even he could forget himself; little splatters of blood showed along his throat.

"The First, High Priest." He handed him a sealed note.

"And it cannot wait?"

Derlac looked down at the disfigured body that lay in the rounded groove of the floor. Wrists and ankles had been fastened to metal rings sunk into the marble, but they showed no movement. "I would not be here otherwise."

Geslik frowned; he disliked the tenor of the younger man's voice almost as much as he mistrusted his sudden rise within the hierarchy of the Church. He held out one red hand without further comment, and Derlac dutifully deposited the message. He then took a respectful step back, but did not leave the room. He had not been dismissed, and he was curious.

He watched as the red seal was broken by fingers still damp, as the scroll unfurled, and the color drained slowly from the high priest's face.

I warned you, he thought, but wisely held his peace. Not yet could he afford to antagonize Geslik.

"Call my guard." The high priest set the note aside. "Now."

"As you command." Derlac bowed again and left the room to follow his superior's orders. He went quickly to the south wing of the palace and summoned six of the Swords; the high priest had, by custom, twenty-four. Some day they would be his.

He followed them to the high priest's chambers, pausing along the way to alert the rest of the council's thirteen members.

"In fifteen minutes we meet in the outer chamber of the high priest."

They looked surprised, for the council was not due to meet for a fortnight, but they nodded and readied themselves.

Geslik had already taken the opportunity to reattire himself. Instead of temple black, he wore his full dress garments, with their high, red shoulders and one red slash across both front and back. He also wore the circlet.

"Derlac."

"High Priest, how may I serve?"

Geslik raised an eyebrow, but Derlac's words were harmless. "Summon the rest of the Greater Cabal."

"It is done." Derlac's bow was punctuation for the crisp, quick reply.

"Then take your seat in the council chambers. We have a matter of great urgency that must be dealt with immediately."

Derlac nodded again and walked to the far end of the room. He paused beneath the arch of the twin doors and looked at the long, empty table, with its thirteen chairs. The high-backed one was the only one he coveted; he was not fool enough to take it yet. He waited.

"You made all of this?" Erin looked up, her face almost at a right angle to the rest of her body.

"Not all." Stefanos replied, as he stood in the shadows of the pillars in the main courtyards. Daylight was almost gone, and soon he could walk freely by the Sarillorn's side.

She glanced quizzically back at him, and he studied the lines of her face; he could still see them perfectly.

"No, Sarillorn." He smiled. "No human hands designed or built the foundations; even these arches are not the product of mortal labor." He gestured toward the east wing. "But Sargoth built that; and even now, when he wanders it, he destroys any new additions—unless they are mine."

"Sargoth?"

"The Second of Malthan. No, the name means little to you because he does not choose often to roam the mortal world. He is different from the rest of Malthan's Servants."

"Mortal worlds?"

"Ah." He smiled. "There are three 'worlds' that you know of, although only one is available to you. The hand of the Bright Heart, the hand of the Dark Heart, and the body of the two."

She nodded.

"There are, or so Sargoth tells me, others—stranger than the three, with their own odd laws. It does not trouble me; only Sargoth has had the patience and time to find the pathways to them."

He walked toward her, risking the touch of the sun's last rays. They were uncomfortable, but weaker in their dying than they were in their beginning.

"But come, you have not seen all of my palace—and only the smallest portion of my lands." He saw her face darken slightly, but she nodded. He couldn't help but smile; his order must already have reached the high priest, and from this eve on, the Sarillorn would know some measure of peace within his walls.

But he did not tell her; not yet. Rather, as she discovered the architecture and glory of his palace, he wished her to learn it for herself. They began to walk side by side down the long, tall cloisters.

Geslik placed the scroll on the council table. "This is the reason I have summoned you."

Serlin, the second most senior member of the Church, raised an eyebrow over the near black of his eyes; he was strong of blood, but old. "The seal of the First. Is there a great danger from the front?"

"It is worse than that." Geslik leaned forward, his eyes darkening. "The First Servant requires us to cease all blood ceremonies within the confines of his palace."

Only Derlac had any suspicion of the news, but even he fell silent as it was confirmed for the first time. As ever, he kept his own counsel.

Serlin found voice first. "Pardon?"

"It is as I said." Geslik handed the offending scroll to Serlin. "Read it if you cannot believe it. You will find it bears his mark."

Normally Serlin would have bypassed such an offer, but the import of Geslik's message did not allow it. He scanned the document, pausing at the last to note the faint glow of the Lord's mark. The scroll fluttered gently to the table.

"Why?" he asked, visibly shaken. "The Church's heart is

within the south wing of the palace. It is here that the nobility
comes to worship; it is here that we deal with the blooded lead-
ers. He cannot expect—''

"He can," Geslik replied bitterly. "He has."

"Surely God cannot allow—" A new voice broke in, younger
but harsher, as befitted the craggy face that accompanied it.

"Don't be a fool, Morden. The Dark Heart does not interfere
with the general of his forces."

"But why would the Lord choose to cripple His Church in
this fashion?"

Uncomfortable glances were exchanged as the question remained unanswered.

"Sarillorn."

She turned her face away from the open breeze that touched
her hair. "Yes?"

"Do you see the lights of my city?"

She nodded. "Yes. But they look so far away."

He smiled. "It is the effect of the spires; they are very tall."
He was not sure why he added the last piece of information; it
was obvious by the way she gripped the stone that she was aware
of it.

"It isn't just the height," she answered softly. "Elliath—my
home—has more light than this, though I doubt it's a tenth of
the size."

"It is smaller, yes. Less grand than my work."

She fought the urge to reply immediately and found it less
difficult than she had expected. "It's darker here."

"Yes. But I do not need the light to see by."

"Oh."

"Would you care to see more of the city?"

"Now?" she asked, looking doubtfully into the dark night
sky.

"It is the only time I can show it to you."

"Oh." It was true, of course. But to wander the heart of the
empire she'd fought so long against, by the side of its ruler . . .
She pulled back from the edge. "I—yes. Yes."

She turned to walk back to the large door and froze as he
touched her arm.

"This way, Sarillorn."

She drew back, and he let her go.

* * *

"And if she is not the cause, what is?"

"But she's only Lernari—and he is the First of God. He could not—"

"He can do whatever he wishes. He has the power for it."

"He cannot wish to allow this—this taint to corrupt the Church. It is not within the realm of the believable."

"Then what else can be the cause of it? She is here, yes." Geslik frowned, recalling the moment of elation he had felt upon first seeing her. That had vanished as soon as the First Servant had made clear that she was not to be given to him. "And she is not dead. She has not graced the altars of God."

"No."

"I begin to believe there is truth to the rumors." All heads turned to face Derlac, who had so far been silent.

"Rumors?" Geslik said testily.

"Among the Swords. The Karnar that accompanied the army attempted to secure the Sarillorn's death. He failed, purchasing his own in the bargain."

"She killed him?"

"No. The First did." Derlac paused for effect. "During the dawn."

Silence then.

The streets were dark, darker than she could have imagined from the heights of the spires. Only once before had she spent time in the darkness of city streets, but that was Karana, and it had fallen. Buildings pressed in at all sides, impossibly tall, impossibly close. She thought them stone, for the most part, with wood used occasionally as an afterthought, but there was little grass, little tree cover, and no forest voices to lessen the night. Erin walked slowly, letting her feet touch uneven cobblestone before taking a firm step. Here and there lamplight made circles upon the ground, but they were small, and Stefanos avoided them.

"Sarillorn, do you see this?"

"Not clearly. It looks like a square."

"It is. And around it, statues that commemorate—" He stopped as she stumbled again. "Why do you not call your light, little one?"

She looked back in the direction of his voice. "Because I know it makes you uncomfortable." *And I don't know if I could stop with light, not here.*

Her answer surprised him, as she so often could. He reached out, touching her right shoulder with his left hand.

She froze again and he released her.

"I see," he said, as if to himself. Very slowly, he held out his arm. "Would it trouble you to accept my aid?"

She looked at the arm he offered. Hesitantly, she touched it with her hand as if skimming the edge of a finely honed blade. She was shaking.

"Sarillorn, you have nothing to fear."

He had said it so often, but in this darkness that was almost complete, she thought she might believe it—perhaps because she wanted to. Her grip was tentative and shaky, but she held on to him as he began to walk toward the center of the square.

He stared down at her, his vision giving him the advantage. Her lip was between her teeth, but she walked within the reach of his shadow. She had accepted his guidance.

"Here, Sarillorn." He stopped in front of the foremost statue. "This is representative of the Second of Malthan."

She shook her head. "I can't quite make it out."

"Touch it, then. Let your fingers see what your eyes will not."

She hesitated, and he touched her hand, gently guiding it forward.

"These," he said, as her fingers ran along smooth, worn stone, "are how the mortals see us."

"Cold," Erin whispered, "and hard. Are they red?"

"No. No more than you are pale green. No more than you are the light." He drew her away, knowing that she was disturbed again. There must be something in his city that would truly please her.

"And I must warn you again, High Priest," Derlac said, bowing his head respectfully, "that your idea is not a wise or prudent one."

"We have no choice." Geslik stood, signaling an end to the meeting.

Derlac ignored this; a breach of etiquette, but not, he hoped, a dangerous one.

"The Lord must have some plan for her that he does not wish to share with us."

Geslik frowned slightly—a bad sign. "What of it? If he wishes to play his games with the Sarillorn, he would be wise to restrict them to matters that do not affect the Church."

No one spoke. Each of the council members avoided the eyes of the others. To thwart the First Servant was never wise. But to cancel the blood ceremonies was also unthinkable; it would cost them too much of the power they needed.

"It is decided, then. In three days?"

Only Derlac spoke. "I caution—"

"Good."

Thus dismissed, Derlac did not care to speak further. He heard the high priest call his Swords and command them to bring five of the slaves from the east wing.

Three days. Derlac thought carefully on all of his options, then nodded quietly to himself. Perhaps this was a good time to visit the lands of his family.

But first he had one duty to attend to.

It was just after midnight when they returned to the palace. Erin was silent; she drifted across the threshold of the gates as a ghost might. The road to the palace proper stretched on nearly half a mile.

"Sarillorn."

She looked away from him. She hadn't realized how hard it would be to wander through Rennath, with its isolated meager light; to know where the nobility lived, in grand and glorious mansions; and know that there, too, dwelled the slaves that had once been free under the protection of the lines.

"Sarillorn." His voice, for all its quiet, held the chill of the dark.

She looked up warily as she passed the gate. Here, at least, light shone in abundance, reflecting the red slash across the black armor of the Swords. No ordinary guards, these. She eyed them warily, but they gave no notice of her passing; she was with the First Servant.

"What—what time is it?"

"Midnight."

She tensed visibly. He thought she might speak; she started to. But she bit back the words and walked on.

Midnight. The time for the ceremonies. She almost asked him to take her back to the city outside of his walls. It was easier in that darkness to imagine that her companion was human. She did not ask it. She was Sarillorn, and in this land she could not dare to ignore the true meaning of darkness.

She listened; she couldn't help it. Even in the north wing, the screams could still reach her. She had become known for her hearing among the line with good reason.

There was silence. It stretched on, like a fabric pulled so taut it had to tear. And she walked along the edge of it, waiting.

The First Servant escorted her back to her rooms. "I have taken the liberty of ordering a meal that we might both partake of. Would it trouble you if I remained?"

She didn't answer. How could it not "trouble" her? How could she eat with the sound of the dying playing its dissonant chords in the background?

She walked, the edge growing fine and sharp beneath her feet.

I made my choice.

But it was hard. She had only managed to stay abed these last few days because she was too weak for combat. But tonight— tonight she should—

I made my choice.

She stopped when he did, realizing that they stood outside her rooms—rooms, so grand and glorious, that had probably housed priests or visiting nobility. Open these doors, and the richness of dark wood, with old, perfect chairs and low tables, would greet her eyes. Beyond that another room, with a fireplace that slaves attended to, and a dining hall, with twin doors that led to a bedroom more spacious than her house had been.

Everything that she had ever learned strained against her control. Soon it would start again. Soon, the priests would have their rituals, their blood, and their slow, agonizing death—and they would gain power from it, power to spread the law of the Dark Heart.

She leaned her forehead against the door, biting down on her lip until she drew blood.

"Sarillorn?"

She turned, then, her eyes blazing in the darkness. He took a step back, but went no further.

Her hands fell to her sides rigidly, ending in small fists. And around her, in his eyes alone, the light twisted and buckled. *No.* He reached out to touch her; she drew back, hitting the door with the force of the step.

He knew what words would calm her, then. Although he had hoped she might discern this for herself, perhaps it was better; this way he might see the easing of the light that looked so strangled.

"Sarillorn." He touched her trembling jaw and she drew her head up, the way a horse might, in anger or fear. "There will be no ceremonies this eve."

He waited, watching for some sign from her. There was none, and after a moment he continued. "There will be none in the palace from this day forward." He drew back as the light continued to twist. *Perhaps,* he thought, as he watched her face, *I was wrong.*

But no, the light suddenly surged; it grew stronger, touching even the lines of her face as her eyes grew slowly wide.

"Would it trouble you if I remained?"

She stared up at him, her head moving slowly from side to side, her mouth wide.

"No ceremonies?" she whispered. "No blooding of the altars?"

"None, Sarillorn. None, where you are present."

As if cut from her supports, she staggered forward, her arms reaching for him.

She felt the darkness that lay beneath velvet within the circle of her arms. To her surprise, there was nothing cold about it. It had been a long time since she had hugged anyone; a long time since arms had circled her shoulders in return.

Thank you. But she could not say it, not yet.

He felt the touch of her light and smiled. That smile remained as she pulled back, looking suddenly at the ground, her feet, the wall—anything but him.

"Dinner?" he asked quietly, as he opened the door to her rooms.

She nodded, still unable to meet his eyes.

This did not bother him. The light shone, this night, for him; it was his. As, in the end, all things must be.

That night, he fed for the first time in nearly two months. He waited until the Sarillorn slept and drifted out of her room, each step taken as if in time to the even, shallow intake of her breath.

He chose, from the dungeons of his palace, a young man for his purposes. The smell of the man's fear pulled at him as the Swords delivered his chosen to the east wing. It had been too long.

He stepped quickly into his personal chambers. They were utterly black, without the taint of even the faintest hint of light, natural or no. He preferred this; only here, without the presence of mortals or the meager torches they carried, did he care to relax and take his pleasure.

"Here." The word came from the darkness that light couldn't travel into.

The Swords nodded in silence. He approved of this; whether they were half blood or no, they felt no pity or sympathy for the human they dragged into death. They forced the struggling human to the brink of the darkness and threw him in. Then they withdrew, the captain's salute crisp and respectful.

The Servant of the Dark Heart crossed the threshold, already stalking his prey. Anticipation curled his lips over the sharp points of his teeth. He could feel the screams shudder through him as the door closed behind his back.

Derlac stood in the dimly lit hall. He could only barely hear the screams that came from behind the closed door; they were shorter, though no less intense, than the ones that usually came from the Lord's chambers.

He waited, glancing around from time to time. His blood was strong enough to allow him to see the detailed work of stone statues that stood posted as a warning at the single, stone door to his Lord's chambers. They were human in shape, one female, one male, and each face and body was contorted in silent agony—simple work; an elegant statement. He turned again and looked down the long stretch of halls that ended with stairs leading upward.

It was absolutely vital that no other eyes saw him here. But rare indeed was the message that would cause any priest to wait outside these doors for long; he looked in vain before turning back to wait.

He wondered how long the First Servant had been thus ensconced. He did not have much time; his coach was already waiting and prepared to carry him to the Valens estate to the south of the city. It was risky, this choice, but seemed to augur best for the future. If he had judged the Servant correctly, his warning would gain him much, not the least of which was permanent relief from Geslik's stupidity and arrogance.

He heard another scream, but again it was quiet; almost subdued. It choked away into silence, as it had done several times. But this time the silence held.

Derlac waited. Often the Servant gave his victim some respite, to play upon a hope and relief he could then use to his advantage. And only once in history had anyone interrupted the Lord before he had finished his feeding. Derlac gave an involuntary shudder at the thought of that fool's fate. Especially now, when he could understand how such a mistake might be made.

He counted time by the heartbeat.

At last, when he was as confident as he could be, he knocked lightly on the Lord's door.

It swung open smoothly and silently into a darkness that even Derlac's Malanthi eyes could not easily penetrate. Outlined by the door, the priest gave a very low, very respectful bow. It was one of the few times that he meant everything that the gesture implied. But he waited at the door; very few willingly crossed into the Servant's territory, and Derlac was not one of them.

"Derlac." The voice that came out of the darkness was low, almost feral in quality.

Derlac prayed seldom; he prayed now.

"Lord." He kept his own voice as steady as he could.

The First Servant materialized inches away from his bowed head. Derlac did not look up; he had not yet been granted leave, and here of all places protocol was essential.

"Be at ease, Karnar—if you can."

No human eyes would have seen the signs that Derlac displayed as he relaxed. But human notice was not his concern here. He looked up and saw the First Servant as few saw him: after the glory of feeding. His entire form, shadowed and dark, glowed with the red of the power he'd gained. Here, in his chambers, he made no pretense of humanity. His face was shadow, his arms dark mist, his body a swirl of silent motion.

"Why have you come?"

Derlac did not look away from the red glow of the Lord's eyes. "To render a service."

Low laughter answered him. "You think to be of service to *me*?" The laughter ceased abruptly. "Call the Swords, then. Have them dispose of the body." He turned and started to dissolve into darkness.

"Lord, a moment, please."

The Servant turned again. "Yes?" he asked softly.

"I have—I have delivered the message you left with me." He almost took a step back then, for the smile that the Servant gave was dangerous.

"I see."

"The high priest called council for it."

"What of it? The council is of little concern to me."

"To you, Lord, no." Derlac drew himself up. "But to the Sarillorn . . ." He watched as the Servant froze.

"The Sarillorn?" Darkness limned in red stepped forward; an arm reached out of the mist as if that were all that remained of a dissolving body. Derlac did nothing to avoid the claw that grabbed his robes and held them in a vise.

"Yes, Lord," he answered, playing as close to the edge as he dared. "I would have informed you at a time more convenient to you, but I find it expedient to visit the estates of House Valens, and I leave at dawn."

The grip tightened. "Priest." The word was a sibilant whisper; there was a death in it.

Derlac spoke quickly then, striving to deliver that death to anyone else.

"Lady?"

Erin looked up in confusion and shook her head, struggling out of the grip of feathered quilts. Then the room coalesced, its high ceiling and quiet tapestries telling her clearly where she was. Sunlight shone openly through the large bay of the window in the northern wall, lighting off the small blue flowers that had been set there.

"Lady?"

"Yes?" She shook the sleep out of her voice and tried again. "Yes?"

"I've brought your breakfast."

Erin's eyes fell upon a young girl in a scoop-necked cream-colored dress. She carried a small tray across long, thin arms and stood just inside the large, mahogany doors.

"Come in," Erin said, smiling.

The girl did not meet her eyes. Rather, she scurried as quickly as the tray would allow. Reaching the bedside table, she laid it down, hiding her eyes beneath a short spray of delicate brown hair.

Laid in white relief against the bare pink flesh of her right arm was a long scar.

"Thank you," Erin whispered.

The girl didn't respond. She pulled back and away, fleeing the room with what dignity her fear would allow her.

Erin watched the slave go. She wanted to call her back. If she had been anywhere else she would have; the fear at least she could have comforted. Even knowing where she was, it was hard to still that urge. But she did, turning without appetite to the breakfast that had been laid out for her.

I have to ask Stefanos if these slaves are mine. She shuddered a little, thinking on it: She would be asking to own slaves.

Yes. She raised the top of the tray. *But if I own them, I can*

decide their fate. I can protect them. And maybe, if they under-
stand that, they might come to trust me.

It would certainly make this morning ritual more bearable.
Restless, she rose, leaving blue-patterned covers askew, to look
out the window. Morning? She sighed. Afternoon, then.

She walked over to her closet; Stefanos had shown it to her
on her first night there, but she had not yet dared to open it.

What do you expect to find there, she chided herself, as her
hand touched the doorknob. *Bodies?*

No, it held finery, dresses such as she had never imagined,
let alone seen. She wanted to laugh then, and surprised herself
by doing so. Only twice in her life had she ever worn a dress.
How on Earth could he imagine that she would ever wear any
of them? They weren't in the slightest bit practical—she couldn't
fight in them—

The laughter died abruptly.

Of course she couldn't fight in them. She wasn't expected to,
here. None of her fighting would be done in the drill circle or
on the field; no sword blow, no physical maneuver, could accomplish the goal that she had set for herself.

But sunlight refused to let all of the darkness in.

No ceremonies. She reached out, her hand brushing against
deep blue velvet and smooth, clean silk. *No blooding of the
altars.*

For that she was willing, even able, to wear what he had
chosen for her.

At least she was willing. But as she pulled a blue velvet dress
out of the closet, she wondered if she was able. The back of it
was a maze of tiny, glittering buttons. She looked at them closely
and thanked the Bright Heart that she'd not had enough experience with jewels to be able to tell if they were all real.

But real or not, there must be at least fifty of them, and most
of them were placed in such a way that she alone would not be
able to close them all.

She put it back, feeling its weight. *They can't all be like this.*
Much to her horror, she found that they were.

How on Earth, she thought, half an hour later, *can anyone
be expected to wear these? You'd need a small army of servants
to—*

Or slaves.

Erin. She shook herself. *He promised there would be no
blooding of the altars. Remember that.*

It helped.

* * *

The chairs, even the single ones, that populated her sitting room made her feel even smaller than she was as she sat very stiffly in them. When the knock on the door came, she leaped to answer it.

"Sarillorn."

Erin looked up to see that the First Servant's face was inches away—as it had been just the evening before. All the words that she had wanted to say for the entirety of the day fled her suddenly trembling lips. She nodded unsurely.

"Are you troubled?" His voice felt like the velvet of the first dress she'd touched.

"No," she managed to get out.

"Do you mind if I enter?"

"N-no, of course not."

He looked at her, the barest hint of red in the depths of his eyes. She was frightened. Almost against his will, he felt a flicker of anticipation at the touch of it. But it was no ordinary fear that she felt; it was tangled with everything that she was. He smiled.

"Sarillorn, I can hardly enter if you continue to stand in the doorway."

"The—" She blushed and took a quick step back. "Oh." She took another step back involuntarily.

He followed. She was afraid, yes. But not in the way that she had been at any other time. The lamplight glinted off the sudden display of his pointed, pale teeth.

You are afraid. He stepped forward again and closed the door very firmly behind him. *Of me.* He felt the force of her fear; heard the sudden clamoring of her heart as clearly as he had heard the few words that she had spoken. *Of me.*

He spoke no words as he took another step toward her; she spoke none as she retreated into a room that was suddenly too small and too crowded.

And this, this was normal. This paralysis, this sudden tension, was something he was accustomed to viewing in the eyes of the mortals who could actually see him—and who knew what his presence meant.

He touched her chin, his forefinger curling gently under the line of her jaw as she froze, the backs of her knees against the low table.

"Sarillorn."

She had never heard such sibilant death in a voice, not even on the first day that she'd encountered him. He was shadow, he was darkness, he was the cold container of red-fire. She felt his fingers bite into the line of her jaw in a sudden, painful clamp.

Her throat suddenly dry, she tried to pull back.

He showed her all the menace a gentle smile could contain. With a strength that could not be denied, he pulled her face toward his.

White-fire seared his unprepared hands.

With a harsh curse, he threw her and she staggered back, her hands trembling in air in a silent language he knew well.

"You *dare*?" he whispered, as red engulfed his no-longer-human hands. "After what I have done for your sake?" His flesh grayed as he cast aside his mortal countenance. He was the First of Malthan, the most powerful of his kind. And she—she was little better than mortal; even the taint of her blood could not save her from age, from death, or from his rage.

She stood, not five feet away, her hands raised against him, her eyes living green. It was her eyes that caught him unprepared.

They were wide, unblinking emeralds. He saw her trace her Greater Ward across the air and noticed that her hands were shaking.

"Stefanos," she whispered, "why?"

He owed her no answers. He walked through her ward with contemptuous ease and reached for her shoulders, striking her raised arms away.

She froze again, as a rabbit does before the hawk strikes. This time he understood her terror well. She was mortal; she was female.

"Are you frightened?" he asked, in a conversational tone. His hands tightened on the shoulders of her robe, and it fell back, exposing the whiteness of her breasts.

White-fire flared again, but this time he was ready for it. It crackled uselessly against a shield of red and disappeared.

She struggled, as many others had struggled, her strength muted by the paralysis of denial. He thought he had long since grown bored with this particular, bloodless sport. It was subtle, and the pain it afforded his pleasure was slow to take root in his victim.

But he felt all her fear; it went deep, into darker regions than the Sarillorn had faced before. He could see the rise and fall of her shortened breath as his hand pressed over her heart, leaving its mark.

Almost intoxicated by it, he forced her to the floor, casually kicking the table across the room. He looked down at her white body as it moved in the frame of gold carpet, her auburn hair a spray of darkness.

It was not the first time she had been afraid—but it was the first time she had gifted *him* with her fear.

Inexplicably, she ceased her struggles, although the fear, if anything, had grown stronger. He lowered his mouth until his teeth pressed into the skin of her throat without ever tasting blood. He pulled the torn dress away, throwing it just out of the reach of her open hands.

Then he stopped a moment, raising himself on his arms to look at her. Her eyes were closed, her lips parted in silence. Tears trailed silently out of the corner of her eyes, to rest against the pillow of her hair.

The taste of his victory turned to ash.

For less of a crime than this he had bisected one of his Swords.

But she is mine.

Her eyes opened, met his, and closed again. She was trembling.

With effort he pulled himself away from her and stood.

"Sarillorn."

She did not, could not, answer. The robe lay, as she did, where it had fallen.

He should say more. He knew it. But he found himself trembling as well. He did not want to destroy her, to destroy her light; but he felt the desire to take and twist the fear that she offered. He took a step forward.

She is mine.

But not—not like this. Not like any mortal cattle that had been paraded before him, for his pleasure alone. For he felt certain that this pain would destroy the light that she alone could offer.

That knowledge was almost not enough.

With a snarl, he turned his back on her prone body and walked to her closed door. He gripped the handle of it, shaking.

Mine.

Another snarl, lower and more visceral. He swung the door open and left the room, slamming it behind him.

He left his mark in the bronze handle.

"With all due respect, Lord, I do not think that you can be of any aid here."

Erin heard the physician's words clearly. Her eyes turned to face the window of her room; night had almost fallen. She gathered the folds of blankets and covers and pulled them up to her chin.

She knew who it was.

He was the only one who ever visited.

Don't—don't let him in. But it was a hopeless thought; the First Servant walked exactly where and when he pleased.

As if to bely this, minutes dragged by. The doctor returned to the room, lighting the three lamps that were gathered near her bed. His face was still and pale as he went about this task.

The Servant had not entered.

Erin relaxed, but only marginally. It was dark here, even with the lamplight.

"Is he . . ."

"Outside the door," the man replied, his hands already closing the heavy curtains.

She wanted to ask him not to leave, but bit her lip instead. If she, the Sarillorn of Elliath, could be so afraid—why was she shaking?—she could not ask anyone else to face the Servant.

"Are you hungry?"

She shook her head; the exact motion that had also refused a morning and afternoon meal.

"Sarillorn."

She looked up. The physician stood no more than two feet away.

"You must eat something." He had difficulty meeting her eyes. He didn't know what had happened, but it was easy enough to guess.

"Tomorrow," she said softly.

He sighed, looking up at the closed door. She followed his gaze and then looked away.

Of all things that she had been prepared for, this was not one. She had fought in her share of battles, taken her share of injuries. She closed her eyes. She was bruised, slightly scratched, but whole. Why—why was she shaking?

It wasn't as if she hadn't been hurt before. Two years ago, she'd taken a wound to her left breast from a spear thrust on the field. Her armor, light and simple, had been torn; although she'd managed to stop the bleeding, she had continued to fight half-naked.

Why was this worse? Her hands crushed the sheets between tight fists.

She knew what he had intended. It had happened to others before, and she'd had to calm and heal any number of villagers who'd had worse done to them than she had.

She curled her knees tightly up to her chest.

He—stopped. She told herself. *He didn't—he didn't . . .*

"Sarillorn."

She shook her head, a tight, sharp snap of motion. Her eyes cleared and she looked around at the points of light the lamps provided. Those lamps stood between her and the First Servant.

The doctor was no longer anywhere in sight.

He saw the shadows that marred the whiteness of her face. More clearly, he saw the broken trail of light that ringed the tight curl of her body.

Something foreign touched him then: relief. He stood barely inside the room, the open door at his back.

"Sarillorn," he said again, more clearly.

He felt all her fear as it reached for him. It was stronger than before, but he expected it now. He held his place. "Have you eaten?"

She almost didn't understand his words. *Eaten?* she thought. *No. No, I haven't.* She looked up, shaking her head when the words wouldn't come.

"I see."

She tensed, but he stayed put, a shadow with no body to cast it against the paneled wood.

"Will you eat?"

She shook her head again.

"Sarillorn." It was not easy to speak. "I told you, you have nothing to fear from me." In spite of his resolve, he found himself a few steps closer to where she sat beneath her cloth shields.

Does she think that they stop me? He pulled himself back. Never before had it been important to still or calm fear; fear and pain were the things in mortals that had, until now, been most beautiful and compelling.

And in her he felt them more strongly than he had felt them in centuries.

He allowed himself to smile at the irony of it.

The smile dimmed.

"Sarillorn."

Her eyes were flat and lifeless.

"It is—it is not easy for me to be here."

She heard the words, but had no response to offer; none but the fear. He hoped that later she might remember what he said.

"You have shown no fear of me; no fear of the death that I mean to your kind, not until last night." He turned away. "I do not understand why. But when I came to you, I had no intention of harming you; no intention of doing other than dining, as we have done these past months.

"I do not understand the nature of the fear you felt before I touched you." He shook himself and reached for the door frame. "But I understand the fear you have now. Understand that I do not wish to cause it. And understand, little one, that we are both drawn to fear and pain—but for different reasons.

"I will leave you in peace this night. I have"—he smiled again, bitterly—"the physician's word that my presence is likely to cause harm.

"But tomorrow on the eve, if you are strong enough, I would be honored if I might remain."

He looked at her then, for the last time that evening.

She saw the hunger in his eyes, but beneath that there was something else. Pain?

Are we both called to it? She watched him leave as relief crawled slowly in.

chapter
thirteen

"Sarillorn?"

Erin smiled almost shyly as she met the physician's surprised gaze. The door framed her almost exactly, and she stood so still she looked like one of the portraits that hung in the grand hall of the priests. No, not so like, for while she wore an emerald-green gown, with the low, square, lace-bordered neck that had been fashionable in the older years, her face was open and friendly, even though her smile was hesitant and questioning. He shook himself and stepped back, opening the door.

"I wanted to thank you," she said, as she entered the small infirmary and looked around at the plain, blank walls.

"Are you feeling well?" His own glance strayed to the row of four single beds, each covered in two plain, white sheets. Sick beds did not suit her attire.

She nodded. "I—"

"Do you want to lie down?"

"No. I just wanted to—"

"Did you sleep, then?"

She laughed. "Doctor, please, I—"

"Why don't you—"

"Doctor!"

He stopped. "Yes?"

"I wanted to tell you that I slept through the evening. It's probably why I'm awake so early." She caught his arm, her smile still quiet. "Thank you. You told him—you told the Servant not to stay. He didn't."

Erin thought the relief on the doctor's face was stronger than the relief she herself had felt. They stared at each other for a moment in happy silence, and if she wore the dress of nobility, and he of well-regarded slave, no one was there to notice. Then, as if only just aware of the surroundings, the doctor drew back.

"Is there anything else I can do for you?"

"I hoped that I might be able to be useful here." She looked around doubtfully at the empty beds. "I didn't want to just lie around my rooms today."

"Understood." The doctor shook his head. "But we don't see too many injured here." His face darkened. "Usually if someone is injured they don't get treated."

Erin was silent for a moment. It was strange to be in an infirmary that was so ghostlike in its emptiness.

"Sarillorn."

She smiled sadly. "If you ever need help . . ."

He caught her hand and held it tightly. "I think," he said softly, "that if you're here, I—"

They both turned at a sudden sound.

The door flew open. Daylight glinted off black surcoats and drawn swords. These uniforms were crisp and clean, and across each, red glittered like a jeweled wound. Six Swords.

The doctor rose immediately, putting Erin firmly behind him. "What may I—"

He never finished the sentence.

Erin had seen Swords on the field before; they were fast, even armored. A weapon swung and stopped in the doctor's body. She reached for her own sword automatically, before remembering that she hadn't carried one for months. Tensing, she began to back away.

The Swords circled her, pressing her back. They did not strike. She stopped wondering why when a man in archaic red robes bent slightly to enter the infirmary. A red hood of stiff silk rose from his shoulders, a misplaced crown for the head of the Karnari. He was tall, even without it, his shoulders were wide, and his face a study of angular grimness. *High priest.*

"Sarillorn." He smiled.

Something about his tone was familiar. She swallowed, recognizing the ancestors of the Malanthi. For a moment the priest's face seemed to gray into darkness and shadow.

She shook herself. This man—this one she understood.

"Karnar." She smiled in return, but it was a frozen, cold expression.

"Dressed for the occasion." His sneer took in the collared velvet and lace. "And unarmed." He motioned to the Swords. "How unwise."

Erin looked at him carefully. Her smile almost faltered when she caught the sudden brilliance of his power; it glowed like the dying sun.

She turned slowly to look at the Swords and sagged. Against the high priest alone she might show her measure, but there were too many others.

Swords took her by the arms. She did not resist.

"Very good," the priest said, as she was dragged past him. "I was afraid that we would have to kill you here—and I am a man who enjoys a more leisurely form of entertainment."

The halls were empty—almost suspiciously so. Nothing stopped the Swords from leading Erin to the south wing of the palace.

"A precaution, Sarillorn. Any slave found in these halls at this time has volunteered for the ceremonies we will perform tomorrow evening."

Ceremonies? Erin shrunk inward. Now she understood why they had come.

But Stefanos said—

She stopped for a moment; the guards dragged her off her feet. Turning her head—which was difficult in the position she was held in—she said, "The First will not be pleased."

"No." The high priest's smile rippled uncertainly before once again emerging whole. "But unfortunately he is not here to consult. He never walks in daylight."

"You can't possibly think he'll accept—"

"Accept what? It is not our duty to guard you, Sarillorn. When you have chosen to flee the palace, what can he do? Hunt you, perhaps. But as Sarillorn of Elliath, you are clever and not without power of your own. I do not believe he will find you when he searches.

"Hurry." His voice grew sharp.

The halls unfolded rapidly before them, turning into the towering arches that lay at the palace's center. Tapestries, all black and red flesh, hung on the wall declaring whose wing the south was. Erin shuddered. The artist that had captured so much human pain with mere wool must have been Malanthi.

She wasn't given the time to take a more leisurely look at them; the doors of the temple were upon her.

Like much of the decor, they were black, with metallic red detailing and ruby work. But even these were not for her eyes; they swung open quickly, revealing almost endless height and majesty. Artists had worked here, too, painting frescoes chaot-

ically from one end of the hall to the other—black, red, and
pale, pale pinks and browns. She could almost hear them
screaming.

Through the doors lay the altar, some sixty feet back. It hung
as if suspended by the red lines that were wrapped around it,
protecting the consecrated ground from light. Like the doors it
was black, and it shone as if it were oiled.

Around the altar stood nine men, in vestments similar to those
the high priest wore. Similar, but lesser, an elegant red silk,
with traceries of black and formal hoods that had been carefully
arranged around their shoulders. All of them glowed distinctly
more brightly than their own power would have allowed.

They prepared for this. I should have been more careful.

"You're late," one man murmured, as the Swords dragged
her up to the altar.

"The Sarillorn was not in her quarters. We persuaded one of
her personal slaves to tell us where she had gone."

"Then let us hurry."

"Are you nervous, Serlin?"

"Impatient."

Geslik laughed. "It is day, fool. The First sleeps in the Dark
Heart's hand. Even such screams as she will make could not
draw him here."

He turned and walked over to where Erin stood. Very gently
he caught her face in his hands. "Strip her."

Her eyes widened involuntarily and she started to pull back.
Fingers dug into her cheeks and jaw.

White-fire flared, too rapidly for the swords that held her to
react. They uttered choked cries and her arms fell free.

"Yes." Geslik whispered. "You *do* have power. But Sarillorn, so do I."

He stood in the center of her fire, regarding its brilliance with
contempt. It shone, a pale reflection in the darkness of his eyes.
Geslik reached through it.

Her hands flared, white torches, as she touched his and tried
to force them to release her jaw. He held her there, a shield of
shimmering red around the whole of his body.

"We have had three days to gain this power, Sarillorn. Do
you fully understand what it means? I fear not, but I am patient;
I will show you.

"Serlin, come."

Red robes and red shields outlined the body of the man who
left the altar to join the high priest. Serlin closed his eyes for a

moment, and the shields sharpened and crystallized until they were gauntlets around his large hands. He drove them through the whiteness of fire and touched the green of fabric.

"She is powerful," he said, his teeth clenched.

Erin was certain that he at least felt the heat of her fire. But it wasn't enough to stop him. Velvet tore away in strips. It hurt; she felt the seams cut into her back and pull her forward.

"Enough," Geslik murmured. His hands still crushed her face, bruising it without drawing blood—not yet. He lifted her off the ground, his arms not even straining with the weight.

Three days, Erin thought. How many people could die by slow and painful ritual in three days?

His power was all the answer she needed.

She struggled against it, regretting her earlier caution. Against the Swords she might have had a quick death and, compared to this, an easy one.

Easy? Her blood forced power outward. No death by enemy hands could be so, and no life taken from one of the lines was easily given—not to these.

Geslik's eyes narrowed. His smile ceased; she was glad of that. With a curse, he threw her down. She felt the stone of the altar against the back of her head.

She muffled a cry.

Hands grabbed her hair and her head hit the stone again. And again. And again.

Erin's struggles grew weaker, but they didn't stop entirely; the power that she had summoned was already diminishing the force of the blows.

"Enough," Geslik said.

Fingers tangled in auburn hair. "Why? You know what her power is. Let us drain it this way."

"If she can heal herself, so much the better—but I will not have her killed so easily. Not for a pleasant death do we take this risk." He stared across at the second of the thirteen council members.

After a moment, the man nodded, and Erin's head fell limply once more onto the cushion of obsidian.

Geslik gestured to one of the more junior of the Karnari, and the man held out a long ebony box.

A grim little smile flickered across Erin's lips. She summoned her power inward, shaping it carefully. Telvar had taught her this years ago, and she had never forgotten. Only once, once in all her years, had she put it aside.

I gave my word to Stefanos. My pain in exchange for their life. I gave no such word to you.

She saw the dagger as it came out of the small casket. It glimmered darkly in the light as if night itself had chosen this moment to visit the temple. Her smile, if anything, grew broader. *Kill me,* she thought. *You will get little satisfaction from it.* Even the First of the Dark Heart had been certain of that.

Her power grew within her like a smooth, soft shield. Even the dull throbbing of her head dimmed and receded.

She saw the light clearly for the first time in months. It grew behind her eyes, coloring the world in a soft haze of white and green.

Geslik raised the knife and began to chant softly. The cadence of his voice was almost pleasant, although it dwindled into silence by the time that Erin caught the fullness of its rhythm. "Now, Sarillorn, let us show you what the Karnari have developed over the years. I have not yet had the chance to purify the taint of Lernari blood. I look forward to seeing you ward. It is always satisfying to see the death of any hope. Will you ward for us, Sarillorn?" Serlin murmured something that Erin couldn't catch. She strained, listening intently. Nothing.

This, this is what her mother must have faced. She thought it without any bitterness. She was tempted to ward, tempted to try her power against them to see who broke first. The red brilliance that each man contained told her clearly who would win.

On the field—on the field they could not have done this. Or could they?

She thought of her mother and lay silent and motionless.

They could stop her power from going outward. They could not take it from where it gathered within her body. Even now, they had not the power of a full Servant.

But her power was not infinite; and once it was gone . . .

No. No, Erin. Concentrate, damn you.

The shadows gathered about the high priest, taking form and substance. He stood, red against black, the very epitome of the wars. The knife came down steadily and surely, its edge caressing the whiteness of exposed skin.

Where it walked, a trail of beaded blood followed, red against white.

Erin felt nothing. But for how long? How long?

She tilted her head back, eyes catching the sunlight that forced its way through thick stained glass. She felt a small tugging at her feet and looked at Geslik, catching his smile, so dark and strong, as he held out a patch of wet, red skin. Her mouth opened, soundless, and she clamped her lips, forcing the corners upward.

Maybe, if she could anger him, he would kill her before her protection gave out and she could feel what he did. Her smile cut through his.

She still had power to draw on. It was morning. By evening she knew they would have to be finished with her, one way or the other. By evening—but the days at this time of year were long.

"Serlin?"

"With pleasure, Karnar." The knife changed hands almost as if it had a will of its own. It looked like a living, wounded thing as Serlin took it firmly.

The blade bit deeper this time, and further up Erin's body. She felt it trembling in the wound it made, but no more.

"Sarillorn," the man said softly, "I do not believe any of the Karnar have been so privileged."

Blood welled up, trickling down her side to grace the stone her body warmed.

"Never," someone said. "Nor will they be so now."

"What?"

Serlin looked up as Erin turned her head in a like motion.

The shadows had gathered. The altar of the Dark Heart was waiting for the pain the Karnari could bring. The darkness had been called.

In the light of day, it answered.

Erin's eyes grew wide. She started to sit up, but stopped; the knife still protruded from beneath her right breast, the hand that had twisted it hanging motionless.

"Stefanos," she whispered, sliding down to the stone again, death forgotten. Only now did she truly realize that but for a sheen of new blood, she was naked.

He stood between the open doors of the temple, sunlight arrayed against him like an undeniable army.

Undeniable?

Erin could see the red that glowed around him; it was so strong that she could barely see the gray of his face. He seemed to be on fire and not in control of it; wisps of smoke, like innocent mist, curled high above the hands that buckled black doors.

Serlin drew back, as did the rest of the Karnari. "Lord—"

"Yessss . . ." He walked into the room. The jaws of daylight closed around him.

Erin rolled shakily off the altar, but no one seemed to notice. She turned to see the Karnari in their resplendent red garments. Shadow was there, at their feet, colder than the marble they stood on. Red lines sprang to life, a complicated net that surrounded even the least of their number. She watched the net grow stronger as the red light they held grew weaker. And she saw fear on each of their faces. Not obvious, not hysterical, but there nonetheless.

She shuddered as she wrapped her arms around her breasts. No Servant walked in daylight, yet Stefanos was here. And he walked. The fire moved with him as he continued to burn.

"More power," Geslik murmured. "The daylight takes its toll even now."

The strands of red grew thicker and stronger as the weave itself began to pulse.

None of the Karnari spoke.

Nor did the First Servant. Any word might show the pain he felt as the day delicately burned its way through the first few layers of his darkling skin.

He approached the barrier and stopped.

The Karnari whispered among themselves.

"Lord," Geslik said, his voice quieter. "We mean you no disservice. But the Church—"

The Servant raised his arms. Claws came out to grip the sharp lines of blood-power. He smiled then. Erin shivered at the sight of it. If it cost him effort, he did not deign to show it.

The barrier fell away, torn to shreds by the greater power the Servant commanded.

Geslik leaped back—too late.

The solid iron of the door had not been able to stand against the Servant—nor, now, did flesh.

The last thing that Geslik saw was the color of the Servant's eyes boring into him even as his claws did. He fell forward, denied even the release of a scream. He had not the throat left to utter it.

The Servant did not appear to notice. He moved on, and quickly, taking each of the priests in turn as easily as if they were waiting in line to greet him. His one regret was that he hadn't the time to give them the death they truly merited.

Erin could only watch.

She knew that were she whole and armed, she could not have covered the space between herself and Stefanos in the time it took him to reach the last man.

And she wasn't sure that she wouldn't have tried.

Deaths she had seen before, and in greater numbers than most. But none of them had been like this. She watched blood spray across the altars, an afterthought for the Dark Heart. Poets talked about red plumes of fountaining blood, and in the future, if she chose, she could do likewise.

She saw him turn, his power only slightly diminished. The death was gone from his eyes, but not the red. It reached out to touch her more surely than the priests had.

She took a step back.

He held out one claw, whether in supplication or demand, Erin could not be certain. It, too, was red.

"Sarillorn," he said softly. His voice was shaking. "Are you well?"

Well?

Her hands fluttered nervously, concealing what they could while they trembled. She was suddenly afraid. This fear even the priests could not evoke. Confused, she moved back again.

He sensed her fear, even through the pain that held him; sensed it, and knew what she knew: that it had not been given to the Karnari.

Once again it came like a gift to him, and him alone. He dared not move toward her.

"Sarillorn." His voice was even weaker now; he should already be gone. But he stayed just a few seconds longer, risking dissipation. "Sarillorn, I have taken the liberty of calling your slaves to you. They will arrive shortly. They are frightened; I had no choice in the aspect I took to command them. But they will see you to your rooms."

He smiled then, grim and dark. "No one will trouble you there."

Then he vanished, turning away from the sun's light to the hand of the darkness itself. The smell of his immortal flesh burning lingered in the air.

"You were very lucky."

The doctor smiled out of a pale face. His hair, what there was of it, rested awkwardly against a pillow—one too fine and soft to have come from the infirmary. The Sarillorn, her hair drawn tightly back into a practical, unlovely knot, touched his hand a moment, then nodded.

She turned to one of the three hovering orderlies. She smiled warmly. "Evan?"

He nodded, no smile in return. His hands had rolled the fold of his white shirt into an endless pattern of dirt, sweat, and wrinkles.

She sighed. "You did well; you did the right thing. I think, if you can keep him abed, he'll recover."

Evan nodded again, the movement still crisp and jerky. But Erin caught the tight lines around his mouth as they relaxed.

"What happened?" one of the other orderlies asked. A young woman, perhaps a year or two younger than Erin herself. Evan spun and turned a dark look upon the girl, one which she chose to ignore. She was dressed in a thick gray skirt and plain white shirt, and looked every bit the fighter. Erin liked her.

"Swords," Erin replied softly. "Swords came." She said nothing else, but the girl seemed satisfied.

"Sarillorn?"

Four heads turned to look at the doctor.

"The name's Marcus." He held out one shaky hand.

"Thank you," she said softly as she pushed him firmly back against the pillow. "Mine's Erin."

"You've spent yourself tending to me; have you seen to yourself at all?"

"I'm fine." It was mostly true. "And anyway, I'm the doctor here, you're the patient. I suggest you worry about regaining your own health before you start asking after anyone else's." But she smiled as she said it. As a healer, she knew how difficult it could be to be a patient.

Marcus appeared to know it as well. He returned her smile wryly.

"But the Swords—"

"Dead."

"The high priest?"

"Dead as well."

Marcus smiled and Erin shook her head. "No, I didn't kill him. He—and the Karnari gathered with him—had prepared for many days. They were able to block any outside use of power I might call."

"You didn't kill them?" he said, as if to himself. "Then who?"

"The First Servant. Stefanos."

He looked at her with a mild frown. "How long was I unconscious for? Have I lost an entire day?" He looked out to catch the red light of sundown.

"No." Erin shook her head. "It was day."

"Day? Bright Heart! He came in the light of day."

She rose then. "I will come tomorrow to see how you fare. But now, I think I must return to my rooms for dinner."

"Sarillorn?"

She hovered in the doorway, wanting to stay, wanting to leave. "Yes?"

"Thank you."

She nodded then and made her choice. The door closed behind her back as she stepped out into the long, silent hall.

When the knock came, she tensed. Her fingers dug into the upholstery of the chair she sat in, and she looked down at them ruefully.

So much for choice.

Clearing her throat, she said, "Yes?"

The door opened smoothly.

In the frame there stood a man, haloed darkly by the shadow that was his mantle. He was more pale than she remembered him.

"Might I enter?"

"Please." She nodded rigidly. "Have you—have you asked for dinner?"

"For two." The door swung shut behind him. "But it will be longer than usual."

"Oh." *Oh? Is that all you can say?* Her jaw seemed clamped so tightly that only forced words would come out of it. *He saved your life. Can't you at least say thank you?*

Her silence answered her.

From where he stood, he could hear the song of her fear. It was fascinating. Beautiful. It made a tapestry of her breathing, her expression, and her stance. No artisan could capture the feel and texture of it; it was a living work.

He shook himself. It was easier than it had been to deny the call of it. Easy or no, he had made his decision. He would abide by it.

As he walked toward his customary chair, he could see her face pale. With precise, even movements he took his seat.

She looked away when he met her eyes.

"Sarillorn."

Auburn hair obscured part of her face as she bent her head. "Yes?"

"I apologize for your . . . trial today. I did not think that the Karnari would dare to touch you. My word on that was clear."

The chill of his voice was not for her, but she shivered at it.

"I was careless. It almost cost your life. Please forgive me."

Forgive you? Erin wanted to shout. *Forgive you for what? You saved my life—you dared the daylight to save* me.

And that's the problem. I don't understand you, Stefanos. I don't understand what you want. For a single moment she could feel his hands, with their delicate, dangerous claws, pressing into her breast. Without thinking, she lifted her hand to her heart as if to push him away.

"Sarillorn?"

"I—thank you." It was awkward, but it was the best she could do.

He stared at her, and again she froze, as she had frozen once before. They shivered at the same instant.

Then he gave her a very rare smile.

"We cannot continue thus," he said softly, the points of his teeth still evident. "Tell me, Sarillorn, what it is that you fear? I will not force you, or force myself upon you." He looked at her oddly. "But that evening, that was not the fear that drove you." His face darkened. "Not, at least, at the beginning."

She shook her head. "No," she said at last. "No—I didn't even think that you would—"

"And now?"

"Now?" she said stupidly.

"You still wear your fear, Sarillorn. But even your fear is strange. It is not, I think, given to many. I am—honored by it."

"Honored?"

He nodded gravely, and Erin realized that he meant exactly what he had said. She felt a blush rise in her cheeks. Before she could speak, he began again.

"But this fear, why do you feel it?" He leaned forward in the chair, coming closer to her without leaving it. "Is it that you do not trust me?"

"Trust you? How am I supposed to . . ." The words faded. She gulped air as if it were water and she were drowning, bowed her head again, lower than before, and brought her hands to her cheeks.

"If you do not, I understand. I will be—patient enough to earn it."

She had never been very good at lying, not even to herself. For a moment two images pulled her; his darkness as he hovered over her, and his fire as he burned for her.

"I do trust you."

He raised one eyebrow, the only visible gesture of his surprise. "Then why?"

The chair could no longer contain her; she rose, wringing her hands tightly in front of her stomach. Her feet padded against the plush, gold carpet as she paced in front of him like a caged animal.

"Why—why did you stop?"

His eyebrow flew again, but her back didn't notice it. Her ears heard the smile in his voice.

"I see," he said softly. "I could say, 'because I wished to.' But I think I understand. We must both answer questions that we would rather not ask of ourselves."

He watched as she stopped at the edge of the carpet, turned, and walked back along its length.

"But indeed, I speak the truth when I say I stopped because I wished it. For the end of it would be your death to me. And I do not wish you to die." He paused, watching again in fascination as a shaky foot touched the ground. "There is a light in you, Sarillorn."

At this she turned to face him.

"But it is not the light of the Bright Heart alone. It is different; perhaps a part of the mortality that taints you. This I do not know." He frowned; he disliked ignorance. "I have tried to find a like incident in the past; there is not one to learn from."

"I don't understand."

"Ah? No, I do not think you do." As she had done, he rose, leaving his chair behind. He moved upon her silently and she backed away. With a smile, he stopped. "But it is there, Sarillorn. It does not hurt me, but I cannot truly touch it. It is . . . different, as your fear is different."

Her fear. He reached out to touch her chin; it trembled. With regret, he withdrew. He did not wish to hurt her—and yet he still felt the desire. "Sarillorn, the one who cannot exercise self-control when necessary is the one who cannot rule. I have already given you my word."

"The word of a Servant."

"The word of the First." But he smiled again. "And perhaps your wisdom mistrusts it."

She took a deep breath. "No."

"Then what do you fear, little one?" Again he reached for the line of her jaw, his fingers playing gently against her skin.

She snapped her head away. "I don't know."

He caught her shoulders and held them. "Do you not? Come, I have answered your question; answer mine."

She couldn't. What she had said was true: She did not know fully what it was that she feared. Or why she feared it so strongly only when he was present, when he looked down at her, when he was touching her.

She tried to pull back; his hands held her firmly, gently, in place.

"I don't know." Her voice was a whisper, a plea.

Her widened eyes, her shortened breath—these spoke a familiar language to him—familiar and strangely new.

"Sarillorn." He caught her chin again, pulling her face up to meet his.

"Please . . ."

But her trembling was the only movement she made.

"Do I hurt you, little one?"

Cold, cold fingers stroked her jaw and cheeks, drawing tiny circles there. His eyes locked on hers and would not leave them.

"N-no."

He cupped her face between his hands, moving slowly, moving gently. Against his will he found himself savoring all the visible signs of her precious fear.

"Do you trust me?"

"Please . . ."

There, again, the whimper that controlled her word. And the word itself struck him, familiar and new as all about her was.

"What do you fear?" His face hovered just an inch above hers. His hands tightened imperceptibly as he felt the call again. He pushed it away, but not all of it would leave; he still felt desire for her fear, for her.

Once again he caught the twisted halo of her light as it struggled with some invisible enemy.

She started to pull away and he held her there.

"No, Sarillorn. From this you will not run. Name your fear."

Her lips moved soundlessly.

"Name it."

But she couldn't. He was too close, too encompassing for words alone to describe.

Moving slowly and deliberately, his mouth came down, lips resting almost gently against her own—almost. Then he felt the strangest thing of a strange evening; her lips, much softer, much warmer, moved also.

In surprise, he pulled back to see the lashes of her eyes flutter open. She was shaking; at least he thought it must be her.

"This," she whispered, swaying. "Just this."

He knew it for truth. Fear, like tongues of flame, burned deliriously close. But it was not unalloyed—he could see that suddenly and felt angry at his obtuseness. The fear was foreign to him because it embodied something else as well: desire, one unlike his own, but suddenly no less tangible.

His lips came down again. A kiss, a long one. Wordless, it spoke around the edges of what he felt driven to. It was not an act of violence, but the violence was there, beneath the darkness that gathered around them.

She still offered him her fear, and this little of it—this little of it his nature would not allow him to reject.

"Sarillorn." His voice was shadow as he swept her off the floor, pressing her just a little too tightly against him.

She said nothing, nothing at all, but after a moment her shaking arms reached up and wrapped themselves just as tightly around his neck. The hesitation and trembling never left her.

He carried her quickly through her chambers to the bed and there laid her down. His lips met hers again; his hands touched cloth, touched flesh. He moved slowly, trembling with the effort of doing so. And his hands, where they touched her, drew no blood and left no mark. She was still, very still; the ocean that hides the undercurrent.

"I will not hurt you," he murmured, feeling the breath leave her throat.

But this night, this one of many, he lied.

She had never been touched so before.

chapter
fourteen

He watched her as she slept.

It was early; the night had just begun. But he knew she would be tired. These past two months she had worked hard to start her clinic. It gave her a pleasure he did not understand to tend to the injuries of her slaves. But it was harmless; if it made her happy, he was willing to allow it.

"Sara," he whispered. She stirred; in the darkness of the curtained room he could see the hint of smile turn the corners of her mouth.

He smiled as well.

I'm Erin.

He remembered clearly the look on her face, half-shy, half-apologetic.

Erin of Elliath. I'm sorry. I just realized I never—you don't know my name.

"No," he said, mirroring the words of six months ago, although no one could hear them. "You are of Elliath no longer."

He saw her face darken for a moment, but he could not—would not—bring himself to use that name. She was his. This he would not give up.

"You are the Sarillorn. You belong here."

Stefanos. She had looked up, the darkness that he hated in her alone already fading. *How would you like it if I always called you "Your Majesty" or "Your Highness"?*

"Those are not among my titles, Sarillorn. They are human conceits."

And he remembered her little snort.

All right. If I always called you "Lord" or "First of the Servants."

"First, little one, of the Sundered."

You know what I mean. Sarillorn is a title. *It isn't a name.*

"Is it not what you are?"

She had thrown up her hands and shaken her head.

You know something? I never could have imagined that you would remind me of Belfas.

And then the silence had come over her again. But he knew her well; knew that this particular silence would hang like a cloud for the night if he did nothing. He did not ask her who Belfas was; he did not wish to know. Her life, or all of it that concerned him, began when he took her, living, from the village that she had tried so futilely to protect.

He walked over to the bed and touched her sleeping face, tracing the line of the smile that still lingered there.

"Let me name you anew, Sarillorn, if you will not have a title." He thought for a while, discarding the few names he knew. She *was* the Sarillorn, and no other word came easily to him. Then he smiled quietly. "Is Sara a name that you will take? It is a human one—common, I believe, among the southerners."

He had watched the cloud disperse and was glad of it. The light shone through it.

Stefanos—I . . . It's a diminutive.

"Yes."

Well—it would be the same as if I called you, I don't know, darkling.

"Darkling?"

"Darkling . . ."

Mortals were so odd.

"Shhh, Sara. Sleep a while yet; it is two hours or more before we leave."

She nodded and reached out to touch him. Then her eyes fluttered open, green even in this light.

"Stefanos?"

"Sara." He sat by her on the bed and pulled her into his arms. He tilted his head up slightly as her light wrapped itself gently around him.

"Is it already time?" She yawned, stretching her arms out awkwardly.

"Not yet."

"Oh."

"Did you accomplish your tasks during the day?"

She nodded sleepily. "Marcus will tend to the servants here while I'm gone."

Always servants—she never called them slaves.

Happily she added, "He thinks Evan will probably be qualified as a doctor soon."

He listened politely; Evan did not concern him.

Knowing this, she changed the subject. "Where are we going
first?"

"Did you not read the itinerary I gave you?"

"I didn't understand it all. I haven't managed to master reading your impossible language just yet."

"Ah. We go to Caras, to see the duke."

The duke of Caras had been seen. The duke of Redford had
been seen. The duke of Alondale had been seen.

She shuddered quietly, pressing her head against the cold
metal frame of the carriage window, striving to control the anger
and the grief that those visits had caused her as she continued
through her mental list.

The baron of Fellhearth had been seen. She remembered him
clearly because of the particularly ghoulish way he had delighted
in his naming of his granted lands. He was not Malanthi—one
of perhaps three who were not—and he didn't know, couldn't
know, who she truly was.

Her smile tightened momentarily. He did learn.

*Stefanos. Why did you bring me here? Why do we have to
keep on with this hideous tour?*

"It is only for a little while longer, Sara," he had said. "Only
a few more weeks, and we shall return to Rennath." The same
words, always the same.

Rennath. Never before had the name seemed quite so welcome, quite so bright.

But why do I need to—

This, too, memory answered. "You do not. But I, Sarillorn,
I wish these men to meet you. I wish them to know who you
are. Bear with my decision."

And she had.

It helped to know that while she visited there were no ceremonies, that while she walked the various grounds, she could
tend to those slaves that might need her help. But it also reminded her of all that she could not do, all that would continue
happening to the helpless when she left.

A third month passed.

She had been almost afraid to go. She remembered it clearly
as she stepped out of the carriage for perhaps the twentieth time,

gathering the ostentatious skirts of yet another dress and holding them high above her laced "traveling" boots.

Stefanos aided her as she stepped down, and she gripped his hand firmly. Another noble—Baron Tremayne—was already bowed to the ground before the shadow of the Lord of the Empire.

Swirling around the velvet of his finery was a thin, red line—another Malanthi.

"Lord."

"Baron Tremayne. You may rise."

The man complied. He was not used to such displays of obeisance, and they suited him poorly; neither his dress, all fine, dark blue velvet with frills and lace, nor his girth allowed for grace. He turned to the guards arrayed at his back and nodded briefly.

"You grace my humble lands with your presence."

"Indeed."

Watching, she caught the hint of cruel smile play around Stefanos's lips.

"Will you require rooms, Lord?"

"Yes. For myself, and for Lady Sara."

Lady Sara grimaced and stepped forward. She could not bring herself to bow, but managed a polite nod.

"Lady Sara." Baron Tremayne stepped forward, reached for her hand, and took a sudden step back as his blood-sight told him who he was dealing with. It didn't surprise her; she'd seen it played over and over again at each stop they had made. She wished that Stefanos had made clear what his visit would entail—and he had been quite adamant in his refusal to do so.

"They will learn at my leisure, Lady. And at yours."

"Will you stop calling me 'Lady'? I don't want people to associate me with the nobility, not in these lands."

"Do you not? I am sorry, little one. But nobility you *will* be, and of greater station than any of these can possibly hope to attain. They *will* respect you."

"Baron Tremayne," she said softly. She couldn't help but smile as he struggled to control his reaction. Maybe a little of Stefanos's amusement had touched her as well. It was a light thought, but it drove the smile from her face.

The baron turned to stare at Stefanos, striving for respect amid his confusion.

This, too, she was familiar with.

She was glad that it was almost over. She longed for home. *Home?* She looked down at her feet. *Lady Sara, Sarillorn of Rennath.* Over the many months, these titles had become familiar.

She reached for Stefanos's hand.

He raised an eyebrow, but lent her his strength.

"May I show you to your rooms, Lord?"

"You may. Come, Lady."

Their quarters were not as grand as those that they shared in the palace, but they were luxuriously equipped; each piece of finely crafted furniture was dark and gleamed in the dim light. A slave might fetch a lesser price on the blocks. At least the baron had been given enough warning to manage this—this, and more.

In the corner of the room, hands behind her back, a young girl lay curled against the floor.

"I see that the rooms are already occupied." Again the First of the Sundered gave a chilling smile.

Mistaking him, the Baron smiled in return. "Yes, Lord. You will find that she is quite suitable for your needs. I will send a detail to remove her after you are finished, should you require it."

Lady Sara did not wait to hear Stefanos's reply. She ran across the room and knelt beside the child. Her pale hands touched pale hair very gently.

The girl looked up. Her face was tearstained and very white.

Nothing cut the lady more than this: the sudden widening of eyes and the resurgence of pure terror.

"Child, child," she said, pulling the girl awkwardly into her lap. She sent out a finger of her power, placing it gently against the fear that she felt so strongly.

The child whimpered and suddenly pushed herself into the lady's arms.

"Shhh. It's all right, it's all right. I'm here now. I'll protect you." Small shoulders strained against the chains that were now visible. A hint of blood around the wrists showed the strength of the young girl's panic. "I'll protect you. Shhhh."

Bitterly she noted that aside from the chafing, the girl was uninjured. No one gave used goods to the Lord of the realm. Her anger caused her to tremble, even as the child did. She looked up and met the baron's eyes, her own green and flashing with a power he knew.

"Sara?" Stefanos said softly, ignoring the Baron's sudden stare.

"Please."

He nodded quietly and walked over to where the two sat huddled.

The child tensed, and Sara stroked her hair with the green of her power. "It's all right. He's a friend. He'll help me take these chains away."

The child quieted. Sara knew it was only because she hadn't the blood-sight that would strip Stefanos of human guise and identify him clearly. She saw only another man, another noble, albeit a tall one in black jacket, black shirt, and black pants. At least they were not the robes of the priesthood.

Stefanos touched the cool steel manacles and gestured with mild contempt. They snapped crisply and fell away. Sara pulled the child fully into her grasp and turned her away; she did not want her to see that the metal smoldered.

"Lord?"

Very slowly, Stefanos turned his head. "Yes?"

"I don't understand. Have I displeased you?"

"Displeased me?" He shrugged elegantly. "That is not your concern. You have displeased the Lady, however." He smiled. "And the Lady chooses to grant her mercy here. Do you question this?"

"M-mercy?"

"Ah, but that is not mine to grant. Lady?"

"Not now," she replied tersely. She pulled the child gently to her feet. "In fact, I think it best if you both continue your discussion elsewhere for a time." Turning her back on them, she carried the girl to the large, regal bed.

"What is your name, child?" she asked softly.

The girl was young, but not so young that she would answer that question when asked by a noble.

The baron, however, was unwise enough to answer for her.

"She's a slave," he said, half-incredulous.

"Oh?" Her voice was cool. "I wasn't aware that I was asking the question of you."

His face darkened. He started to step forward and Stefanos caught him by the arm. Sara heard the baron's gasp of pain. She couldn't help it; she smiled almost viciously, an expression that vanished completely as she turned to speak with the child.

"My name is Lady Sara, but most people just call me Sara,

unless they happen to be nobility.'' She grimaced with distaste at the word.

"I'm a slave,'' the girl said cautiously. Sara smiled, encouraged. These were the first words the girl had spoken. She applied a little more of her power, but not too much; she would still have her tour of the house to make, and there were many, she was sure, that would require at least as much attention.

"I know,'' she said. "But that isn't your fault.'' The fear vanished under the weight of her power. "Do you want to go home?''

The child nodded.

"Well, then,'' Lady Sara said, taking the child's hand. "If you think you can walk, I'll take you. What is your mother called by the other slaves?''

The child stood on her toes and whispered something. Sara nodded. She braced herself for the fear that would follow when she met the girl's parents; fear mingled with hate of the station that Stefanos had granted her.

Little fingers wrapped themselves suddenly around hers. It helped. She smiled down.

Without another word to the two who watched, she left the room.

Stefanos helped her into the carriage. He watched as she waved her silent good-byes to the windows of the large mansion; watched in surprise and acceptance as those windows, ringed by slaves, acknowledged her passing. Hope he knew, and hope he saw in the faces that watched.

This was why Elliath had always been a danger to him. But that danger was secondary.

He looked down at the Sarillorn's weary face and wrapped her gently in the anonymity of his shadow. *Do you not see,* he thought, as his hands stroked her hair, *the effect that you have had?* He did not think so—else why would she be so weary, so tired?

"He was the last, little one. From here we return home.''

She sighed, nodded, and closed her eyes. Her breathing alone told him that she did not sleep.

"All things are in preparation in Rennath; they will be waiting for us.''

"Waiting?''

"Yes.''

She was silent a moment, as she always was when she was trying to understand something. "Stefanos?"

"Yes?"

"Why did we come here? Why did we tour Veriloth?"

He smiled. "Must you always question all that I choose, Sarillorn? Can you not just accept that it was necessary?" But he knew the answer to his question; he asked it only out of habit.

"Very well," he said, when her silence grew too long. "I wished them to know you, Lady. I wished them to understand your position. I wished to force them to accept what will soon be a known fact: You are my consort. You are my chosen Empress. Under my command, you will rule by my side."

Again her silence answered him; her silence and her sudden stiffness.

"You—you told them *that*?"

"Not, perhaps, in so many words. Why?"

"You—you told them that I was—that I'm—" She pulled away from him, not an easy maneuver in the confined space of the carriage.

Once again she had managed to surprise him. He looked at her pale, shocked face, at her wide, unblinking eyes. They spoke of a tremulous horror that he could not understand. Had he not just granted her more power than any of her kind had ever known? Had he not indicated how important she had become to him? Had he not acknowledged to her that she was no slave, to come and go entirely at his whim?

This rank, this title—it was a gift that the nobility would kill for. Why then did she not show the appreciation that was his right?

He was angry and he fought to stifle it. Here, alone in the darkness with her, he could take no chances. Control came with difficulty.

"Did you even think of asking *me*?"

His teeth glimmered in the shadow; it was not a smile.

"*Asking* you, Sarillorn?"

"Asking me."

He felt her own anger, so much less dangerous, in every syllable. There was a snap as one of the gilt-edged windows broke away beneath his fingers.

"I have," he said with difficulty, "bestowed upon you a rank that no half blood would dare to think of taking. I have honored you above even my own brethren. You dare to ask me if—" Another snap. He bit back the remainder of the words.

She was trembling, but there was no hint of the beauty of fear about it.

"What if I don't want to rule this—this empire? What if I don't want to be associated with the nobility and the man—the Servant—who created it?" Her own hands gripped the side window out of which she looked. Landscape, obscured by nightfall, passed by her narrowed eyes.

He touched her shoulder. Very softly, he said, "Is it not too late to ask that?"

Her sudden tears dissolved his anger completely.

"Sarillorn, Sara, why?" He touched her chin, turning her face toward him. "Am I cruel to you? Do I hurt you?"

"It isn't me that I worry about." Her voice was bitter and very distant. "It's never me that I have to worry about." Her head sagged forward without resistance. "Why do you want to do this to me?"

"Because I desire it. If I am to honor you, all of my subjects will."

"*Honor* me?" She laughed then, almost hysterically, and she would not speak again.

"Oh, Marcus, I'm so glad to be back!"

The doctor smiled. He looked both weary and happy as he nodded to the beds in the infirmary. Three were occupied.

"I'm not sure what you said, Sarillorn, but we've been open for business these last three months—and no one's said a word against it."

Her smile wavered. "It isn't what I said," she told him sadly, "but who I said it to."

"I thought it might be." He put an arm around her shoulder and steered her firmly to one of two chairs. "Was it hard?"

She nodded. "I—I think I've just been sheltered in Rennath. I—everywhere we went there was just so much ugliness. And I knew while I stayed I could change things, but does it help them when I've gone? What does a day here or there really mean when they have to look forward to years of slavery?"

He didn't press her for details.

"But the worst—the worst of it is here. Stefanos wants me to be Empress." She laughed. Marcus did not.

"Empress?" he said softly.

"Empress." The word was flat. "Of the empire he's built. And I can't do it, Marcus. I can't." She stood suddenly and walked over to the window; it was glass. She pressed her cheek against it. I've given up everything I can. I don't know if there'll be anything of me left if I do as he wants.''

"What would he ask you to change?''

"What else would he have to? I wasn't raised and trained by Elliath to rule at the side of a Servant!''

"Not even one you love?''

"L-love?''

His eyes met hers.

"I can't love him.'' But she smiled, quietly and sadly, all anger suddenly quenched. "What about him is there to love?''

"If you have no answer for that, Sarillorn, there is not a mortal alive that does.''

"And is love meant to be such a selfish thing, then? That I care about what he grants to me, when I know it is only to me that he grants it?''

Marcus was very thoughtful. He was old; he had the experience that she lacked.

"Love, Sarillorn, is not easily defined. But only the love of the Bright Heart Himself is not motivated by mortal things. It *is*, in some ways, selfish. And in some, selfless.

"Were your lover human, I would counsel you as you counsel yourself: to seek another. Often, what one will do to others, they will one day do to you. But that isn't, I think, the case here.'' He stepped closer to her. "Sometimes I think you are more afraid of the kindness he offers than of the death he could give.''

She nodded, the same smile pulling her lips down. "I am.''

"Then this is the hope that must guide you: that the Servant *can* give these things. Perhaps for now, they are only given to you—but maybe, in time . . .''

"Do you really believe that?''

"It isn't important if I do, Sarillorn. Do you?''

"I try to.'' She looked down at her hands. They were shaking. "But it's hard. I keep thinking—I know what he does. I know it and, if I accept it, I must be a party to it somehow. I can almost see the blood on these hands.''

He closed his eyes. "I know,'' he said gently. "But if that's the case, then ask yourself what *you* really want.''

"I have. I still don't know. Six months ago, I might have said 'to go home.' Three months ago, even. Now . . . I just don't know.''

"Sarillorn, do you love him?''

"Do I?" She looked at the walls as if she could drag answers from them.

Dinner was a ritual. Food was laid out on a short, low table, each tray appealing in its presentation. Two silver plates decorated either end of the dark wood; cutlery, in the empire's odd style, lay on the left side. On the right, two goblets, each worth more than a small farm's yearly harvest.

A ritual. She greeted him at the door, taking care to see that the large skirt of silk and the crinoline beneath it weren't crushed against the wall.

He asked, "Would it trouble you if I remained?"

She shook her head, out of habit, really. Was that all that ritual held? He took her arm as he led her to the table, even though they both knew she was capable of finding it on her own.

She stopped once, to adjust the lamplight, and then continued on to take the chair that he pulled out.

Ritual; she had taught him this, and he had accepted it. But as she looked across the full table to meet his dark eyes, she knew that more than habit lay beneath it.

It was the first thing I taught you.

He filled her goblet with a vintage he had chosen; a good one, although initially this had not always been the case. Not that it had made, or did make, much difference to his lady; she herself had known precious little about wine. She watched as the liquid, cool and clear, spilled gently into one goblet.

Soon they would drink it; soon they would eat. She would talk of her day, he of very little.

Then, afterward, they would retire, perhaps into the sitting room. He would speak more there, and she less. He would touch her, taking her face very gently into his winter hands. He would kiss her, less gently, and she would know a moment of fear; the same fear that was always present for the beginning of each night.

He would dim the lights, but not completely, and let the shadows touch them both.

Rituals.

Do I love you?

This was not a question she could ask him. He was First of the Dark Heart; what little he knew of love was cold and cruel.

Cold and cruel . . . She put her fork down, swallowing slowly, aware of him, as she was always aware.

"Sarillorn?"

She shook her head, picked up the fork again, and watched it shake, the light gleaming off the silver.

What do I want?

Not to be Empress. Not to rule.

No?

She had already done much in his name, and with his permission: the clinic, the dismissal of the Church from the palace proper. What more might she hope for, if she had the courage to remain?

But she knew she must be honest with herself. She didn't know if courage alone kept her in this place.

Do I love you?

No answer came, and she took refuge in the dinner proper.

"Sarillorn."

"Hmmm?"

"Are you well?"

She looked down at what remained of her dinner: most of what had been put upon her plate.

"I'm fine."

"You have hardly eaten anything. Are you sure?"

She shook her head.

He rose, leaving rituals behind. Very quietly he came to stand beside her chair, one hand resting upon her shoulder.

"Is the thought of being consort to the Lord of Empire so terrible?"

She thought, for a moment, that she heard the smallest of catches in his voice. "I—I already am, aren't I?"

He smiled. "Yes. And I wish the rest of my subjects to know it."

She didn't ask him why. She said nothing for a long while. And then for no real reason, as she often did, she made her decision. She caught his hand, took a deep breath, and laid her cheek gently against it.

"I love you, Stefanos."

Her words were a sigh.

She didn't see his eyes widen, couldn't see the way the touch of her light leaped up like a sudden flare to dazzle his peculiar vision. Nothing he had seen yet had prepared him for this.

Love? He watched the steadiness of her inner light, wondering where the twisting current and eddies of it had gone.

Love? He touched her face very gently, amazed that he could do so. And he understood for the first time all that she offered, and all that he wanted. He understood what he had seen the first time they had met; knew that it had not been for him that the light had shone.

He knew that it shone for him now.

In wonder he met her green, green eyes.

Could such a one as this truly co-rule all that he had built? In all history, no one, human or half blood, had dared to offer a Servant of the Dark Heart this gift. All that he had been certain of before left him with nothing save the desire to hold this light aloft for any to see, could they choose it.

"Sara."

She nodded quietly.

"I wish them to know that I have chosen you. I wish them to know that you have chosen *me*." He drew her gently to her feet. "But if—if you choose against it, Lady, I shall abide by your decision." He could offer her nothing less.

She wrapped her arms around him, hiding her face in his chest. He heard her muffled voice as clearly as he felt it.

"They will know I've chosen. I'm afraid that they'll think I— I love this world you've made." She took a deep breath and drew back so he could once again see the starkness of her expression. "But no love should exist with shame. If I love you, I will do it without being ashamed of it." Her eyes were shining, a sad, bare brilliance.

"How, then, Sarillorn, do your people express this love?"

Her eyes widened. "My people?"

"The lines." He rarely asked anything about her former life. "The Malanthi have little that could capture it; the Servants of the Dark Heart, none."

She bit her lip, and he wondered if in asking the question he had brought a pain he did not seek to inflict.

"There are—there are the rites of bonding, rituals, simple ones. I mean, when two people choose each other. There are other ways that we love; we love our parents, we love our brothers or our sisters, we love the Lady." She took a deep breath, steadying herself. "But if there are two who wish to make their bond known, they call the rites, in front of people they care about. I—it's not easy to explain."

She looked at the dinner, now cold, laid out before her.

"But I could teach you."

"Teach me, then. I would learn it."

* * *

The train of the dress shimmered around her feet, hinting at beads of crystal and pearl. They had been sewn very carefully into large, glinting circles, edged with silver trim.

Emilee, one of the servants who had tended to Lady Sara throughout her long stay, adjusted the dress for perhaps the fiftieth time.

Sara looked at the long, oval mirror. Her reflection stared back, robed in pale green, with a long, white sash and a white border around both trailing sleeves. These were the colors of the lines in celebration. Her hair was a mess, but Emilee insisted it be a beautiful one—all pulled high and strung through with the same pearls, the same crystal, that lay at her feet.

Embroidered in silver thread at her right breast, the circle of the initiate caught the fading sunlight.

"Where's Marcus?" she murmured.

"The sun hasn't set yet. He'll be here when it does," Emilee replied—as she had done for perhaps the last half hour. She straightened the smooth dress once more. "I've not seen a dress like this in tens of years, Lady." Her voice was quiet with awe. With memory.

"I've never seen one like it." She smiled. "But simpler ones, yes. I didn't realize what I was asking for."

"No," the woman murmured. "But Helda, now Helda was happy to do it."

Lady Sara smiled, remembering the look on the elderly seamstress's face.

Aye, I can do it, Lady, and with pleasure. It's a welcome change from the robes I'm used to making. And aye, I know the style of dress. I used to make 'em earlier. I used to be the best.

The best—Sara could well believe it; it explained why Helda was spared the brunt of slavery in her old age.

"I wonder where Marcus is."

Emilee sighed, but she had no heart for frustration; not on an evening like this. She could understand why her lady was nervous.

Tonight, before the assembly of lords, priests, and slaves, the Dark Lord would take her as bond-mate.

It's a two-edged thing, Emilee thought, as she pulled the sleeve out of Sara's tight hands and smoothed it down. *But you're a better mistress than any we'd hoped for, and with you at his side, he's a better master.* She could even think of him, in his black and red, without shivering or falling silent. *Mind,* she added to herself, *it's taken the better part of two years.*

She wanted her lady to be happy, if happiness was granted to anyone in the empire who wasn't born black-blooded. If not for the scar on her right arm, Emilee might have even been completely content to serve such a one.

Sara knew this, and knew it further as the praise that it was.

There was a knock on the door, and the nervous lady in question turned round so violently that Emilee left off thinking and began to straighten out the train once more.

"Be still, lady. I'll answer it."

Before she could leave, the door swung open.

There was a moment of silence.

"Marcus?"

The doctor smiled at the incredulity contained by the word. He gave a low bow. "At the service of my lady."

"Is that you?"

"Indeed." He turned, allowing her to see the back of the green velvet jacket he wore over a single ruffle. "Do you like it?" A walking cane, of dark hardwood and gold handle, tapped the ground in time to his words.

"I—where did you get it?"

His smile deepened. "The Lord himself sent me to Helda, no less, to be fitted. If I am to be worthy of being your escort, I must look the part, must I not?"

He walked over to where she stood and offered her his arm. His smile faded a little. "I haven't done this in years," he said softly.

She knew who he was thinking about. In silence she took the offered arm.

"But not tonight." He made an effort and was surprised to find that the smile that returned to him was genuine. "I'll not mar your evening with foolish musings."

"Thank you," she said quietly.

"No, Lady. Thank *you*." He began to lead her out of the room, and Emilee stopped him.

"Marcus, you lout, have you forgotten?"

"Forgotten?"

"You'll need both Trin and Tanya to carry the train. If you'll wait for a moment, I'll summon them—they're in the other room being as nervous as she is."

Sara grimaced. "That obvious?" she whispered to Marcus.

"About." His arm tightened encouragingly. "I'd be."

Two young girls, dressed in less complicated visions of green and white, were ushered firmly into the lady's presence by a clucking Emilee.

"Now mind what I've told you, and don't drop the train until the Lady's met up with the Lord. Understood?"

They nodded quite solemnly, although Lady Sara caught the doubtful glance that Tanya gave to the long, complicated train.

"Good, then. Off with you; I've only a short while to reach the galleries myself and I don't want to miss a thing." She smiled warmly at her oldest charge.

"Lady Sara, Bright Heart bless you." She bowed quite low and then left the room in a hurry.

Trin and Tanya each took part of the heavy train, and Marcus led her out of the room.

The halls had never seemed either so long or so empty.

"It's quiet," she whispered, but even this seemed to echo.

"Should be." Marcus smiled. "I don't know how you managed it, but I think every palace slave, and the ones that tend the outer grounds as well, will be in attendance for you. You might be nervous, but I think they're jubilant. No, this way, remember?"

She nodded, obviously not remembering.

He stopped for a moment and hugged her. It was a careful, gentle gesture—he didn't want to be the one to ruin Emilee's solid labor.

"Don't be too afraid, Lady."

"I'm trying."

"I know. But I mean what I said; the slaves here are almost ecstatic." He looked down at his velvet-covered arm. "We've grown to know you; you've earned the confidence we offer. And this rite is the best way to tell us all that you'll not be leaving us. Even if the rite of bonding means nothing to the nobility, those below know it well." He drew back. "Are you happy?"

"I think so."

"Then come. They're waiting."

Waiting? Yes, I guess they are. The halls that seemed so long and endless suddenly dwindled into inches. They opened up to pale, large doors of wood, with gold inlay that followed their peaked arches and danced around their handles. This simple design had replaced the black ones that Stefanos had all but torn off their hinges once. She liked them better.

There were guards on either side, but at her request, they had been chosen from among the regular troops. She wasn't certain they were much better than the Swords, but at least they were not Malanthi.

It was one of the many requests that the Servant had granted her. She looked at the doctor, resplendent in his formal attire.

They nodded smartly, and the door rolled open.

She froze for a moment as she looked in. The pews were full, lined with faces that she did not recognize. She saw curiosity there, mingled with hostility, envy, and fear: the nobility of Rennath, of all Veriloth.

She raised her head as she passed beneath the arch of the doors. Let them see her then, as enemy, as foe. Not for them had she walked this far. As she looked up, she saw the galleries. She had never seen them occupied—and could never have imagined that they could hold so many.

Most of the people were on their feet, and many of the children were nearly leaning over the balcony. One, a boy she recognized from her time in the clinic, had the temerity to wave and smile before his mother caught his hand to still him. He did not, however, make any noise.

These slaves were her people. These were the ones she cared about, these and one other.

She looked straight ahead for the first time since entering the chamber and saw him standing where once had stood an altar. As that altar had been, he was cold and dark in its place. Robed in black and red, he waited for her.

The white and the green of the Bright Heart walked quietly to meet him.

"Stefanos."

"Sara." He took her hand. It trembled in his. He looked carefully at her, seeing for a moment the silver and gray that the Lernari wore into the fields.

No other had worn the white and the green thus in his presence. Although he had known what she would wear, he found himself nonetheless surprised to see it.

Very gravely he bowed his head to her, and they both turned as one to face their audience.

"You must address them, Sarillorn, as initiate of the Bright Heart. This at least, I will not do."

He kept to that intention firmly, as she knew he would. For a moment, staring out into the pews, her memory failed her. These nobles of differing stations—these were not meant to share what she wished to make known.

"Lady?"

She looked up once again, to the still and silent faces in the galleries. She saw the hope that Marcus had promised shining down like rays of dawn between the clouds.

To them she could speak.

She'd practiced her lines many times in the last few months, but even as she began to speak, she realized for the first time that they were out of place. She looked up at Stefanos and saw his unwavering eyes as he waited.

"Friends, family, and those who wish us well," she began. Her voice stopped as she thought of Belfas. Although she could never wish the life of the empire upon him, she missed his presence sorely. And Katalaan would never see her bonded either—she'd be angry, if she knew. Swallowing, Sara continued. "We have asked you here, and you have honored us with your presence.

"Today, before those of you who have made our life more complete, we wish to make our oath known, that you might witness it, and see in it some measure of the joy we feel."

She stopped speaking, and Stefanos tightened his grip, as if to lend her his strength, or the odd warmth of his purpose.

May the Bright Heart bless you, as he has blessed us. May the light of his love shine between us; let the bond that we feel be a vessel for it. Oh, yes, she had practiced the words well, and often—but she found that they would not leave her lips, not in Veriloth.

In this place, to speak of the Bright Heart was to invoke the Dark Heart as well. She looked at Stefanos, and he raised an eyebrow.

No. Today, the only two hearts that concerned her were not bridged by blood-wars, but by love.

"Bless us," she said softly. "Wish us well. We have come to a road that many, and none, have walked; there are shadows here, and mysteries, but we have the light of our love to guide us. Help us, if you know the way."

She nodded quietly to Trin, and the young girl approached her carefully with a simple silver goblet.

Sara took it carefully and murmured a few words. Her hands passed over it three times. In answer, the water contained therein began to glow very, very gently.

Stefanos saw this; he could not fail to. But he smiled nonetheless and nodded to still the momentary uncertainty in her eyes. *It is only a little pain, Sarillorn. I will bear it.* But although he had told her this many times, he knew that she was still uncertain.

Slowly, cautiously, she held it up to his mouth. He steadied her with his cold, still hands, and allowed the bright liquid to pass his lips.

It burned as it slid down his throat; the smile that touched his lips froze in place. Tonight he desired to share no pain with her. He closed his eyes. The pain went deep, but not as deep as he expected. He traced its passage, summoned his power to deal with it, and then held back.

He had touched her once with the finger of the Dark Heart, and she had borne it. Could he do any less?

He opened his eyes to see that she had not moved.

Ah, Sarillorn. The light . . . He wanted to touch it, to keep it. Without thinking, he cupped it in his hands and found himself holding her face.

Without pulling back, she lifted the goblet to her lips, and drank as he had done.

Then, smiling, she turned to give it back to its bearer.

"Our love, like the water, flows between us."

"Our" love, Sarillorn? He knew it was important to her to be spared none of the truth. But was this not mortal love? Did he not honor her above all others, desire her in a way that not even Sargoth, most learned of the Sundered, could have guessed at?

"Like the waters," he answered as she had taught him, although the pain they had caused still burned at his blood.

She took his hand.

"Above all others, I have chosen you. If you will have it, I will swear my oath, and we shall be bonded."

He said nothing, and she continued, "But before you answer, know this: That all of life is endless change and endless growth. We will face our adversity, our sickness, our battles, and these will contrive to hurt us by dimming what we feel now. Love is not for the weak at heart, nor is it an act of destiny. It is what we choose, and to keep it alive, we will have to choose often."

Her smile was softer, but beneath it he felt the determination in her ritual.

"Know then," he said, touching her cheek gently, "that I have chosen *you.*" He smiled as she started. *No, Sarillorn, they are not the words of the Lernari ritual; they are mine, as you are.*

She shook herself slightly, her smile bearing a hint of wryness as she realized she could expect no less from the First of the Dark Heart. That smile changed as she continued. "Then take my oath, as I shall take yours."

"I shall."

"I will remain with you, in trust and faith."

"I will remain."

"We will know the passing of years, and the growth and change that it brings. Let our love give a value to the years we have chosen, that neither age nor time will tarnish. Let us choose no other, nor let another come between what we have chosen for ourselves."

He was silent a moment then, his face suddenly still. He reached out to touch her again, to feel the soft, smooth warmth of her living skin. His nod was quiet and intense.

"Let no adversity, no illness, no injury, come between all that we are."

"None shall. None."

Her voice dropped. "And when death parts us, one from the other, let us wait for each other at the bridge of the beyond, and we shall cross together."

He almost didn't hear her, for her words, the words that had seemed mere mortal ceremony, had a sudden, grim reality. *Time . . . age . . . death.* These were not things that he had ever feared; he was of the beginning, of the time before man and before the taint of life. No mortality had ever touched him. And none ever would.

He felt her arms around him and saw the pale blur of her face as she tilted it, just so. He kissed her, but quickly, then pulled back, holding her to study the lines of her face.

There was clapping in the galleries. Perhaps something of the same from one or two isolated individuals in the pews. It didn't matter. For he saw what his perfect memory had not yet made clear to him—the years on her face. Two years, and they had changed her. And the years that would follow would change her more, until at last, like the oldest and weakest of slaves, she succumbed to death and the beyond.

No. No. She is mine.

Looking at her, seeing the strength of her light—her love, as he knew it—he was determined to make sure that time and death understood well the claim that he made.

"Behold," he said, raising her hand in his own and addressing a point beyond the audience. "The lady of the Lord of the Empire."

"First of the Sundered."

Stefanos turned, already knowing whom he would see; no

other came into his private chambers without announcing his presence first. "You answered the summons quickly."

Sargoth smiled, shadow mixing with gray over a glint of sharp teeth. It was a disconcertingly human expression for one who was farthest removed from human things, but Stefanos understood it for what it was; he smiled in return.

"Pleasantry, Stefanos? Your time among the mortals shows. Who among the lesser Servants would not hasten to your summons?"

"Indeed." He inclined his head, waiting for a moment. If Sargoth had no other weakness, he had his curiosity, and Stefanos enjoyed allowing it to burn at him.

Sargoth's smile faded; he understood the game. "Why have you summoned me, and why with such urgency? It has been only a few years since I last walked this plane, and I am involved in my research."

"It has been, old friend, a human generation."

"What of it?" Sargoth moved restlessly. "I am still Second, Stefanos. I am not Valeth, to be held till dispersal at your whim."

"No." Stefanos nodded almost genially. But it was forced, and they both knew it. "Very well, Second. I need the knowledge that you have spent time hoarding."

"Ah. It is too much to hope that you wish to travel as I have traveled."

"Indeed. My concern is here, near our Lord."

"Ah, well. Perhaps when you have conquered, and you tire of it, you will truly begin to learn."

"Enough."

"Ask, then. The fire awaits me."

Stefanos nodded. "I wish to cure the taint of mortality."

"The taint of mortality?"

"Indeed. Among my subjects, there is one that I do not wish to die."

"And that one?"

"It is not of your concern, Sargoth." His voice was cold. "But if it is necessary to know it, she is half blooded— Lernari."

"Ah," Sargoth whispered, as if to himself. "That would explain much. As half blood, she is very strong; I am peripherally aware of her presence, though I have not searched for it." He looked up to meet the eyes of the First.

"No. Do not ask me why. Perhaps in time I will tell you, but I will not tell you now."

Sargoth's frustration was visible and immediate, but he said nothing, duly noting Stefanos's mood. He turned his mind and experience to the question; in and of itself, it was fascinating. How did one remove the taint of mortality from the mortal?

Stefanos waited.

With some annoyance, most of it directed at himself, Sargoth said, "I am afraid that I cannot immediately answer your question."

"You?" A hint of surprise in the First's voice did nothing to still the Second's annoyance.

"Indeed. I must . . . look into it."

"Then look. But know that I am waiting—and know that you do not have long." He rose, then, and left Sargoth alone.

"Stefanos?"

He felt her fingers brush gently against his chest as he stared up at the blue, curtained canopy. "Yes?"

"What is it? What's been bothering you?"

He looked down at her, seeing her face as she moved, day by day, closer to the death that would separate them. Normally she would have been sleeping by this time. "It is nothing, little one. Sleep."

He felt her warmth as she curled around him.

"I can't. This thing—whatever it is—it's been bothering you for the last four weeks, since the rite."

He sighed. When had it become so difficult to hide his thoughts from her?

"Sarillorn." His voice was quiet. "You are aging. Even as I watch, I can see the march of days."

She was startled, and then silent a moment as she absorbed what he said. "I forget that you are a Servant," she said at last. "I think the Lady saw as you see. But what of it? I'm mortal, love."

His grip tightened.

"I didn't think of it before, I'm sorry. But I am mortal. I've always lived with it."

"Mortal. And you will know age; you will know death."

"Yes." She shivered.

"No." He pulled away from her suddenly and rose.

"Stefanos!"

But he did not stop. Like a shadow he drifted out of her room, leaving her alone in the darkness.

Sargoth.

* * *

It was a full month before the Second of the Sundered returned with the answer to his question.

"To change her nature is impossible. The taint of mortality *is* her life; to remove it would kill her."

The First was silent in the face of the words of the Second.

And then Sargoth smiled; two could play a game of waiting—but only if one held information that the other needed. With the First, however, the wait had to be short. "There is another way."

"Speak it, then. Quickly."

"She is half blood. And half of that blood—the blood, I believe, of the Lady of Elliath—is not in and of itself prey to mortal whim. Through that half, Stefanos, you might choose to bind her to you."

"Bind her? I do not understand."

Sargoth allowed himself another, smaller smile. "It is not an easy thing; it requires, I believe, at least the blood of a Servant. But if you have that at your disposal, you might learn to use it as a link between yourself, our Lord, and her blood. You are the stronger; you would be the focus of it. Through the part of her that is not mortal, you might bind her life to yours."

Stefanos leaned forward, almost transfixed. "Tell me, then. How?"

And Sargoth did, while Stefanos absorbed each word. At length he sat back, feeling more at ease than he had in nearly two months.

That ease shattered as Sargoth spoke again. "Of course, she is not Malanthi. The Servant required would not be among us." The words were almost casual.

Stefanos closed his eyes.

chapter
fifteen

It was cool in Rennath, but the chill that bothered Sara had little to do with the weather. Nor was it the bleak, interminable stretch of city landscape; the gray of the city was something she'd adjusted to; and Stefanos had succeeded, in the end, in his attempt to convince her of the beauty inherent in subtle shades of shadow. Beneath the closed doors of her balcony she could hear the murmuring of her people as they walked between their homes and the market, their colorful clothing welcome contrast to reds and blacks. She smiled momentarily at the knowledge that even in Rennath the market was not a quiet place. Then the smile dimmed; Rennath was still Rennath, and in her four years here she had done little enough to change it.

She began to pace the carpeted floor of her bedroom, crushing the standing blue wool beneath her weary steps. At least here, in her quarters, color prevailed. Stefanos always thought it loud and impossible—much like its sole occupant. Again she smiled, and again the smile faded, but this time more rapidly.

What am I to do? She wrapped her arms around her shoulders, shivering. Her first impulse, and her last, was to call the First Servant into her presence and ask for his advice; for four years he'd been at her side in any situation she considered a crisis. She hadn't called him yet, and she wouldn't, not this time.

Belfas, why did you have to come?

Although he wasn't with her, she shut her eyes against the pain and confusion that was his parting gift to her. He had always had an expressive face. She could still see him clearly, as he walked toward the door of the room, placed one hand upon the knob, and stopped. He kept his face pressed against the wood of the door as he spoke.

Erin, Sarillorn, what has happened to you?

"Nothing."

Not nothing, Erin. I know you well enough to know that. You don't even look pleased to see me. Doesn't my news mean anything to you?

He'd turned then, his face a mask of white over the white of his power. White, radiant, brilliant—everything Sara had struggled so hard to put aside for too many years. She looked inward, saw a light that matched his, and felt the sting of tears take her eyes. He held out his arms then, and she stood immobile, half-comprehending, half-fearing. Belfas's arms, clothed in the indifferent rags of slavery, fell to either side.

"Will you help us, Sarillorn of Elliath?"

She knew what it cost him to be so formal—it wasn't his way, and it couldn't be the product of time. She opened her mouth to comfort him, and the words came out wrong.

"I don't know. I don't think you have a chance against him."

"Sarillorn, Kandor of Lernan is with us."

She shoved aside the memory, turned abruptly, and walked over to the balcony. With an almost furious tug, the paned doors flew open. Outside, Rennath sprawled in a familiar, tangled web. *When,* she thought, *did this cease to be a prison? When did I learn to value the small light that it holds?*

And as always, the doubt returned, stronger for the visit of Belfas, and more painful.

Have I lost the light? Lernan, Lernan, help me.

There was no answer, nor did she expect one. But today the use of His name gave her no peace, no respite.

Year-mate, line-brother, forgive me, but why, God why, did you have to come now?

His answer, complete with its mix of determination and worry, returned to echo around the empty walls of her room.

"We come to kill the First of the Dark Heart."

And years ago, four years ago, Sara knew that she would have willingly been among them. She wanted to tell him then that the First was also her bond-mate, rited and promised. But silence held sway in the face of her fear and the echoes of shame that she suddenly felt.

We come to bring home the Sarillorn of our line.

Home? This was home, this strange and ugly city with its legacy of death and violence, with its dark and grim Lord. Her stomach twisted, and her hands shot out to grip the gilded iron of the balcony railing.

They're right, all of them. Without the First Servant, Rennath will fall, Veriloth will fall, and with it the threat of the Dark. The Lernari will be able to heal the wounds that are left. She knew that it would be better for her people; they would know freedom again—a freedom that she could not completely give them, even now. But the First was also bond-mate. She struggled to keep the opposing images apart, even as she struggled to put them together.

"Sara?"

She wheeled around.

"Does something trouble you?"

"I—" Words fell away as her feet tripped lightly across the floor. He stood in the center of the room, silent as ever, cloak unfurling naturally to let her in. Without thinking, she brought her arms up and held them out as if to embrace him. Before she could, his own hands, strong and sure, gripped her shoulders.

"Sara, what is this?" Very gently his fingers brushed her cheek. "Tears, Lady? Dry them. Soon, someday soon, the work you wish to do with this city and this land will be yours to accomplish as you see fit. I swear it."

She shook her head. "Darkling."

She felt herself being pulled into his arms, felt the coolness of his chin as it rested against her hair.

"Lady, when the Empire of Veriloth is complete, I will give it to you. If the land is too difficult for the day, close your doors and shut it out."

This man—this Servant—was responsible for so much of the destruction that had swept the land. Three kingdoms had fallen to his attack in the last century; more beyond that, she was sure. How many more would fall, how many people would die or be delivered into slavery?

They're right. She thought it again, felt it resonate too deeply within her for expression. *He must die. If I love him, does it change that fact?*

But her arms curled tightly around him in denial. She knew why the Lernari had come and that on the morrow she would learn how. She knew what the results of their intended action would be—had she not been Sarillorn of Elliath?

But she knew also that Stefanos had not walked, in the manner of his kind, for almost four years, that he could dwell under the unforgiving glare of sunlight and open day, and that for her sake he had banished the ceremonies of Malthan from his palace—from the core of the Malanthi Empire.

Almost without her knowledge, the bands of her light crept

slowly outward. She could not see the smile of wonder and appreciation that turned the corners of her Lord's mouth upward in a gentle smile. The light, her light, was always new to him. It came wrapping itself around him as tightly as Sara's small arms.

Lernan forgive me. I love him.

Dinner was a subdued affair. Although Sara smiled and spoke as usual, her eyes were shuttered and impassive.

"Lady, what troubles you?"

"Nothing. Why do you ask?"

"Curiosity, Sara, only curiosity." But although he was unwilling to press her further, he watched her closely for the rest of the meal, and she was aware of each passing minute. For the first time in four years she longed for the comfort of anonymity.

She asked him a question, and dimly acknowledged his answer, but it meant nothing at all to her. The tines of her fork stabbed aimlessly at pieces of food as she pushed them around her plate.

At last, when she could suffer his scrutiny no longer, she rose, pulling the creased napkin from out of her crepe-covered lap.

"Stefanos, I'm—I'd like to have a little time to myself. I'm going to go back to my room."

" 'Stefanos'?" He smiled. "You are indeed troubled, Lady. You have used nothing but my chosen name for the entirety of our meal together. It is more formal than you are given to being."

She grew rigid for a moment; Stefanos could almost hear her muscles lock before she forced herself to relax. With a wan smile and a mumbled word of apology she left the great hall for the comfort of her quarters.

Stefanos watched her go. A faint, faint shiver touched his neck as he contemplated her action.

It has been long, Sarillorn, since you have been so troubled. It is almost as if . . .

Rising, he, too, left the hall.

I am waiting, Kandor.

She pulled her robe in a tighter circle around her upper body. She had long since ceased to pace the confines of her room; there was no answer in the movement and it wearied her. The doors were firmly shut, and the curtains had been tightly pulled. The shiver at the base of her spine spoke of a meeting to follow that no prying eyes should see inadvertently. What they saw if they were careful or cunning she could not prevent, but she did what she could, as always. The sun had faded from sky, leaving the clarity of cloudless night in its wake, and still she waited.

Kandor, she thought, staring at the wall without seeing it, *come now, come if you must.* She was dimly aware that she should feel some dread at the coming interview, but could gather only a numbness in response.

If you were dead, they would be free. And if I did not love you, I would help in your destruction for their sake. It is why I am Sarillorn; it is what the lines are sworn to. How selfish am I allowed to be?

Then, as she maintained her vigil, the air in the room began to shift. A soft breeze, sweet and clear as the air in the Woodhall had always been, touched her cheek and her memory. She felt for the direction of it, turning her face instinctively to catch the crystal sparkling of a foreign lattice in the room. It robbed the night of shadow, touching the walls, the bed, and the woman with gentle fingers of equal brilliance.

Kandor. She sighed, moved by his appearance in a way that she had not expected. Only twice before had she seen the arrival of Lernan's Servants, yet even as she watched she felt that she was seeing something new and precious unfold before her. The very room seemed to welcome his presence.

"Sarillorn."

Kandor, cloaked in form and shape so welcome to the lines, stood before her, his light both weapon and armor. His hands were at his side, but she felt that they were open, calling her to enter the ring of his arms. She had forgotten how beautiful a true Servant could be. *No, not forgotten,* she thought to herself. *My memory couldn't retain this. I don't think any human memory could.*

"Sarillorn." He said it again, the timbre of the word resounding in her stillness. "You are well."

"I am, Kandor of Lernan." She bowed then, low and formal, her knees trembling beneath her.

"We feared the worst, little one. How come you to be here, and safe?"

"Stefanos of the Enemy keeps me at his side."

"Stefanos? Is that not the name of—"

She felt a blush rising in her cheek.

His brow, so flawless in complexion, creased slightly. A frown, rare for the Servants of Lernan, touched his lips, but

Sara was certain that it was not directly connected to her words.
His eyes fell upon her, and she was reminded of the one other
Servant who had looked at her that way—the Lady of Elliath.
There was sorrow and resignation in eyes that should have held
nothing but peace and beauty. Without stopping to think, Sara
stepped forward and laid one hand against his breast.

"Kandor."

He reached up then, cupping her face between his hands.
They were cool and bore the faintest scent of orvas.

"It may be," he said as he looked into the green of her eyes,
"that my path differs from that of the Lady. I must try, little
one." But his words lacked conviction.

"What is it that you must try, Kandor?"

She knew what his answer would be and felt it keenly as his
words touched her mind.

"The destruction of the First of the Enemy."

She pulled her face away and turned her back upon him.

"Sarillorn, in this your help is necessary."

"What can I do? I've tried to escape the confines of the palace
before and I'm still here."

"Yes. And that troubles me."

She heard his words clearly and felt a growing ache as they
echoed into silence. Trembling, she turned to face him again.
He looked at her for a long while, his eyes unmoving and unblinking. At last he stepped forward, the light following his
movement.

"I do not understand what has happened here, Sarillorn, but
be at peace. Either my hope will come true, or the Lady's. If
you have a choice in either, make your choice free of guilt or
regret; we each must do what we perceive possible. For my part,
I must contest the Servant of the Enemy. I ask for your help,
but if you are unable to grant it, I ask only that you do not
interfere. Do not warn him of our presence here."

"I—" She bent her head. "Kandor, Servant, I will do what
I am able to do. But I—"

His fingers touched her trembling lips, stilling their movement. "Hush, little one. For you the road must indeed be hard—
I did not understand that until this moment. But I will trust what
you are. Do you the same."

Mutely she shook her head from side to side, but the movement was so slight that Kandor appeared to have missed it. He
continued to speak, his voice unbearably gentle. Tears touched
the corners of Sara's eyes, trailing listlessly down her cheeks. It

had been long since she had heard a voice completely free from the shadow of the Enemy, and she discovered with pain and surprise that she had missed it.

"On the morrow, Sarillorn, the initiates of Line Elliath will come with me to the palace. There we will confront the Dark Lord and attempt to bring about his destruction. He does not know of our presence—at great cost to Lernan. With surprise on our side, we should be able to accomplish our task.

"If you will help us, do so. If you will not, absent yourself from the company of the First of the Enemy if you have that option.

"But regardless of your choice, I bid you be at peace. Lernan alone knows what you have seen these four years, and to Lernan alone must you answer."

He bent his head then and gently kissed her brow. Leaning slightly into the comfort of the pressure of his mouth, she closed her eyes, and by doing so missed the look of pity that briefly touched his features. His arms enfolded her, cradled her in their warmth.

That warmth lingered as the Servant of Lernan faded into the night as quietly as he had come, but with his passing the chill returned.

In all her life, Sara, born Erin of Elliath, had never felt so alone.

The morning came, gray and unrelenting. Sara pulled herself reluctantly from her bed and over to her closet. She opened the door weakly, sunlight at her back revealing the clothing that hung so lifelessly along the wall.

Sara always dressed in such a way as to alleviate the gloom of Rennath, but for the first time in years it was not the darkness outside that she feared. Without thinking she pulled one robe out of the closet and brought it to her bed, where it was casually laid aside. She unfastened the ties of her nightclothing and stepped out of it, thinking about the day ahead. She would have to see to the infirmary, then journey out to the market's center, to the place of judgment, where she would sit beside her Lord and listen to the pleas of those who had made it this far.

Kandor. The name slid into her mind effortlessly, but it was not as easily dislodged. Shaking herself, she bent and began to fold her nightgown, placing it to one side of the bed. Emilee would come for it in half an hour, and in the eve a new gown would be available.

Kandor. What must I do?

Blindly she turned to the bed to lift the day's clothing in tired hands. Only then, with the sunlight glinting off a circle of silver, did she see clearly which of her robes she had chosen. Picking it up, she clutched it tightly to her breast and cheek, waiting for tears that would not come.

Stefanos stood at the end of the hall. Sara saw him clearly as she rounded the corner only minutes after leaving the physician's rooms. She caught a glimmer of the sun from one of the high windows and, tracing that beam to the floor, sighed. Late again, as always.

"Lady." Stefanos bowed, low and formal, as she approached him. "The time draws near. Will you travel with me to the place of judgment?"

"I will." Her answer was automatic; she could say it without thought, as she had said it every week for the last year. The place of judgment was something she had taken from her people and, with no small effort, implanted here. Stefanos had been curious about it, the Church furious. She was never sure which of those two things had decided him.

He offered her his arm and she took it, walking woodenly at his side. He noted the robes of his Enemy's priesthood, but forbore to comment on them; something troubled Sara and, if those robes gave her comfort, she was welcome to them.

But as they walked out to where the carriage waited, he noted the lag of her step. *She grows old,* he thought, chilled by it. He pulled his own robes more tightly around him as the glare of open sunlight touched his face. A strange pride touched him, and he lifted his face to the sun's rays. Mere years ago, a blink of time, he would not have thought it possible. *But now,* he realized, helping Sara to her seat with a quiet intensity, *now anything is possible.*

The carriage moved quickly down the cobbled streets, and Sara hated the fact, for she could hear the rough shouts of the men who drove and see pedestrians leaping out of the vehicle's path. Their faces flickered by too quickly for Sara to catch their expressions, but she was familiar enough with her people to know their fear or panic.

At least we won't hit anyone.

She drew a weak comfort from that, remembering clearly the body of the child that they had left in the wake of their first ride. She had stopped the carriage and stumbled out, too late to help the child, too noble to be of comfort to the parent who sat blindly cradling the tiny corpse.

Her eyes fell upon Stefanos's impassive profile. *You stopped those deaths. For me.* Silent, she leaned into his side and felt his arm slide round her shoulders.

"Sara," he said into her hair, "if you wish, we may shorten the hearings."

She shook her head.

"Or you may absent yourself from them altogether and wait for me in the carriage."

She shook her head again, more forcefully. She knew it was not the First of the Enemy that they came to make their pleas to. She would find the strength to hear them out and to help them, for although she was weary, she was still Sarillorn.

"Very well." He held her the more tightly, as if to shield her from some future ordeal. "We are almost at the pavilion."

Nodding, she let the rest of the landscape pass her by in a gray blur, her face pressed into her Lord's side. He was cold. Normally she found a warmth beyond touch at his side. Kandor came between them this time.

The carriage came to a halt, and a doorman appeared on the instant to allow them out of the coach. Stefanos stepped down and turned to aid his lady—something no guard or slave dared do while he was present. He felt her stumble slightly and braced her arm while she completed her tentative steps to the ground.

"Sunlight becomes you, Sara." He began to lead her to the pavilion. "One day I shall capture the sun for you, and it will shine for your pleasure alone."

She smiled then, moved by the forced lightness of his words. "And I, my Lord, will set it free at that moment, to let it touch all faces alike and to marvel at their beauty."

"And will you take nothing for yourself?"

"I have what I need." But her smile slipped away. She looked up, then, to the deep blue stripes of the tent, twisting around lines of darker gray. The flaps were open upon two ornate chairs, one large and tall with gold leaf and inlay, the other light and simple. She listened to the dying chatter of the market, noting that people, clutching their purchases in baskets or under arms as befitted their station, walked quickly away from the perimeter of the area. Those that did not move quickly enough were escorted by guards, but here again no violence was offered.

And that, too, was your gift.

She walked in the enforced silence until she reached the dais.

There she took her accustomed chair, and Stefanos joined her in his own. His posture was almost regal, but in the darkness of his robes and the shadow of the tent flap, he looked, in truth, like the creature he was.

He looked at Sara, and she sighed.

"Ready," she murmured.

Turning, he nodded to one of his men.

"The Lord and Lady will now hear those who have come before them to be judged." His voice was loud and monotonous—like that of any mediocre herald. Sara tuned out the rest of the speech; it had something to do with proper behavior, and she abhorred it. It was not what the people had come for and seemed to her to be just another obstacle to justice.

At last the herald fell silent, and the crowd began to shuffle. Most of the people here were spectators; Sara saw a few familiar faces, and caught a shy, young smile. She returned it then let her attention drift back to the opening among the people.

A man stepped forward. His clothing was in ill repair as only that of a fugitive can be; there were tears and rents that were so old they looked natural.

He stumbled a little before he reached the foot of the dais. There he stopped and bent forward in a harsh bow, knees snapping. Sara started forward involuntarily; from where she sat she could feel that the man's arm was broken and caused him great pain. She restrained herself before her Lord could, sinking with gritted teeth into the prison of her throne.

"Your case will be heard."

The man looked up. At this distance, almost close enough to reach out, Sara could see a long seam that marred his features. She had thought him old, but recalculated; what appeared to be wrinkles at a distance were minute scars. She could feel his eyes upon her alone as he opened his mouth.

"Bring him water," she said curtly to one of the guards. "He'll be able to speak when he's had something to drink." The men were well enough acquainted with her presence that they did not look askance at their Lord when he did not interrupt. They obeyed, their faces locked in gray neutrality and indifference. Water was brought to the man, and shoved roughly to his dry lips.

"Gently." Sara kept her voice even, hating the guards, hating the empire. "Drink slowly."

The man nodded, the most he was capable of, and let the water linger a few seconds in his mouth before swallowing. It was warm, but hopefully clean; and if the hearing did not go well, it would also be the last he would taste.

He did his best to heed her words, but felt the eyes of the guards boring into him.

"Please." Sara held out a hand. "Stand if you will be more comfortable."

Slowly and gratefully he got to his feet, gingerly avoiding the use of his right arm. As if by accident his eyes glanced furtively out to the crowd.

It was no accident. Sara could see that by the easing of his tension, and she sought out the eyes of the watchers herself. Someone or something waited there, important to the man who had come before her. She looked carefully but no one started guiltily, and too many eyes were upon the claimant to be able to single out any one person.

What she was attempting must have been obvious to the man, for he cleared his throat loudly, drawing her attention away from the search.

"My Lord." He bowed awkwardly. "My lady." His speech was oddly accented and shaky.

He came closer and once again assumed a kneeling posture, but this time he sat directly in front of Sara.

Stefanos did not fail to notice this.

"It is customary," he said, leaning slightly forward, "to give your name before you make your plea."

Stiffly the man nodded, but again in Sara's direction.

"Lady, you hear the plea of Ranin."

"Of what house?"

"I am with no house, Lord." The man was trembling.

"I see." Stefanos nodded, raising one hand to touch the tip of his chin meditatively. "What house claims your protection, then?"

Ranin was silent a few moments before answering. Sara felt a shock of fear travel through her. It evoked an answering shudder, and she held out one hand in the direction of the First Servant.

"My Lord," she said softly, "let him speak freely."

Stefanos nodded, eyes shuttered, and Sara *knew* what the man's fate would be. She paled slightly, took a deep breath, and turned again.

"Why have you come before us?"

"To ask—to beg, if the lady wills it, for your aid and mercy."

Sara could see an echo of her own knowledge in the man's face and bearing.

"Show us your arm."

Sara cringed at the tone in Stefanos's voice. She met the open plea in the man's face and turned away ashamed. Weakly he lifted his left arm.

"The other one."

"Stefanos, his arm is broken; it causes his pain. Please—"

Without looking at the Sarillorn, Stefanos continued. "The other arm."

Ranin attempted to comply, clamping his lips shut as he did. Pain flared around him, seen clearly by Sara's eyes alone. With an audible curse, she thrust herself away from the confines of her chair, stepped off the platform, and came to stand at the man's side. Her hands, still as white as they had always been, came up on either side of Ranin's shoulders, and she opened the gate between his pain and her power. Effortlessly she flowed outward, and the pain receded at her touch.

"My thanks, Lady," the man whispered, but his voice was bitter and broken. "But you have wasted your energy; I do not believe you will sway your Lord this day."

She started at the strange sound of his words and paled further when she realized that the tongue was not the one used by citizens of the empire. She knew well the punishment for such a crime.

He must have seen her start, for his expression changed subtly. "Indeed, Lady, I am newly brought to the empire, from Segan. I know the robe you wear, but not how it has come to be here."

"Why did you—"

"Not because I knew you to be initiate. Because I had heard that you might sway the will of the ruler of Rennath. Seeing you, I might well believe it—but seeing him thus, I cannot." He straightened, pulling away from her hands.

"What crime do you seek mercy for?"

He gave a brief, bitter smile. "The crime of remaining as true to Segan as I have been able."

The sound of metal against metal touched her ears, and she looked up. Two of the guards were walking toward them. Wheeling, she faced her Lord; her cheeks bore the twin flags of anger and shame.

"First Servant, I ask you not to pronounce a judgment before you have heard the case."

"Lady," he replied, all steely politeness. "I have seen with my own eyes two crimes committed here. This man that you seek to save is a slave, not in itself a crime. But he has named himself, and he speaks to you in a tongue that I have declared dead. He has earned my judgment for breaking laws that are mine."

She knew the cast of his features. Anger welled up, and she fought it down, but it was hard; she had not felt it truly for years. With one deft movement, she inserted herself between the man and the approaching guards.

"Sarillorn, Lady," Stefanos stood. "In other matters I have granted you leeway. I have conceded much to you, but this must fall outside of that domain. I will rule the empire. It is *mine*. Should I give ground to you in this case, it will only weaken the foundations that I have laid. And they are strong, but young. They need their time to grow."

The guards drew closer, their faces still completely neutral. Sara still barred their way, and as they reached her, they came to a nervous stop.

"Lady, please stand aside."

Sara met the eyes of each of the guards before turning to face Stefanos. "Lord." She bowed slightly, a tinge of bitter mockery in the gesture. She did not do as he requested, but was well aware of the futility of her defiance.

"Lady?"

She looked at him then, her eyes touching the harsh contours of his pale, shadowed face. His mouth was set in a grim smile that gave her nothing.

"Lord," she repeated, then added, in a lower voice, "Stefanos . . ."

He shook his head once, sharply. "Not in this, Lady." Very gently, he added, "My laws must be followed if I am to govern this world."

Again he motioned to his guards, and they took a step forward, but Sara could see their hesitance. She knew well the dilemma they found themselves in; their Lord had given a command, albeit wordless, and yet should they harm her at all, it was worth their lives.

After a few minutes, Stefanos stepped down from his throne, to join his lady. There was nothing friendly in the movement, but nothing threatening—not for Sara.

She could feel the trembling of the man at her back, although he, too, kept silent as the nightwalker approached.

For a few seconds, caught between one who needed her aid and one who denied it, she felt again the strands of an old call. She had thought it dead, and realized that it must be as inseparable from what she was as this mockery of justice from him.

And Stefanos drew back as the bands of her light, so necessary and so familiar, flickered in an awkward and ugly rhythm. *No, Lady, I know what I do.* He shook his head and stepped forward again, catching her face in his hands. *I cannot give you this yet. But soon . . .*

He turned to look at the man with a cold distaste. For a moment he longed to give her what she asked for, but steeled himself against it. To cease to feed was a thing that affected only himself directly; to cease to judge was to lose control of Veriloth, the only true goal in his existence.

"Little one."

Her eyes opened slowly.

"I am sorry. I cannot give you this slave's life. He seeks to prove a point by breaking my law before my people, and he shall indeed prove it." His grip on her tightened, and he nodded again to his guards. This time they moved quickly and efficiently to their goal.

Sara struggled briefly against the cold vise that held her. Tears, caught and held in, made her eyes shine with a preternatural brilliance. *You don't understand!* She opened her mouth to say it, but the words remained locked with the tears that she would not give up.

As the guards secured the man, Stefanos released her, his fingers lingering against her cheek. He turned and walked back to the dais while Sara stood still in the center of the square. She watched his back as it receded.

"Wait!"

Both the guards and their Lord turned at her words, stopping at the command inherent in them. With a few quick steps she approached Ranin, the captive slave.

The leader of the guard stepped in front of her before the hand she reached out could make contact. He offered her no violence and no threat, but would not move out of her way.

Turning rapidly, she sought the eyes of Stefanos and found them, as ever, upon her.

"My Lord, please let me speak with your prisoner. I've no choice but to accept your judgment, but I—"

Silent, he motioned and the captain stepped away, eyes betraying none of the curiosity he must have felt.

Ranin met her eyes with his own bleak, gray-brown ones. He gave a tremulous smile and spoke again in the tongue of his youth.

"Priestess, I thank you for what you have tried to do. I should have known that it is still the Lord that rules."

"Yes." Her voice was soft and gentle, but contained all of the bitterness she felt. Reaching out, she again touched his arm, her fingers dancing along skin bare through rents in his tunic.

"What are you doing?"

She tried not to meet his eyes, knowing the cost to herself, but she failed because it was in her nature to do so. Her tears, controlled so far, spilled over to adorn her face and the fingers that were tentatively raised to catch them.

"I am dulling your pain. For later."

He nodded.

In a rush, before she could lose control of her voice, she said, "I don't believe you came here just to make a point. You came for something. Ask it; as long as it is not your life, I will grant it."

He closed his eyes on the hope that she offered and then shrugged his arms free of the guards who loosely held them.

"Lady . . ." His voice was so quiet that had she not been so intent upon the words, she would have missed them. "In the crowd, my wife and child are watching. For myself, I can ask nothing, and maybe it is better so; I am—"

She touched his lips with the tip of her fingers, and he nodded against them.

"My wife is of your height, but her hair is darkened. The roots are pale and blond; you will see them as you approach. My child—my daughter—the same, but she is smaller. She is dressed as a boy; she speaks but little.

"We were slaves in the House Calvar and worked from their summer home, two days' journey from the city."

Sara nodded; the name meant something to her.

"My daughter was to be given to Deven of Calvar. To spare her that, we have traveled to you."

"Deven? But he's just a boy."

"Yes. And out of the three that have been given to him previously, not one has survived the week."

"So you—"

"We risked our lives for the chance of your intervention. Even if we failed, my daughter's chances would be no less, and her death more pleasant." He lowered his voice. "We had heard

of you, even in House Calvar—that you listened to the pleas of
the poor in your city, you judged fairly, and that you granted the
Lord's mercy. You were our only chance. And I knew that to
approach you here, as a free man, would cost me much.'' Suddenly he grabbed her arms. One of the guards started forward,
and Sara gave a vicious shake of her head.

"Save my child. Take her for one of your own. I have seen
you; I know what you are. If you cannot take my wife, she will
understand; we have spoken and she has agreed." He released
her then and turned to his executioners. They began to walk
away.

"Ranin."

All five stopped at the word.

"What are their names?"

"Names?" He laughed bitterly and turned again.

His laughter hung in the air. Chilled, Sara turned to the crowd
and began to scan the faces it held. She saw the mixture of fear,
respect, and satisfaction that mingled in the unknown spectators, and passed them by; she knew what she was looking for.
Ranin's description had not been clear—any number of women
matched it—but Sara knew she would have no difficulty.

One face, perhaps two, would hold the emotions of shock
and bereavement, and she would not return to the dais until she
had found them.

Once her eyes swept fruitlessly across the crowd, and once
again, but on the third pass, at the very edge, she could see one
stiff, still figure, with another huddled beside it.

She focused on the two of them and began to push her way
through the crowd. People parted only slowly, and she felt the
hands and fingers of many brush against the gray of her robes,
and heard the whisper of plea or prayer that accompanied the
gestures. *Not now.*

The huddled figure drew closer, and as it did, it straightened
suddenly and looked up.

Contact.

Pain. Anger. Fear—the last, so strong and fierce and pure
because it was fear for another, born out of love and desperation.
The blue, blank eyes gave way to a storm that streaked out to
touch the Sarillorn of Elliath, to call her forward.

The smaller figure pulled at the larger one, wordless, and the
larger one—caught by Sara's eyes—pushed her away.

The little one, whose face was still soft with the contours of
youth, whispered something that Sara could not catch. The older

woman spoke, her voice harsh but low. The girl nodded and held out a hand, which her mother took firmly. Her eyes never left Sara's face.

As Sara reached them, she gave a half bow; the only public acknowledgment she could make of their loss. Nor was the bow returned, but she hadn't expected it to be.

The woman stood her ground; she did not flinch as Sara reached out and gripped her arm with one strong hand. She touched the child in the same way.

"Come," she said softly.

"Where?" The woman spoke the tongue of Veriloth.

"To the Lord. I—" Her voice broke as she turned her eyes away from the woman's pain. She caught herself and forced words past stiff lips. "I wish to—to claim your ownership."

"We are already owned." As if to make the point more clearly, the woman raised her right arm. Her sleeve rolled away to reveal the mark of the House Calvar. She nodded at her daughter to do likewise, but Sara had a firm grip on the girl's arm, and not for such a statement would she release it.

Taking a deep breath, Sara said, "You bear the mark of House Calvar. Yet you are not in their holdings now."

"What matter? We will be returned there soon enough." At this, the woman's eyes flared briefly to life as they darted to the child she and her husband had failed. Her husband . . . Sara caught the wave of her pain and her grip tightened.

"You will not be returned to them. They have proven their . . . dereliction of ownership. You should know that anyone can claim ownership of you now. Come. Please."

The woman began to walk forward, but suddenly stopped, grasping tight the hand that held her.

"Lady." She fell awkwardly to her knees, bowing her head to hide her expression. "Lady, if you claim us . . . we'd heard that—will you—" She took a deep breath. "This is my only surviving child. She has been a good slave of the high nobility since she turned four. She will serve you well if you will take her for your own." Her grip faltered then, as did her voice.

Sara started to speak, stopped, and took a breath. When she began again, she whispered in the tongue of the condemned man.

"Lady, you came to me for mercy, at the cost of your husband's life. I cannot save him, but he knew this before he came forward. But both you and your child I can help. By the law that condemns your husband, I can claim you."

And if your husband had not come to me in the place of

judgment, had he stopped me on the street or in procession, I could have saved you all.

She pushed the thought away, but it stung her deeply. He could not have known this; he could only know that she would preside, with their Lord, over the judgment, and that only free men could plead their cases.

As a free man he had come, for the first and last time.

She was determined to make him understand that his courage had meaning. More brusquely than intended, she pulled Ranin's wife forward, lapsing once again into the harsh tongue of Veriloth. "Come."

This time the woman followed with no further comment. The child was reticent, but took her lead from her mother.

Sara strode through the opening in the crowd, her face set and grim. She walked the path that any supplicant might walk, her eyes searching for the guards and their precious prisoner. Already he was almost beyond hearing; what she had to say must be said quickly.

She stopped at the foot of the dais and turned to her two followers, releasing them. "Give me your arms."

The tone of her voice left no question as to which arm she referred to. Mother and child, in one movement that spoke of years of slavery, did as they were told, turning their sleeves back to reveal the scars beneath them. Sara gripped one arm in each hand and raised them both.

"Lord, I have found two slaves of the House Calvar in the common market. I claim them for my own." Her voice was that of a priestess: loud, clear, and too resonant to be missed.

Watching her from the dais, Stefanos frowned. "They are running from their house?"

"Their house is my house now. They will not run from me."

The frown increased slightly. "They bear the brand of Calvar."

"Yes. But they are not in Calvar holdings." She met the dark of his eyes with defiance. "And by *your* law, what Calvar cannot hold, they cannot keep. By your *law*, and the *laws* of your land, I claim the two for personal service."

Stefanos watched the tears that formed at the corners of Sara's eyes, watched the intensity of the corded light that flared from an invisible center to weave round each of the two slaves. His eyes flickered back to the guards that held the slave he had declared criminal.

Calvar is a powerful house, Sarillorn. Can you never see the cost of your decision? His fear was not for himself.

But he knew she would accept any cost; the light told him that. And because of the light, he would accept any cost, for he knew that to refuse her this, when it was within the bounds of the written law, would be to lose her.

He raised one hand, gave one order, and the group escorting the slave halted, turned, and faced them.

"Very well, Lady Sara. I accept your claim. These two are yours; you may do as you see fit with them." Calvar he could deal with far more easily than the Sarillorn's pain.

She lowered the branded arms, feeling the tremors in the older one. Her eyes flitted outward to Ranin; she could still see him clearly, although he was almost out of the square.

Quietly she bowed, this one low and formal; it was the salute of Elliath. He could not return the bow; he was anchored by guards on either side, but she saw the slight bob of his head. More she could not see; his face was too distant.

He smiled, she thought. *Please, Lernan. He smiled.*

And then she was crying. She tried to keep her knees from touching the ground. Darkness enveloped her; cold arms circled her shoulders and waist.

Oh, Kandor, she thought, unable to hold herself from her Lord's support. *Kandor, it's so dark. It* is *so dark.*

chapter
sixteen

The carriage ride home was uneventful, or so Sara believed; she remembered little of it. She left her Lord at the front gate, shunning his offered arm as if it could brand her as her new slaves had been branded.

"Sara."

She shook her head from side to side without turning back.

"Sara!"

This stopped her, although it took a little while to realize why. His hands were upon her shoulders before it came to her that Stefanos had *shouted*. In all her years at Rennath, she had never heard him do so; if he raised his voice at all, it was to ensure that feeble human ears received proper orders if they were too distant.

"Lady, why are you running?"

For a brief instant she leaned her back against his chest and felt the circle of his arms around her waist. *Was I running, Lord?* It was an almost idiotic thought. She closed her eyes as his cheek brushed against hers. *I've not run from you for—*

She saw again Ranin's desperate, broken face in the darkness against her lids, heard again Kandor's gentle voice and wrapped it around his mission: *We must save the people of Veriloth. I am here to destroy—*

With a harsh, sharp breath, she broke away.

"Sara?"

She wheeled around, her cheeks flushed with anger and guilt. "Damn you!"

He took a step backward at the unfamiliarity of the guttural words. A mild surprise flitted across his face—that and something else, both of which Sara ignored.

"Why wouldn't you spare his life? You know why he came

to me! You could hear every word he spoke!'' Her hands shot up to grip the folds of his robes.

Neutrally he said, ''Lady, you know the laws of my land.''

''I know that they're *your* laws; you made them, you can break them!''

''And yet you have said that my word, once given, should be binding.''

It was true; Sara could not deny it. In the first few months of her stay, she had tried so hard to make him understand how the value of the given word, a Lord's promise, would not weaken his rule. His assertion did nothing to assuage her anger; instead, it heightened it.

''That was a question of honor—this is a question of justice and mercy! That man was doing the only thing he could to save his daughter from—''

''In my empire, slaves have no rights to the lives of their children.''

''Yes!'' She was close to tears. ''In *your* God-cursed, damnable *empire*!'' She threw her hands up, releasing him as if the contact burned her.

We must save the people of Veriloth. Sarillorn, will you aid us? Erin, we're here to free you. What's wrong?

Stop it! She brought her hands up to her ears. *Just stop it! I know what you're saying!*

She felt a roiling darkness within her, as pain mixed with sorrow and fury.

Stefanos stood, completely still, in the silence in front of her.

''Stefanos, please . . .'' The anger fell away from her voice. ''Please, give me some reason . . .''

''Lady, do not—''

''Give me one reason. Please, if it's not too late, give me this one life. Let me know that you understand.''

He caught her hands.

''Lady, why is this one life so important today? You must know that this happens—''

She tore her hands away as he opened the wound of her guilt. ''I know what happens!'' For so long, the knowledge of all the death and pain that she couldn't *see* or touch, had eroded the joy she felt when she was able to help.

''Kill him, then. Do what you want, Lord. You're a Servant of the Enemy; it's what you do best.''

She turned and fled across the courtyard, sunlight twisting her shadow along the cool, perfect stone. This time he did not stop her. Her words lingered in the air, and around them, the cold of her absence. Once he started forward, stopping himself before he could take a step—and hated the lack of control the action showed, although none but himself was witness to it.

Once she had entered the castle, she leaned against the gray of the walls of the north hall, her cheek cooling against the touch of stone. She longed to escape to her room, but there was one more thing to do: Claim her new slaves from the slavemaster Kadrin's tender mercies. She was exhausted; her hands and arms shook as she pressed them tightly against her body. She took a few moments to steel herself against the pain in the eyes that she walked to meet and brace herself against the gratitude that showed her more clearly than anything else the magnitude of the empire's crime.

The empire, Sara? Say rather, the First Servant. Say Stefanos.

Her fist struck the wall and slid downward. She cursed, knowing that the two would be waiting under the fear that she had proved false to her word. She could see the mother's arm wreathed tightly and protectively around the daughter's shoulders, see the way they would cringe upon sighting her, their eyes full of hope and the expectation of the loss of even that.

But even knowing how they must feel, she could not quite gather the strength to leave the silent hall. Bitterly she thought, *Am I never to have a moment of life to call my own? Is there never a day when I can lay aside responsibility? Must I always have to be so damnably strong?*

The answer returned to her.

Sarillorn, you have changed.

And because acknowledgment of that silent voice demanded more strength than facing the slaves, she ran from it, her feet striking the floor. But it echoed within her, the way the worst of fears always does.

Kadrin looked up as Lady Sara burst into the room. She could see the faint hint of surprise across his rounded features as the door slammed once against the wall. Taking a deep breath, she schooled her expression.

"Kadrin, I've come to see to the two slaves that were brought in from—from the market."

"They are here, Lady." He rose from behind the desk he

occupied, straightening his brown tunic as was his habit. "Wait but a moment, and they will be with you."

She nodded and he left.

True to his word, he was back in a moment, turning to say a few words that she couldn't quite catch to someone the door obscured. He entered the room, and behind him trailed the woman and child that Sara had seen earlier.

The woman looked up warily, and in her eyes were all the emotions that Sara had expected. The foreknowledge stopped her from flinching.

"Lady." The woman gave a low, cringing bow, one that her child was quick to copy. In the daughter's face, angular and thin, the mother's heritage was obvious. Sara watched their foreheads touch the ground at the same moment and shuddered.

She looked away from them to the only other person in the room and met the dark concern of his eyes.

Sara, you've got to practice more control. Her mouth folded awkwardly into the semblance of a smile.

"Lady?"

"Return to your duties, Kadrin. After I have spoken with these two, I shall send them to you for housing and general instruction."

He bowed. "I understand they are to serve you personally?"

She nodded again, this time more emphatically, feeling the woman's eyes upon her.

"Very well, Lady. Do you wish to use this room to conduct your meeting, or will you speak with them elsewhere?"

The question was pure formula; Kadrin knew well that Sara spoke with new slaves in her personal rooms. He gave her a soft smile in acknowledgment of this and was troubled when it slid off her face without changing it.

"I'll talk to them in my rooms." In a falsely bright voice, she added, "They'll have to know some of the geography of the palace, so they might as well begin now. That way they won't be in the same straits I was for my first year or so."

Kadrin smiled, forbearing to correct his lady. It had been perhaps fourteen months before she could wander anywhere in the castle without getting lost.

Again his smile had no effect. "Lady, does something trouble you?"

Her eyes met his, and he took a step back.

"Come," Sara said softly, holding out one hand to the child. The girl gave her mother a nervous look, and her mother returned a forcible nod—both of which made Sara regret the openness of the gesture. Timidly the girl walked forward and placed one of her hands in Sara's. It was cold and shook visibly.

"Come, little one. Your mother follows us. There is nothing to fear."

She said it, knowing that she would not be believed, not yet. *But this is what I'm good at.* She sighed, taking little comfort from the truth of the thought.

Silent, they walked down the hall toward the steps that led to her rooms. There was a grim air about the walk, as if it were a funereal procession.

Which it is.

She felt tears start and pushed them back in near fury. Why did anyone choose to love in the empire? Its cost was so plain and so unavoidable. She saw it in the face of the two that walked with her, a shadow that no amount of light would ease.

And then she caught the direction of the thought and turned her face away from the child at her side to allow a few meager tears the escape they demanded.

I've changed.

She could not see the way the girl's face tilted up at the sight of her or the curiosity flickering amid the pain and loss.

They walked in a silence made of bated breath and sorrow.

At length they came to the wing that was Sara's. She turned to her young charge and watched her as they passed the various tapestries that lent warmth to stone.

Although the child kept her head forward, Sara could see her eyes flicker from side to side, trying to take in the elements of the woven tales all at once. This was one of the reasons they had been put here, and as Sara's eyes joined the girl's, she drew on the second reason—memory. For along the walls was much of the history of Elliath, from the death of Gallin of Meron, whom all lines could claim, to the founding of the seven lines. She looked at the face of Gallin, so painstakingly, mortally woven, and met his cloth-bound eyes. As always, the contrast of eyes and face surprised her and humbled her, for his features were distorted by extreme pain—one of his limbs was caught in the process of burning away—but his eyes were full of a deep and endless peace.

Did the women who wove your countenance truly capture you so well, or do I imagine you as clearly as the line knows you existed?

He had no answers; at least the lifelike quality did not give him speech, although she often expected it.

She turned to the child, and the child's glance darted almost guiltily away. She did the only thing she could; she kept walking. The girl relaxed.

Yet again Sara stopped, toward the end of the hall. And once more, eyes captured her—but this time, they were no mortal eyes.

Lady.

Sara resisted the urge to bow, although she normally did so when unaccompanied. Her free hand went up and stopped just short of the flat, silken face.

Mother of Elliath. The Lady looked outward, through her lost granddaughter, and beyond the tapestries that hid the walls on the other side. She was robed in the simplest of white, a gown unadorned by even the circle that symbolized the continuity and wholeness of the line. Her arms fell out to either side upon the knees of the legs crossed beneath her.

And in her palm, a cut that did not bleed lay bare, turned upward to catch a beam of sunlight.

She did not look mortal.

What do you see, Lady? What vision haunts you?

Again no answer. Sara expected none, but were this pale visage to speak, she would not be surprised.

What could you see that would send me to Veriloth? She searched the face, as she'd done countless times, for some hint of sorrow, anger, or pain; for some hint of triumph, defeat, or planning. But the Lady's eyes touched something that her face could never express.

Nor her words—at least not well. Sara sighed once, refusing to give in to the anger that lay beneath the surface of the thought. *I am still here, Lady. May I not betray whatever fate you saw me serving.*

She turned and stumbled slightly, then blushed, remembering that her hand was still anchored to a young child.

"Sorry," she said softly. "I, too, find the tapestries distracting. Come, my rooms are beyond the doors."

So saying, she walked up to the set of double doors, freed her hand momentarily, and opened them. She tried not to notice the child shrinking into her mother.

The mother whispered something softly—something Stefanos would have heard from half a hall away—and the child walked quickly forward, following Sara's shadow into a large sitting room.

"Come in." Sara spoke to the mother. The mother followed without hesitation, eyes darting side to side to see if all was safe, although she knew she could do nothing about it if it were not.

"Please, take a seat, both of you."

A suspicious glance at Sara in no way changed the instinctive obedience that followed the request.

Blithely Sara continued as if unaware of the tension of her two spectators. "These rooms will be a part of your duties. They're to be cleaned when I leave them in the morning; I'll provide a schedule for you if Kadrin's lost his, which is likely."

She waited, and after a moment the woman nodded.

"If you would prefer it, you and your daughter may work together in the tasks that are given to you when you are not tending to me; I'll also speak to Kadrin about this."

The child looked curiously at her mother.

Sara smiled softly and nodded. When the child made no move, she said, "Go ahead, child. You want to ask your mother a question; feel free to do so."

The girl blushed and her mother whitened.

"It's all right. No question she could ask would give offense, not here."

Still the child remained where she sat.

"Whisper, if you have to. I shan't mind. Well, go on. Consider it an order."

At this, the girl inched toward her mother. Her mother's trembling arm shot out around the girl's shoulder, drawing her closer. The girl whispered something and the woman's brow furrowed. Quietly she shook her head.

Again Sara smiled. "Yes," she said softly, catching the girl's attention. "Kadrin is a slave."

She could feel the two sets of eyes upon her as she continued. "He is also slavemaster. He was given the position because he knows—better than the low-born free—what a slave must suffer at the hands of the wrong man or woman. It is up to him to watch his charges carefully."

The woman looked confused, and Sara sent out a wave of sympathy, not knowing if it would reach her.

"If you have any difficulties with the visiting dignitaries—" This said with obvious distaste. "—you are to tell Kadrin; he will come immediately to me. I will speak with the people involved to ensure that they understand the rules of this palace."

Neither spoke.

"I think that's about it. I've taken the liberty of having some food sent up to you; it should be here soon."

"Here, mistress?"

Sara smiled at the shock in the woman's voice. *At least she's speaking.* "Here. And to be truthful, I didn't exactly arrange the food, Kadrin did. He knows my routines well enough to anticipate me—and he knows I live in terror of Korten." She laughed. "Korten's the head of the kitchen."

The child leaned over to her mother again.

"Child, you can ask me the question, and ask it without fear. I won't hurt you here; no one will."

The mother met Sara's eyes, locked on them, and nodded without looking away.

For the first time, Sara heard the girl's voice. It was deeper than she would have expected, and she revised the estimate of the girl's age up by a couple of years. It was also smooth, almost melodious. Without nervous cracks—evident between almost each syllable—the child's voice would have been beautiful.

"Is the head of the kitchen a slave?"

"Yes, child."

The girl took a deep breath and straightened out. Without looking at her mother, she said, "Then why do you call him by name?"

"Because to me he has one. He is my . . . slave. If I choose to name him, that is only my concern now. In doing so, child, I break no laws." Her voice broke on the last word.

The girl was silent a few moments. She bent her head, and when it came up again, her eyes were filmed.

"No slave has a name."

"Not outside of this palace."

"My father—"

The mother hissed out a one-word warning, and the child subsided, with difficulty.

Sara stood and crossed the distance between them too quickly to be a menace. When she reached the girl, she knelt in front of her. "Little one, I do all that I can—" She wavered. "—all that I'm capable of." She heard her own voice crack, but continued. "In the palace, by right of rank, I am given the chance to let my laws govern in some small way. But outside of it—"

The woman's eyes widened in recognition and surprise as she realized what Sara was asking for. She shook her head in bewilderment, and the movement cleared her mind. For the first time she saw Sara as one lone woman, robed in gray with the symbol of a circle glimmering in the fading light.

"Mistress."

Sara turned her head without rising.

The woman held out a hand, and without hesitation Sara accepted it as if it were an anchor. "My name is Mattie. My daughter is Rasel."

The words fell into silence, but the expression on Sara's face gave the woman everything she needed.

"Thank you, Mattie."

Rasel turned to look at her mother as if she had gone insane. Both women met her gaze without speaking.

"I think it's all right, Rasel." Her mother's arms reached out in a half circle, but the girl pulled away.

"How can it be all right? This is the crime my father *died* for!" She leaped up.

"Rasel—"

She gave a hysterical laugh that fell abruptly into sobbing. She covered her face, huddling downward for a few seconds. As Sara approached, the girl's face shot outward like a bolt.

"Why didn't you save *him*? Why didn't you tell him it was all right to speak his name?"

"I tried, Rasel."

But she was weeping again, not expecting an answer.

Sara turned to face Rasel's mother, tightening her grip on the woman's hand to reassure her. *Or to be reassured?*

She shrugged, not knowing if there was really a difference between the two.

"Mistress, he knew what he was doing."

Sara nodded mutely.

"We have what—" Her voice cracked, and she shut her eyes. "—what we came for."

"For how long, Mattie?"

"For now. That's all we can ask."

Yes, here in Rennath, that is *all you can ask for.*

Seeing the woman's muted pain, Sara cursed herself bitterly. Her nails bit into the palm of her free hand as she struggled with her thoughts.

We can change this. We can—maybe—bring it all down. If he dies. Lernan . . .

Perhaps the empire could be changed, if she could make the right choice, if she was willing to help Kandor and her brethren of Elliath. The image of Stefanos, seated like ebony upon the throne of judgment, loomed above her. Her imagination needed to add no distortion to the picture: There he sat, and with few words condemned an innocent man to death for the crime of loving his child too dearly in an empire where love exacted so high a price.

But the man's death bought his child's life.

Yes, but if not for Veriloth, his death would not have been required—if not for Stefanos.

He changes. In four years he has changed much.

And is the price in innocent life worth the hope of change? Can you make that choice and condemn God alone knows how many people?

I do not know.

She was too tired to cry; her eyes remained dry even as she shut them. There at the heart of her pain was the indecision of hope.

You have changed, Sarillorn.

We all change.

She started to stand, and Mattie clutched almost blindly at her hand. Sara returned the pressure and resumed her kneeling position on the floor. What good would pacing do? It couldn't change the course her thoughts had chosen.

I feared to change too much.

Ah, Kandor, Belfas, I fear what your coming presages.

She bent her head, touching the older woman's lap with the cold white of her forehead. Almost absently, the older woman responded to the need that Sara unwittingly projected; her hands, soft for all they were callused, began to stroke the auburn head.

"I'm sorry," Sara murmured, as Mattie drew her gently into her lap. "I'm so sorry."

"I know, child," Mattie answered, half in amazement that she could know any pity for this lady. "I know."

Then she heard Rasel's sobs blend with the ones she kept locked between her lips and the lap of a woman who had just lost her husband.

There was a knock at the door. It was light and hesitant, enough so that Sara did not hear it at first. Rasel, however, displaying years of rigorous training, fell immediately silent. Hearing this, Sara raised her head.

"Someone's at the door."

Nodding, Sara drew herself up to her full height. She was embarrassed and ashamed of her need to take comfort from a woman who deserved only to receive it.

"I'll get it," she said lamely, to no one in particular. Her feet dragged across the carpet as she approached the door. She took a deep breath, then another, and her hand gripped the doorknob for support.

"Who's there?"

The knock came again, no louder than before.

"Who is it?"

"Lady."

She tensed, realizing just how much she did not want to see *him*, especially not now, with Ranin's wife and child as witness. "Lord, I do not feel up to visitors at the moment."

There was a pause, then he spoke again. "Yet I hear, Sara, that you have two."

She felt a small surge of anger, knowing the tone of his voice quite well. "Yes."

She still made no move to open the door, knowing that he would not enter without her leave.

"Lady—" The word was curt. "—I believe a third 'guest' will not harm you. Please allow me to enter."

She turned to look helplessly at Rasel and Mattie; both of them watched her with fear across their closed faces. They had composed themselves as they were able, and Sara was guiltily aware that she looked worse than either of them.

"Very well, Lord. You may enter."

"Thank you, Lady."

She felt the doorknob turn and released it, stepping away.

A man stepped into the room; his dark clothing torn and dirty, his hair red-tinted and disheveled.

Sara's jaw dropped, and behind her two women drew breath to cut the silence so sharply it nearly bled.

"Mistress?"

"Ranin." One word, half-spoken, half-whispered. The man flinched slightly. Unconsciously she reached out to touch the bruises on his face. He bore the touch as she robbed him of his pain.

"Mistress, I am commanded to report to you."

She tried to speak, but words would not come.

"Is there anything you require of me?"

She shook her head, meeting his eyes. There she saw a question too fierce to be expressed verbally. Almost giddily she stepped aside, her arm flying in a wide arc to indicate Mattie and Rasel. He saw them, his expression mirroring the relief of his discovery more eloquently than words could.

Mattie stared at the man who was her husband. Sara could see the tension that took her, although she sat perfectly still. Rasel, although younger, showed all of her mother's control—except for the eyes, which were round with hope.

"Please, enter."

Ranin did so. He walked awkwardly, as if another pulled the strings that moved his legs.

Sara gave him a small smile—one that could not express all that she suddenly felt. "Go on, that's an order."

He looked at her then, his face completely open.

"Go."

Nodding, wordless, he walked to the couch that held the two people he loved in all his world. Rasel contained herself only until he was a foot away, then sprang up, arms flying out, face already touching the breadth of his chest. "Father!"

The word was muffled against the torn coarseness of his tunic. His own arms came out in response, and then he was holding the daughter that he had almost died for.

Mattie's eyes left her husband and child for a moment, to meet Sara's. There was an odd wonder in her expression. Again Sara smiled, but this time her lips trembled and she looked away to give the three the privacy that they deserved; their reunion, unseen and unhoped for, was not a thing for "noble" eyes to witness.

In the hall outside the door was the First Servant. He looked colder, grimmer than Sara remembered. He remained still as Sara walked out of the room.

"Stefanos."

"Lady."

She walked to him then, closing the door to her room. Her hands reached up to touch the ice of his face, and he flinched at the contact, but did not pull away. His eyes, as he watched her, were neutral.

She started to speak, fell silent, and felt herself thaw. The ache of the afternoon vanished as she thought of Ranin's reunion with his family. Were it not for Stefanos's dark countenance, she would have smiled openly. But he was grim. "Why?"

In answer, he reached down and pulled her into his arms. There was nothing gentle about the motion, but Sara responded softly, resting her arms around his waist. She could sense the anger that he held in check, and knew who it was aimed at and why.

"Thank you, darkling. Thank you." She buried her face

against his chest and after a few moments felt the weight of his chin against the top of her hair.

And as her pain diminished, he knew again the warmth of her light and he relaxed. She held him on all levels, bands of her brilliance touching his face, his arms, and his chest; a smile against his shoulder and with it the warmth of tears that eased her heart.

Ah, Sarillorn, the light. His hands came up of their own accord, to smooth her unruly hair. For the moment, he felt at peace, and the moment was enough.

It came at too high a price, but he paid it and knew in the future that he would pay it again—not easily, and only barely willingly.

For you, Sarillorn. His arms tightened. He heard the clear sound of laughter and tears that came from behind her closed door, the rustle of clothing and the minute movements of air that spoke of an embrace given and one returned. He wondered, for a moment, if her slaves felt as he did in the circle of Sara's arm.

Then the moment passed. *What does it matter if they feel thus?*

And the answer came quickly. *It matters to the Sarillorn. It brings her peace.*

He felt he would never understand it, and as her face rose from the cushion of his shoulder and he met the brilliant green of her eyes, he thought it did not matter.

Oh, hells. Sara grabbed at the gray silk gown she had chosen for the evening meal. *When did the sun go down?* With quick, precise movements she tossed off her robe and stepped awkwardly into the dress. It was simple compared to the current court styles of Rennath, but it was still more difficult to negotiate than the simple robes she wore during the tasks of the day. She had half the buttons done when she cursed softly, stepped out of the dress, and went in search of her undergarments. *Everything* in Rennath was complicated.

She looked out at the muted light that struggled through her curtains.

Why didn't I hear the dinner bells? For she was certain they had chimed. It wasn't the first time she'd missed the call, and it certainly wouldn't be the last. *Why on Earth did I tell Kadrin to keep the servants from coming to get me?* It was something she only wondered when she was late. She cursed again, knotting one of the ties of the simple cotton undershift.

If Stefanos smirks at me, I'll kill him myself.

She started to smile, then her face froze.

In the half-opened crack of cloth at the balcony a familiar face flickered in the dimming light.

Belfas.

She caught a glimpse of a nervous smile, and then it was gone. Not bothering with the rest of her clothing, she rushed to the window and flung the curtains back, but he was nowhere in sight. She walked out, not particularly caring who would see her; a few people walked casually in all directions beneath her searching gaze—but none of them was familiar.

She returned to her room and continued to dress, but more slowly this time. She listened for any unusual sound, but the room was quiet.

The words of the Servant of Lernan returned to her. If Belfas had been at her balcony, she was certain he was within the palace. And he was counting on her, as he had done any number of times when she was the third of Telvar—as he had done, unwittingly, on the field of Karana when she had first earned her circle.

With quiet deliberation she fastened the buttons that remained undone and then headed toward the hall. Once she stopped, shook herself, and resumed walking; her face was set and grim.

Remember the place of judgment, Erin.

It was the first time in years that she had used her given name; it felt distant and yet familiar in the way that very old friends do after years of separation.

She walked down the hall, her eyes again falling on the tapestries that lined it. She met the Lady of Elliath, lost in the depth of a trance too difficult for a mortal mind to undertake, and she dropped to her knees in front of her.

Lady, please, please guide me.

No response.

Lady, he spared the life of Ranin, because he knew what it meant to me. Might he not, in time, do the same for another?

Again no answer. She almost regretted Stefanos's change of heart. But she thought of Mattie and Rasel, and the regret drifted. What did it matter if her decision had been made, once again, so difficult? They were happy; they had each other.

Lady, I will do as I am able. Please . . .

She stood and walked quickly down the hall.

She shook herself again as she reached the stairs. There would be people below, and she would have to face them as brightly as ever.

Come on, Erin. They're waiting for you. You're late, as usual. Her feet took the steps automatically, bringing the main hall closer.

"Ah, Lady Sara."

She turned slowly at the sound of the voice, the hair on the nape of her neck sparking outward. With a patently false smile, she greeted the high priest. He had two rooms in the palace, although he used them infrequently. Derlac, for some reason, was one of the few that Stefanos could tolerate.

"Derlac."

He returned her smile, failing to notice that she had not used his title. She never used it; he never noticed; it was a game they both played that each heartily despised, although for different reasons.

"I am gratified to note that I am not the only diner to be somewhat tardy. If it would not be too much trouble, I would be pleased to arrive with you." He offered her his arm; she ignored it. Another step in their silent fencing. Nor was he ruffled by her refusal—although that had not been the case when he had first accepted the rank and "responsibility" of his office.

"As you wish." She walked, looking straight ahead.

He fell into step naturally.

"I heard that there was some sort of difficulty in the market today."

She pointedly ignored his "idle" chatter, quickening her walk. *Not that it's going to inconvenience him,* she thought. He was a full foot taller than she, and she was grateful for the fact that she had never once been forced to keep pace with him.

"Nevertheless, the word I received was that the difficulty in the *market* had been suitably dealt with."

Sara clamped her teeth down. She knew what Derlac was doing. He had done all in his power, which was considerable, to assure that the place of judgment was not created. Failing that, he used one of her own famous gambits. He refused to notice the change.

"Come, Lady Sara." Ironic inflection colored every word. "You cannot hope to save every slave in Veriloth. It does not befit your station." He was well pleased; to his mind the First Servant gave far too much to this, a ranking member of their greatest enemy. To order the death of a man she saw fit to plead for—yes, Derlac was satisfied. Perhaps there was hope for the

Lernari's death yet. But he remembered the cost of the last "hope," and he was not fool enough to undertake its realization.

Sara was suddenly angry; of all nights to play at useless confrontations with the high priest, this one was least welcome. She let a hint of satisfaction show through her face as she responded. "Not every slave, Derlac. But I did manage to save that one. *Ranin* is now in my personal service, or didn't your informants tell you that?"

When he did not reply immediately, she pressed the point home. "And yes, I do intend to save every slave in Veriloth, if it takes me all my life."

"I see."

His voice was cold and neutral. Sara gave him a sidelong glance, already regretting the words.

He didn't know, and not only did I inform him of the fact that Stefanos went against his word to spare Ranin, but I rubbed his face in it. She felt the juxtaposition of regret and satisfaction. Regret won.

Stefanos, my position here is still not as strong as you would like it. Must I always make it worse?

Still, at least he's stopped talking.

It was true, but it didn't make her feel better; Derlac silent was Derlac plotting, and although he was too canny to act directly against the First Servant of his God, he was still not a man to antagonize. She knew well that he considered her a weakness, and a dangerous one—the fact that Ranin was still alive proved it yet again.

Master, he thought, *this Lernari woman will poison you if she is not . . . removed. I have done all I can to lessen her influence, but it has proved useless. Perhaps it is time . . .*

He shuddered. Going against the First Servant's orders usually left a man a lifespan that could be measured in seconds. Yet he could not just stand idly by to watch the destruction of the Church at the hands of its enemy—and he was certain as to what the Sarillorn intended; she had never been anything less than clear.

He shook his head to clear it and walked a little more quickly. It still amazed him that one with such power could possess so little understanding of the uses to which it should be put.

"Lady," he said, and she turned. "I believe we must walk more quickly. The Lord has never liked to be kept waiting."

Except by you.

chapter
seventeen

The dining hall was unlike any other room in the palace; al-
though the ceilings were high, the arches were smooth and clean;
no beams cut across them, and no frescoes colored them. The
doors were rectangular, not peaked, and were of simple wood.
Thus had Sara described the hall of her home; Stefanos had not
managed to capture the longing her voice had given to detail,
but was moderately pleased with the rest.

He looked up as Sara and Derlac entered. He smiled almost
maliciously at her as his eyes flickered over the high priest, and
she rolled her eyes in response. Derlac missed none of this, and
his face grew somewhat more red, but he held his peace; it was
one of the reasons he had become high priest, and he never
forgot it.

"It pleases me to see that you could be spared from your
duties in order to join me."

The high priest gave a low bow.

"Your pardon, Lord. I was detained."

"By whom?"

Rising, Derlac shrugged and took a seat. "It is a minor problem, Lord, unworthy of your time or attention."

"Most problems with the Church are. But few cause you to
be late."

Derlac nodded again, ill at ease. "Yes, Lord. But it is not a
problem with the Church precisely; rather, with the Swords.
Gerdonel and Lampret are struggling for position, and the division between their associated units is causing . . . unrest."

"I see. But surely both are under the command of—let me
think—"

"Karver and Morden, Lord." Derlac inserted the names, well
aware that his Lord knew who they were.

"Perhaps I shall have to speak with them."

The black robes he wore highlighted the sudden white of his long face. "Lord, you have trusted me with the keeping of the Church; I have already spoken to both men, and at length. I assure you that they will cause you no trouble."

"I see." With those two words of dismissal, Stefanos turned to regard Sara. Derlac let himself relax slightly. Although he would never admit it, there were times when the presence of the Sarillorn was a boon, and this was one of the few. He remembered clearly the events that had occurred three years past—he had narrowly avoided being caught up in the uprising of the Church's upper hierarchy. The purge that had followed had left numbers sparse, and Derlac wished strongly to avoid any further pruning.

"Lady Sara," Stefanos was saying, "you cannot tell me that after the events of the afternoon, you—"

"I was tired, Stefanos. I'm sorry I'm late, I just didn't hear—"

"So you have said." He waved an arm. "But please, do not let me keep you standing if you feel so. Take your place." He smiled softly, then clapped his hands twice.

Sara had time to find her seat before the serving slaves entered the dining room.

They began to serve her first, and she moved slightly to give them more room. The young boy who held the first tray smiled shyly at her. She returned his smile, but said nothing, knowing how intensely Stefanos disliked it.

They ate in silence. Sara was aware, as always, of her Lord's gaze and met it firmly, almost warmly—even though Derlac also watched.

Master, he thought, appetite lost, *can you not see how she weakens you?* His fork skidded across his plate, and he corrected his shaking hand with some chagrin.

Because he avoided the Sarillorn's eyes, he missed the change in them. Not so Stefanos, who paused in midsentence when her head moved upward as if pulled. "Lady?"

Her eyes grew unfocused as they pondered something—perhaps some memory—beyond the table. For a moment he thought the clarity of the green grew opaque. Her lips clamped shut, and the fingers that held cutlery let them drop noisily to table and floor.

From somewhere, the smell of a familiar breeze touched Sara, and she knew that this was the moment. Her blood rushed outward to cheek and fingertip, called by the force of kinship. *No. Not now!* But it was *now*, more immediate than she could have foreseen.

"Sara?"

She heard his voice as if by habit, but it was distant and distorted when it reached her ears. She swung around to gaze at him—slowly, so slowly twisting the white of her neck, as if the movement itself could break her.

And she saw him more clearly and more truly than normal sight permitted. Shrouded in shadow, the velvet folds of darkness wreathing his face and hands where they showed through his clothing, he sat at the head of the table. She could not see his expression clearly; folds of gray that denied the light twisted his lips and eyes into a parody of the concern she *knew* must be there. His mouth began to move, but the words his lips formed were lost to time—and to the sight of his teeth, the only gleaming light that remained within him. She saw them clearly and wondered, almost ludicrously, how it was that they had never drawn blood when she had kissed the gray of his lips.

Turning again, this time quickly and effortlessly, she saw the glimmer in the air, the beauty that danced in little sparks through the hall. But this time it was larger, somehow complete in its pattern. She knew that Kandor would appear—but not alone, not this time.

She knew that God's power was dimmed and the Gifting invoked. Everything seemed to happen so slowly; she thought that Stefanos would notice, by now, the approach of his doom. But he did not; his face was still turned toward her among the shadows, although she could only catch it from the corner of her eye.

Blood-spell. She knew it for truth; even the Malanthi priest moved slowly and sluggishly in her sight. Only Kandor and those of Elliath would have the speed necessary to do what they had come to do.

And I, she thought bitterly, *am of Elliath. The blood chooses its course.*

But as she thought it, she knew it to be wrong. The choice, damned and damnable, was still her own. The blood flowed faster through her veins. She stood, turning to her Lord, and caught the start of an expression of astonishment curve around his lips.

Nightwalker. She took a step forward, then another, knowing that he could not yet react to it. She read his face—what she could see of it—harshly and honestly; reviewed her life in Rennath ruthlessly. All of the details crept back, all of the lost lives, the people she had not been permitted to save, and the screams that had kept her awake for her first few weeks in the palace—screams that no longer sounded here.

Servant of Malthan. The name held venom, a poison that was only now being flushed away by the touch, by the grace, of Kandor of Lernan.

Breathing in once, deeply, she caught the taste of the orvas flowers along her tongue, washing away the stain of the city and the curse of the empire. She could almost see the Woodhall, standing in storm and sunshine as it had always stood, weathering the passage of season and human kingdom alike.

She let the feeling overwhelm her, and a laugh broke through her clamped jaw; a laughter that told her, and any who would hear it, that she was truly *alive* and still very much Sarillorn of her line.

"Erin!"

Wheeling, arms outstretched, she caught the flicker of hope that danced across the face of Belfas. And his face was all light, shining in the circle of Kandor's power; dear to her, more so than any other, because it was a light that she'd saved on her first battlefield years ago. She could see, beneath his glow, the tattered rags that passed as slave garments, and letting her sight dance across the others—three—could see a similar garb.

Only Kandor, standing in their center, looked as he had always looked; clothed all in white, the youthful glint of skin and pale-gold hair a song of his birth at the dawn of time. He stepped forward quickly, his brow creasing.

"Sarillorn, well met."

She bowed to him then, sweeping the gray of her skirt to one side.

He left the Lernari behind, covering the distance from the corner of the room to the table almost too quickly for Sara to perceive.

Belfas and Taya also broke, running visibly toward the high priest. The others, Carla and Rein, turned their backs upon her, to face the doors of the room. They were nervous, she could see it—and feel it at the base of her tingling spine.

Hurry, she thought, turning again for sight of Kandor.

Kandor stood in front of Stefanos.

Stefanos.

She could see his arms, moving slowly against the grip of

time, and the red flash of his eyes. His mouth struggled with something—some word, some spell of power—as the seat fell away from beneath him, resisting the pull of gravity and losing to it inch by inch.

His eyes unexpectedly found hers, and even though his movement was slowed in her vision, she saw the quick fan of shock spread and ripple outward across his face—knew that it would cost him time he didn't have as he evaluated the situation.

Kandor's arms crossed his chest on their tangled upward sweep and a beam of light broke forth from him. His brow creased slightly as the white of it pierced the red cleanly and absolutely.

Sara heard the beginning of a scream take shape from the throat of her captor. It was cut short before it could fully blossom, but that—that was his way. No pain in the face of the enemy, even if that pain gave no satisfaction. She understood it well.

Her hands curled into little fists as he fell—again slowly, agonizingly so—to the floor. The red around him still pulsed frantically, but it was weakening. Kandor was doing his work, and well.

She felt a sharp pain and looked down to her hands. Little drops of blood lingered on her fingernails. She looked away again, to see Belfas, arms raised, begin his attack upon the Malanthi high priest.

I should leave.

She thought it, senselessly, as her legs locked her in place. So she waited, not knowing what it was that she waited for until it came, drawn out, covering more of her than either she or her Lord could have expected.

He called her name, just once, into the odd silence of the battle zone. But once was enough.

And she turned to him again, caught his eyes, and held them as if to provide an anchor for him before she realized fully what she was doing. She saw him—as she had seen him daily, as she had seen him this afternoon—her chosen, her bond-mate, nightwalker, Servant, and darkling. She felt the coolness that lingered over cheek and brow in the morning, felt the concern that had been his first thought when Kandor and the priests of Elliath were launching their assault.

It hurt her, more than walking through red-fire, for it was a darker and deeper pain.

"Erin, *don't!*"

But she was already running the short distance between herself and Kandor—arms outstretched as if to embrace him. There was no time for tears, no leisure for anything but automatic action, as her hands gripped Kandor's tightly, wrenching them into a direction that would, for a second, free Stefanos.

Nor was she prepared for Kandor's reaction. His hands shuddered once, twice in her grip, but he made no move to pull free.

"Sarillorn."

It was the first time he had spoken aloud to her, and she knew what it meant; he was tired, his power was failing. *Yes,* she thought uneasily, *that's what it must be.*

Then he gently, but firmly disengaged her hand. "It is over. Rest."

She turned then, wildly, to see Stefanos standing, glowing brightly with the ugliest of light haloing his body.

"This the Lady saw." Bending, he kissed her forehead. "And I am ready. Stand aside, little one."

"No." She turned and met Stefanos's eyes. "Please, please no."

"Sara." He bowed once, no hint of his torment marring the gesture. "Thank you, Lady. Now we will meet on equal ground."

Kandor bowed, also. "Not equal, First of Malthan. But come, I have done what I can to defy the Lady's fate; I will defy it no longer." The saddest of smiles touched his lips, and he turned to look at Sara.

Derlac's loud cry filled the hall, robbing Kandor's last words of sound. But Sara saw his lips move, saw a tremor of something shudder through his eyes. And when he turned to face his enemy, he was Servant of Lernan once more, with all the majesty, and all the power.

Stefanos laughed once. "You were a fool to come here; this is the seat of my strength."

"I was a fool, yes," Kandor replied, mildly. He raised his arms high, and the light that flooded the room blinded Sara.

She cried out, "Stefanos! Don't!" knowing that she would hear nothing in return. Nothing? She choked as the sound of wood striking wall rang through the room, followed by the scrape of metal against metal, and the loud, dissonant clang of armor. She heard the scuffling of feet and bodies as she tried to clear her eyes.

"Erin, *why? why?*" The agonized question was followed by a grunt and a silence punctuated by heaving breath.

When her eyes cleared, she was still in the hall.

"Lady."

She could not face him.

"Lady." His arm touched her shoulders, drawing her close. "Thank you."

Avoiding his eyes, she turned to see the still form of Kandor upon the floor. Dodging Stefanos, she darted toward it and knelt.

His hand, ivory and pale, was motionless in hers, limp, all of the life he had carried into the hall vanquished.

Kandor, please—understand me.

He had; she knew it. She drew the body closer, wondering why it still existed in the mortal realm.

Lernan, God, forgive me. I am Sarillorn of Elliath no longer. And she wept, salt tears warming the chill of her face. Beyond, the voice of her Lord broke through.

"Captain, take them to the north wing. Confine them until I—"

She stood, leaving Kandor on the floor. "Stefanos."

He turned to her as the guards began to carry out his orders, and beyond his back she could see that Rein was bleeding profusely. The other three were unscathed—physically. She tried to capture Belfas's gaze and failed; he turned his face away without speaking another word.

"Lady?"

"Please, Stefanos, please let them go."

He grew remote, his eyes black against the gray of his natural pallor. "They are my enemies, Lady. There is an understanding in this. They have failed; they know the price."

"They wouldn't have failed if I had not—not—" *betrayed them.* But the enormity of the words stuck in her throat, refusing her the relief of releasing them. "Please, Lord. I saved your life. Please grant me this one thing. I won't ask for anything else."

He caught her trembling chin in his fingers. "Sara, I—"

"You'd be dead if I hadn't interfered!"

"I am not alive now."

Dropping to her knees, she caught the hand beneath her chin and grasped it so tightly that the blood ran out of her fingers. Bowing her head, she said, "First Servant of—of Malthan. I ask you, *beg* you if I must, for their lives. Please."

He studied her for a while as the hall emptied, saw the tears upon her cheeks, etching themselves into her countenance as if they were acid. At length he knelt in front of her, pulling her into his arms.

"Sara, Sara, I understand. You ask me to lessen the price you have paid tonight.'' His hands ran through her hair, changing shape and color as they did so, until he stood before her, once again Lord of Veriloth—as close to human as a Servant could become. ''Lady, why did you choose as you did?''

She shook her head, wordless, and he let the question fade, knowing the answer, marveling at it.

''I will not earn your hatred this night, Sara. Rise. Return to your rooms. The Lernari are free to go; they have lost the strongest of their number; they have lost the Third of Lernan.''

She trembled, but this time brought her face up. Tears still fell, and her face was no less troubled, but he could see a glimmer of light in her eyes.

Weakly, her arms came up and around him.

''Thank you. Thank you, Stefanos.''

She tried to stand, and he caught her as her knees gave.

''It is I who should thank you, Sara. Come.'' He lifted her. ''I will take you to your rooms; you may rest there. In the morning, all shall be as it was.''

He carried her out of the hall, cradling her gently as she curled against his chest. Together they made their way to the north wing of the palace and from there to Sara's rooms.

Sara seemed to sleep; her breath came shallowly and evenly as the First Servant traversed the final hallway that she'd covered so carefully with her tapestries. He had seen them many times and had no need to pause to reexamine detail; it was all in his memory, and with a thought he could summon it up. Given a night he could sit in his chambers, counting each individual thread and each careless flaw.

Nonetheless he stopped at the end, to gaze fully at the loom-drawn Lady of Elliath.

Lady. He did not bow, but would have had he not carried Sara. *Your eyes see your doom. Does it wear my face?*

I do not know if you sent the Lernari, or the Third of Lernan, but I am grateful for both. I shall use them well. He tightened his grip on Sara, a wordless statement. *When we meet again, I shall remember your gift to me.*

He nodded once, crisply, and then carried Sara to her bedroom. She stirred once, and he cradled her until she was again still. Then he pushed her covers back and laid her carefully in her bed, arranging the pillows beneath the spread of her hair.

His lips brushed her forehead once.

Then he raised his arms, passing them three times over her still form. His eyes glinted red in the darkened room.

Sleep, Sara. Sleep until dawn. He spoke a few words, each one carefully chosen to reverberate across her. *It is done.*

Bending down, he kissed her again, lightly on either eyelid. Then he stood and walked briskly out of the room, closing and locking her door behind him.

He walked quickly down to Kadrin's quarters and rapped on the door. Kadrin emerged, paling slightly at the sight of his Lord; it was rare for him to make a personal appearance.

"Lord." He bowed, dropping to his knees.

"The lady sleeps. She has had a troubled evening. Post two of the slaves near her quarters and make sure that she is not disturbed under any circumstance.

"And send someone for the high priest. Tell him he is to meet me in my chambers immediately."

"Yes, Lord."

Stefanos held the man's eyes for a minute, then nodded curtly. Kadrin rose from the floor and scrambled awkwardly—but quickly—down the long hall. The First Servant was already gone.

Derlac opened the door to his master's chambers and walked quickly in.

"You are here."

"Master." Derlac gave a low bow.

"I require your assistance for the evening." He rose, almost impatiently. "We must move quickly; the work will be long and it cannot, under any circumstance, outlast the darkness."

Derlac nodded, rising.

Stefanos was already at the door. "Quickly, High Priest." He had no need to make a threat; Derlac understood his position too well.

"Where do we go, master?"

"To my temple."

A look of surprise, followed by satisfaction, swept across the high priest's face. "Will we need a congregation?"

"No."

Derlac shrugged. Not a full ceremony then—but it didn't matter. The First Servant, for the first time in over three years, was willing to perform blood rites.

"Is there anything that you require?"

"The blade."

"Done."

"And the Lernari. Bring also the body of the Third of Lernan. Both are necessary."

A slow smile spread across Derlac's face.

"Immediately, master." He bowed again, genuinely. "I shall meet you at the temple with the things you have requested."

Stefanos nodded absently.

You trusted me, Sarillorn. And why should you not? In the past four years I have never broken my word to you.

He felt uneasy, and buried the feeling beneath a sharp and sweet elation.

Just this once, Sarillorn, I must do so. Then you, too, will be free of the dictates of time. As I am.

I will never lose you to so impersonal an enemy.

He opened the door and began his journey to the temple. And his eyes were deep and red, a dark red that showed no light, nor allowed any to pass.

chapter
eighteen

Stefanos looked about his small personal temple, noting the marks that the passage of time had left upon it. Here, a cobweb, hiding perhaps a spider or two, there, dust in an even, undisturbed blanket upon the unused altar. He felt momentarily annoyed at the sight; he would have to find the time to make sure that the temple was clean. Not that it would take long, but the darkness of evening was a precious commodity.

With a wide, deliberate gesture and a few curt words, he let his displeasure take form. A strong wind swept through the room, tearing away cobweb and dust alike. Small spiders scurried away from the ruins of their daily labor, and he let them pass.

He walked to the altar, tracing a familiar path easily and cleanly. The stone was cool to the touch, even to his, and black with the faintest threads of gray running through it. It was an elaborate monument, the more so for its plain, unadorned elegance. He had always liked it, although the labor had not been his; Sargoth had constructed it almost whimsically during one of his few visits to the mortal plane.

His arms swung across the length of the stone, inches above the surface. His eyes and the altar glowed red at the same time, and then the color faded into natural black.

I am ready.

As if hearing his thoughts, two men walked through the door. By their uniforms, it was clear they were Swords of the Church, Malanthi, but not strong enough in blood to aspire to the priesthood. Between them they carried a limp, pale body—Kandor's.

"Lord."

"Put it on the altar. The left side."

The man who had spoken nodded sharply, with only a slight

297

trace of fear—it was not, after all, his blood that would grace the altar this night. Still, it always paid to be careful when dealing with the First Servant of God.

They deposited the body clumsily on the stone altar, but before they could straighten it out, their Lord waved them away.

"That will be all. You may go now."

Nodding, the Swords left.

Stefanos went to the body and began to unfurl it almost gently.

Third of the Enemy, know that your essence will be used to aid one of the Line Elliath.

I know it.

Ah. He was aware; in some way still attached to the plane. *If there is pain—*

First of Malthan, do what you must. The Lady herself has foreseen what has come to pass. If she had seen more clearly, you would not triumph in so bitter a fashion for either of us.

Stefanos stood back for a moment, unsettled by the vague hint of pity that underlay his enemy's thoughts. For a moment he feared a trap, but he shunted that fear aside; trap or no, this opportunity itself could not be wasted.

The noise of approaching guards came down the halls again, and with them a familiar footstep.

Derlac. Good. We must begin soon.

The doors swung open, and Derlac walked into the room, step crisp and formal, followed by seven Swords—each wearing the high priest's insignia—and their four captives. Three of them walked with a quiet, desperate dignity; the fourth was dragged, half-conscious, along the floor.

Derlac gave a low bow and, kneeling, handed the First Servant a long, thin, ebony box.

Stefanos accepted the offering and quickly set the box down, passing hands over it before flipping the hinged lid open. He clasped the dagger firmly in his left hand and lifted it out of the box.

"The injured one."

Two of the Swords separated from the main group, dragging the half-conscious man to the altar.

"Release him." He nodded as the men did so, and the Lernari slumped to the floor. "Stand aside."

He began to chant, his form outlined by a pulsating red that all in the room could clearly see. The body began to rise awkwardly, a tangled mess of arms and legs. It floated higher and higher until it hung, suspended by the ankles, over the still form of Kandor.

Stefanos walked forward, dagger ready, his voice never ceasing its odd litany. With a quick, precise movement, he drew the dagger shallowly across the captive Servant's chest. Then, without halting the knife's motion, he brought it up in an arc that ended Rein's life. It was quick, clean—and every instinct within the First Servant cried out against the fact that it was painless. But he had not come this far by being slave to instinct.

As the blood drained from Rein's throat, he turned again, and the chanting ceased. Almost as an afterthought, the corpse drifted away from the altar, coming to rest in a heap before it.

Stefanos raised one gray claw, leveling it at one of the Lernari, the youngest by human reckoning.

"Come."

She hesitated, and the Swords fell behind her immediately, cutting her off from her companions. She turned once, caught a pair of friendly, resigned eyes, and nodded, all wordless.

As she approached the altar, her feet rose until she was gliding on air. Then slowly, delicately, she was rotated until her hair brushed across the blood on Kandor's chest, becoming matted and dark at the ends.

The First Servant reiterated his guttural chant, gripping the knife firmly as he again approached Kandor. Another shallow cut, and the knife swung upward—and hesitated for just an instant at the look in the girl's eyes. Green eyes, like Sara's, shone cold and clear with hatred and fear. He brought the knife back almost defensively and sighed. Reaching out, he touched the tip of her chin, and she moved her face away.

"Do not be afraid. You have met your enemy on the field, bravely and strongly. There will be no pain." He saw the tears begin to form in her eyes and her lips begin to tremble. But she was Lernari, he was Servant to Malthan. He lifted the knife, knowing his hands trembled, and began to chant anew.

Her blood flowed downward, masking her face in a red, ugly sheen. He waited, hearing the sound of it as it struck Kandor's chest. And when it was over, her body, too, came to rest before the altar, but it was deposited almost gently.

Stefanos passed his hands before his face, trying to erase the image that remained; the ghost of green eyes in the air. He tried to judge the time, not knowing how much of the darkness had elapsed. He felt unaccountably weary.

It is the magic, he thought, knowing it to be a lie. He turned once again.

Derlac nodded to the Swords, and they selected the second woman. She was older; a scar seamed her face, and the light in her eyes was firm and solid. They brought her forward. Unlike the girl, this Lernari attempted her warding spells. They failed; she had known they would, but it was not her way to walk resigned into death. She was brought to the altar, and held the same way that her two comrades had been held.

"I do not know," she said, through gritted teeth, "what game you play, First of the Enemy. But know this: The blood of Elliath can never be used against the circle."

"I know it, Lernari. I know it well." And then he cursed; the response had broken the chant.

"Lord."

He spun, the irritation showing plainly on his features, and Derlac took a step back. Only a step; in the temple he was still high priest, and that counted for something even when facing the First of God.

"My Lord." He bowed deeply, more to avoid the smoldering red in the Servant's eyes than to show subservience. "I, too, do not understand what transpires here. If you cannot consign the Lernari to God, you can at least attempt to draw out their pain on His altar."

"Fool!" Stefanos almost spat the word out.

"Lord." Derlac bowed again, torn between anger and fear. Before he could rise from the bow, the Servant spoke again, this time more smoothly, but no less angrily for it.

"High Priest, I do what I do here for my own reasons. If you cannot refrain from questioning them, you may leave the temple."

Leave the temple? Anger won. A feeling of betrayal stirred in Derlac. *You've opened your temple for the first time in three years—and blooded the altar in the bargain. But her influence holds you regardless. She weakens you, and through you she weakens the Church and our God.*

Yes, Lord, I will leave the temple. But I will return, and we will see an end to this sacrilege.

He did not bother to salute or otherwise pay the price that courtesies to a superior demanded. Wheeling, he left the chamber and stalked down the long, empty hall.

At the farthest edge of his earshot, he caught the low dissonance of the First Servant's chant. He quickened his pace; he would have to time his reentrance with care.

With sure steps he traced the path to the north wing of the castle. He brought a torch with him out of habit, although in the north wing, at any time of day or night, light was not necessary.

His anger grew again as he passed the tapestries along the Sarillorn's walls. He hated them; the more so because their expense had come out of Church coffers.

Never mind. Soon enough they'll be gone.

Her door, gilded and wide, loomed in the torchlight. He hated this as well; these had been the high priest's quarters before she had come to Rennath. He doubted that she was aware of this fact, and pride had never allowed him the expense of informing her.

He raised one hand, hesitated, then knocked, firmly and loudly.

A slave came cringing out of the shadows nearest the door.

"High Priest."

Derlac turned slowly, his irritation at the interruption plain across his features. "I am here to speak with the lady. Leave. Now."

The slave took a step back, but it was clear that he had no intention of leaving. "I'm sorry, High Priest. But it's the Lord's orders."

"What orders?"

"The lady's not to be disturbed by anyone—not even the Lord himself."

"The Lord himself sent me."

The slave shook his head. "I'm sorry, master. The lady cannot be disturbed."

"I see." He did, and it didn't please him. "Very well; the business is urgent, but it will have to wait until the morning." He turned away from the door as the slave breathed an audible sigh of relief.

As the slave turned to go, Derlac's hand slipped into his left sleeve. A silver sliver flashed in the torchlight, connecting with the slave's spinal column.

All in all, too easy a death. Derlac set the torch aside, quickly drew the body to one side, and placed it in an alcove. Then, glancing quickly around, he knocked loudly on the door.

No answer.

He tried again, and then tried the door.

Locked.

Cursing, he began to draw upon his own power.

He twisted the door, and this time, although it resisted him, he managed to open it enough to squeeze through. But it cost him. Bitterly he acknowledged the fact that it was a lesser ward; had the First Servant wished to spare the power, he could not have entered the room unless he brought a crew of men to break down one of the walls—the stone walls.

He hurried through the darkened rooms to the bed. Lady Sara slept, but not a natural sleep. This his Malanthi eyes could discern easily.

Damn.

He knew the spell; it was a strong one—one of the strongest that Derlac himself would have been able to cast.

Damn the door.

He drew out his dagger, edged with the blood of the dead slave.

If I'd known, he thought, gritting his teeth as he brought the blade sharply down into his palm, *I would have killed the slave more slowly, damn him.*

But he hadn't; he only hoped that the man's lifeblood, weakened by the easy passage into death, would still grant him enough power to wake the sleeping Lernari. Blood welled into his palm and he began his silent litany.

Everything moved slowly. Sara turned in one direction and then in another, and in each she felt and saw billowing clouds of darkness. They clung to her like webs, and she began to kick out—short, sharp thrusts—in an attempt to weaken them. She could feel a heavy stickiness in her mouth, and began to spit and choke as she realized that the web of darkness clung to her insides. Her hands came up, knives of flesh, and she began to make the motions of the Greater Ward—hoping they would have some effect against this unknown danger.

The going was slow; twice the clouds caught her wrists, breaking her gestures—and twice she began them again, determined. It was hard to make the sweeping pass across her heart; harder perhaps because it had been so long since she'd used the ward itself, but blood remembered, and she was of Elliath. She pulled her arms up, her fingers making the last, subtle arcs, and then—

She leaped out of her bed and rolled to one side on the floor. Her eyes snapped open, and she could see one black outline, slightly bent, leaning over her.

But she could move, and her hands already fell into a familiar cadence.

The shadow backed away, offering her open palms.

She called upon light, and it came, flooding the room. Derlac flinched and pulled away, withdrawing his hands, but not before Sara caught sight of the crimson liquid cupped in them. She stood, slowly, her ward unrelenting.

Derlac was very tired. Fatigue bent his back, and he struggled against it just to stand straight. "Lady."

"Derlac."

"Believe me, Lady, I mean you no harm."

She looked skeptically at the hands that he'd curled into fists.

"This?" He lifted the offending hand. "This is why I have come." He took a deep breath, allowing the very real anger he felt to show. "Lady, this blood is the blood of the Lernari captives."

The words took some time to penetrate her sleepy mind.

Derlac took a step forward.

"I do not lie to you, Lady. The Lord has opened his temple again—and I cannot say that this displeases me."

"He opened a temple?" She put one hand to her forehead.

"Yes. And if you've any chance of stopping him from killing the rest of your companions, you must come, and quickly."

She was almost out of the door. Her gown, pale and simple, swirled in the light around her body. For the first time, Derlac could truly appreciate that this one had been Sarillorn of Elliath, not just a minor priestess. He turned to follow her, keeping a careful distance; contact with her when his power was so low could be very painful.

He stopped an inch short of running into her.

"Derlac, why are you telling me this? What reason have I to trust your word over Stef—over the First Servant's?"

Again he allowed his anger to show, but this time he could also be truthful.

"Let us be honest, Lady. I want your death. Nothing would please me more. You weaken our Lord, and through him, my Church."

"Understood."

"If you try to stop the Lord, as I believe you must, there is a very real chance he will finally kill you."

"I see."

"And think on this: If you choose not to believe me, your companions will almost certainly perish. Even now they may

be dying on the altar. Can you take the chance? You know me
well enough to understand my position; regardless of how I feel,
or how my priests or Swords feel, I will not be able to take any
action against you; it was tried once, and the cost was far too
high. I lead you into no trap."

She was uncertain; he could see her face mirror her attempt
to disbelieve him. For the most part, it succeeded, and Derlac
was satisfied. The more she believed the good of her Lord, the
more unpredictable she would be.

He thought she might attack the First Servant when she was
forced to face fully the truth of his words. And the First Servant,
while severely weakened in the act of casting the spell, would
still be more than a match for her fury. But the full extent of his
aim was more subtle.

*I want you to hate him, Lady. I want you to remember that
he is your enemy, as he will not remember that you are his.*
"Come."

She followed as he began to jog down the tapestried hallway.
For the most part, Sara was angry.

*I don't know what game you're playing at, Derlac, but I warn
you—if this is just another of your cruel schemes, I'll see you
pay.*

She was mostly convinced that she would find nothing in the
temple but cobwebs and dust. Still, a thin thread of uneasiness
ran through her—enough to bring her chasing after Derlac down
a mostly disused hall, rumpled and bleary-eyed from sleep.

She wondered what type of apparition she would appear
should the wandering eye of a slave catch her running past; the
image made her smile almost whimsically.

Then the smile froze and shattered.

From out of the small side door to the temple—the castle
entrance—she could see cracks of flickering light. She stopped
dead in her tracks.

"Come, Lady. There is more yet."

The darkness hid the edge of his grim, satisfied smile. He
walked at a more leisurely pace to the door, and then stood to
one side of it.

Sara came up to the door. For a moment her hand rested
nerveless against the handle.

"What are you afraid of, Sarillorn?"

Had she the time—or the power—to spare, she might have
lashed out at the high priest. Instead she gathered her anger and
shock, and pushed the door open as forcefully as she might.

Belfas hung, like a dimming candle, over the altar of the Dark Heart. His feet touched air, and his head brushed against the blood-spattered body of Kandor.

Sara stood, white against the open door, as words swirled away in a rush, then returned to her open mouth in a single syllable.

"Nooooooo!"

The First Servant of Malthan turned at the sound, but slowly, as if he were exhausted—or casting.

Sara didn't see him clearly, for Belfas's eyes flickered open as well, catching sight of her. He didn't speak—but he couldn't; he had no throat left for it, and very little life.

Too little. Even as Sara began to run, heedless of Swords, across the temple, she could see his light dim and fade.

"Belfas!"

"Sara!"

She turned then, knowing she could do nothing else, to see Stefanos, robed in black, start toward her. His hands were open and red.

She took a step backward. All in the room could see her begin to glow. Her hands swept upward and out, in a large, wide circle.

Two of the Swords ran forward, weapons drawn.

The First Servant began to call them back, but Sara's white-fire raced outward in one deadly, brilliant arc. The Malanthi fell screaming beneath it, and the remaining Swords retreated.

Sara made no sound as her arms came up again and fanned outward. Her eyes, when they could be seen at all, were white and gleaming.

"Sara!"

"You *lied* to me!"

The fire raged outward, and the First Servant fell back, gesturing his own red circle into existence. White-fire beat ineffectually against it and then guttered abruptly as Sara drew it in again.

He could not look at her. His hands danced complicated arcs in the air, a quick, smooth counterpart to Sara's rage.

Delicate fingers of red wreathed the corner of the room that Sara occupied, seeking purchase. They fell away, and Stefanos cursed, but silently.

Lady, Sara, Sarillorn.

The red grew in strength and began to curl around the circle that Sara had drawn.

I have no time to spare. I have come this far; I will not lose all now.

He was unprepared for the bolt that she shot across the room, and his defense staggered inward, only barely holding. He was mildly surprised; Sara had never once thrown the full weight of her blood-power in his presence. The red net died as he enforced his own shielding.

"Sara!"

"They were *right*!" she cried back, as the white-fire grew impossibly more powerful. "They were right about you!"

He heard the hysteria in her voice; that he expected and accepted—for now. But when it was over—

Derlac. It could only be you. You will pay for this.

"Sara—"

"No! I've listened and I've trusted you—and I'll not make the same mistake again!"

Yes, hysteria was there, but beneath it, something darker and more implacable. He felt cold fingers trace themselves along his throat, and words deserted him. Keeping his shield up, he began to advance toward the Sarillorn of Elliath. "Lady, you cannot hold this fire forever."

He could feel it weakening, but gradually. And time was against him in this. If the dawn came before his work was complete, everything that had passed this eve, even Sara's anger—especially Sara's anger—would be for nothing. And that he could not accept.

Turning only his head, he barked an order at the guards, and they complied. The red lace of power in the room grew marginally stronger.

Someone snarled, low and guttural, and Stefanos stopped his progress. Sara.

Her power swept outward with such force that his shield once again pushed into him. The sound of screams and choking surrounded him briefly, and the red net faded.

"Five. Most impressive, Sara. They were defending against you."

He watched her, but her light still shone too brightly for close inspection. *I have no choice, then.*

He felt a shadowy anger come upon him and began to pull power from the lifeblood of his unfortunate sacrifices. Only a little; that was all he needed—but even the little jeopardized his chance of completing the spell he'd so laboriously begun. He used the power thus pulled to strengthen his defense and diverted his own power outward.

Red-fire flared in the room as he gestured. Each movement was concise and economical. The light surrounding Sara drew inward as she frantically brought her own hands up. Red-fire ate away at the white in her, and it ebbed into the gray of stone and the orange of torchlight.

Stefanos could see her face clearly for the first time since she'd entered the room. With a curt, downward motion, he killed the red-fire.

Sara looked around the room, her gaze measured and hard.

"What will you do now, Lord? What will you do to one who has tried to *kill* you and failed?"

Her voice was tight, cold, and focused in ways that it had never been. Her hands were furled into small, white fists.

"Sara—"

"No. I'm not Sara."

"Lady—"

"Not that either. I choose to be Erin, lost to Elliath, but Sarillorn nonetheless."

He met her eyes, then, and took a step back. He felt a sudden lurch, a pain of a sort that had only touched him through the dim shadow of fear. It was strong, as the fear had promised it would be. The light was gone.

In its place stirred something too close to hatred and darkness for a creature of the dark to mistake. He stood back, raising one hand as if to stop what was in her eyes.

The light was dead.

He faced her, not knowing how to. She didn't flinch, didn't move a finger, just stood, cold, smooth alabaster—the corpse of what he'd come to desire.

The blood that remained on his hands burned. He looked down as if seeing it for the first time. Confusion blurred his thoughts.

"Sara—"

She could not, would not respond. Even the tears that often accompanied her darkest moods were absent; absurdly enough, he had accomplished at least that goal. Looking down, he noticed that small patches of red marred the fabric—whose blood, exactly, he could not say.

He took a step forward, then another, almost stumbling toward her. She remained where she was, and he saw in her face her precious lines, and the type of defeat that the lines could acknowledge—all hard, all cold, a bitter, noble pride—but nothing, not one hint, of warmth or light.

Not even when he brought his hands up to cup her face.

He caught her chin roughly, knowing that he would hurt her, but unable to stop.

"No. The light *cannot* be dead. I will not allow it."

Her mouth opened and closed again.

He bent his power outward, more subtly this time, probing her, searching for things that eyes alone could never touch. He pulled at her, at the thoughts she kept hidden, at the sense of personality that slid like water away from his grip. Nothing.

He caught her arms and shook her hard enough to make her neck snap backward without breaking it.

"Lady, I do this for you—I do it because—"

"You did not do this for *me*."

He saw a hint of fear in her, but could not bring himself to exploit it. Pain, he knew well, would not bring back what was lost. Power would not. Death would not.

And thus he learned the first lesson of his Enemy: that only the thing truly given is precious; that this thing that is precious can never be forced.

He bowed his head, brushing convulsively against her chest. Almost of their own accord her arms went out, trembled against the air, and fell to her sides.

"First Servant, you have already killed me."

He looked up. She looked away. And in the motion, everything. His confusion dissipated; his pain did not. But now the way was clear.

"Finish it. Or I will finish it. There are things even I cannot live with."

His fingers brushed her cheek, gently, and she knew she should not have spoken. He stood, straight and tall, the lapse in his control a thing already of the past.

"Come, Lady."

Quietly, she followed him to the altar.

There he turned, again catching her face. "Lady."

She was trembling.

He was Stefanos, First Servant of Malthan, ruler of half the world. Twice challenged, he had left the dead behind, with a determination and strength that marked him as First still.

To lose was not his way.

He bent down and kissed her forehead, so she would not see the red of his eyes as they blazed with the strength of the dead.

His arms shot out to catch her as she crumpled, to hold her as she would not now allow him if she were conscious. He carried her quickly to the altar, and there kissed her sleeping mouth. The approaching dawn did not allow for more.

Quickly he picked up the dagger that lay exposed on the stained altar. He cut his hand neatly and smoothly, and repeated the operation upon hers. Trembling, he brought her hand to his and pressed them firmly together.

And then he sought her memory; the core of what she'd seen; the thing that had killed the light. He found it easily and began to blanket it in his shadow, dimming it and then carefully cutting it away from the rest of her life. When it was done, he pulled away, nearly exhausted.

Almost, he woke her then; the temptation was strong.

And if you wake, what then, Lady? The world is still the world; and it is still mine. Will you not suffer the more to continue to see what I must do?

He pulled away, still clutching the dagger.

Let me finish my task. Let me take what is mine by right of power. And then, perhaps, I can return it to you—a gift for my lady.

He approached her again, uncertainly.

Then the uncertainty vanished. For in the future, a human decade away, maybe more, the Lady of Elliath would have to be dealt with; and all of the lines that did her work. And he would have to face again the loss that had almost overwhelmed him this evening.

No. I will not lose her—not that way. Nor any other.

He stepped away from her, and leaned over the body of Kandor.

First of Malthan. The voice of the Third of Lernan was no more than a whisper.

The dagger tossed torchlight against the ceiling.

You are indeed the One. Your time is short; I feel the dawn, and it is close. Will you truly do this thing?

In reply, the dagger came down, point first, wearing an aurora of pure red.

Kandor's body jerked violently as the point hit his breast and slammed down. The knife went up twice more, and the voice of the Third of Lernan was lost to the mortal plane.

Stefanos lifted Sara's hand and cupped the Servant's blood in it, letting it trickle into the wound in her palm. Blood ran through her fingers into the nest of his own cut hand. It hurt, but he let it in.

Now, Sara. He began to chant. *Your life and mine.*

He raised his free hand and chased a pattern of fire through the air. The pattern fell around the three of them, drawing them closer and closer together.

I free you from mortal time.
I release you from death.
For as long as I exist, you shall rule beside me.

He held her thus until the blood ceased to flow. Then, without pause to exult in his night's work, he carried her out of the temple to the north wing of the castle. There he did what he could to clean her, washing and bandaging her hand and carefully brushing her hair.

When he was finished, he tucked her gently into bed.

Sleep, little one. I shall waken you.

He made it to the door by effort of will and then stopped dead.

"May I stay, Sara? It will be dawn; I can see the sky change. I shall not hurt you."

He walked back into the room, turned the covers down, and after removing—with great care—the robes he wore, he slid in beside her.

She was warm as she lay in his arms. Her breath fanned his chest, as it had done many evenings while she slept. But something was missing.

Am I not to have the comfort of your company before the campaign starts? Sara, Lady, forgive me. He woke her, eyes glinting weakly.

She stirred against his chest.

"Sara?"

"Hmmmm? Is it morning already?"

"Not quite."

"Good. Sleepy."

He was silent for a few minutes, aware that if he did not cast his spell soon, he would not be able to—the black of sky had given way to transparent navy blue.

"Sara?" His arms tightened.

"What is it, darkling?"

Warmth shot through him.

"I wish you to know, Lady, that I am what I am: First Servant of your Enemy."

"I know." Her voice was still heavy with sleep.

"But I—" He kissed her, fully, and she responded. He told her what he must; for he finally understood it as true. "I love you as much as I am able."

"Darkling." She said it in sleepy wonder, her hands brushing against his shoulders.

"Will you remember this?"

"Of course."

"Will you love me?"

She was silent a moment, and then he felt it: The bands of her light were glowing with life and strength. They touched him, pierced him, and passed through him with such sweet clarity that her words were lost.

And then his eyes flickered red one last time, and Sara's smile was surrendered to sleep.

He lay holding her, a feeling of peace upon him.

"Sleep, Lady. Sleep. I will watch you; I will plan for the time when the world can be as you desire."

And she did.

epilogue

It was almost time.

The Lady of Elliath stared at length into the placid waters of the fountain that had been stilled for a century. Caught there, her reflection stared back at her, already flat and lifeless.

She was a Servant, the First of the Bright Heart. Memory hung about her in sharp crystal shards that could not be avoided.

She glanced behind her, saw the sword and the satchel as they rested by the fountain. All was ready.

Yes. It is almost time.

The Dark Lord of the Empire waited without; his army of Swords, priests, and mortals arrayed on the new field. Her people, her descendants, were dead or scattered, the first of the lines to fall.

Only the first. It would continue, and the lines would pay all the price that she had once seen. But she would not be present for those losses; the burden would no longer be hers.

She rose, looking at the fragile beauty of her garden. It glowed with an enchantment and life that had taken much of her power to cast. And here it would wait until the return of the last of the children of Elliath.

She had no tears; even regret was dim and distant. She had set events in motion, cast the net of Lernan's Hope as widely as possible.

It was time to discharge the last of the responsibilities that she had chosen—the last, and the easiest. The only farewell she made to the Woodhall and the life it had once contained was a quiet backward glance.

Her power entered the field; it caused pain, it brought death. For a moment her blood stirred at the combat; the Light against the Dark. But only for a moment. Arrows flew, swords were raised, the tiny gnat of fire the priests could send came forward, but these she could disregard. Even the field, spotted by shrubs and trees over the rolling hills, seemed withered and gray; life was already beyond her.

Then he came, Lord to her Lady.

All around him, his troops grew quiet. The arrows ceased their gentle storm, the traces of red were withdrawn.

He faced her, and she saw some of what she felt mirrored in his dark face. Here he wore no human guise, and here she discarded hers. They were Light and Dark, as in the primordial beginning.

All around them the twisted bodies of lesser mortals lay in grotesque tribute to the roots of their heritage.

She held her power, waiting. So, too, did he hold his.

No song came to them to fill the empty victory, the empty defeat. No true enmity took fire, no true hatred.

"We have both been changed by the mortal world."

For a moment his power flickered sharply, his eyes danced. He saw in her only an echo of the past, no more.

"Yes, Lady." He could not say why, but the change in her disturbed him deeply. She had always been his equal, and not for this sudden chill had he come this far.

They stood above their power, then.

"Stefanos."

"Alariel."

She smiled, no exultance in it. "Do you remember the first time we met?"

He nodded, his smile a match for hers, devoid of the wrath and the pull that had driven him to destroy her. "Well."

They were silent again, the army forgotten. "It was before the gray of the world." He shook himself and stood taller. "But we had heard, Lady, that you had dared the veils. And it has availed you nothing, in the end, but death—a true death, not a sojourn with your God."

Her eyes gazed beyond him, seeing too much, seeing too little. "Yes," she answered. "You heard truly."

"After Kerloth's example?"

"Even so." She shivered, but he knew it was not caused by him. "I went where the Twin Hearts could not go, at the behest of the Bright One. This I foresaw; this and your victory." Her face suddenly grew very still, her eyes glowing a brilliant green in the dark of the night. "Do you remember, Stefanos, the time when we each walked the void? I wanted, not long ago, to be cleansed by fire. And in some wise I have been granted that.

"You know what you must do. I know it, and I have accepted it. Come, let us have an end."

"Alariel." He said her name for the second time and met her eyes, red against green. "Know this: We have nurtured common blood. You were a worthy foe; when the empire is the world, your blood will always be remembered by it."

She smiled sadly, her face no less peaceful. "And is the empire still so important?"

The question stung him; for a moment it was not the Lady he saw, but her granddaughter's vulnerable face.

"It is *mine*."

"That is all the answer I need." For a moment, old fires rose in her. Wind carried the smell of smoke and blood and lifted her hair. "And you will pay a price for it, in the end, that is as heavy to you as the one I have paid. The two, you cannot have; and you will be torn between them."

His fire lashed out then; her shields went up. Both flickered and dwindled.

"You do not know pity yet, Stefanos." She was weary. "Come, end this."

Still he stayed his hand, troubled. This was not the First of the Bright Heart, not as he remembered her.

"Brother," she said softly.

He stiffened. This fight, this battle, this war—for the moment all were hollow. How dared she make a mockery of his power by her acquiescence?

But he, too, was suddenly weary.

"Is this the death you deserve, Alariel? Is this the death you foresaw for yourself?" There and then he swore he would never do as she had done.

"It is . . . peace." And her shields fell.

Bitterness sang all around him as his fire flared out for the last time. True power, that God alone might match; a world in miniature, seen through the cold, red haze.

As she wished, she was cleansed. No pain seemed to escape her before even the form she had shown was blown away in a red, red wind.

He turned when it was finished and walked away into the darkness, ignoring the rustle of mindless chatter at his back.

Sara. He yearned for her; beside this the desire to feed was as nothing. *Sara* . . .

But Elliath was only the first of the lines, first and most powerful. Six still remained, and those six he must also destroy before seeking, once again, the comfort of her light.

A century of darkness was longer than Stefanos, First of the Sundered, had ever thought possible.

How much longer?

He shook himself, whispered three words, and passed through the darkness to Rennath. Let the army do as it would without him; he would return to them soon enough. He walked into the shadows of his rooms; walked into the darkness that no light penetrated.

And there, under a halo of gentle red, she waited for him. In silence he stood, while the time drifted by. Days passed thus, stretching out. What of it? He had time. They had time.

He touched her hand; it did not move.

Very gently he lifted her body, cradling it in his dark arms.

Is this what you feel, Sara?

Is this what you feel when you cry?

about
the author

Michelle Sagara was born in 1963. Her parents were either thrilled or disappointed enough to try again, and she now has one sister, two brothers and affectionately frazzled, wiser parents who don't plan to provide her with any more siblings.

Although she's worked at a variety of part-time jobs in both the corporate (IBM) and retail world, she's been a student for most of her life, and now manages Bakka Books, Canada's oldest science-fiction and fantasy store. She figures she's got time to do all the interesting and exotic things writers normally do. Check this space in a few years for future developments.

She loves reading, folk music and debate, and she has a particular fondness for computer nerds, which is why she's happily married to one.